Wizard Defender

Book Eight

Intergalactic Wizard Scout Chronicles

Rodney W. Hartman

ISBN-13: 978-0-9982166-7-6 (R&K Publishing)

ISBN-10: 0-9982166-7-4

Cover Design by Angie Abler

Editing services by The Pro Book Editor

DEDICATION

This book is dedicated to my nephew Jason. You're a good man, and the world is a better place because you are in it. I'm very proud of you.

ACKNOWLEDGMENTS

This book could never have been completed without the assistance and support of family and friends too numerous to mention. However, I would be amiss if I did not give special thanks to my wife, Karen Hartman, for her support and encouragement.

HARTMAN

Other Books by Rodney W. Hartman

Intergalactic Wizard Scout Chronicles

Wizard Defiant   Book One
Wizard Cadet   Book Two
Wizard Scout   Book Three
Wizard Omega   Book Four
Wizard Rebellion   Book Five
Wizard Betrayed   Book Six
Wizard Redeemed   Book Seven
Wizard Defender   Book Eight

Wizard Scout Trinity Delgado Series

Trinity Unleashed

Ring Defender Series

Fire Defender   Book One

CHAPTER 1

[Begin Transmission]

The convoy of six heavy hover-vehicles made their way down the double-wide street. Deadly looking barrels of 20mm phase auto-cannons stuck out of the fully armored cupolas atop each vehicle. The cupulas swung back and forth seemingly searching the crowd of pedestrians on both sides for any signs of hostile activity. A dozen light hover-vehicles armed with air-to-ground weapons circled three hundred meters overhead, barely staying above some of the tallest buildings. Like mother hens watching over their chicks, the airborne vehicles remained vigilant as the convoy snaked its way through the crowded streets of the Conglomerate's self-proclaimed capital on Risors.

Wizard Scout Richard Shepard stood on the sidewalk a block ahead of the vehicles, at the outer edge of a group of pedestrians waiting to cross the street. He glanced at the lead armored vehicle as it turned the corner and rumbled in his direction, doing his best to act nonchalant and blend in with the pedestrians around him. He doubted he was succeeding.

"Relax," said a voice in Richard's head. *"The gnome's polymorph spell is holding. I calculate a sixty-seven percent probability the facial-recognition security system on those lampposts have identified you as Jerry Tennerson, non-descript store clerk on his way to work. He passes this corner every day at this time, so don't sweat it, buddy."*

"Easy for you to say," Richard thought in the space of his mind that he shared with his battle computer, Nickelo. *"You're safe on the* Defiant *with the other battle computers a quarter of a light year away. If we're discovered prematurely, the guards will be shooting at us wizard scouts, not you battle computers."*

"Then I highly recommend not getting discovered," replied Nickelo. *"Like I said, there is a sixty-four percent probability the security computers think you are Jerry Tennerson."*

"Hey, I thought you said you'd calculated it at sixty-seven percent," Richard said thinking that for once he'd caught his battle computer in a mistake.

"Oh, that was so ten seconds ago, Wizard Scout. Input data changes. You've got to learn to go with the flow."

Not for the first time, Richard wished he could throttle his battle computer. The only thing stopping him was the fact that he knew Nickelo's plans usually worked out.

"I calculate the fact that I am not on Risors limits your ability to strangle me as well. Not to mention I am a gas-based life form encased in a brerellium steel chip inside your battle helmet. I don't even breathe, so trying to choke me is not very logical."

"Whatever," Richard said ending the conversation on the subject. *"Now stop reading my thoughts."*

"Then stop thinking in our shared space. I keep telling you that a lot of your thoughts aren't all that interesting. I would just as soon you kept them in your private space."

Ignoring his battle computer, Richard pulled Power from his reserve. He formed an active scan, wrapped it in a stealth shield, and probed each of the heavy hover-vehicles in turn as they came around the corner. As intel had reported, each of the massive vehicles was armored in brerellium steel mixed with energized titanium flakes. The embedded titanium made the vehicles nearly impervious to creatures that could shift into the void.

"My scan can't penetrate their armor," Richard said, having second thoughts about the advisability of the snatch mission his team had been assigned. He well knew the life of his bondmate Jeena, not to mention the lives of his friends Trinity, Jerad, Tam, and Stella hung in the balance.

"You forgot about Calatron, the leader of the Defiant's *gnome mages,"* said Nickelo. *"He's with Jeena."*

"I didn't forget," Richard said. A little of his irritation crept into his thoughts. *"I've got a lot on my mind. Now, are you sure our target's in the third vehicle?"*

"Uh, define sure, *Wizard Scout."*

"Forget it," Richard said. He had no doubt his battle computer was on the verge of swamping him with technical details and probabilities calculated out to infinitesimal percentages. *"I'm not in the mood for games."*

Richard concentrated on the third vehicle in the approaching convoy—the one battle computers Margery, Danny, and Nickelo had calculated would most likely hold their target. Richard wasn't quite as confident as the three battle computers, but it was too late to back out now.

"All right, Nick, tell the other battle computers to get ready. We'll hit the convoy as soon as the lead vehicle makes it to that stoplight. Make sure you tell Danny to inform Jeena. Are you sure you can stay in contact with him? That ring on Jeena's finger isn't a battle helmet, and my bondmate's the key to this whole ambush."

"Relax, Wizard Scout. Danny is a battle computer whether he is inside a helmet, a ring, or free as a bird in outer space. We battle computers will do our job. I calculate that you carbon-based life forms are the ones that need to concentrate on your tasks."

The idea of throttling his battle computer grew even more desirable, but Richard kept the thought in his private space. He flexed his left hand in anticipation of grasping his phase rod. He knew things were going to happen quickly once the ambush started. There was no room for mistakes.

"That is correct, Wizard Scout," said Nickelo. *"It would have been better if you wizard scouts could have had your equipment with you, but it was too risky. Our intel indicates those vehicles are equipped with the best security sensors the Conglomerate has at its disposal. Not to mention the fact that there are at least two wizard scouts somewhere in the convoy."*

"Yeah, don't remind me," Richard replied. *"They'll be in battle suits. We won't."*

"Don't complain. At least you'll be able to summon your equipment. Trinity, Jerad, Tam, and Stella aren't going to have that option."

"I'll complain all I want," Richard said, growing a little

irritated at his battle computer's slightly superior attitude. *"Just because I can summon my gear doesn't mean I'll have any time to put it on."*

Nickelo laughed, which did nothing to soothe Richard's irritation. *"I calculate nothing is perfect, Wizard Scout, so suck it up."*

The lead vehicle reached the stoplight before Richard could think of a suitable retort. Although the light was red, two civilian police officers had the side streets blocked off. An officer standing in the middle of the road waved the lead vehicle through with his left hand while keeping his right hand on the butt of a standard-issue plasma pistol holstered at his waist. Several pedestrians in the crowd of which Richard was a part frowned at the delay, but they remained on the sidewalk even though the crosswalk sign had illuminated.

When the first two hover-vehicles were completely in the intersection, Richard sensed a buildup of magic in the ground beneath the pavement. He didn't need his passive scan to know the magic's frequency was Jeena's. The area around the intersection glowed blue with magic as the asphalt in a twenty-meter section of the road began bubbling. Within seconds, the crossroad resembled molten lava more than the hard pavement it had been. The first two vehicles in the convoy sank into the bubbling mixture all the way up to the base of their turrets. At the same time, the two police officers flew into the air as their pistols were ripped out of their holsters and dropped into the molten pavement, sinking out of sight. The two officers flew through the air and landed gently on the ledge of a nearby building. Richard sensed the gnome Calatron's frequency on the levitation spells affecting the police officers. Screams of pedestrians filled the air as frightened people scattered in all directions. Soon only Richard remained standing on the street corner.

"See?" said Nickelo. *"I told you it would work. Those heavy hover-vehicles have too much weight to support themselves over anything but solid ground. And neither of the officers was harmed. I love it when a plan comes together."*

"You mean you love it when one of your plans comes together," Richard said as he sprang into action. With surprise no longer a necessity, he thought the command to summon his battle helmet,

dimensional pack, and phase rod. Reaching out, he caught them in midair and slung the pack over his shoulder. Once secure, he shoved the battle helmet onto his head. At the same time, he gripped the phase rod in his left hand and flicked the activate switch to full destructive mode. The meter-long length of brerellium steel with its creallium core shot out the handle as miniature red lightning bolts of phase energy began running up and down its length. Unlike a few weeks earlier, no feeling of hunger accompanied the phase rod's activation.

"Your special phase rods with the demon essence were destroyed during your battle to close the gate to the demonic plane," Nickelo said, obviously assuming his wizard scout needed reminding. *"You're stuck using normal phase rods just like all the other wizard scouts."*

"That's not exactly true," Richard said. *"My nephew Brachia modified all of my phase rods years ago. Their phase energy output is a good twenty-five percent higher than the phase rods of other wizard scouts."*

"And a good thing he did," replied Nickelo. *"I calculate you're going to need every bit of that extra damage capability right about now. So get to it, Wizard Scout. Daylight's burning, as they say."*

Taking off at a dead run, Richard made for the third hover-vehicle. The armored behemoth was attempting to back up but couldn't get far due to the proximity of the vehicle behind it. The turret swung in Richard's direction, and he sensed a buildup of energy inside the large caliber barrel of the auto-cannon.

"Don't give it time to fire, Wizard Scout," said Nickelo. *"Just a suggestion."*

Drawing Power from his reserve, Richard sent it out in the direction of the armored vehicle. *"I'm going to need some help, Nick,"* he said, not being one of those wizard scouts who insisted on doing everything on his own.

Richard's brain suddenly went into hyper-mode. He sensed his battle computer guiding his line of Power into the barrel of the auto-cannon where it wrapped around the phase round in the weapon's breach. The deadly round fired and began traveling down the length of the barrel. Using telekinesis, Richard slowed the phase round just enough so that it was still in the barrel when the second phase round left the breach and began moving up the auto-cannon's tube. The two rounds made contact.

Boom!

The auto-cannon's barrel exploded, sending bits of metal flying.

"Incoming," warned Nickelo.

Sensing energy approaching from his rear, Richard dove to the sidewalk, barely avoiding streams of phase rounds from the two hover-vehicles mired in the intersection's molten asphalt. A wall of the molten material rose into the air, momentarily stopping the enemy's fire. Richard sensed rather than saw two fist-sized streams of the liquefied asphalt reach into the barrels of the hover-vehicle's auto-cannons.

Boom! Boom!

Thank you, Jeena and Calatron, Richard thought as he jumped up from the sidewalk and took off in a crouched run toward the third armored vehicle. As he closed the distance, he reached over his shoulder and into his dimensional pack with his right hand. Touching something inside, he pulled out a bundle of seven deactivated phase rods tied together with an elastic band. He tossed the bundle of rods high into the air. Lines of Power reached out for the phase rods, the elastic band broke, and the rods shot off in four separate directions. Based on the frequencies, he knew Tam, Jerad, and Trinity had each taken control of their phase rods using telekinesis. The remaining four rods flew in the direction Richard knew the four-armed Stella was located.

When he was close to the third vehicle, Richard leaped into the air. By boosting the height of his jump with telekinesis, he landed on the turret feet first. Out the corner of his eye, he saw the turrets of the rearmost three vehicles in the convoy turning their auto-cannons in his direction. Before the weapons could fire, a shield composed of pure Power surrounded all three of the heavy hovercraft, sealing them inside a translucent dome.

Tam, Richard thought.

The auto-cannons of the three vehicles opened up, spraying 20mm phase rounds at Richard. The rounds didn't go far. They hit Tam's defensive shield and began ricocheting around inside the energy field until their momentum was spent. After the initial burst of fire, the weapons grew silent as the vehicles' crews apparently realized the futility of their situation.

It pays to have friends who are defenders, Richard thought, thanking the day he'd met Tam so long ago during their time in the Intergalactic Wizard Scout Academy.

"Yes, it does," said Nickelo monitoring his thoughts. *"You're fortunate Tam's shield defends against both physical and energy attacks. Naturally, I included that in my calculations on mission success."*

"Naturally," Richard thought back.

With the three rearmost hover-vehicles temporarily neutralized, Richard pulled the dimensional pack off his back while sending the specs for a twenty-kilo funnel mine to it. *"Here's hoping Brachia and Dren have the teleporters on Storage working again."*

"You got the phase rods for the other wizard scouts from your pack, so I calculate a one hundred percent probability the teleporters are working. What you really need to worry about is if there are any twenty-kilo mines left. The Dragars' attack on Storage two weeks ago wiped out eighty percent of the equipment warehouses. Your niece and nephew are still trying to get a list of available items to me."

Although he hadn't been there, Richard's niece and nephew had filled him in on how a Dragar dreadnaught had orbited the planet Storage, intent on destroying the entire planet's population. From what he'd been able to surmise, the Dragar warship had been sent to capture the special demon-essence phase rods in his equipment cache. Thanks to Sergeant Ron and the crew of the *Defiant*, the Dragar dreadnaught had been driven off, but not before it had destroyed a majority of the equipment warehouses and over thirty percent of the Storagean population.

"The Storageans are a peaceful but resilient race," said Nickelo, sounding hopeful for a computer. *"They're mourning their dead while reorganizing as much of the undamaged equipment as possible into the remaining warehouses."*

Hoping for the best, Richard reached under the flap of his pack. When his ungloved hand touched metal, he pulled out a fully-functional funnel mine. Once the heavy mine was out of the pack, he set it on the vehicle's turret with the mine's funnel pointing downward.

"Open me a channel to the wizard scouts' battle computers that are accompanying the convoy," Richard told Nickelo using command voice.

"Compliance." A nanosecond later, Nickelo said, *"'The One' has connected us to battle computers Thomas and Ivan. They belong to Wizard Scouts McDonald and Palovich respectively."*

Richard had never met Wizard Scout McDonald personally, but he'd heard good things about the man. Wizard Scout Palovich had been in the Intergalactic Wizard Scout Academy two classes ahead of his own. He knew her by sight but had not had much interaction with her otherwise.

"This is Wizard Scout Shepard," Richard said into his helmet's communicator. "I know you're in there with Felix Deloris. Come out and surrender your weapons. I give you my word of honor no one will be harmed. I have a twenty-kilo funnel mine on your turret. I'll use it if forced. You've got fifteen seconds to make up your minds. One way or the other, you're coming out, so you may as well make it easy on yourselves."

"I'll do you one better," replied the stern voice of a man over the intercom on Richard's battle helmet. "I'll give you ten seconds to leave before our hovercraft circling overhead blow you all to pieces."

"Incoming," said Nickelo.

Four orange blips on the heads-up display of Richard's battle helmet gave warning that a quad of the light hover-vehicles was lining up for a strafing run. Even as he looked at the four blips, Richard sensed a disturbance in the void. He sensed multiple disturbances. Richard smiled. It was a smile that would've made the two wizard scouts in the armored vehicle nervous if they could only have seen.

"Well, you were right, Rick," said Nickelo sounding almost disappointed. *"Sheba, Sheeta, and the pups got here in time. I didn't think they'd make it. You are one lucky wizard scout."*

The quad of hover-vehicles had already begun diving for their strafing run. Only partway into their dive, the four light hovercraft began wavering and drifting off course. Richard detected small explosions in their cockpits as the ejection seats activated and then the pilots shot out of their fighters. They tumbled for a half-dozen heartbeats before the anti-gravity units in the seats took over. The pilots' freefall turned into a gentle drift toward the ground below.

"The other eight pilots have also ejected," said Nickelo. *"I guess none of them liked being in close quarters with your spirit-*

wolves." The spiraling hover-vehicles suddenly leveled off. *"Now that the pilots are out, we battle computers have taken over the fighters' flight controls. What are your commands, oh greatest and luckiest of all wizard scouts?"*

Ignoring his battle computer's attempt at humor, Richard spoke into his helmet's communicator. "Your fighters are now under our control. You have five seconds before I blow this mine. Decide now or forever hold your—"

The front and rear hatches of the armored vehicle popped open. Out came two fully equipped wizard scouts with activated phase rods blazing.

Reaching out with his mind, Richard located the links to the two wizard scouts' Power reserves. He twisted the links back on themselves, basically cutting off the two's ability to draw Power from their reserves. Without giving the attacking wizard scouts time to recover, he sent lines of Power into the base of their spines and snapped their spinal cords. The two charging figures stumbled but recovered when their battle computers took over control of their suits. Knowing full well that he couldn't defend himself in hand-to-hand combat against two battle computer controlled suits, Richard wrapped Power around both battle suits and levitated them into the air using telekinesis.

The smaller of the two battle suits drew a Deloris model phase pistol and fired point blank at Richard. A shield of magic interposed itself between the wizard scout and Richard. The attacking wizard scout's phase rounds ricocheted into the air.

"You shall not harm my bondmate," shouted a feminine voice as lines of magic wrapped around the two battle suits and their helpless wizard scouts, lifting them even higher into the air.

Richard turned to see a silver-haired elf with molten-silver eyes running on the sidewalk toward him. She was dressed in a black jumpsuit and carried a blackened staff in her left hand with a glowing blue stone at its tip. Her right hand held a deadly-looking Deloris phase pistol.

"Jeena, no!" Richard shouted. "Don't hurt them. They're already helpless."

"I calculate that is not precisely a hundred percent accurate," said Nickelo. *"The two wizard scouts aren't completely helpless. Their battle computers could—"*

Jeena stared up at the two hovering wizard scouts and raised her staff. The blue gem at its top grew brighter. "They were trying to kill you, Rick. They deserve to die." A blue glow enveloped the two floating battle suits as they rose to a height of twenty meters.

Richard sensed the magic in the blue glow surrounding the two wizard scouts form into a spell. He didn't know what spell his bondmate was preparing to cast, but he doubted it would be beneficial to the wizard scouts.

"No, Jeena. Please," Richard said in an attempt to reason with his bondmate. He sensed anger coming through the bond link connecting her to him. Based upon his bondmate's emotions, he wasn't sure she was in a reasoning mood.

"Geesh," said Nickelo. *"And I thought you had a temper problem. If you're going to calm her down, I calculate that you had better act fast. Based upon the speed of movement of the molten silver in the elf's eyes, the wizard scouts don't have much time."*

"What about their families?" Richard shouted using a technique of asking unexpected questions that he'd seen one of Silverton's elf lords use to defuse situations.

Jeena took her eyes off the two wizard scouts long enough to ask, "What families?"

"Their families," Richard repeated as he pointed at the two battle suits floating overhead. "The Conglomerate's board of directors is holding those two wizard scouts' families hostage. The board's threatening their loved ones to force them to obey. These two aren't our enemies. We'll need them in the future. I'm asking you not to hurt them. Please."

The elf's molten-silver eyes stared at Richard for a full dozen heartbeats. Finally, the movement of her eyes' molten silver slowed, and the blue glow surrounding the two battle suits dimmed. With a wave of Jeena's staff, the two wizard scouts began floating downward before landing in the molten asphalt near the two lead hover-vehicles. The wizard scouts' heavy battle suits sank into the bubbling liquid until only their battle helmets remained exposed. Before the battle suits could do anything to extract themselves, the molten asphalt returned to a solid form.

Jeena looked away from the two scouts and locked eyes with Richard. "I will allow them to live, but only because you asked. I will not allow anyone to harm you, Rick. Not while breath is in my body."

"Understood," Richard said, thankful the beautiful high priestess was on his side. "As I you." Switching his attention to the front hatch of the hover-vehicle, he shouted, "Come on out. You won't like it if I have to come inside and get you."

A hand reached out of the hatch, followed by the head of a gray-haired, balding man in his fifties. "I'm coming out. Don't shoot."

The thin frame of Felix Deloris scrambled out of the hatch to stand on the hover-vehicle's surface. The man straightened and stared at Richard before speaking in the voice of someone resigned to their fate. "I suppose you're going to kill me the same way you killed my sister. Well, get it over with. I told the board they were wasting their time trying to get me out of the city. If Diane couldn't stay out of your clutches, I knew there wasn't any way I was going to remain safe."

Richard shook his head. He thought back to how the now deceased Empress Diane Deloris had been sacrificed by the elf Kreathin, also known as Lord Crendemor, along with Richard's own brother, Gaston Myers.

"I didn't kill your sister," Richard said, "and I'm not going to kill you. Something's coming that is far worse than anything you can imagine."

The balding Felix's eyes narrowed. "Words are cheap. Why should I trust you? For that matter, why are you even wasting your breath talking to me? I'm already your prisoner."

"We don't have time for this," said Nickelo in their shared space. *"Trinity, Jerad, Tam, and Stella have the other hover-vehicles neutralized, but I detect that additional forces are on the way. If you want to get away from here without killing someone, the time to leave is now."*

"Roger that," Richard said. *"Sound the recall. Have Asquan and Timerman bring the X-shuttle in. It's time to go."*

Wasting no more time on Felix Deloris, Richard nodded his head at Jeena. She holstered her pistol before waving her right hand and saying a word he heard but quickly forgot. A blue ball of magic shot out of her hand and struck the thin man in the chest.

Felix stiffened before falling to the hover-vehicle's metal

surface.

A roar behind Richard announced the arrival of the X-shuttle. He turned to see a shimmer in the air as the shuttle materialized and settled down on the city street. Debris was still blowing in all directions when the shuttle's rear ramp dropped. Richard's fellow wizard scouts immediately began running toward the shuttle. As they ran, he glanced behind them to see three more hover-vehicles up to their turrets in molten asphalt along the city street.

Pointing at the stiff form of Felix Deloris, Richard glanced at Jeena. "Take him onboard the shuttle."

His bondmate's raised eyebrows were immediately accompanied by an emotion of irritation coming through their bond link.

"Uh...please, Jeena. I'll be along in a second."

The high priestess's eyebrows lowered as she cast a levitation spell on the paralyzed brother of the deceased empress. Richard watched long enough to see her run toward the X-shuttle while dragging the levitated Felix behind her, using a form of magic-based telekinesis.

"You need to get on the shuttle as well," reminded Nickelo.

"Give me a second," Richard said. *"I've got something to do first."*

Jumping off the hover-vehicle, Richard sprinted to the intersection where Jeena had trapped the two lead vehicles. He stopped in front of the two wizard scouts also trapped there. Only their battle helmets were above ground, but Richard sensed the suits' occupants alive and well inside. Kneeling down, he spoke to his brother and sister in arms using the external speakers of his battle helmet.

"I disconnected the links to your Power reserves. That's why you can't self-heal. You're both too dangerous to set free right now. As soon as I'm a safe distance away, I'll undo what I've done to your links. Once I do, your self-heals will repair your spinal cords."

A male voice came out of the external speaker on the right-most battle helmet. "You've just killed my family, Shepard. I swear I'll hunt you down wherever you go. There's no place to hide where I can't find you."

Richard stared through Wizard Scout McDonald's visor. He

could just make out the man's angry eyes. "I've got a message for the Conglomerate's board of directors. I want you to give it to them personally. Tell them that Wizard Scout Richard Shepard said if they so much as harm one hair on your or any other wizard scouts' family, on my word of honor as a wizard scout I'll take every one of the board members to a place that's as close to hell as they can possibly imagine. The demons there will torture them for thousands of years. Not even death will be able to release them from their agony. You tell them that if they test me on this, it will be the biggest mistake they ever make."

"Rick, come on," came Jerad's shout.

Richard glanced over his shoulder to see his friend standing on the ramp of the X-shuttle. Jeena stood next to him waving with her staff.

He turned back to the two scouts. "The empress is dead. We didn't kill her. Those who did are coming, and when they get here, there won't be a safe place in the galaxy for any living creature to hide. Our only chance is to work together. That means the Empire, the Trecorians, the Conglomerate, the Carsoloians, and every other race including the Crosioians. I want you to tell the board of directors that Matthew Deloris is going to contact them. When he does, they had better listen, or I swear they'll regret it for the rest of eternity."

Richard stood and switched the visor of his helmet to clear. He gave what he hoped was a friendly smile. "By the way, the next time we meet, I'll show both of you how to defend against the trick I used to disable the links to your Power reserves. We're on the same side. When you see our real enemies, you'll know I'm telling the truth. Until then, you'll just have to take my word for it." With that, he took off running for the X-shuttle's ramp.

The teenage elf-pilot Asquan hit the emergency close for the ramp. The rapidly shutting ramp sent Richard flying forward onto the shuttle's deck. Before he could stand, the X-shuttle shot up into the air, throwing him back hard into the rear ramp.

"Hmm," said Nickelo in their shared space. *"I calculate your friend Tia has been showing Asquan and Timerman how to take off without wasting time. I'll bet it makes you feel all warm and cozy on the inside knowing that the younger generation is teaching each other, doesn't it?"*

"Yeah," Richard said, finally regaining his feet. *"I—"*

"Hang on!" shouted the teenage orc Timerman sitting in the copilot's seat. "I'm activating the hyper-drive…now!"

Richard got another close-up view of the X-shuttle's metal deck. "You know what?" he said to no one in particular as he rose to all fours and crawled to his seat. "Next time I need a quick escape, I think I'll take a hover-tram."

CHAPTER 2

As the X-shuttle made its way to the rendezvous point to meetup with the *Defiant*, Jeena traded Power with her bondmate who was sitting next to her in the shuttle. Neither Richard nor she was low on Power at the moment, but given the circumstances, she had no desire to waste any opportunity to recharge.

The red-gemmed ring on Jeena's left hand tingled. *"I calculate that is a wise course of action,"* Danny the battle computer said in her mind. *"We are at war. A fight could pop up at the most inconvenient time."*

"Is there ever a good time for a battle?" Jeena asked. *"If it was up to me, Rick and I would settle down on the Thoraxens' family farm and raise medicinal herbs for the rest of our lives. I would be quite content living such a life with my bondmate."*

"Well, do not get your hopes up," replied Danny from where he was embedded in Jeena's ring. *"I calculate Rick has awhile before he needs to start worrying about his golden-retirement years. Also, I am not so sure you should plan your future on raising medicinal herbs. Wizard Scout Terrie Shatstot was left in your elf city of Silverton to start a training school for elf healers. If Rick is right, Terrie should be able to train your medics to heal elves using pure Power instead of magic."*

Jeena hoped the ex-battle computer was right. Too many elves had died over the years because they couldn't be magically healed.

"We're two minutes from the rendezvous point," came Timerman's voice from the front of the shuttle. "I'm deactivating the shuttle's stealth shield so Sergeant Ron will be able to see us."

Jeena cast a wordless spell and reached out with her senses. She detected a disturbance a half-dozen light seconds ahead. She turned on the bench seat to look at the orc teenager. "The *Defiant* should be coming out of hyperspace at your one o'clock. Be prepared just in case it's not her."

A sight reticle appeared on the forward screen as Timerman targeted the forward missile tubes and gun arrays on the spot. The orc angled the shuttle's shields for optimum efficiency. Jeena was impressed.

Richard leaned over on the bench seat next to her and whispered in her ear, "He's picked up a lot in the short time he's been in the *Defiant's* crew. Heck, he knows a lot more about the weapons and shielding on the *Defiant* and the X-shuttle than I do. So does Asquan, for that matter."

Jeena smiled. One thing she'd learned about her bondmate during their short time together was that he occasionally had a slight inferiority-complex problem. She turned and whispered in his ear, "That is their jobs, my bondmate, not yours. Each of us has our specialties. I discovered long ago that elves...err, and humans and orcs working together are able to do a lot more as a team than any of us are able to accomplish individually."

"Don't forget Sterilians," hissed Stella through the translator on her battle helmet.

Jeena's smile grew larger. She'd forgotten how sensitive Sterilians' ears were. She looked over at the lizard-looking wizard scout sitting on the bench seat across from her. Stella was just pulling on her battle suit's boots. Jeena noticed the other wizard scouts putting on their battle suits as well. Her bondmate had finished changing a few seconds earlier.

"I could never forget either Charlie or you," Jeena assured her Sterilian friend. She laughed. "Anyone who has seen you swinging those four phase rods at the same time could never forget to include you as a valuable member of their team."

Jeena thought back to the time when Stella, the dragon Bright Wing, and her had infiltrated a Crosioian space station to retrieve bottles of DNA gas. Stella and she had been forced to take on four Crosioian scouts by themselves. The memory of the Sterilian's skill with her quad of phase rods was still fresh in Jeena's mind.

"It's the *Defiant*," said Asquan from the pilot's seat as he slowed the X-shuttle down to maneuvering speed.

Looking past the elf teen's shoulders, Jeena noticed the *Defiant* solidifying to their front. The little recon ship did a one-eighty and presented her backside to the shuttle. The makeshift clamps Sergeant Ron had installed to secure the X-shuttle to the recon ship's back looked like a mighty small target to Jeena.

"Do you think you can hit those securing clamps?" asked Richard.

"I better," laughed Asquan. "If I do not, Tia will have my hide the next time I see her. She made me practice it in our halo-simulator about a thousand times before she left for Trecor."

Thinking back on the young Trecorian fighter pilot, Jeena wiped at her eye as she remembered the tearful goodbye between Tia and the human male, Matthew Deloris. Tia had left to rally the Trecorians and convince them to end their part of the civil war against the Conglomerate. For his part, Matthew had been ordered by Richard to return to Risors and take charge of the Conglomerate's forces.

"That is no easy task," said Danny in her mind. *"Matthew's mother might have been the empress and the de facto leader of the Conglomerate, but according to Sergeant Ron, there are forty-eight people vying for the Conglomerate's leadership. Matthew is way down the pecking order."*

Although Jeena didn't know what a "pecking order" was, she understood the gist of her battle computer's comment. *"Which is the whole reason we are here,"* she said, nodding toward Felix Deloris strapped into the bench seat across from her, next to Stella. His wrinkled business suit contrasted sharply with the battle suits of the wizard scouts sitting around him. *"We will soon see if Sergeant Ron's theory about taking out the top ten contenders will motivate the other thirty-eight to clear the way for Matt."*

"Affirmative," replied Danny.

Timerman turned around in the copilot's seat. "The force field's in place. I'm lowering the ramp. Don't linger getting through the access tube to the *Defiant's* cargo bay. If we're attacked, Asquan and I are raising the ramp and taking off with no questions asked. Those of you without environmental suits would hate to be stuck outside admiring the vacuum of space if the force field goes bye-

bye."

"He's joking, right?" asked Felix Deloris, his face looking a little white.

With a shrug of his shoulders, Richard unbuckled and moved across the aisle to unhook the thin businessman. "Timerman's an orc. I haven't quite figured out his range of humor yet. My recommendation is not to give us any trouble. The sooner we get you into the cargo bay of the *Defiant,* the better."

Jeena noticed the deceased empress's brother move with a purpose for the rear ramp with Richard's gloved hand holding the man's left arm just above the elbow. As soon as Felix's foot touched the ramp, the businessman started floating up.

"Help!" cried Felix.

"Calm down," said Richard as he pulled the man back onto the ramp. "I've got you. The gravity unit doesn't extend to the ramp. The magnetics in my boots are keeping me down. Or don't your luxury space yachts work that way?"

The now completely white-faced Felix closed his eyes and grabbed onto Richard's arm for dear life. "I hate space travel, yachts or otherwise."

Watching closely to make sure Felix Deloris didn't try anything foolish, Jeena remained in the shuttle and covered her bondmate. Within seconds, both he and his prisoner disappeared down an opening in the *Defiant's* skin that had appeared near the end of the shuttle's ramp. She waited until all the remaining occupants of the shuttle had departed except for the teenage elf and orc pilots.

The ring on Jeena's left hand tingled. *"You may as well go now,"* said Danny. *"Asquan and Timerman will be staying onboard to do their post flight."*

"I'm going," Jeena replied as she tentatively placed a foot on the shuttle's ramp. When she did, her foot tried to float upward. She hastily stepped back, eyeing the ramp.

Two sets of laughter sounded behind her.

"It's perfectly safe, Jeehana," said Asquan. "Even if you floated completely free of the ramp, the force field would keep you from drifting more than a couple of meters."

When Jeena turned to glare at the two teenagers, they both hastily turned back to their control panels and pretended to look at their instruments.

"He is right," confirmed Danny. *"I calculate only one chance in a hundred-thousand that the force field will deactivate while you are outside the shuttle."*

Never fond of being laughed at, Jeena drew Power from her reserve and formed it into a one-word levitation spell. The magic wrapped around her, giving her a feeling of stability. Taking a step forward, she used the spell to maintain contact with the ramp. Hurrying into the access opening at the end of the ramp, she slid down the ladder as fast as she could while doing her best to avoid looking at the vast emptiness of space.

"You will get used to it," said Danny. *"Look at me. Moving around in the vacuum of space does not bother me at all."*

"You're a gaseous life form inside a brerellium steel chip in my ring. You don't even breathe. I'm the one who would be harmed if the force field stopped working."

Her battle computer laughed. *"That is true. I calculate that is why it pays to be a gas-based life form instead of a carbon-based one."*

Before Jeena could reply, her feet made contact with the bottom of the access tube and she felt the force of gravity again. With a flick of her left hand, she released the levitation spell. As she turned to enter the cargo bay, Jeena heard loud voices.

A red-faced Sergeant Ron was facing Felix Deloris. "I had nothing to do with the death of my daughter," said the *Defiant's* captain. "I wish I could've helped her, but you know how stubborn she is."

"Was," said Felix. "My sister's dead. Remember?"

"Don't ya think I know that?" said Sergeant Ron. "Don't ya think I would've given my life to save my only daughter's if I coulda?"

Felix shook his head. "Words are cheap, Father. What are you going to do now? Kill me to regain control of the company? Well, you're wasting your time. I might own half of the Deloris Armaments Corporation on paper, but I don't know squat about the company. Diane took care of everything. I just signed whatever she stuck in front of me."

Sergeant Ron looked at the metal deck before glancing back at his son.

Although Jeena rarely detected emotions from the humans on

the *Defiant*, she sensed a wave of sadness wash over the captain and then noticed the red heat of anger in his face disappear as he spoke.

"I'm sorry I wasn't there for you, Felix," said Sergeant Ron, sounding meeker than Jeena had ever heard the contrary old man speak. "I'm more sorry than you can imagine, but things are going on that're bigger than the both of us. Matt needs to take charge of the Conglomerate. We need you to help him do it. You've got the political know-how. He's got the knowledge of the company's inner workings and the drive to make it happen."

"Ha!" laughed Felix. "Jaqual Thoris and Ycckomar Minist have already consolidated their grasp on the political power in the Conglomerate. Why do you think they were trying to get me off Risors? I was in the way. They were sending me to a comfortable but secure house arrest on Thandar Five. Those two will never let Matt take charge. I suspect they've got my nephew under arrest for treason by now, if they haven't already had him executed."

This time Sergeant Ron was the one who laughed. He looked at Richard before glancing back at Felix Deloris. "That's where you're wrong, Son. As of two hours ago, both Thoris and Minist are sitting in a prison cell on Diajor waiting for a military tribunal to be convened. They were both up to their eyeballs in Governor Jenkin's battle plan. They helped betray the Empire on Estos." Scratching his beard, Sergeant Ron gave Felix Deloris the once over. "I'm assuming you had nothing to do with that disaster."

The balding businessman glared at his father. "You know very well I didn't. I may not be the smartest man in the galaxy, but even I know you'd have me on the way to Diajor by now if you had any doubts about my involvement."

Felix Deloris glanced at the others in the cargo bay, staring at Jeena for several seconds. His eyes took on a glassy look before he shook his head and hastily looked away. After seeming to take interest in his scuffed shoes for several seconds, he raised his head. Jeena noticed he made sure to avoid eye contact with her, seeming to take great pains in concentrating on his father instead.

"So it's true," said Felix. "Diane told me you were working with mythical creatures."

Heat rose to Jeena's face. "I am not—"

"Jeena is an elf," said Richard, placing a hand on her shoulder.

20

"She is also my bondmate and my wife, so watch your tongue."

The balding man raised both hands in a stopping motion. "You've got me wrong. Diane told me that Gaston was conducting missions on a planet with elves, dwarves, dragons, the whole works. I didn't believe her until now." He jerked a thumb over his shoulder at a two-meter-long silver-winged creature resting on a nearby crate filled with magic globes of energy. "Between the elf and the miniature dragon over there, I'm convinced."

"You don't know the half of it," said Richard. "There's a dark side filled with vampires, werewolves, demons, and every kind of nasty you can think of. The demons are our real enemies. The Conglomerate and the Empire need to work together again, or we're all dead."

"The Conglomerate is the Empire," said Felix standing straight. "You're the traitors. I'm not the one in charge, so it doesn't matter what I think, but if I was, I wouldn't help you anyway. I don't care what you say or do to me. My sister's dead. I think you killed her." The thin man pointed a finger at Richard. "She warned me about you, Wizard Scout. And don't try to frighten me with children's tales of demons or whatever. I've never been a religious man. Demons are just contrived tales to scare the uneducated into compliance. I don't believe in them. I seriously doubt you do either."

Sergeant Ron opened his mouth to speak, but Richard raised a gloved hand before the *Defiant's* captain could say anything. "Then I'm gonna make a believer out of you...*Felix.*"

Jeena sensed something on the edge of her scan. Something was coming. She wasn't sure what it was, but she sensed it under the ship's steel decking.

"Not under it," corrected Danny in her mind. *"It's in the void. Check the frequency of the creature."*

Reaching out with a scan spell, Jeena felt for the creature with her mind. She found it readily enough and immediately recognized its frequency.

"Rick, what are you going to do?" Jeena asked, growing suddenly concerned. "Are you leaving me?"

Her bondmate turned and smiled. "Just for a minute. Felix here and I are going to take a short trip. We'll be back soon enough."

Also seeming to grow concerned, Sergeant Ron said, "He's my

son, Rick. I don't want—"

"Relax," replied Richard. "Trust me. We'll be right back. He won't be harmed."

With those words, Jeena sensed her bondmate reach out with Power and wrap it around Felix Deloris and himself. The Power vibrated. As she watched, Richard reached out with his left hand and grabbed onto Felix's arm. Both the businessman and her bondmate shimmered before turning translucent and sinking into the floor. Jeena got a vivid view of two large round eyes as Felix Deloris disappeared into the steel deck. His final scream echoed off the walls of the cargo bay as his head sunk below the surface of the metal floor.

Sergeant Ron glanced at Jeena, stress lines punctuating the corners of his eyes. "What's Rick up to?"

Jeena shrugged her shoulders. "I'm not sure. His spirit-horse is in the void right below us. I can sense your son and Rick mounting the stallion now." The sensation of the life forms in the void disappeared. "They are gone now. Do not ask me where. Richard said he would be back in a minute. We will just have to wait."

A minute passed. Then another. Ten more minutes passed before Jeena sensed a disturbance in the void below the cargo bay's deck.

"The void is not below the deck," said Danny. *"It is the space between dimensions. How many times must I explain it?"*

Jeena banged the back of her left hand against a metal supply crate, making sure the red-gemmed ring on her finger took the brunt of the blow. *"Quiet, Danny."* Catching Sergeant Ron's eye, Jeena said, "They are back."

A dozen heartbeats later, the forms of Richard and Felix Deloris rose out of the metal deck. Jeena sensed Power dissipate from around the pair. An ashen-faced Felix collapsed to his knees with both hands clasped in front of his face. The business man's lips moved, but Jeena's normally sensitive ears picked up no sound. *Is he praying?* she wondered.

With an unexpected tenderness, Sergeant Ron knelt by his son's side and wrapped a protective arm around the man's shoulder while patting his back. The *Defiant's* captain looked up at Richard and demanded, "What did you do to him?"

Richard's gaze met Jeena's and he stared at her for a second before turning back to Sergeant Ron. "I showed him who our real enemies are. I took him to the spiritual dimension. I've got a feeling he'll help us now."

"The spiritual dimension?" Jeena asked. "You mean where your dolgars live?" Her bondmate had told her about the lava-spewing, barren land of the spirit wolves.

Shaking his head, Richard looked down at the still praying Felix. "No. Deeper than that. I took him to the demonic plane. I showed him our real enemies. He's seen them first hand now."

Hoping she hadn't heard correctly, Jeena said, "The demonic—"

"Just the upper-most level," said Richard as if that made a difference. "My soul was drawn there during the battle at the Presence of the Lady when I healed the elf children. I saw our real enemies then. I saw the massed demon armies waiting for the command to wipe out every living thing in the three galaxies." Pointing at the kneeling Felix, he said, "Now he's seen them too."

As Jeena looked at her bondmate, he knelt beside Felix Deloris. Placing a hand on the thin man's shoulder, Richard glanced over at Sergeant Ron kneeling on the other side of his son. He and the *Defiant's* captain traded glances. Sergeant Ron sighed and then nodded. When he did, Richard turned his attention back to Felix.

"I'm sorry you had to see that," said Richard in a soft voice, "but it was necessary. The time for our petty hidden agendas and narrow-minded goals is past. We've all got to work together to have any chance against what's coming."

Felix Deloris shook his head, then bent over until his head was almost touching the deck. "It's hopeless, I tell you. Nothing can stop them. Everything's lost. We're all going to die."

The hopelessness in the man's voice hit Jeena hard. Whatever the man had seen had obviously overwhelmed his senses. In spite of her determination in the struggle to save the three galaxies, she began wondering if their fight really was hopeless. Apparently sensing her growing despair through their bond link, Richard looked up at her, catching her eye. She saw him shake his head slightly before turning back to Felix Deloris.

"If I thought it was hopeless," said Richard still kneeling beside the businessman, "I wouldn't have wasted my time taking you to see what's coming. I'd have gathered my friends and run to the farthest corner of the galaxy and lived out as many years as I could before the demon armies overwhelmed us."

An image of billions of demons overrunning the three galaxies flashed in Jeena's mind, followed by the thought of running to a safe area with her bondmate. She struggled to push the thought away, but it persisted nonetheless.

As if sensing her internal struggle, Richard stood and stared at her for a long heartbeat. He turned and looked at the others in the cargo bay. When he spoke next, it was in a voice full of conviction. "I tell all of you here and now that it's *not* hopeless. I'm not going to run and hide. I'm going to fight what's coming as long as there is breath in my body. I've got freewill. One thing I've learned during my missions for *'the One'* is that nothing is set in stone. Working together, and by that I mean *all of us* working together, we've got a chance. We just have to put aside our differences. Each of us has to swallow our pride and prejudices and use every asset at our disposal to hold the line against what's coming."

Jeena felt the ever-growing determination of her bondmate through the link they shared between them. His determination and courage became hers. She gathered strength from his words. *No, not just his words,* she thought. *There's more to it than that.*

"He's forming a Circle," came the thought from Danny in her mind. *"I do not think he even realizes it, but he is."*

At her battle computer's words, Jeena realized Danny was right. She sensed a line of energy reaching out from her bondmate and connecting everyone in the cargo bay in a continuous ring of Power. Even the dragon Bright Wing was included. As Richard's determination and courage jumped from one person in the Circle to the next, it increased with each successive jump. She felt her own resolve grow as it fed on that of the others in the Circle. The feeling of despair at the words of Sergeant Ron's son fell to the wayside where it belonged.

I am a living creature, Jeena thought. *I think. I can fight. I will fight against all who seek to come against us.*

Jeena looked around the room, catching the eyes of everyone there. She had a feeling if the demon armies could see what she saw in the eyes of the *Defiant's* crew, the armies of the dark would have second thoughts about attacking the lands of the living. Even Felix Deloris rose from the floor and stood ramrod straight. He stared into her molten-silver eyes before turning to her bondmate.

"What do you need me to do?" asked Felix in a voice that sounded surprisingly resolved.

Richard smiled and patted the thin man on the back. "I want you to do the same thing the rest of us are going to do. Fight with every breath in your body and with every tool at your disposal."

"How?" said Felix. "Where?"

"How?" said Richard. "Sergeant Ron will tell you what you need to do. Where? On Risors. That's where your battle lies."

"What about you?" asked Felix.

"Me?" said Richard giving a tired smile. "My battle lies elsewhere. I have to fight it alone."

Jeena smiled. She didn't know what her bondmate had in mind, but one thing she knew for sure was that he wasn't going to be alone. She would be by his side no matter what.

And that's the way it's supposed to be, she thought. *That's the way it's always going to be.*

CHAPTER 3

Newly promoted Lieutenant Tianika Bistoria, or Tia to her friends, sat watching her father, War-King Bistoria as he spoke to the assembled council of the Trecorian Alliance. The thirty-meter-wide situation room in the royal palace on Trecor was barely large enough to hold the hundred and fifty admirals, generals, and civilian leaders present. Her father pointed at the star map in the center of the room. It displayed the Trecorian Alliance's part of the galaxy. The war-king waved his hand to include the blue dots that denoted the locations of the combined Trecorian and Empire fleets. Other dots in a lighter shade of blue indicated the additional ships provided by the United Galaxy Alliance that had arrived from the magic dimension.

"Our forces are spread thin," said War-King Bistoria. "All of you can see what we're up against." Waving his hand, he indicated the red, yellow, and orange dots that were the locations of the Conglomerate, Carsoloian, Crosioian, and Balorian Pirates' fleets arrayed against them. Her father gave everyone time to think about what they were seeing.

Only a fool would fail to see that there were a whole lot more red, yellow, and orange dots than there were blues ones. The map certainly gave Tia a lot to think about.

"That's just including the Crosioian fleets we know about," said her father. "The Crosioians' empire stretches into parts of the galaxy we don't even have mapped. Our military intelligence analysts tell me that we can only guess at how many additional forces they have at their disposal."

Tia noticed a movement from her left as someone in a white naval officer's uniform stood to address the council. The officer was her sister, Admiral of the Combined Fleets Elizabeth Bistos.

Humph, Tia thought. *She looks mighty spiffy in her admiral's uniform, but she'll always be plain old Liz to me.*

"Our troops will do their duty," said Liz as she walked to stand near the star map. "We are still consolidating our fleets after the trap in the Criterion star system, but as you can see, we have dispatched ships to harass our enemies. I'm hopeful we can keep them off balance long enough to allow additional reinforcements to arrive from the United Galaxy Alliance. Once those additional UGA ships are integrated within our combined fleets, we will start our own offensive."

Despite being a mere lieutenant, Tia stood. Being the daughter of the war-king, she was far from being intimidated by higher-ranking personnel, especially her sister. "There will be no more ships coming from the United Galaxy Alliance."

"What's that?" asked a large red-bearded man wearing an ill-fitting business suit. The man looked at War-King Bistoria. "I thought you told the council we could expect additional ships from the magic dimension. My miners are spread out on asteroids from one end of the alliance to another. Without additional ships from the UGA, how can you guarantee our safety?"

Tia recognized the man as the representative for the miners' union.

"Lieutenant Bistoria oversteps herself," said Admiral of the Combined Fleets Elizabeth Bistos. "I spoke with the representatives from the UGA three days ago. They assured me that fleets were being assembled in the magic dimension to come to our aid. They should be here by the end of the week."

"They aren't coming," said Tia despite a warning glance from her sister. "I tried telling you earlier, Liz, but you were too busy…err, *Sir.* The winds of politics have changed in the United Galaxy Alliance. The Dragars are escalating strikes against the UGA. There's talk the Dragars will start their invasion soon. Before Rick…err, Wizard Scout Shepard sent me back, he said the UGA made it known that they are depending on reinforcements from our physical galaxy to support them in the Great Battle that threatens their galaxy."

"We're supposed to send *them* ships?" asked the red-bearded man. "We barely have enough warships to hold off the forces arrayed against us as it is."

"That's not quite—" began Tia.

"Enough, Lieutenant," said Liz. "You will sit down and be quiet, or I'll have you removed."

Tia looked at her father, hoping he would overrule her sister. When he remained quiet, her military discipline kicked in. She sat down. After all, Liz *was* the Admiral of the Combined Fleets.

A familiar feminine voice sounded from the other side of the room. "Well, I for one would like to know what the lieutenant has to say."

Tia looked over to see her mother, Kristen Bistoria, standing near her younger sister. Although only nine years old since her birthday last month, Tia thought Chloe looked every bit a Bistorian in her newly issued cadet uniform.

I never thought she'd make it in the military, Tia thought. *I guess being one of only a half-dozen diviners in the Trecorian Alliance adds a lot of self-confidence to even the meekest of souls. I suppose that's another reason I have for trying to do what Rick asked me. He's helped my family a lot since we first met.*

"Very well," said War-King Bistoria deferring to his wife. "Finish what you were going to say, Lieutenant."

With all eyes on her, Tia stood. She drew strength from the green-gemmed ring she wore on her right hand. She felt a tingle in the ring as a feeling of warmth passed over her. Tia knew the warmth for what it was. Matthew was sending her encouragement from wherever he was through the matching ring he wore. She remembered how they'd gotten the rings during their battle on Storage and smiled. Matthew and she were linked now and forever.

"You smile," said Liz. "Does our situation amuse you?"

Tia dropped her smile, wondering if all leaders eventually turned into jerks. She had a fleeting thought that her sister used to be nice.

"No, Sir," Tia replied. "I don't think it's amusing. I do think we're in better shape than it appears at first glance. Even as we speak, Matt is—"

"We cannot base our hopes on the son of a traitor," said Liz.

Tia felt her face grow warm. "He isn't a—"

"Enough," said War-King Bistoria glaring at both of his daughters. "Traitor or not, I don't believe Matthew Deloris has the wherewithal to convince the Conglomerate to surrender to us."

"Rick didn't ask Matt to have them surrender," Tia blurted out before remembering she was talking to the war-king and not her father. "Rick's plan is to have them ally with us and fight against our foes."

"Never," said Liz. "The Conglomerate was in league with the Crosioians. Tens of millions of my fellow Empire soldiers and sailors died as a result of the Conglomerate, as did many of Trecor's finest. I once thought we could make peace with the Conglomerate, but that was before I saw firsthand the destruction and misery their betrayal cost our side. Nothing short of unconditional surrender will suit us now."

War-King Bistoria grew red as the muscles on his face tightened. Slowly they relaxed. "Do you now speak as the war-king, Admiral?"

"Uh...no, I...err," said Liz, her face growing redder with each word.

The war-king nodded his head before giving a slight smile. "That's good. I thought perhaps the council had taken a vote in my absence and replaced me with you."

Liz turned even redder.

Tia was pretty sure the change in color wasn't from anger.

"Sorry, Sir," replied Liz. "I spoke out of turn."

As Tia watched, her father walked to the star chart and stared at it for a dozen heartbeats. No one in the room spoke while he did. When the war-king finally turned back around, he had a strange look in his eyes. She also saw wrinkles on his face that she didn't remember being there before she'd left to serve on the *Defiant*. His shoulders also seemed to sag. The mortality of her father suddenly hit her. *He's always been a giant of a man,* she thought. *It never occurred to me that anything could get him down.*

"We're all under a lot of stress," said her father. "That's all the more reason we must work together and not squabble among ourselves."

Tia met her father's gaze as he looked at her.

"While I have the utmost respect for Wizard Scout Shepard," he continued, "he isn't the war-king. Neither does he command the combined Trecorian, Empire, and UAG fleets."

Her father straightened, standing ramrod straight with shoulders back. Suddenly the version of her father Tia had always known was back.

"We will continue to operate on the assumption that the Conglomerate is working hand in hand with the Crosioians," said War-King Bistoria. He looked at Liz. "Admiral Bistos."

Tia's sister snapped to attention. "Yes, Sir?"

"Until further notice, you will hold our forces on the Conglomerate border in a defensive posture. Be prepared to attack if the council so decides, but make no offensive operations against the Conglomerate for the present."

"As you command," said Liz, looking none too pleased. "What about the Crosioians, Sir?"

"Our latest estimates are that the Crosioians captured a hundred million Empire and Trecorian troops during the battle on Estos. Another hundred million were taken prisoner on the other planets in the Criterion system. I don't know how long those bats will keep our troops alive. I want you to come up with a rescue plan. We need to save as many of those prisoners as we can, while we can."

Tia was shocked. From what she'd found out on her return to Trecor, the combined fleets were barely holding their own against the Crosioians. The war-king's order to come up with a rescue plan for two hundred million POWs was an impossible task, in her opinion. She didn't envy her sister. *Actually, I don't envy anyone who's unlucky enough to get stuck helping her accomplish it either.*

"And...," said War-King Bistoria, "I want you to assign Lieutenant Bistoria to your staff to help plan the operation. She's been to the magic dimension twice now. She'll make a good liaison to the UGA forces."

An empty feeling made itself known in Tia's stomach.

"Yes, Sir!" said Liz.

War-King Bistoria looked at Tia.

She snapped to attention and saluted along with her sister. "Yes, Sir!"

Tia's father returned their salutes, then smiled. "I have one additional order for both of you."

"Sir?" said Liz.

The war-king winked. "Both of you will have dinner with your mother and I tonight. That's an order."

Tia smiled. *That's one order I won't mind obeying.*

CHAPTER 4

The supreme leader of the Crosioian Central Command spread her wings. Hissing and clacking noises in the council's cavern on the capital planet of Fealty came to a halt. The three-hundred-plus Crosioians in attendance retracted their wings to give their supreme leader the acknowledgement and respect she deserved. When she sensed everyone's ears in her direction, the supreme leader spoke.

"Estos was a setback. We were betrayed by the Conglomerate. They should have attacked the Empire's forces on a second front. Instead, they ran and hid. But no matter. We will wipe the Conglomerate out as soon as we are finished destroying what remains of the Empire and Trecorian fleets. Our forces in the outer realms are even now assembling our reinforcements. We are coordinating for more ships and soldiers from our sisters in the Andromeda galaxy. Once these military units arrive, we will be in a position to strike a blow that will wipe the human species from every star system in this galaxy once and for all. The other races will fall in line after the humans are gone. Crosioians will rule the galaxy from now until the end of time as we are destined."

Hissing erupted from the hundreds of assembled representatives of the Crosioian Empire's tribal districts. The combined flapping of their wings caused a breeze to whip up in the cavern, bringing the delicious aroma of ammonia to the supreme leader's nostrils. The smell reminded her of home. She was eager to go back into retirement and leave the future of the Crosioian Empire to the younger generations, but knew she couldn't leave yet. After the fiasco in the Criterion star system and on Estos, the council had enticed her to leave her well-deserved years of rest with her family and return to active duty to take control of the situation. Although she would never admit it to the younger bats present, she knew better than anyone that the battles that lay ahead before complete victory could be achieved would take more years than remained in her lifespan.

Unless, she thought. *Unless we can crush the humans in one decisive blow. I have stripped the outer and inner realms of troops and ships. I will make our sisters in the Andromeda galaxy understand this is their battle as much as ours. They will come to our aid if I have to drag them here by the ear like newborn hatchlings. I will gather the largest armada the galaxy has ever seen and guide the younglings to ultimate victory. My plan will work. I know it will.* She thought of the newborns in her home cave. *My plan must work so they may live. I owe it to our newborns to ensure their safety and that of our future generations. The humans must be destroyed as a species. That is the only way our younglings can ever know true peace.*

A bat only a few years younger than the supreme leader stood and spread her wings. She was the oldest representative of the Long Wing tribe. The supreme leader knew her well. She was called Charge-In-The-Face-Of-Great-Odds for good reason. They had been friends since their youth, during scout training. At the sight of the Long Wing rep spreading her wings, the cheering of those assembled subsided until the cavern was silent.

"With all due respect, it is a dangerous game you play, Supreme Leader," said the Long Wing representative. "Our outer realms are not without dangers of their own. The same can be said for the territories of our sisters in Andromeda. Once we strip our defenses, our worlds in both galaxies will be susceptible to attack. The humans may take advantage of the weakness in this galaxy and attack our rear even as our fleets move to engage their primary districts."

The supreme leader gave a bat's version of a smile. "Ah, it is good to hear your voice again, old friend. I thought for sure you would be in your tribal cavern, surrounded by younglings as you regaled them with the exploits of your long-ago youth."

Charge-In-The-Face-Of-Great-Odds hissed a smile in return. "As I you, Supreme Leader." She waved a wing encompassing the crowd of bats in the cavern. "When duty calls, a bat always answers no matter their age. I was asked to serve, so I am here."

The supreme leader nodded in approval. "The loyalty and commitment to duty by bats of all generations is why the Crosioian race will achieve final and total victory over our foes. As for your concern, I share it, *but*...I have set fruit in a trap that the humans cannot resist." When the supreme leader sensed she had everyone's undivided attention, she hissed, "Unlike Crosioians, humans and their allies see no shame in surrender. As you may know, our forces captured a little over two hundred million of the humans."

The cavern filled with hissing and the sound of flapping wings. That any race could endure the shame of surrender was unfathomable. More than a few in attendance shouted, "Kill them! Kill them all!"

"Yes," hissed the supreme leader using a voice high-pitched enough to be heard over the noise of the crowd. "I share your disgust, but the humans' shame works to our advantage. We have assembled the prisoners on the planet Estos. Most of them were there already, when they fell into our trap. The residual radiation of the magic nukes we were given by the Conglomerate is slowly killing them. We are sending down enough food and medicine to the planet's surface to keep them alive, but their time is short. The humans will be forced to act to save the prisoners before they succumb to the radiation."

Charge-In-The-Face-Of-Great-Odds hissed her disbelief. "Even humans would not be foolish enough to fall into a second trap on Estos. Their forces barely escaped as it was. Surely they would not risk their ships and troops a second time to save those who deserve to die for their dishonor."

The supreme leader hissed laughter. "You give the humans too much credit, old friend. The emotional ties between them are strong. As a Crosioian scout, I spent many years conducting missions deep in the humans' star systems. Their weakness has always been their attachment to even the frailest of their species. Trust me, they will come. When they do, our fleets will be there waiting."

Another bat stood and spread her wings. "Our fleets were

waiting last time. Yet our forces suffered even greater losses than the humans."

The supreme leader recognized the bat as the representative from the Blood Claw tribe, the honorable Spear-Through-Your-Heart. The supreme leader's chest turned dark gray. *The Blood Claws are ever the ones to voice discontent and stir up trouble,* she thought. Getting control of her anger, she kept the thought to herself. With effort, she said in a calm voice, "Yes, the generation below us mistakenly relied on our master computer too much. After analyzing the data, our techs have discovered that the master computer was infected with a previously unknown virus so subtle, it was only found after the fact. The younger leaders also allowed magic users and demons to play too large of a part in the battle. We have rectified that situation."

Sending a radar ping to scan the crowd, the supreme leader merged the results with her passive scan. She identified twenty-four scouts besides herself in the assembly of bats. None of them had their stealth shields activated out of respect for the sanctity of the council cavern. Next to her own Power reserve, the reserve of the Long Wing representative glowed brightest. The reserve of the Blood Claw's rep was not far behind.

"Twenty-five scouts counting myself are in this room," said the supreme leader. "Each of you would recognize the scent of the remains of the virus we found. It is the same scent as that from *the Hole.*"

Hissing and flapping of wings erupted in the cavern once more.

"Impossible," said the Long Wing representative, Charge-In-The-Face-Of-Great-Odds. "Our guards have secured *the Hole* ever since its discovery on the Blood Claw's home world of Astaris a hundred thousand years ago. For generations our scout candidates have entered *the Hole* to prove their worth before being teleported to Velos for their DNA modification. Every hundred years, the best of our scouts have entered *the Hole* to ensure that the rift to the plane beyond cannot be used by the demons to come to our dimension."

"Nevertheless," said the supreme leader, "one did. It infected the master computer. At the peak of the battle for the Criterion system, the demon virus was destroyed, though we do not yet know how. What we do know is that the destruction of the virus left our strategic computers in disarray. The humans took advantage of our momentary weakness. Our techs have regained control of our computer network by using a backup master computer. Our part of the tele-network is functioning normally again. This time our fleets will overwhelm the human forces and destroy them once and for all."

The Blood Claw rep, Spear-Through-Your-Heart, stood again and spread her wings, flapping them to get everyone's attention. "Perhaps our fault was in not utilizing the demons and magic users to their full potential."

Charge-In-The-Face-Of-Great-Odds bristled as she flapped her wings and gnashed her teeth. "Are you that foolish? Fifteen millions of my Long Wing tribe died on Estos due to the participation of the demons and their filthy magic users. Our younger generation relied on them instead of the abilities of our soldiers and sailors. The demons and magic users are the reason we suffered defeat instead of victory over the humans. That is why the first thing the supreme leader did after she was sworn in was order their termination."

"Yes," said Spear-Through-Your-Heart. "The few demons that provided the stealth shields for our fleets have been destroyed along with their mage caretakers." She swiveled one ear at the supreme leader before turning it back to the Long Wing rep. "I argued against that action, but orders are orders, and so it has been done." She furled her wings and tucked them behind her back as she wove her way between perches and made her way to the cavern floor. Once there, she spread her wings and faced the rest of the flock that was spread throughout the cavern. "However, I offer an alternative version of the Estos battle. I say the reason we failed was not because we used a few demons and magic users, but that we did not use enough. At the master computer's suggestion, we kidnapped one demon from *the Hole* and forced it to summon a few of its kind to cast stealth spells around our fleets. We brought only enough magic users from their dimension to cast illusion spells on Estos to fool the Empire's wizard scouts. I say the mistake was not that we used a few demons and magic users, but that we should have used more. If I had been in charge, every Crosioian regiment and every warship larger than a shuttle would have had a demon and a contingent of mages to supplement our forces. Then the trap would have worked. The Empire would no longer exist."

Charge-In-The-Face-Of-Great-Odds spread her wings, demanding the attention of the crowd. "Have you not been listening? A demon infected the master computer. It was not one of the demons we allowed to be summoned. It somehow made its way into our galaxy on its own and took over our part of the tele-network. What the demons did once, they may do again. A hundred years have passed since the last indepth recon of *the Hole*. In six weeks, it will be time to do so again. We must be sure the rift is still secure before we launch our attack on the humans."

"The rift is secure, as is *the Hole*," said Spear-Through-Your-Heart. "The best of the Blood Claw tribe guards *the Hole* as we have guarded it since ancient times. Say the word, and I will personally enter *the Hole* and lead a team to recon the rift if you need that assurance. I consider it an affront for anyone to accuse my tribe of allowing a demon to escape." She turned both ears on the Long Wing rep. "Is that what you are suggesting?"

Charge-In-The-Face-Of-Great-Odds said nothing. Her continued silence made her opinion of the Blood Claw's guarding abilities more than obvious.

The Blood Claw rep's chest turned a deep gray.

"No one is suggesting such a thing," the supreme leader said. "The Blood Claw tribe has ever been the faithful guardians of *the Hole*. But let us not forget that even though *the Hole* was found on your home world of Astaris, all tribes share in responsibility for its security." She swiveled her ears at the Long Wing rep. "You know that as well as the rest of us, old friend. If a demon somehow slipped through the rift, all tribes would share equally in the blame."

Charge-In-The-Face-Of-Great-Odds tucked her wings tightly behind her back. "As you say, Supreme Leader. Still, I must again stress our need for a recon of the rift. Demons must never again taint our fighting forces. We do not need them or their pathetic magic users."

The supreme commander was not surprised by her friend's heated defense against the use of demons and magic users. The words of her friend were aligned with her own thoughts. The use of any demons had been a mistake. As the supreme leader, she would not allow the same mistake to be made on her watch. Releasing a sonic wave, she touched every bat in the cavern. Both the Long Wing and Blood Claw reps lowered their wings as was proper. Once everyone was quiet, the supreme leader spoke.

"As my friend Charge-In-The-Face-Of-Great-Odds has said, the time for the next recon of the rift is due. I have no doubt all of you know there is a problem. Since the destruction of the DNA center on Velos, we have not had any new scouts. With the loss of the bottles of DNA gas at our research center on the space station *Last Hope*, any chance of creating more scouts has disappeared. Like the Empire, we have only those scouts that currently exist. There will never be any others. I mean no slight to those long-time scouts present when I say our best scouts have been lost. What scout remains that is young enough and strong enough to lead the recon into the rift?"

"It is true," admitted Charge-In-The-Face-Of-Great-Odds. "The best of our scouts are gone. My own grandaughter died during the battle on Estos. The heads of two Empire scouts reside on my tribe's Wall of Honor due to her efforts. She would have been our best choice to lead the recon."

"Alas, as you say, she died during the battle as is honorable," said the supreme leader. "Many others also died. Your grandaughter would also have been my choice to lead the recon if she'd survived. She was our best hope after the death of your daughter on Veturna in the Empire's Drako system. The wizard scout and his allies destroyed the best of our best."

At the mention of the hated wizard scout, the Long Wing representative and every other bat in the cavern hissed their desire for revenge.

Charge-In-The-Face-Of-Great-Odds waited until the hissing stopped before speaking. "Yes, my daughter was the best of our scouts and my granddaughter the best after her. The heads of five of the Empire wizard scouts are on the Long Wing's Wall of Honor due to my daughter's efforts. If she had lived, I have no doubt she could have taken a team all the way to the rift, as could have my grandaughter. However, they are gone. We must hold a tournament to select a new leader for the recon of *the Hole*. It will need to be done quickly. Our time is indeed short, and our need is great. I believe what our supreme leader says is true. The humans will be assembling their fleets to rescue their comrades on Estos soon. We must assemble our fleets as well and prepare our trap even as we conduct the competition to select the leader for the recon of *the Hole*."

The supreme leader nodded her head. "As always, old friend, we think along the same lines. Even now preparations are being made for the competition. The best of our remaining scouts are on their way to the Onstarian star system in the outer realms. Once they arrive, the competition will begin. Let us hope that we find a scout as good as your granddaughter to lead the recon team. It will do us no good if our recon team gets all the way to the rift in *the Hole* but is not strong enough to return with word of what they find. If the rift is opening, we must know it so we can find a way to block it once and for all."

"That would be a mistake," said Spear-Through-Your-Heart. "If there is an opening in the rift, we could use it to bring enough demons to our galaxy to conquer our enemies in one fell swoop. We could—"

"Enough!" the supreme leader said. "As long as I am your supreme leader, Crosioians will never again use either demons or magic users. We will speak of this no more."

The Blood Claw rep nodded. "As you say, we will speak of it no more as long as you are the supreme leader."

CHAPTER 5

Rubbing her eyes, Telsa looked around at the dozen elf scribes hunched over stone desks littered with scrolls and tomes. Like her, they were poring over the aged parchments in an effort to unlock the secrets of their ancient ancestors, the Letian elves. She was tired. More than that, she was bored and growing more so by the hour. The dim light of the subterranean chamber located ten levels below Silverton's main library wasn't helping.

Glancing at the cavern's roughly hewn rock ceiling ten meters overhead, she frowned at the bluish glow emitted from the dozens of magical light globes embedded in the ceiling. The glow from overhead provided enough light to see, but in her opinion, it did little to make the long hours of translating Letian documents into intergalactic standard an enjoyable endeavor.

"You obviously do not appreciate the elves' magic," said Raj in their shared space. *"The light is designed to preserve the writing on the scrolls and books. It wasn't designed for the comfort of non-elves."*

"So you've told me," Telsa said. She wasn't in the mood for her battle computer's logic no matter how reasonable it might sound. She longed for the fresh air and sunshine located ten levels above the part of the library designated for the oldest of the elves' books and scrolls. In her opinion, she'd already spent far too much time searching their most treasured documents for clues about what had happened to the Ecarian giants and their yellow gem. Even with the elf scribes' expert help, they'd come up short.

Leaning back in her chair, Telsa gave a big stretch. She winked at the thin elf boy sitting at the desk next to her. "You know, if you all paid your electric bills once in a while, maybe you could keep it a little brighter down here."

The elf boy, Therso, was one of the scribes at Silverton's main library. He'd been assigned as Telsa's liaison by the chief librarian. At Telsa's remark, the young elf took his eyes off the manuscript he was studying long enough to look at her. "Elect...what?"

Telsa laughed at her little joke even if it did go over the elf's head. "Never mind. I was just complaining about the lack of light down here. Not everyone has night vision."

"All elves do," said Raj speaking over the external speakers of Telsa's battle helmet. "Besides, as your battle computer, I'm the one doing most of the translating. All you have to do is monitor our shared space. It's not like you have to stare at the paper or anything."

"Regardless," Telsa said. "It's nice every once in a while just to look around and see something besides dank stone walls."

Therso placed his stylus on his desk before turning in his seat to look at her. "I will admit it is a little dark down here, but it is hardly dank, Wizard Scout. Our oldest scrolls and books are kept in these subterranean chambers. A few are over a hundred thousand years old. Even with the preservation spells the ancients cast on these storage rooms, the writing is gradually fading, not to mention the paper is deteriorating. Keeping the lights low helps to slow the aging process." The thin elf boy leaned toward Telsa, "Or so I have been told by Chief Librarian Elisinsar. To be honest, I have often wondered how he knows for certain. Some of us younger scribes are of the opinion that bright lights do not affect the deterioration at all."

"Hmm," Telsa said, thinking of a half-dozen controlled experiments she could conduct to test the chief librarian's theory. "Perhaps I could—"

"No, you *cannot*," said Raj in no uncertain terms. "Wizard Scout Shepard assigned us here to translate the ancient Letian tomes in the hopes we could discover the location of another of those yellow gems. We have access to blue, green, and red gems on Storage. We are short the yellow gem. If we are able to find one, then perhaps the elves' gate to the demonic plane can be closed permanently."

Telsa glanced at the stack of scrolls on her desk. "Well, we aren't having much luck so far. The last three documents I've translated have been content lists for warehouses long turned to dust. I doubt we're helping much in the war effort."

Therso shook his head. "That is where you are wrong, Wizard Scout Telsa. Each and every thing your computer and you have translated from ancient Letian adds to our knowledge. I dare say the two of you have translated more text in the past week than an army of scribes have in the last fifty thousand years."

Telsa shrugged. "Maybe, but it's still boring." She pulled a scroll off her desk, unwound it, and scanned the first couple of paragraphs. The ancient Letian writing passed through Raj's translation program, appearing in intergalactic standard in the shared space of her mind.

"Take this, for instance," Telsa said holding up the scroll to the elf. "It's a report of some kind for a mining company. Looks like something about rafts." She grinned. "Now why would a mining company need rafts?"

Therso frowned. "Rafts? Are you sure?"

When Telsa handed the scroll to the young scribe, he rolled it out. Then he placed a translation sheet Raj and he had been creating on the desk next to the scroll. After thirty seconds of peering at the parchment, Therso laughed. Taking his stylus, he changed a symbol on the translation sheet.

The elf looked over at Telsa. "I am afraid your battle computer and I made a mistake in our earlier translation of this symbol. I see the problem now, thanks to you. The word is rifts, not rafts."

"Rifts?" Telsa said getting out of her chair to peer over the elf's shoulder. "What kind of rift?"

The elf shrugged, adding a smile before he spoke. "My specialty is translations. I pretty much leave mining questions to dwarves. They are the experts."

Telsa sat back on her seat. "I don't suppose there's any dwarves hanging around Silverton, is there?"

"Nay, I am afraid not, Wizard Scout Telsa," said Therso. "A few of their emissaries visit from time to time, but it has been a good decade since their last visit."

Smiling, Telsa straightened up the stack of books and scrolls she'd been studying. "Well, too long to wait for the next visit, I'm thinking." She looked at Therso, catching his eye. "By the way, I told you to call me Telsa. Adding wizard scout to the front makes it sound too formal."

"As you wish, Wiz—err, Telsa." The elf returned her smile. "Are you leaving?"

"Yep. I think Raj and I have done all the damage we can here for one day. I promised Terrie I would try to make time this afternoon to see how the new Academy of Healers is coming along." She winked, giving the elf a smile as well. "I think he just wants to brag a little, to tell the truth."

Instead of smiling, the elf's face took on a serious expression. Actually, he looked sadder than anything. Telsa wondered why her attempt at humor had fallen flat.

"Wizard Scout Terrie and his bond—err, I mean wife, Angela, have done more for our race than I think you know. Almost all other races on Portalis are able to be healed magically. My elven race has never been so blessed."

Before Telsa could speak, Therso said, "Please do not get me wrong. Elves have been blessed in so many other ways that I have no room to complain. Plus, our medics can do wonders with herbal healing. Still, many elves that could have been saved over the years have died due to our inability to be healed magically. What Elf Friend Richard and Wizard Scout Terrie have done for us is beyond anything we expected."

Telsa thought back to the battle in the Presence of the Lady. Rick had healed several elf children who by all rights should've died. Combined with Terrie's healing abilities, the elves were appreciative to the point of embarrassment. Their appreciation even affected the way they treated her since she was also a wizard scout. She'd tried telling them her specialty was Power projection and not healing, but the elves of Silverton paid her no heed.

"I'm sure you'd have done the same for us," Telsa said.

Therso shook his head. "To my shame, you are wrong. Prejudices against humans have run deep in elves for tens of thousands of years. Thanks to the elf friend and Wizard Scout Terrie, those attitudes are changing, especially among the younger elves. Nevertheless, my race still has a long way to go before all humans are accepted."

Telsa didn't know what to say.

The young elf looked at her. "My father and mother were killed in an orc ambush a century ago. Our medics did all they could to save their lives, but it was not enough. Once the first batch of healers graduate from our new Academy of Healers, then perhaps other elf children will not be faced with the loss of their parents as was I."

Telsa reached over and touched the elf on the arm. "I hope it all works out. Terrie's the best wizard scout healer I've ever known. If anyone can train your healers, he's the man."

The elf nodded his head without speaking and turned back to stare at the parchment on his desk. Telsa noticed something wet fall on the aged paper. Beating a hasty retreat, she turned and made for the stairs.

Once outside the library doors, Telsa stopped on the stairs and leaned against the elaborately carved, white-stone guardrail. It was positioned in a manner to prevent careless pedestrians from falling off the stairway without detracting from the beauty of the library's architecture. One look over the side, to the ground fifteen meters below, convinced her that the railing was needed considering the number of elf children she'd seen visiting the library.

"Actually, it is fourteen point seven meters to the ground," said Raj in their shared space.

"Thanks for the update. I'm not sure I could've made it the rest of the day wondering exactly how far it was."

"Then it is a good thing I told you, Wizard Scout."

Telsa wondered in her private space if it might be nice having a battle computer that understood sarcasm. Facing to the north, she took in the single-story, white-stone buildings that made up the majority of Silverton. The low structures gave a clear shot of a blue-roofed, hundred-meter-tall, white obelisk that was blackened in spots. She knew the black spots were from the scorching blasts of energy used during the attack on the Tree of Light two weeks earlier.

"I'm surprised the elves haven't painted it white to cover up that smoke damage," Telsa said. *"They've repaired most of the other damage from the demon's attack."*

"Oh, I gather from listening to the conversations of the elves you have been around that they will not be painting the black

marks on that obelisk or the damage on the other three either. The elves' mages have spells at their disposal that could easily return the stone to its original condition."

Telsa turned slowly to look at the other three obelisks. The one to the east had a red roof; the southern obelisk had a green roof; and the western obelisk's top was yellow. The white stone of the other obelisks was only slightly less discolored than their blue companion to the north. *"I'd think if they could repair the damage with a simple spell that they'd have done it already."*

Once again, Telsa thought she detected a hint of emotion from her battle computer. It was barely discernable, but this time she was almost certain it was there. *Is Raj being emotionally corrupted?* she wondered in her private space.

"First off, Wizard Scout, I calculate no spell is simple. From what I have read, an elf child studies magical writing for almost a hundred years before they are allowed to cast their first spell. As for why they haven't repaired the damage to the obelisks, I heard Leethor tell his children the obelisks would remain as they were to be a reminder for future generations that they should never let their guard down. He told them an attack by forces of evil could occur at any time or anywhere."

Telsa laughed. *"You've been eavesdropping again, haven't you?"*

"Humph," said Raj. *"I do not eavesdrop. Can I help it if the amplifiers on your battle helmet are so sensitive they can pick up whispers from a hundred meters away?"*

"Forget it," Telsa said, knowing she couldn't win the argument. She started down the stairs toward the white cobblestone street below. *"Enough dillydallying, as Nickelo would say. I've got things to do."*

Once on the street, Telsa headed toward Silverton's center. A family of elves, two adults, and a child appearing to be about five or six in human years, passed going in the opposite direction. The two adults nodded politely. The child smiled and waved. Telsa waved back.

"I don't know what Therso was talking about," Telsa commented to her battle computer. *"The elves seem friendly enough to me. I'm human, and I don't see any signs of prejudice."*

"I calculate you do not for several reasons," replied Raj. *"First*

off, you are short for a human adult. Based upon the reactions of adult elves in your presence, there is an eighty-four percent probability they think of you more as a tall gnome than they do a small human."

"I don't look anything like a gnome. I've seen several over the years, what with my trip back in time with Rick to stop the Dragars from sacrificing unborn dragons."

"Nevertheless, I am just informing you of the probabilities. A second reason for their acceptance of you is your battle suit. Face it, even deactivated as it is and with your helmet in half mode, you stand out in a crowd. You are instantly recognizable as an associate of Wizard Scout Shepard's."

"Whatever," Telsa said, growing more than a little bored with the conversation.

"Do you want to hear my third reason?"

"Not particularly," Telsa said before Raj could get started.

"Humph," said Raj. *"That is what I get for trying to provide useful information. Speaking of useful information, your course is not taking you to the Academy of Healing building. It is farther to the east."*

"Shows what you know," Telsa laughed. *"I'm not going to see Terrie yet. I want to find Rembis. The gnome magic user should be at the Mages Guild around this time. I'd like to pick his brain about the yellow gem. I think I'll ask about rifts while I'm at it."*

A map of Silverton appeared in the shared space of Telsa's mind. A green path went from her current location to a building she knew was the Mages Guild.

"What's the map for?" Telsa asked. *"Are you afraid I'll get lost?"* She sensed an emotion in her shared space that was unusual for her battle computer. *"Hey. Did you just laugh, or am I imagining things?"*

"It must have been your imagination. I am a computer. I do not laugh. I also do not get afraid. I do, however, get concerned. As it so happens, I am concerned you are not taking the most efficient route to the Mages Guild, so I plotted a recommended course on a map for you."

"Very kind, but also very dull," Telsa replied. *"We're in a city full of elves. Where's your sense of adventure. We may never get to experience anything like this again. Look at the buildings. Leethor*

and Meshoan told me a lot of them are tens of thousands of years old. A few are almost a hundred thousand. Despite their age, they appear nearly new."

"*Preservation spells,"* replied Raj. *"It is an efficient way to build things. The elves build something well once and keep it in good shape for as long as it is useful. Of course, that would never work with humans or a lot of the races in the physical dimension."*

Telsa stopped in the middle of the cobblestone road to admire a small shop made of white stone and embedded with glow-stone chips. The small chips reflected the afternoon sun, making the walls of the building explode with every color of the rainbow as she moved her head.

"What do you mean it wouldn't work with humans?" Telsa said. She suspected her battle computer was making a snide comment about her species, but she wasn't exactly sure how.

"What I mean is that preserving buildings, or preserving anything for that matter, is not in a human's nature. Your species is too commercial. The entire economy of your race depends on manufacturing and building things. If humans made things too good and preserved them with spells, before long, all the manufacturing plants would close down. People would lose their jobs. Chaos would ensue."

Telsa frowned. *"That hasn't happened here. The elves seem to be getting along fine."*

"True," admitted Raj. *"On the other hand, Portalis is a special case. It has been stuck in what would be considered the middle ages back on Earth for a hundred thousand years. Based upon what I have discovered reading the planet's history at the library, any time things start to advance too much, either a natural disaster or some big invasion sets things back."*

"I repeat, that hasn't happened here in Silverton," Telsa said, determined to win the argument. *"Like I told you, some of these buildings are a hundred thousand years old."*

"The elves have maintained a static population for tens of thousands of years," said Raj. *"Their birthrate is low compared to humans. I calculate that is one of the reasons for their animosity against your species. As the human population has grown, the elves have been pushed out of their territory. Wars have been fought in the past for that very reason."*

Telsa looked at the growing crowd of elves on the road as they walked to conduct whatever business elves did. *"I see several children on the street. I've seen a lot during the two weeks I've been here, so I'm not sure I buy your theory about elves not being prolific."*

Raj laughed.

Telsa recognized it as the canned laughter battle computers sometimes used to appease humans' need for humor. It wasn't the emotional laughter she thought she'd felt earlier.

"For a genius who has spent the last week at the library, you sure miss a lot when you read," Raj said. *"The birthrate of the elves has been increasing over the last five hundred years. I have read about previous increases of birthrates in the histories at the library. They have always preceded a period of war."*

"What's that?" Telsa asked. *"Are you saying the elves are having more children because war is coming?"*

"Based upon other cycles of birthrate increases, I would say that is a logical conclusion. Take the elves Leethor and Meshoan, for instance. They already have two children with another on the way. A thousand years ago, an elf family with three children was unheard of. About five hundred years ago, the birthrate for the elves started to increase. High Priestess Jeehanathoraxen's family was one of the first to have three children. Now it is more common. The first of the children born in the birthrate increase are now of military age. I calculate the younger children may be replacements for those who are killed in whatever calamity is headed the elves' way."

Telsa didn't want to consider what might be heading the elves' way. She supposed it was because she knew that whatever it was, it was also headed for her human race. Turning, she began walking the most efficient route to the Mages Guild as recommended by her battle computer. She no longer felt like sightseeing.

Twenty minutes later found Telsa standing outside a squat, black-stoned building.

"Are you sure this is the place, Raj? It's not even twenty meters square. From what I heard, the guild has dozens of children training on most days." Telsa leaned forward, peering closer at the building. *"For that matter, it doesn't even have a door."*

Before her battle computer could reply, a white-haired gnome wearing a black robe walked out of the center of the wall nearest the street. The gnome's wide belt was stuffed with a half-dozen wands along with a small dagger. The butt of the handle on the dagger contained a blue gem. A necklace in the shape of an eye with a red gem for the iris adorned the gnome's neck.

"Rembis," Telsa said. "Just the gnome I wanted to see."

Rembis smiled. His blue eyes sparkled with just the hint of mischievousness Telsa associated with gnomes of all ages.

"Telsa," said the old gnome. "Well met. When our guards saw you approaching, they sent word right away. They assumed you were coming to see me."

Reaching out with her passive scan, Telsa searched for any signs of invisible guards. She found none.

Raj spoke to her in their shared space. *If their stealth shields are good enough, then you would not spot them.*

While Telsa had a high regard for elves in general, she'd been around them enough during the past two weeks to know their stealth shields were nowhere near as good as that of a wizard scout's. She kept her opinion to herself anyway. The last thing she wanted was a lecture from Raj on types of stealth shields.

Glancing left and right before looking back at the gnome, Telsa said, "Guards? I don't see any guards."

Laughing, Rembis waved a hand at the black building. "That's because there aren't any out here. They are inside the dimensional pocket, using scrying devices. If you had been an enemy, you would've been met by a dozen guards and mages instead of me."

"Hmm," Telsa said. "I'm afraid that I'm not exactly sure what a dimensional pocket is."

Grinning, Rembis bowed before turning toward the black wall. "Then allow me to show you. Uh...that is if you have the time."

More than a little curious, Telsa grinned back. "Oh, I've got the time. In fact, your guards assumed right. I did come to see you. So lead the way. We can talk while you give me the grand tour."

Waving a hand in the air, Rembis said a word Telsa heard but quickly forgot. The black wall turned slightly translucent as the gnome stepped through. She followed close on his heels, unsure what she'd find on the other side, and felt a cold tingle as she passed through. Two steps later found her in a brightly lit chamber two hundred meters in length and half as wide.

In the area immediately in front of the doorway sat half a dozen elves in black robes concentrating on round globes twice the size of basketballs. In the globe closest to her, Telsa saw the street outside the black building. Four elves wearing chainmail and carrying spears and shields stood on either side of the six mages. She noticed another dozen guards off to the side, sitting at a table. Their spears and shields were leaning against the wall, but each of them still wore a longsword on their hip. She sensed magic coming from all the guards' weapons and armor.

"The entire place reeks of magic," said Raj. *"I'd be on my best behavior if I were you."*

"Aren't I always?" Telsa said in their shared space.

"Most of the time," conceded Raj. *"However, I calculate some of Wizard Scout Shepard's bad habits have rubbed off on you over the years."*

Telsa smiled. She didn't think that was a bad thing.

Rembis spoke with one of the guards. The gnome motioned Telsa to follow as he walked between two metal posts. Once again she felt a cold tingle until she was on the other side. Glancing back over her shoulder at a globe near the two posts, she saw an outline of her body similar to the output from security sniffers at spaceports or other high-security facilities. Her weapons were outlined in red while her battle helmet glowed orange on the image.

Rembis laughed. "I think your battle computer has confused our security spell. It's not sure whether it is a weapon or harmless."

The black-robed elf mage sitting at the table holding the security globe eyed Rembis. "Are you vouching for her?"

"Yes, yes," replied Rembis as he grabbed Telsa's arm and dragged her behind him. "She's a wizard scout. She's with me."

The gnome passed a large set of black-stone stairs leading downward. Globes of white light embedded in the ceiling of the stairs allowed Telsa to see all the way to the bottom.

"It must go down at least two hundred meters," Telsa said. "How big is this place?"

Rembis waved his hand at the inside of the building. "I told you, this is a dimension pocket. It's as big as the spellcasters need it to be. Administrative offices and some of the more classified areas are ten floors below us. The rooms above them are libraries, classrooms, training areas, and things of that sort. What I wanted to show you, though, is over there." The gnome pointed at the far left corner of the first floor. Thanks to the light globes in the ceiling twenty meters above, Telsa was able to make out the entire area easily enough.

A group of fifty elf children in sets of two were lined up in the center of the first floor, facing one another. The elf children wore gray robes with white belts. As an adult elf in a black robe approached the first pair of children, one of the gray-robed elf children raised a hand and shouted a word Telsa quickly forgot. She sensed energy form in the child's hand before shooting out at the second elf child. The second elf raised his hands and formed a shield of magic energy. The incoming ball of energy ricocheted off, heading straight for Rembis and her. Reflexively, Telsa drew Power from her reserve and formed a shield to her front. The child's spell never reached her defensive shield. It hit a wall of magic a dozen paces to her front.

Laughing, Rembis pointed at the shield of magic. "Give us a little credit, Wizard Scout. That shield is strong enough to absorb even ninth level spells. The center area where the novices are practicing is our primary hands-on training area. Even our master mages practice there. The shield of magic is refreshed every day by our best mages. If it wasn't, I dare say walking around the first floor would be more than a little hazardous."

Telsa dropped her defensive shield to conserve Power. "No kidding. I sensed the shield with my passive scan, but I didn't want to take any chances. Is this what you wanted to show me? The children training, I mean."

Shaking his head, Rembis said, "No, although it is interesting in its own right. What I wanted to show you is a little experiment I set up in the far left corner of the room."

The word experiment drew Telsa's curiosity more than anything she'd seen thus far. The challenge of creating logical experiments to prove or disapprove theories had always fascinated her. She followed the old gnome as he weaved his way past pairs of younger elves in gray robes being supervised by older black-robed elves.

Telsa pointed at the sparing elves. "Assuming the elves in the gray robes are the novices, you've got a lot of students. I count a good hundred just on this floor alone."

Nodding his head, Rembis stopped and looked back at her. "You assume right. The beginners wear white robes. They are still studying reading and writing of magic spells. I am told it normally takes a hundred years or so for the beginners to advance to earn their gray robes as a novice. Then and only then are they allowed to begin casting the simplest of spells." He smiled at Telsa. "The elves spend many years becoming mages. I suppose that's why they are considered the best. Of course..."

When the gnome remained silent, Telsa prodded him on. "Of course what?"

"Oh, you know. As good as they are, they are nowhere near as competent as the elves were during the time I was born twenty thousand years in the past. The height of their skill was a hundred thousand years ago. The elves nowadays don't even know how to protect the links to their Power reserves."

Telsa unconsciously sensed the link to her Power reserve. Dozens of locks and traps lined the link protecting weak points. She silently thanked her friend Rick for taking the time to beef up her defenses. "Well, to be honest, the links of most wizard scouts aren't protected either. As far as I know, only Rick knows how to defend or break links."

"Don't kid yourself," said Rembis. "Others do as well. I will admit that most of those who do, received their training back in time like me, but they exist nonetheless."

Telsa nodded. "Yeah. Rick taught me how to fend off attacks on my link when we were on the mission to destroy the Dragars' temple. Since I'm not a diviner, I can't set traps on my link or anyone else's. I also can't break anyone's link."

"Nor can I," admitted Rembis. "Still, you and I are in better shape than any of the elves in Silverton as far as protecting our links is concerned."

Telsa had no argument against the gnome's observation, so she said nothing.

Shrugging his shoulders, Rembis turned and led the way toward the far left corner of the first floor. As they drew closer, Telsa made out miniature buildings surrounded by a white wall no higher than her little finger. A tree twice the size of her fist was in the center of the miniature city. Reaching out with her passive scan, she detected magic around the entire mockup.

"It's an illusion of Silverton, isn't it?" Telsa asked, enthralled by the detail of the miniaturized city. As far as she could tell, every minute detail of the elf city was captured by the spell.

Nodding his head, Rembis walked into the illusion and began pointing out various buildings. "That is correct, Wizard Scout. Here is the palace, the library, and this little black building is the Mages Guild where we're currently located."

As she stepped into the illusion, Telsa made out miniature figures walking down the white-stone streets. "Is it real time?"

Shaking his head, Rembis said, "No. That would be a complicated spell indeed." He laughed. "Don't suggest it to Master Jathar. He likes challenges way too much for his own good. Besides, it's not needed for my purpose."

Telsa remembered the gnome's words about an experiment. "What exactly is your purpose, if you don't mind my asking?"

Grinning, Rembis said, "Mind? Not at all. I value your opinion." He gave her a wink. "Uh, as one scientist to another, so to speak."

Laughing, Telsa had a hard time thinking of the little gnome as a scientist.

"Do not laugh," said Raj in their shared space. *"He is not much smaller than you."*

"Mind your own business," Telsa snapped back. *"At least I've got a body."*

"Ah, yes," said Raj sounding sympathetic. *"That's the burden you have to bear for not being a gaseous-based life form. Just so you know, I do not hold that against you, so take heart."*

"You're talking to your battle computer, aren't you?" asked Rembis. "You have that same 'I am not in this room' look Rick gets when he talks to Nickelo."

Telsa felt her face grow warm. "That's right. Raj was discussing how much better it would be to have a carbon-based body than to be a gas."

"Liar," said Raj over the battle helmet's external speaker. "I was arguing just the opposite."

Rembis laughed.

Telsa thought the old gnome laughed a lot. She supposed that was why she liked him so much. He reminded her of her.

"I can see advantages to both sides, Master Raj," said Rembis. "Perhaps you can spare a couple of minutes to help Telsa and me with a problem."

"A problem," said Raj. "I think at nanosecond speed. Give me the data and I will process it into a possible solution before you can say Alakazam."

"Alaka-what?" asked Rembis as he reached up to scratch at his long beard.

"Ignore him," Telsa said. "That's what I do. Nickelo has been teaching him to use phrases from his 'cute sayings' book. I'm not sure I like it."

"Well, nevertheless, I could use both of your opinions," said Rembis, turning his attention back to the illusion of Silverton. He pointed to the western quadrant of the city. "You will notice the obelisk with the yellow top. I have set up a scenario in the illusion so that the obelisk is empty." He pointed to the remaining three quadrants of the city. "The illusions of those three obelisks contain their respective blue, red, and green gems."

Telsa thought back to the battle on the planet Storage two weeks earlier. To their good fortune, the warehouse containing the blue, red, and green gems Rick had recovered over the years hadn't been damaged during the fight. Although she hadn't seen it herself, Telsa remembered Dren explaining how a place in the warehouse was reserved for a yellow gem, but that it was currently empty.

"So you're setting up the illusion as if you're using the blue, red, and green gems on Storage?" Telsa asked. "I guess that makes sense. To what end?"

"Watch," said Rembis as he stepped outside the illusion.

Telsa followed and stood beside the gnome facing the miniature city. As soon as she was clear, Rembis pulled a wand from his belt and waved it at the illusion. The simulated blue, red, and green obelisks began glowing. Beams of blue, red, and green light reached out and touched the Tree of Light. The tree began oscillating between the three colors with the change in colors speeding up with each change. Suddenly the Tree of Light erupted into a ball of yellow fire so powerful that it consumed the entire city. Only a black hole remained where the tree had once been. What remained of Silverton resembled blackened ruins more than it did the vibrant city it had been only seconds earlier.

Telsa wasn't sure what to say. "Uh, I'm guessing that's not the outcome you were striving for."

Grinning, Rembis shook his head. "Not hardly." He waved his wand at the illusion. It wavered momentarily before returning to its original form. "This time I have set the illusion with a yellow gem based upon specifications provided by Dren and Brachia. Naturally, they had to make assumptions on the composition of the yellow gem, but it's the best we can do."

With a wave of the gnome's wand, beams of blue, red, green, and yellow light shot out from the four obelisks and merged at a point just above the Tree of Light. The tree began oscillating between the four colors until the changes were happening so quickly they became a solid black color. The now black Tree of Light wavered and disappeared. Only a flat clearing of blackened rock remained.

"Uh, what just happened?" Telsa asked. She stepped into the illusion to get a better look at the place where the Tree of Light had been.

Rembis walked over to stand beside her. "The illusion of the gate below the Tree of Light has been permanently closed. The Tree of Light merged with the energy of the four gems to close it."

"What happened to the tree?" Telsa asked. "Where'd it go?"

The speaker on Telsa's battle helmet clicked. "I believe I can answer that," said Raj. "I realize this illusion is just a controlled experiment, but even so, I calculate that once the purpose of the tree is fulfilled, its presence on this world will no longer be required. From a logical standpoint, whatever entity makes up the tree would have nothing left to do here, so it would go back to wherever it originally came from."

Telsa thought of Rick's friend Shandria who was the Lady of the Tree. "Maybe we should keep this little experiment to ourselves for now. I'm not sure Rick would take it well."

"My thoughts exactly," said Rembis. "That's why I wanted to show you. The end result is that we need a yellow gem to close the gate. That's all there is too it."

The mention of the yellow gem reminded Telsa of why she'd come in the first place. "I've spent the last week practically living at the library. Chief Librarian Elisinsar has every available scribe looking for any references to yellow gems. Except for the story of the destruction of a yellow gem of great Power in the keeping of the Ecarian giants, we've found nothing. I was hoping you might know something."

Waving his wand at the Silverton illusion, the gnome reset the spell to its original form. Once the miniature Tree of Light was reformed, Rembis turned to face Telsa. "You were there when I told Rick everything I knew about the gem. You have to remember that although I was born twenty thousand year ago, most of my adult life was spent living with Queen Emerald and her dwarves in New Drepdenor over a hundred thousand years in the past."

"So you haven't been there recently?"

Rembis laughed. "Not unless you call a hundred thousand years recent. I only know how it was when I left. I'm told the place has been uninhabited since the time of Queen Emerald. From what I remember, the guardian dragon doesn't like intruders. I imagine the guardian only put up with Queen Emerald and the rest of us because we were friends of Rick's."

"So what happened when Queen Emerald died? Surely the dragon didn't force everyone else out."

The gnome looked at the Silverton illusion before turning to respond. "I'm told there is no record of Queen Emerald's death in the Silverton library. She and her dwarves stopped communicating with the outside world shortly after I was captured. I'm also told that adventurers and even small armies have tried forcing their way into the caverns beneath New Drepdenor over the millenniums, but that none have ever succeeded. At least not as far as the elves know. As I said, the guardian dragon doesn't appreciate intruders."

"So there might be a yellow gem in New Drepdenor that we don't know about?"

"I would not bet on that," said Raj over the battle helmet's speakers.

"Nor would I," said Rembis. "I heard no mention of a yellow gem being in the caverns before I was captured."

"You said yourself that was a hundred thousand years ago," Telsa said, refusing to give up her hypothesis so easily. "One *could* be there now, right? Perhaps your Queen Emerald didn't tell you everything."

A stern male voice sounded behind Telsa. "Does any leader ever tell their subordinates everything?"

Spinning to look behind her, Telsa spied a tall, white-bearded elf wearing a black robe with silver trim. Although she could see the elf plain as day, she detected nothing with her passive scan.

"Good stealth shield," commented Raj in their shared space. *"It is almost as good as yours."*

"Master Jathar," said Rembis. "I didn't sense your approach."

The elf gave a half smile. "You honor me, Master Rembis. If one as skilled as you could not detect my stealth shield, then all the practice my instructors forced me to do over the years has been worth the effort."

The elf turned to face Telsa. "A few weeks ago, I would have said the idea of a human being allowed in the halls of the Mages Guild was preposterous. Yet here you are."

Rembis shifted on his feet. "Uh, perhaps I should have—"

Waving his hand in a gesture of dismissal, Master Jathar said, "Do not fret, Master Rembis. As the elf friend told us before he departed, we must learn to work together even if it means associating with those we considered enemies in the past."

"Sir, I assure you that I'm no enemy," Telsa said.

"Of course you are not," said the elf. "If I had even the slightest concern about your loyalty to our cause, I would not have left word for our guards to allow your entry should you ever pass our way. I am honored that one of the elf friend's fellow wizard scouts has chosen to seek wisdom here before going to the Priest Guild."

"Hmm," said Raj in their shared space. *"It sounds to me like there is a little inter-guild rivalry among the elves."*

"Hush," Telsa said before returning her attention to the elf mage. She gestured toward Rembis standing to her left. "I came hoping to find more information about the yellow gem. Rembis was kind enough to show me his experiment with the Silverton illusion and the gems. I believe it is more important now than ever to find another one of the yellow gems."

Glancing at the illusion of the elf city, Master Jathar nodded. "I tend to agree with you, Wizard Scout. On the other hand, you may have set yourself an impossible task. As I am sure Chief Librarian Elisinsar has told you, there has been no mention of a yellow gem of Power since the disappearance of the Ecarian giants."

"The elf is right," came Raj's thought. *"I told you as much."*

Ignoring her battle computer, Telsa pressed on. "Perhaps I

should go to the home of the giants and see if I can find anything out."

The elf didn't laugh, but Telsa thought the corners of his lips twitched as if he was fighting the urge.

"I am afraid that would be difficult," said Master Jathar after getting control of his expression. "From what we know of the Ecarian giants, they were destroyed by a catastrophe fourteen thousand years in the past. A series of earthquakes ravaged the Thandarhar Mountains and much of our continent. Elf Friend Amirithoda and his giants calmed the earth before our lands were destroyed, but the damage to the home of the Ecarians was irreparable. Nothing in the histories of any of the civilized races in Slyvrastra ever mentions the Ecarian giants again. I fear their fate and whatever they knew about the yellow gem is gone forever." The old elf frowned and rubbed his chin. "Perhaps…"

"Perhaps what?" Telsa said, eager to hear anything that didn't predict total failure.

The old elf actually smiled. It wasn't a teeth-revealing smile, but it was a smile nonetheless. "I was just thinking that New Drepdenor's guardian dragon might have the knowledge that our histories do not."

Telsa frowned. She looked at the gnome before looking back at the master of the Mages Guild. "Rembis was just telling me the dragon guarding New Drepdenor isn't all that friendly. He mentioned something about small armies being unable to gain entrance to the mountain."

This time the master elf's smile showed his full set of teeth. "I doubt even large armies could enter the caverns under the mountain without meeting their doom. The dragon is renowned for guarding the treasures of the dwarves. However, you would be seeking answers, not treasure. The dragon guardian might allow you to live long enough to answer a few questions."

Telsa grinned back. "Somehow that doesn't give me a warm and cozy feeling."

Gesturing toward the Silverton illusion, the elf mage said, "I tend to agree with Master Rembis that acquiring a yellow gem of Power is an urgent priority. Whether another exists, I do not know." He turned back to look at Telsa. "In my opinion, if one does exist somewhere, it is worth taking a risk. The guardian dragon has let others before you approach and live. Has the high priestess not told you how her life was saved by the guardian fifty years ago?"

Out the corner of her eye, Telsa saw Rembis shrug.

"Obviously he doesn't know any more about that than me," Telsa told her battle computer in their shared space. *"What about you, Raj?"*

"Oh, yes," replied Raj sounding eager to share his knowledge. *"I know all the gory details from listening to conversations of the elves we have been around. To make a long story short, the elf Leethor was in charge of a recon team that found the high priestess after Wizard Scout Shepard freed her from the Dalinfaust. With a magical gag ball in her mouth, she was in danger of dying. Leethor's team took her to the dragon guardian who saved her."*

"So the dragon is a healer?" Telsa asked.

"Far from it," replied Raj. *"I told you this was the short-story version. Do you really want me to recite the whole tale now? The end result is that the dragon can be reasonable if you are not trying to steal the dwarves' treasure from its mountain."*

The last thing Telsa was interested in doing was stealing treasure from a dragon or anything else, for that matter. Treasure mattered little to a wizard scout. "So you think the dragon can be reasonable?" she asked the elf. "If so, how do I get there? Is it a long walk?"

"It is definitely a long walk if you choose to travel that way," said Master Jathar. He glanced down at Rembis. "Your friend does not get around much, does she?"

The old gnome winked at Telsa before replying to the elf. "Oh, she gets around, but things work differently in the physical dimension. She's not used to having a master mage for a friend."

Telsa wasn't sure whether the gnome was referring to himself or Master Jathar. She liked the old gnome, but the word friend seemed a little strong for their relationship.

"Oh, do not be so picky," said Raj in their shared space. *"You need every friend you can get; especially one who knows how to cast a teleport spell."*

"Are you talking about teleportation?" Telsa asked, directing her question at the gnome this time.

"Naturally," replied Rembis. "I am a master mage of the ninth circle. Unless Rick's niece and nephew have gotten the primary teleporter for *'the One'* on Storage working reliably enough to transport living beings again, I'd say a teleport spell is your best bet for traveling on Portalis."

"Master Rembis is right," said Raj using the battle helmet's external speaker. "Brachia and Dren are still working on Storage's primary teleporter. It is reliable enough to send equipment to Wizard Scout Shepard's dimensional pack, but the risk is still too high for life forms. The time differential component is also down."

Telsa didn't mind the last part. She had no desire to travel in time again. Things got way too confusing. She looked at Rembis. "All right, so will you teleport me to New Drepdenor?

"He will," said Master Jathar before the gnome could speak. "We have a few preparations we need to make first."

Telsa cocked an eye at the elf. "We?"

Master Jathar smiled. "Yes. We. Rembis and I will both accompany you. I will have a talk with High Lord Trenadine and see if we can also get Commander Leethor to come with us. He is somewhat familiar with the guardian."

"So when do we leave?" Telsa asked, finding herself suddenly eager to get going now that they had a plan.

"Tomorrow," replied Master Jathar. "Tomorrow morning will be soon enough."

Telsa hoped the old mage was right.

CHAPTER 6

The fifteen people in the conference room grew quiet as the acting president of the Conglomerate finished reading the names of the latest members that were missing.

A pot-bellied, gray-haired man with bloodshot eyes stood. "If Councilmembers Thoris and Minist couldn't protect themselves, what are the rest of us supposed to do?"

A thin woman in her thirties took a large gulp from a half-full glass of light-brown liquid. She tried to rise but fell back into her seat. "The empress promised us protection," she said, slurring the words. "Why aren't our wizard scouts out hunting down these assassins?"

"Here, here," added an older, bald man. "I wasn't involved in the empress's plan to betray the Empire. Now I'm apparently being hunted down by death squads mounted on horses that walk through walls. Our wizard scouts need to be doing more to protect us!"

The acting president eyed a nearby glass of the same brownish liquid that was in the thin woman's glass. He was tempted to chug down an entire decanter of the potent liquor and be done with the whole affair. *I didn't want any part of this in the first place,* he thought. *I'm a merchant, not a politician.*

Steeling himself to ignore the liquor glass, the acting president stood. It had been a long night, and he was growing more tired by the minute. "The empress is dead. So is the chief of security."

"Rumors," said the thin woman. "No one knows for sure."

"That's no longer true," said the acting president. "The bodies of the empress and Wizard Scout Myers were brought to Risors earlier this morning. DNA testing has confirmed the identities of the bodies. The empress is dead."

"Who brought the bodies?" asked the pot-bellied man. "The last report we had was that she'd been kidnapped by some demon-cat or whatever it was."

"The empress was taken to the magic dimension where she was killed on a planet called Portalis," said the acting president.

"So, Wizard Scout Shepard murdered the empress," said the pot-bellied man. "Did he kill his brother as well?"

"The killer wasn't Shepard," said the acting president. "We have an eyewitness."

The thin woman took another drink from her glass. "Who?"

"The same person who brought her body to us," replied the acting president. "That person is none other than her son, Matthew Deloris. He saw the whole thing."

The bald man whispered into the ear of the pot-bellied man sitting next to him. The pot-bellied man nodded before standing back up and facing the acting president.

"I assume you've placed the empress's son under arrest. Perhaps we can use him as leverage against that rogue wizard scout. It's about time we stopped letting traitors kill our Conglomerate staff with impunity. We should—"

"No," said the acting president surprising even himself with the strength of his denial. "We will not act against the empress's son." He glanced around the room, paying particular attention to the increasingly red face of the pot-bellied man. "We have been given an opportunity to get out of the mess the empress left us." He pointed at the bald man. "As you said, we were not involved with the empress's betrayal. Thoris and Minist were her main backers along with Jenkins."

"Jenkins is dead," said the bald man. "Thoris and Minist probably are as well."

The acting president shook his head. "They aren't. Felix Deloris said they are being held on Diajor, awaiting trial as traitors by an Empire military tribunal."

"We are the Empire," said the pot-bellied man. "I haven't approved any such tribunal."

The bald man looked at his pot-bellied counterpart. "The

empress's betrayal of the Empire regular forces failed. The majority of the Empire's fleet along with a large force of ground troops escaped. The Trecorian alliance has cast their lot on the side of the surviving Empire rebel forces. You've all been briefed on the part that ships from the magic dimension played in the fight. No Conglomerate warships fought in the battle against the Empire fleets. Only the empress and her fellow traitors took action against the Empire." The bald man glanced around the table. "We are business people, not warriors or politicians." He locked eyes with the pot-bellied man. "Are you sure you want to align yourself with those who decided to betray the Empire?"

The pot-bellied man glanced at the bald man before turning to address the acting president. "Naturally, I had nothing to do with the empress's plans. I, uh, only want what's best for the Conglomerate and, uh, the Empire, from a business standpoint."

"I have no doubt," the acting president replied. He eyed his glass of brownish liquid and pushed it away. "I have taken the liberty of asking Felix and Matthew Deloris to attend our meeting. They are waiting outside. That is, if there are no objections."

After five seconds of silence, the acting president nodded at a guard standing next to the conference room entrance. When the guard opened the door, Matthew Deloris and his uncle, Felix Deloris, walked inside. The acting president motioned at the head of the table where the empress normally sat. Instead of moving to the head, Felix Deloris sat down in a chair on the side of the table. Matthew Deloris walked to the chair at the head of the table but didn't sit down.

"My mother is dead," said Matthew wasting no time on preliminaries. "We can go into details later. There will be no state funeral. Both my mother and...my father will be disintegrated in a quiet ceremony later today. In the meantime, we have important work to do." He pulled a folded piece of paper from his pocket and stared at it.

The pot-bellied man began growing red in the face again. He glared at Matthew before turning to look at Felix. "I will not be told what will be done by some young popinjay. If you have something to offer us, say it and be done with it. I've got a few ideas of my own I'd like to discuss with the board before—"

A crumpled ball of paper flew through the air, hitting the pot-bellied man on the chest. The paper landed on the table in front of the man.

"Read that," said Matthew.

The pot-bellied man's face turned beet red. "You arrogant—"

Felix Deloris stood and spoke in a surprisingly stern voice. "I'd suggest you read that before you say anything else. The paper contains a list of names. You'll notice the first ten names are marked off the list." Felix smiled at the pot-bellied man. "If you look close, I believe you'll notice that your name is number eleven on the list."

The pot-bellied man glanced down at the paper before jumping to his feet. "I could have you both shot."

"Yes, you could," said Matthew from his position at the head of the table. "If you did, our deaths would be quick. I can assure you that yours would not." He glanced around the table. "Each of you has a choice. I'm not going to mince words. The Conglomerate can either come back to the Empire's fold in a peaceful manner, or everyone on that list will live to regret it. Regardless of what you do, the Conglomerate will return to the Empire. It would be better if the return was voluntary, but it's going to happen nonetheless. To that end, I am taking charge of the Conglomerate. You can either join me in an endeavor that will prove very profitable for all of you, or you can fight me and share the fate of Jenkins and his cronies. Either way, the Conglomerate will once again be part of the Empire."

The pot-bellied man opened his mouth to speak, but the acting president spoke first. "What do you mean by profitable?"

Felix Deloris sat back down. "What my nephew means is that the Conglomerate stands in a unique position if the board is ready to seize the greatest business opportunity our galaxy has ever seen."

"What are you talking about?" asked the bald-headed man. "What business opportunity?"

Matthew Deloris placed a small, metallic pad on the conference room table. A beam of light shot upward to display an image of a galaxy.

"Very pretty," said the bald man. "I've seen holograms before. What's your point?"

Matthew smiled. "My point is that you haven't seen this before.

This isn't a hologram, and the image isn't being generated by technology. The pad contains a magic spell that projects the image." Pointing at the pad, Matthew said, "These can be made for half the cost of a holographic projector, and the image is every bit as good. From my experience, I've found that some things can be done cheaper or better using magic, while in other cases, technology is the better choice of the two."

"Magic?" asked the bald man.

Matthew nodded, then raised his hand to indicate the image. "This isn't our galaxy. It is our sister galaxy in the magic dimension. In that galaxy are trillions of potential customers who depend on magic to do everything. Once this war is over, our galaxy's technology will be in high demand there, as will their magic items in ours." Reaching down, Matthew touched a protrusion on the metallic pad.

The image changed from a galaxy to a legal form.

The acting president leaned forward. "What is that?"

Matthew smiled. "That is a trade agreement between the Conglomerate and the United Galaxy Alliance in the magic dimension. It makes our Conglomerate the primary suppliers of technology to the magic galaxy and the main subsidiary for the sale of magic items in our physical galaxy. You'll notice the contract has been signed by Uncle Felix and I as authorized representatives of the Conglomerate."

The pot-bellied man tore his gaze away from the contract to look at the wrinkled piece of paper in his hand. He glanced at Felix Deloris before looking back at Matthew.

"Just what are we expected to do for this err...consideration?" asked the pot-bellied man.

"Nothing more than loyal citizens of the Empire would naturally want to do," said Matthew. "The Conglomerate will place our military at the disposal of the Empire's High Command. I think you'll find most of our commanders will be more than willing to do so. They were just as shocked by my mother's betrayal as I'm sure most of you were. We will also send a delegation to the magic dimension to begin coordinating the trade agreement."

The acting president pushed his glass of brownish liquid farther away. "Our navy is positioned to begin attacks on the Empire forces in order to begin taking back the rebel districts. There have already been skirmishes. Even if we try to stand down our military, who's to say the rebels and their allies will allow us to do so?"

"Let me worry about that," said Matthew. "In the meantime, we'll send orders to our fleet commanders to withdraw to defensive positions and attempt to make contact with their counterparts in the Empire fleets. This civil war should never have happened. It's going to stop now. It *has* to stop now." Matthew glanced around the room, making contact with everyone before saying, "There is no profit in it."

The acting president took a last look at his glass of liquor before picking it up and dropping it into the trash disposal slot on the table. "I make a motion that Matthew Deloris be elected as interim president of the Conglomerate until our full council can be assembled to discuss electing a permanent leader."

"I second the motion," said Felix Deloris.

One by one the council members at the table nodded their heads. The last to vote was the pot-bellied man. He glanced down at the wrinkled paper in his hand, then looked up and nodded his head.

"All right," said Matthew Deloris. "Then let's get down to business."

CHAPTER 7

A streak of light in the sky announced the arrival of another Crosioian troop transport. It came to a hover fifty meters over Estos' frozen landscape, directly above the POW camp Wizard Scout Trinity Delgado had been observing for the last thirty minutes. From the smaller size of the starship, Trinity could tell it was one of the battalion-size troopships and not one of the frontline divisional assault craft. Although not the largest of the bats' transports, there was still an obvious problem in Trinity's mind.

"My passive scan's picking up less than fifty life forms inside," Trinity said in the space of her mind shared with her battle computer.

"I calculate the Crosioians are using it for something other than transporting personnel," replied Jennifer.

Doors slid open on the sides and rear of the troopship and dozens of truck-sized cargo containers spilled out, falling to the tundra below. At least a dozen of the crates cracked open on impact. The broken boxes spewed cartons of food and other supplies into the air. A spray of plasma rounds erupted from one of the three bottom gun ports, hitting ten meters in front of a group of unarmed POWs who were apparently getting too close for the Crosioians' liking.

Trinity increased the magnification of her helmet's visor until she could make out the supplies littering the landscape. *"It looks like the ship's dropping food, cold weather clothing, and medical supplies to the POWs. From the actions of the prisoners, I'd say this isn't the first supply drop. What gives? The bats should've taken our troops off the planet by now, to the gulags near their home worlds. After all the nukes that were set off during the battle for Estos, the radiation is deadly even in relatively clean spots like the one below this ridgeline."*

"If the situation was reversed, I calculate the Empire would be doing as you say," said Jennifer. *"Unfortunately for the POWs, the Crosioians are not like your species. Based upon what you have seen over the last two days, I calculate they are bringing more POWs to Estos instead of the other way around. That makes no logical sense, but the parameters of the equation are what they are."*

"Unless they are assembling them all here to die," Trinity said. *"I wonder if they are bringing all two hundred million of our captured troops to Estos."* The heartlessness of such a plan went against everything she'd been taught to value during her career as a wizard scout. *"How long can the POWs last on Estos?"*

"Assuming the Crosioians continue to resupply our troops with food and medicines, they might last two months before the radiation in the clean *areas starts to take its toll,"* said Jennifer. *"Do not hold me to that. I have limited data to base my calculations on. Your helmet's video is picking up some anti-radiation pills in the crates that broke open. My calculations are based upon the Crosioians providing enough of the pills for all the prisoners."*

The situation confused Trinity. *"If the Crosioians want to kill their prisoners, all they have to do is leave them on Estos and make sure no ships land to take them off. It looks like they're intentionally trying to keep them alive and bringing more POWs to share their fate. Why resupply them if they are going to die in two months anyway?"*

"Insufficient data to calculate the Crosioians' motives, Wizard Scout," replied Jennifer.

All three bottom gun turrets on the troopship opened up, firing more warning shots at some of the increasingly desperate POWs trying to get closer to the supplies. Trinity made out a score of Empire officers and sergeants trying to hold the prisoners back with only limited success.

"I calculate the discipline among our soldiers is beginning to deteriorate," said Jennifer. *"If their commander is not careful, these food drops may turn into a free-for-all."*

"Can you blame our troops?" Trinity asked, thinking of the masses of captured soldiers crammed into the thousands of poorly provisioned camps spread out over Estos. *"A hundred million POWs are scattered around the planet in zones where the radioactive contamination is less but still deadly."*

"As I told you earlier, I calculate the Crosioians are bringing all two hundred million prisoners here," said Jennifer. *"I am surprised the bats are keeping them alive in the first place. Based upon information in my databanks, the Crosioians consider surrender an act of cowardice. They normally kill their prisoners outright, except for the unlucky ones who might have information the Crosioians need. My calculations indicate the Crosioians must have a reason for keeping our troops alive, even if only for two months."*

Trinity took another survey of the POW encampment below the ridgeline. There were over ten thousand POWs bunched into a few hundred tents that had apparently been provided by the Crosioians. She sensed small energy sources coming from a lot of the tents.

"Heating units," said Jennifer. *"The Crosioians must have provided the tents and heaters when they initially captured and disarmed our troops. My sensors are not picking up any weapons among the POWs."*

Trinity nodded her head. The Crosioians were nothing if not thorough. They'd obviously disarmed the survivors before herding them into the small camps. She had no doubt a lot of the soldiers still had some fight left in them, but she wasn't sure how long that would last. The cold was a terrible enemy.

"Very true," said Jennifer. *"If I was one of the Crosioians' tactical computers, I would have recommended letting the cold convince the Empire troops to trade weapons for tents and heaters. I calculate that would have been effective against seventy percent of the soldiers. It would have been more effective than trying to take all the weapons by force."*

"What about the other thirty percent?" Trinity asked knowing the answer already.

"I calculate a few tactical nukes from orbiting warships would

have convinced the others to surrender. It would only be logical."

Sometimes Trinity hated her battle computer's cold logic. Low-crawling another three meters forward, she moved to a semi-covered position for a better view of the encampment.

"Be careful," warned Jennifer. *"Your stealth shield is good, as is your battle suit's camouflage unit, but they are not infallible. Your orders were to teleport from Velos to Estos and pinpoint the locations of any remaining Empire troops. You have remained undetected over the last two days, but I calculate your luck will eventually run out given enough time. I recommend that you request teleport extraction so you can make your report to Admiral Bistos. The Crosioian warships orbiting the planet make sending messages over the tele-network too risky. You will need to make your report in person."*

"Not yet," Trinity replied as she increased the magnification of her battle helmet's visor to get a better look at the hovering troopship. *"I need to analyze the amount and type of supplies so Liz can make a reliable estimate of how long our soldiers can remain alive on Estos."*

As Trinity watched, the troopship continued dumping crates of supplies out its side and rear doors. She looked past the hovering ship to see other troopships in the distance making similar drops at other camps.

"I don't understand what they are trying to accomplish," Trinity said, making the same old argument to her battle computer. *"Why give the prisoners supplies if they want them dead? It makes no sense. Maybe we should make contact with the POWs and see if they know what's going on?"*

"Negative," said Jennifer in a surprisingly firm tone. *"We have had this discussion before. Our orders were not to interact with the POWs. I calculate attempting to make contact with the prisoners will only expose you to an unacceptable level of danger while providing no useful data."*

Trinity wished Jerad were with her so they could discuss options together. Beneath her battle suit's gloves, she sensed the warm presence that she associated with her husband in the blue-gemmed wedding band on her finger. Jerad wore a matching ring on his hand. The rings had been given to them by Richard on their wedding day. She was tempted to try and communicate with her husband using emotions but refrained. She didn't want to distract him.

He's got his own mission to worry about, Trinity thought. *I've got mine.*

"Very sensible," said Jennifer. *"Now what do you want to do, Wizard Scout?"*

Before Trinity could answer, a stream of plasma rounds shot out the side door of the nearest troopship. She spotted one of the bat-winged Crosioians in the doorway with a rifle raised to his shoulder. Another burst of plasma rounds shot out the barrel of the bat's weapon, toward a group of POWs frantically running for cover. The stream of plasma rounds slammed into the chests of two men, knocking them to the ground.

"That bat's shooting them for sport," Trinity said as she aimed her M12 toward the troopship's door.

"No," said Jennifer. *"You will give away your position. The ship's primary weapons are not firing. I calculate the door gunner is not authorized to—"*

Trinity didn't care if the bat in the doorway was authorized to fire or not. He'd just killed two unarmed prisoners for no reason other than pure bloodlust.

"Assistance," Trinity said using command voice as she aimed the M12's sight at the still-firing door gunner.

"Compliance."

Trinity felt the left arm of her battle suit move slightly as the index finger on her right glove pulled the M12's trigger. The weapon bucked against her shoulder as a single ball of plasma energy left the barrel and streaked toward the troopship's side door. When the round hit the Crosioian firing the rifle in the chest, the bat fell back into the ship, dropping his rifle in the process.

"The ship's primary weapons are traversing in your direction," said Jennifer. *"I highly recommend you find another location to plan your next move."*

Jumping to her feet, Trinity leaped off the rim of the rock outcropping just as a stream of heavy plasma rounds smacked into the rocks where she'd been hiding. Pieces of broken stone and jagged chunks of ice filled the air around her as she fell twenty meters to the ground below. Wrapping herself in Power, she slowed her rate of descent before making contact with the frozen ground. Tucking the chin of her battle helmet into her chest, she summersaulted once before rising to her feet and running for all she was worth.

Balls of plasma energy blew ice and frozen dirt high into the air.

Trinity drew Power from her reserve in preparation for forming a defensive shield, but she only kept it at the ready. A glance at her heads-up display showed sixty-nine percent Power in her reserve.

I'm far from empty, Trinity thought, *but I'm not going to use Power unless it's absolutely necessary. I don't know how long this little skirmish is going to last.*

"*There is a ravine located a thousand meters to the west,*" said Jennifer. "*You might be able to break contact with the gunners if you can make it there before they get in a lucky shot.*"

A shrill whine behind Trinity told her she probably wasn't going to get lucky. Reaching out with her passive scan, she noted two sets of life forms leaving the troopship and heading in her direction at a high rate of speed.

"*Fighter-shuttles,*" said Jennifer. "*Based upon the energy signatures, I calculate they are Furgerson class shuttles modified with phase auto-cannons and anti-personnel rockets. You can't outrun them. What are your orders, Wizard Scout?*"

Skidding to a stop, Trinity turned and began firing a steady stream of plasma rounds from her M12 at the left-most of the approaching fighters.

"*Range is eighteen hundred meters,*" said Jennifer. "*By the time the fighters are within our effective range, they will already have fired their rockets and auto-cannons.*"

"*Good,*" Trinity said still holding down the trigger of her M12. "*That's what I want.*" She noticed four rockets leave the right-most fighter's wing pods and streak in her direction.

"*Well, you have got your wish,*" said Jennifer. "*The left-most fighter is keeping its shields up to avoid your small-arms fire. I fail to see what you hope to accomplish.*"

Drawing Power from her reserve, Trinity sent a line of Power toward the fighters. She split the Power into four separate lines the way Richard had taught her. Touching each of the incoming rockets with a line, she used telekinesis to shove the missiles into the path of the phase rounds coming from the right-most fighter's auto-cannon.

Boom! Boom! Boom! Boom!

The balls of fire from the exploding rockets combined to form a single giant ball of burning plasma. Both fighters banked in opposite directions to avoid the flying shrapnel and plasma energy. Trinity held the trigger down on her M12, spraying plasma rounds into the bottom of the right-most fighter.

"It's too heavily armored for your M12, even without a force field activated," said Jennifer. *"You are going to have to come up with another plan."*

Reaching toward the fighter banking left with another line of Power, Trinity sought out the pilot. Locating the bat-creature, she reached into the left side of the bat's chest cavity and wrapped Power around the heart.

"Crosioians have two hearts," said Jennifer. *"Just a friendly reminder."*

Splitting off another line of Power from the main line, Trinity sought out the second heart. She found it and wrapped it in Power before jerking hard on both organs using telekinesis. The fighter-shuttle wobbled in the air, rolled onto its back, and dove into the ground where it exploded in a massive ball of fire. Plumes of flame and smoke billowed into the air.

"Shield," said Jennifer.

Throwing up a defensive shield, Trinity turned to see the second fighter lining up for a strafing run. Balls of phase energy streaked out, hitting her shield dead on. The first three balls of phase energy were absorbed by the shield. The fourth and fifth balls found weak points and penetrated. Trinity twisted to avoid the first of the two rounds. The last phase round caught her on the right shoulder, throwing her back a dozen meters with blood spewing out of the double-finger-sized wound, onto the snow. Trinity's M12 flew out of her hand as she went tumbling across the snow and ice. Rolling to a stop, she heard the fighter roar past overhead.

"You should have angled your shield," said Jennifer in a chastising tone. *"The good news is that you were knocked out of the field of fire before additional rounds hit you. I recommend that you request an emergency teleport out before the fighter can line up for another pass."*

Doing her best to ignore the pain in her right shoulder, Trinity mentally yelled, *"Drugs!"*

"Compliance."

A cool liquid shot into Trinity's right arm, traveling up to the wound in her shoulder. The worst of the pain disappeared. She tried to focus on her surroundings, but tears made everything a blur. Reaching out with her passive scan, she located the remaining fighter. It was halfway through a turn five hundred meters to her rear. Probing the fighter with her mind, she located the rockets underneath the fighter's wings. After wrapping the warhead of one with Power, she squeezed inward with telekinesis. Nothing happened. She squeezed harder.

Boom!

"The fighter is destroyed," said Jennifer. *"I have the emergency teleport code ready to go. Do I have your permission to signal mission abort?"*

"Negative," Trinity said as she picked up her M12 and used it to leverage herself to her feet. *"If I leave now, that troopship will take its wrath out on the POWs. I've got to draw it away somehow."*

"I highly recommend against that course of action, Wizard Scout. Your best bet is to teleport out now. You are down to forty-two percent Power in your reserve. The Crosioians' tactical computers are bound to know you are a wizard scout based upon the way you destroyed their fighters. I calculate a ninety-one percent probability the troopship will request a nuclear strike on your current location from one of the orbiting destroyers. That will kill you and all of the POWs. You need to escape while you have the chance. Let me send the emergency teleport code."

The last thing on Trinity's mind was bugging out and leaving the POWs to their doom. She dropped her stealth shield and began running as fast as her battle suit would go in the direction of the ravine her battle computer had mentioned. With the hole in her battle suit's right shoulder, the suit's integrity was gone, but thankfully all the hydraulics were in working order. She drew in a deep lungful of the cold Estos air and immediately regretted the action as her lungs started to freeze. The Power from her self-heal repaired the damage as fast as it came, but breathing still hurt.

"Why did you drop your stealth shield?" said Jennifer. *"The Crosioians will be able to track you easily now."*

Despite the pain in her shoulder and lungs, Trinity smiled.

"That's what I want. I've got to draw them away from the POWs. That's their only chance. I'm not going to make them pay the price for my actions."

"That is not logical. I told you there is a ninety-five percent probability the Crosioians will request a nuclear strike on your location."

"I thought you said ninety-one percent."

"That was before you dropped your stealth shield. By the way, you still have six hundred meters to go before you get to the ravine, not that it will do you any good. With only forty-two percent Power in your reserve, your self-heal will be unable to keep you alive from a close hit by a tactical nuke."

Trinity had no doubt her battle computer was right. She'd survived a couple of nuclear attacks before, but they'd always been at a distance. Making a quick estimate of the time required to request a nuclear attack from the orbiting ships and the time it would take for a missile to get to her location, she knew she'd never make the ravine before the weapon exploded. She sent a feeling of love to Jerad through the ring on her finger. It was the best she could do to say goodbye.

Continuing to run at max speed, Trinity saw the ravine drawing closer. With each step, she waited for a telltale streak of energy to come out of the sky in her direction. The ravine was four-hundred meters, then two hundred, then only a hundred.

What are they waiting for? she wondered.

* * *

The commander of the Crosioian troopship spread her wings as she turned to her communications officer. "Denied? What do you mean denied? The wizard scout will be able to escape if the ravine is reached. I need that nuclear strike now."

The communication officer tucked her wings tightly against her back as she turned the sonic tablet toward her commander. She touched an indentation on the tablet's side. "You can hear for yourself, Captain. Our orders are to let the wizard scout escape. The orders are from the admiral herself. We are to take no further action against the wizard scout. We are to finish dropping our supplies and return to the supply convoy to refill our ship for another run."

The troopship's commander lowered her wings. The sonic transmission from the tablet backed up her communication officer's words. Although the skin around her upper chest turned a darker gray, she did the best she could to hide her irritation from her crew. Orders were orders.

Turning to her bridge officers, the commander said, "You heard the admiral's orders. Finish dropping our supplies and prepare for orbit. The sooner we get off this Creator-forsaken planet the better."

CHAPTER 8

The *Defiant* came out of hyperspace a quarter of a light year from Diajor. The dull light reflecting off the planet formed a dim halo around its moon, which was the *Defiant's* actual destination. Richard stared out the front windscreen of the cockpit from his position in the navigator seat. The teenage elf Asquan sat in the copilot's chair while Sergeant Ron occupied the pilot's seat. Jeena was located at the communication officer's station across from Richard.

Glancing over his shoulder, Asquan said, "Margery told me only the most dangerous prisoners are kept on Diajor's moon."

"Most dangerous indeed," said Nickelo over the external speakers of Richard's battle helmet. "The prison on the moon only consists of thirty-five cells. Only one prisoner is being kept there at the present. The information in my databanks indicates the other prisoners were transferred to maximum security cells in the main prison on Diajor. The transfer was accomplished as soon as the warden received word a Crosioian scout was headed his way. From what I can determine, the central computer's escape algorithm determined the scout's odds of breaking out of her cell were too high to keep other prisoners or even guards nearby. Everything's been set on automatic. As an additional precaution, the moon's prison has been wired with a nuclear weapon containing energized flakes of titanium, just in case the warden needs to activate a self-destruct."

Richard whistled. "Creallium? Why?"

Jeena spun in the communication officer's chair to face him. Her silver eyes sparkled as she flashed him a smile. "For someone so powerful, you occasionally fail to put simple things together to form a logical conclusion."

"That's our Rick," said Nickelo. "He normally prefers acting first and thinking about what he's doing later."

Richard frowned. He wasn't fond of criticism, especially when it came from his battle computer. The feeling of loving tolerance coming down the link between his bondmate and him softened the blow of her comment.

"Hey, what can I say?" Richard said, ignoring his battle computer and speaking to Jeena. "My mind can be a screwed up place sometimes. So what am I missing?"

Jeena nodded toward the moon. "I am assuming the Crosioian scout imprisoned on yonder moon is as skilled as you. If the situation was reversed and the bat-creatures had you locked in their prison, I am more than confident you could eventually break out of your cell. If you did, you could shift into the void. The Holy Metal, or creallium as you call it, that is in the nuclear self-destruct weapon would ensure you would be so damaged in the blast that your self-heal would be unable to keep you alive."

Richard was surprised. "You figured that all out by yourself? Considering we've only been in the physical dimension a couple of weeks, you've picked up a lot. I'm impressed."

Jeena gave a wink and laughed as she raised her left hand and flashed the red-gemmed ring on her finger. "I'll admit I have been talking to Danny. Battle computers can be quite informative if you pay attention." She winked again. "I am sure Master Nick does his best to keep you informed."

A laugh came out of the external speakers of Richard's battle helmet. "I try my best, but sometimes it's a losing battle." Nickelo laughed again before taking up a more serious tone. "Danny and Jeehana are right, though. If the situation were reversed, you could break out in nothing flat. If the Crosioian scout is a shifter like you, she can do the same. Assuming she is a shifter, I calculate the only thing stopping her is the fact that she'd still be stuck on the moon with nowhere to go."

Sergeant Ron turned over the ship's controls to Asquan and spun in his seat to look at Richard. "From what the prison's warden told me, they aren't sure whether their prisoner can shift into the void or not, but they aren't taking any chances. As Nick said, the entire prison on this moon has been fully automated. There are a lot of automated weapons stations, but no guards." After scratching his beard, Sergeant Ron said, "Are you really sure you want to go down there, buddy? Why take the risk?"

"Why?" Richard said. "To be honest, I'm not sure. I just have this feeling that I should do it."

Sergeant Ron frowned. "Well, at least let us land the ship and send a security detail along with you."

Richard shook his head. "No. I think I need to go alone."

Molten-silver eyes flashing, Jeena crossed her arms and shook her head. "Then think again, because I *am* going with you."

Proving he was as stubborn as his bondmate, Richard said, "No, you're not. That's final."

A flash of fire in his bondmate's eyes was accompanied by a feeling of defiance through their bond link.

"I mean it, Jeena," Richard said trying to sound firm. From their short time together, he well knew the elf had a temper when pushed too hard.

"Look who's calling the kettle black," said Nickelo in their shared space. *"You're not exactly Mr. Congeniality yourself."*

Ignoring his battle computer's poor attempt at humor, Richard locked eyes with his bondmate. "I need to do this alone. When you voted to elect me leader, you promised to obey my orders."

Jeena shook her head. "Do not put words in my mouth, bondmate. That is *not* exactly what I said." An emotion of determination passed through the link from Jeena to Richard. "I am going with you. You may as well accept it and stop wasting precious time."

"Perhaps you should try talking to another prisoner instead of the scout," suggested Margery over the ship's intercom.

"No," Richard said. "The prisoner on Diajor's moon is the only Crosioian scout the Empire has ever captured. The others on Estos killed themselves rather than be taken prisoner. Heck, if this one hadn't run out of Power and been knocked unconscious, we wouldn't even have her."

Jeena stood and walked next to Richard's chair, placing a hand on his shoulder. "What exactly do you hope to accomplish by speaking to her? If what you told me is true, Crosioian scouts are as loyal to their cause as are wizard scouts. I doubt she is going to tell you any information that will help the Empire. The scout considers you her enemy."

"I calculate the high priestess is right," said Nickelo over the battle helmet's external speakers. "The scout will not tell you anything that we cannot surmise ourselves."

Richard took his eyes off Jeena and looked out the *Defiant's* windscreen at the moon. It was growing increasingly larger. "I don't want her to tell me anything. I want her to take me somewhere."

Jeena stepped between Richard and the windscreen, bent down, and locked eyes with him. Her molten-silver eyes churned furiously as an emotion of concern traveled down their link to Richard.

"Where exactly do you want her to take *us?*" Jeena asked.

The molten silver of his bondmate's eyes pulled Richard in. Each time he looked into her eyes, he felt they held all the answers if he only knew the right questions. Only this time, he knew his answer lay elsewhere. It lay with the Crosioian scout.

"The capital city of the Crosioians," Richard said. "That's where I need to go."

Sergeant Ron jumped out of his seat. "Are you out of your freakin' mind? That's crazy. No one even knows where it is."

Richard pictured an image of a bat-shaped creature in his mind. "That's not exactly true. You've just got to ask the right someone, and that's exactly what I'm planning to do."

* * *

"Fasten the latch where the power-suit's pants connect to the chest armor," Danny told Jeena. *"You do not want to start leaking air when you are only halfway down to the moon."*

Locking the latch in question, Jeena noticed the light on her helmet's heads-up display change from red to green. *"I could have used a spell to provide my air and thrown up a defensive shield to stop the radiation."*

"Yes, you could have," agreed Danny. *"On the con side, that would have used Power from your reserve. Just because Rick and*

you can create Power when needed, does not mean you should rely too heavily on recharging your reserves. The commandant always made sure his instructors at the academy stressed using technology first and Power second. Even though you are a magic user and not a wizard scout, it is still a good philosophy."

Jeena didn't argue the point. She knew her battle computer had previously belonged to the commandant's wife, Janice. From past experience, she knew saying anything against the commandant's teachings was likely to result in a long rebuttal from the battle computer.

"I put the suit on instead of casting a spell, did I not?"

"Yes, you did," conceded Danny. *"However, I must point out—"*

The intercom on the wall of the cargo bay crackled. "It is time to enter the ejection tubes," said Margery.

Turning slightly so she could see her bondmate on the opposite side of the cargo bay, Jeena nodded her head. Richard nodded back before climbing up the ladder to the entrance of the portside ejection tube. She followed suit, climbing the ladder for the starboard-side tube.

The ring on Jeena's left hand tingled. *"Your heart rate and breathing are up by twenty percent,"* said Danny. *"You have done this a dozen times in the halo-simulator. There is no reason to be frightened."*

"I am not scared," Jeena said doing her best to control her breathing. *"I do not expect you to understand. There is a big difference between doing something in a simulator and actually doing it for real."*

"That is not logical," said Danny. *"I have run a comparison algorithm a dozen times. There is no logical difference between the two."*

"I died three times in the simulator when I did not slow down my rate of fall fast enough."

"True," laughed Danny. *"The good news is that your last two times were successful. There was no time to do any more practice runs, so unless you are too scared to go and want to back out, I recommend you take your position in the ejection tube. Rick is already in the portside tube."*

Biting her lip hard enough to draw blood, Jeena scrambled up the ladder as fast as she could make the power-suit move. Since the top of the ejection tube was already open, she placed both feet into the dark opening and slid into the hole while holding her staff as close to her left side as she could. As soon as the top of her helmet passed below the lip of the opening, the hatch swung shut, cutting off the light from the cargo bay. Everything turned pitch black. Even her night vision didn't help her in the confined blackness.

"The inside of the tube is smooth and painted black," said Danny. *"There is nothing to see."*

Reflexively, Jeena tried bringing her right hand in front of her visor, but the tube was too tight. Both of her arms were locked tight to her sides.

"Your heart rate is up another ten percent," said Danny. His voice took on a note of concern. *"I calculate you are a tad claustrophobic. If it helps any, so is Rick. Try thinking of something else to take your mind off where you are. Nickelo says that is what his wizard scout does. We still have another minute to our drop point, so you need to get control of your emotions."*

Jeena took a deep breath in an attempt to slow her heart rate. When she did, her helmet bumped into the inside of the tube. *"It is too close in here."*

"The tube is designed to conform to the size of the occupant's suit," said Danny. *"It is supposed to be tight."*

"Then it is working perfectly," Jeena said, trying to force a laugh. The sound that came out sounded anything but humorous. She tried to force her mind to think of something besides her confined space but wasn't surprised when she failed.

A warm feeling came rushing down the link she shared with her bondmate. Concentrating on their bond link, Jeena traced it back to Richard and used him as an anchor point against her fear of tight spaces. She'd done the same thing once before to overcome the base emotions of a crowd of human males. The technique had worked then. It worked just as well now.

"Your heart rate is returning to normal," said Danny. *"By the way, the drop point is thirty-two seconds away."*

The thought of thirty-two more seconds trapped inside the ejection tube brought on drops of sweat that rolled down Jeena's forehead and into her eyes. She shook her head inside the helmet and focused on the memory of her bonding night. She remembered the fear she'd felt when she'd knelt before the human male dressed in his strange black armor. She'd offered herself to him in bonding only to have him initially claim he didn't know her. The image in her mind switched to the black-armored human kneeling before her in the Hall of Meetings with the entire Council of Light watching as he performed his part of the bonding pledge.

That was a very good day, Jeena thought. The memory made her smile. She sent her feelings down the link to her bondmate. The feeling of warmth coming up the link instantly increased.

"Five seconds," said Danny. *"Get ready."*

Jerked back to reality, Jeena stared at the blackness before her. Suddenly, the floor dropped beneath her feet as a blast of compressed air shot her into the vacuum of space. The blackness of the tube was replaced by a flash of dull silver as the *Defiant's* hull whipped past. Thousands of points of light on a background of deep black took the ship's place.

Stars, Jeena thought as the vast emptiness of space began to make her miss the confines of the ejection tube.

"Arch your back and roll over," said Danny making the words sound like an order. *"You are facing the wrong direction."*

Sending out jets of compressed air from the steering tubes on her power-suit, Jeena rolled over, arched her back, and spread her arms the way she'd practiced in the halo-simulator. The surface of Diajor's gray moon replaced the emptiness of space.

"Why do I need to arch my back?" Jeena asked, trying to take her mind off the fact that she was hurtling toward the rocky lunar landscape at breakneck speed. *"The moon does not have an atmosphere. There is no air to slow me down."*

"True," replied Danny, *"but I calculate it will give you something familiar to do. I think it best for you to do something that will take your mind off the fact that you are falling at a high enough rate of speed to crush you like a rotten apple when you hit the surface."*

The image of a lunar crater growing increasingly larger through her visor brought her battle computer's words into perspective. *"Thanks for the reminder."*

Danny laughed. *"That is what I am here for. I live to serve."*

The voice of her bondmate came over the headsets built into the helmet of Jeena's power-suit. "We are at six thousand meters.

You're doing great. Do you see the prison?"

Fighting an urge to scream, Jeena forced herself to concentrate on the approaching surface of the moon. A green blip appeared on the inside of her visor.

"I have taken the liberty of highlighting the prison in green on your visor's heads-up display," said Danny. *"Do you see it?"*

Increasing the magnification of her visor, Jeena took in the details of the prison. It was a small two-story affair with a landing pad located a short distance from the gray-steeled building. White strobe lights flashed to mark the outline of the pad.

"I see it," Jeena told her bondmate. "It looks like we are going to fall short of the target."

"No," came Richard's reply. "This is where our telekinesis comes into play. The entry point through the force field is on the north side of the landing pad. We've got to come in at a low angle. Don't forget to squawk the IFF code to get through the opening."

"Danny?" Jeena thought.

"I have activated the correct Identification, Friend or Foe *code in your power-suit,"* said Danny. *"I recommend casting your levitation spell now. We are passing below three thousand meters and closing."*

Drawing Power from her reserve, Jeena cast a single-word, no-hand-gesture version of a levitation spell that her bondmate had helped her write. The spell was only half as potent as a full-version of the spell, but confined as she was in the power-suit, she was taking no chances on messing up a hand gesture. She sensed the spell convert her Power into magic. Wrapping the spell's energy around her body, Jeena began slowing the rate of descent to match that of her bondmate located a bowshot to her right.

"Excellent," said Danny. *"Close the distance to Rick a little. Make sure you do not bump into him. That could be disastrous."*

Levitating horizontally, Jeena drew within ten meters of her bondmate. *"How come he is not in a spread-eagle position?"*

"Because he is more experienced at this than you," said Danny. *"Once you do this a few hundred more times, I will not insist that you arch your back and spread your arms either."*

"I would just as soon not become an expert at this, thank you very much. I wish the warden had not forbid us from landing the Defiant *on the moon. I think it would have been much safer."*

"I calculate the warden made the right decision," said Danny. *"The risk is too high that the prisoner could escape and commandeer the Defiant. I have no doubt Rick could do it if the situation was reversed."*

"You have a lot of faith in Rick, don't you?"

"Of course," replied Danny matter-of-factly. *"He is his mother's son, after all. By the way, I calculate you are getting too close to Rick. I recommend you slow your rate of descent. We are passing a thousand meters now."*

Pulling back a little from her bondmate, Jeena reached out with her senses and located the wall of energy ahead. She felt for a lessening of the energy in the force field. After probing for a couple of seconds, she found a small area of reduced energy between her and the landing pad.

"The entry point is just ahead," said Richard through her helmet's headset. "I'm putting on the brakes, so watch out."

Jeena did her best to match her bondmate's deceleration. She nearly touched his boots with her helmet at one point, but succeeded in pulling back at the last second to avoid contact. A tingling through her body told her they'd successfully passed through the force field.

"Your IFF code worked," Jeena said. She didn't fully understand how the identification system worked, but she was thankful her battle computer had gotten the code right.

"Of course I got it right," said Danny sounding insulted. *"What do you take me for, an amateur?"*

"Sorry," was all Jeena had time to say before she noticed her bondmate rotate into an upright position. She rotated as well, feeling more than half tempted to slow her rate of speed to a more manageable rate too, but she resisted the urge. If her bondmate didn't need to slow down more, then neither did she.

Twenty meters above the brerellium-steel deck of the landing pad, Jeena sensed Power surround her bondmate. His rate of descent slowed significantly. She followed suit and reduced her rate of movement to match his.

"Recommend you reduce your speed more," said Danny.

Jeena ignored her battle computer. *"No way. If Rick can do it, I can do it."*

Her boots hit the metal deck hard. The knees of her power-suit bent, taking up some but not all of the force of the hard landing. Throwing her arms out, Jeena tried to keep from hitting the landing pad with her helmet. She didn't quite succeed.

Smack!

"Are you all right?" asked Richard, reaching out to help.

Jerking her arm away before her bondmate could grab it, Jeena stood on her own. "I am fine, thanks."

"I warned you to slow down more," said Danny. *"I swear you are as stubborn as Rick. He is in a battle suit. His suit is designed to take hard landings. Yours is a civilian-model power-suit. The specs are not nearly as high."*

"Whatever," Jeena said using her bondmate's favorite word for ending a conversation. Noticing her bondmate looking at her, she clenched her teeth as she spoke into her intercom. "Not a word, bondmate. Not a word."

CHAPTER 9

The Crosioian scout cocked her head and strained to hear if the sound would be repeated. She swiveled her ears in all directions to no avail.

The noise came from the direction of the landing pad. I heard it at the same time I sensed the disturbance in the force field. There is only one answer. Someone is here. They must be using a stealth shield.

Lowering herself to the floor from the bar on the ceiling that was her perch, she walked to the part of the wall she knew contained the door. Touching the metal wall with the tip of the point on her right wing, she sent a concentrated line of Power into the wall. Converting her line into an active scan, she weaved the line of energy between the particles of creallium embedded in the walls of her cell.

The builders of this prison did not expect it to hold a diviner. I was able to pinpoint the primary locks and automated gun-control systems the first day I was here. If the humans had been foolish enough to keep live guards at this prison with a starship, I would have escaped long ago. As it is, I have been forced to bide my time. She bared her fangs in a smile. *Perhaps my waiting is over.*

Releasing a series of sonic waves, the scout intertwined the waves with her active scan. She listened for any changes in the environment around her. Before long she picked up two sets of vibrations coming from the prison's main hallway.

Ah, I have two visitors. I will kill one to intimidate the guards

*watching from the monitors. Then I will use the other as a hostage.
I may be able to convince the guards to give me access to a
starship to save their companion. If I was imprisoned by
Crosioians, my plan would not work, but the humans are
sentimental fools.*

Even as she thought of her plan, the scout knew the odds of
success were low. The humans' emotions were their weakness, but
it all depended on who was in charge. From experience, she knew
some humans were smart enough to sacrifice the lives of a couple
of hostages to keep her from escaping.

*It does not matter. The dishonor of being taken prisoner is too
much to bear. Death trying to escape is preferable to life as a
prisoner of the pathetic humans.*

The scout thought back to her capture. After destroying the
hyper-drives on two Empire dreadnaughts during the ambush
around Estos, she had been picked up by a Crosioian troopship. As
luck would have it, the troopship was one of the first two ships to
actually land on the planet Estos.

The trap for the Empire should have worked, she thought. *The
one who killed my mother is the reason it did not. I sensed him as
soon as I got off the troopship. He was using a stealth shield, but
his Power was low. He was unable to avoid detection by a diviner
such as myself.*

She remembered running as fast as she could from the
troopship, outpacing the soldiers around her in her eagerness to
reach the wizard scout first. She gnashed her fangs as she
remembered what happened next.

*He must have detected me. The tactical nuke he fired destroyed
my troopship. I was caught in the blast. My reserve was too low
from my battles on the dreadnaughts. My self-heal was unable to
keep up with the damage from the nuke. If I had only had a little
more Power in my reserve, I could have remained conscious. As it
was, my unconscious form was discovered by one of the last
Empire units to escape the trap on Estos. They took me prisoner
and kept me unconscious until I awoke in this cell.*

The shame of being taken prisoner washed over her again. *The
tractor beams in my cell prevent me from killing myself as would
be honorable. If the two visitors heading toward my cell are
foolish, perhaps by killing them I can regain at least some of my*

honor before I die.

The scout thought of her mother. *She at least died honorably fighting the wizard scout on Veturna. Unlike my mother, the wizard scout had no honor. I have studied the surveillance videos. If the two demon-hounds and the human children had not aided him, my mother would have killed the wizard scout. His head would even now be a prized trophy on the Long Wing tribe's Wall of Honor.*

The scout regretted she would be unable to take the head of the wizard scout who had killed her mother. *My mother was the best. She trained me well. I regret I will not be able to kill the wizard scout who killed her, but the lives of these two visitors will have to do. After I escape my cell and kill them, the humans will undoubtedly activate the nuke I detected below the prison. It does not matter. A life without honor is no life at all.*

The thought that her grandmother would never know of her small victory in killing the two approaching humans bothered her. She thought of the shame her grandmother must be feeling if she had heard of the capture of her granddaughter by humans.

Would that there was some way I could reduce her shame by escaping and taking the heads of these two humans as trophies back to our tribe's Wall of Honor. At least that would be some recompense toward undoing my shame at being taken captive.

The scout shook her head. She knew her grandmother would never know of her final fight against the two visitors. *I will soon be atomized particles of dust forever scattered over the surface of this moon. My ashes will not be placed beneath the heads of my enemies on the Long Wing Wall of Honor.* Shrugging her wings, she decided it didn't matter. *All that matters now is killing these two humans, if humans they be.*

Between her active scan and sonic wave, the scout sensed the two visitors come to a halt outside her cell door.

Their stealth shields are good, but they make no attempt to hide the vibrations of their steps on the metal floors of this prison. I know where they are. If they are foolish enough to open my cell's door, I will kill them. Whatever happens after that will happen. It matters not.

The scout sensed a line of Power reach through the wall, toward the link to her Power reserve. She knocked it away with a line of her own. The moment the two lines touched, hope flared in the scout's chest.

It is he. I can sense his frequency from his scan. He did not wrap it in a stealth shield. Why, I care not. All I know is that if I can kill him, my mother's death will be avenged. Perhaps my grandmother will hear how I killed the wizard scout before I died. Perhaps that will erase the shame of having her granddaughter taken prisoner.

Another line of Power came through the wall and separated into two lines with both heading toward the link to the scout's Power reserve. She succeeded in knocking one line aside, but the other line touched the link to her reserve before pulling hastily back.

The scout bared her teeth in a moment of rare humor. *The wizard scout senses the traps my mother placed on my link. He fears to try and break my link now. If I can lure him inside my cell, I may be able to kill him. He may not be wearing a battle suit. We shall soon see.*

Stepping back from the wall, the scout sent out another line of Power feigning weakness. She probed for the wizard scout but could not locate him through his stealth shield. She almost gave up hope that the fool would enter her cell when part of the wall shimmered and disappeared. Through the opening came a sphere of potent energy. The scout threw up a defensive shield, diverting the ball of energy to the side. The energy felt strange.

Magic, the scout thought. *How?*

The magic spell spread outward, filling the cell with its energy. The air grew intensely cold. The scout reached out with a line of Power toward a female carrying a staff in her left hand with a paw-sized gem at the top. Before the scout's line of Power could find the female's heart, two lines of Power reached out from a male wizard scout wearing an Empire battle suit. One line knocked her line away from the female. The scout sensed the wizard scout's other line reach into her neck, seeking out her spinal cord.

Charging forward, the scout aimed the point of her wing at the female, intent on skewering the magic user's throat. Before the point made contact, the air solidified, filling the entire room with a solid block of ice. Unable to move, the scout formed another line of Power determined to kill the wizard scout's companion before she died. Again her enemy knocked her line aside with one of his own. At the same time, the wizard scout's first line continued to seek out her spinal cord. With a third line of Power, he began probing the link to her reserve. In desperation, the scout sent a line of her own to defend her link, but a line of magic from the female knocked her defensive line aside.

Drawing half the Power from her reserve, the Crosioian scout sent a blast of pure energy toward the wizard scout and his companion. Even as the energy closed on the two, she sensed the wizard scout continue to probe the traps on her link. At the same time, a wall of magic formed around her two opponents. She sensed the gem on the female's staff blaze with magic as it reinforced the female's defensive shield. Due to the block of ice, the scout sensed more than saw her Power rebound back, shattering the ice encasing her. She was thrown into the back wall of her cell, knocking the air out of her lungs.

Scrambling to her feet, the scout charged forward just as the wizard scout's line of Power did something to her link. She stumbled as the connection to her reserve disappeared. At the same time, a ball of magic energy hit her in the chest. The scout fell to the floor. She tried to move her arms, legs, and wings to no avail. Something warm reached into the back of her neck. She heard a snap, then all sensation from her shoulders down ceased.

The wizard scout snapped my spinal cord. He must also have disconnected the link to my Power reserve. My mother could do that, though I cannot. Now my self-heal is not working. My mother's traps were not enough to stop him. They only slowed him down.

Shame washed over the scout as she realized the wizard scout had defeated her. *No,* she thought. *He is the one without honor. He had help, just like he did when he fought my mother. If he had been alone, and if I had been in my fighting-suit, I could have beaten him.*

She knew her thoughts were only that, thoughts. She was helpless before her enemies. The sounds around her began to dim as lack of oxygen began taking a toll on her senses. She tried to breathe, but between the elf's magic and her snapped spinal cord, even that simple task eluded her.

Waiting for death, the scout hoped she would meet the wizard scout in whatever place she was going. *The next time, I will beat you. I swear it.*

HARTMAN

CHAPTER 10

Richard eyed the Crosioian scout lying on the cell floor. She was tall even for a Crosioian. He sensed her life force fading as her body used up the last of the oxygen in her blood.

"This one is dangerous," said Nickelo out loud for the high priestess's benefit. "I highly recommend you allow her to die. We can find another prisoner to take us to the Crosioian capital if you insist on pursuing your plan. This one needs to die. She almost got your bondmate."

Glancing out the corner of his eye, Richard saw his bondmate standing to his left, just inside the door of the cell. She had removed the bulky power-suit and helmet. Blue light from the glowing gem at the top of the staff in her left hand reflected off her silver hair, turning the walls of the cell into a rainbow of colors.

Glancing down at the still form of the scout, Jeena said, "He did not almost kill me. I could have protected myself if necessary. I knew Rick would guard me from harm, so I concentrated on my spell." She looked away from the scout and into Richard's eyes. "Master Nick is right about one thing though. You should allow the bat-creature to die. She is too dangerous to let live."

Richard knelt next to the scout. "No. This is the one we need. I recognize her scent." He heard his bondmate sniff the air.

"Uh…what scent?"

"My wizard scout does not mean a physical scent," said Nickelo. "He is referring to her frequency. It is similar to a Crosioian scout he fought and killed on Veturna. I calculate this one is related to that scout."

The room brightened as the light from the gem in the Staff of the Lady of the Tree grew more intense. "Then all the more reason for her to die. I do not enjoy taking another's life, but I will not allow her to kill you, my bondmate."

Richard had no wish to die either. He also knew the scout had come closer to killing his bondmate than she admitted. *I barely knocked the scout's line of Power away in time,* he thought in his private space. *Maybe I should let her die.* For the merest moment, he considered allowing the last of the scout's life force to flow out of her body, but a persistent urge to save her kept him from doing so.

"I think *'the One'* wants me to use her to complete my mission," Richard said.

"You keep insisting I am part of *'the One,'*" said Nickelo still speaking out loud. "I have nothing in my memory banks indicating she should live."

"Doesn't matter," Richard said growing ever surer the scout was the key to his plan. He looked up at Jeena. "I'm going to heal her spinal cord. Do you still have the paralysis spell on her?"

"It is still active," said Jeena. "I also have a disintegrate spell Master Jathar taught me ready to go. At the first sign of attack by the bat-creature, I will use it."

Richard nodded. "Fair enough. Nick, I'm giving you full control of my battle suit. If the scout attacks, do what you need to do."

"Compliance."

Removing his right glove, Richard touched the Crosioian's shoulder. He imagined how the scout's body should be and compared that with how it was now. Pulling the difference into himself, he heard a popping sound from the back of his neck. All feeling from his neck down disappeared. He struggled to breathe on his own, but the muscles of his chest wouldn't move.

"I am taking over your breathing," said Nickelo.

A second later, Richard sensed air flowing through the tube that was part of his battle helmet, into his lungs. The feeling of oxygen starvation disappeared. He heard a deep breath and noticed the chest of the scout moving in and out.

"Your spinal cord will be healed in 5...4...3...2...1," said Nickelo. "I am giving control of your battle suit back to you."

Richard took three breaths on his own before raising his helmet to three-quarters mode. The tubes in his mouth and nose disappeared back into the helmet. He took deep breaths, smelling a musty, ammonia odor. He looked at Jeena. "I'd forgotten how the bats smelled. It's not unpleasant, but I can't say I'd want scented candles of it in our home."

Jeena wrinkled her nose. "Nor would I." She caught Richard's eyes with hers. "Now what?"

Replacing his glove, Richard pointed at the lone cot in the room. "Put her over there."

Jeena said a word Richard heard but immediately forgot. Magic wrapped around the scout and lifted the bat-creature into the air and to a sitting position on the cot.

"Nick," Richard said. "I want you to activate the translator on the battle helmet's speakers. I want to speak to the scout."

"Compliance."

Removing his dimensional pack, Richard pulled out two folding chairs. He placed one near the cell door and the other chair an arms-reach in front of the scout. Pointing to the chair by the door, he said, "Jeena, that one is yours."

"I prefer to stand," said Jeena shifting her staff to point the gem at the scout. "I would also prefer to be by your side in case the bat tries something."

At each of their words, Richard heard a hissing sound come from the battle helmet's speakers. He noticed the scout's ears twitch.

"She is listening," said Nickelo.

Ignoring his battle computer, Richard looked at his bondmate. "Jeena, please sit. You can cover me from the door."

Jeena's molten-silver eyes churned, and she opened her mouth to speak. Before she could say anything, Richard sent a feeling of need down the link to her. His bondmate nodded her head and walked to the cell door. He noticed her position the chair a step to the side of the doorway before sitting down. She removed the phase pistol from her holster and held it in her lap.

Getting a better field of fire, Richard thought. *Well, nothing wrong with that.*

Sitting down in his own chair, Richard stared into the scout's eyes, barely visible through her thick facial fur.

"The Crosioians do not use their eyes much," said Nickelo in their shared space. *"They* see *with their ears and sonic waves."*

Richard ignored his battle computer and concentrated on the scout instead. "My name is Wizard Scout Richard Shepard. I once fought a Crosioian scout with a scent very similar to yours. That was on the planet Veturna. Did you know her?"

Richard waited five seconds. When nothing came through the battle helmet's translator, he said, "I placed a kink in the link to your Power reserve. Your link was trapped, but I found a weak point that was missed. Did you place the traps, or did someone else do it for you?"

Again Richard waited five seconds. The only noise in the cell was the sound of Jeena's boots shifting position on the metal deck. He looked back at his bondmate.

Jeena spread her hands as if to say, "What are you hoping to accomplish?"

What indeed? Richard wondered.

Turning back to the scout, Richard made another attempt at communication. "You are a diviner. So am I. So was the scout I fought on Veturna. I viewed the video report of your capture on Estos. You were picked up near the point where I was located on the planet. I have a feeling if the nuke I shot off had exploded a few seconds later, we'd have met under more honorable circumstances."

At the word honorable, the bat's ears twitched.

"Hmm," said Nickelo. *"I think you hit a sore point."*

"I believe you're right, old buddy," Richard thought back.

Deciding to pursue the matter, Richard said, "If we had met on Estos, we could've fought as two scouts should, with honor." He noticed the bat's ears lock on him. "After I killed you in battle, I would have told stories of your prowess. As it is, if I kill you now, neither of us will receive honor. It is a shame you were taken prisoner."

Although Richard wasn't an empath, he still felt a rise of emotions in the scout. She remained silent, but he knew he had her full attention.

"I was thinking about having my battle computer send copies of the video of your capture to every Crosioian warship within range. I'm sure your friends, assuming you have such, would be interested in seeing your fate. I think that's the only *honorable* thing to do."

A feeling resembling anger came from the scout.

"I think you just pissed her off," said Nickelo in their shared space.

"I certainly hope so," Richard thought back.

"What would you know of honor?" came a husky voice out of the battle helmet's external speakers. "My mother could have beaten you if you had fought her by yourself, as a warrior of honor should. Even captive as I am, you needed a pathetic magic user to beat me. That is why we will win this war, and why your species shall cease to exist. We need no one other than ourselves to be victorious."

"Wow," said Nickelo in their shared space. *"She's quite a speechmaker when you get her talking. Keep on her, buddy. I calculate pride is a definite weakness in her species."*

Richard leaned toward the scout and gestured with his thumb over his shoulder. "Pathetic? Really? You don't know my bondmate very well. I think you'd find her a formidable foe under any circumstances."

The scout said nothing.

"You are losing her," said Nickelo in their shared space.

"This magic user is my ally and bondmate," Richard said. "I think the truly pathetic ones are those who serve at the beck and call of demons and their magic-user lackeys. Or are you going to try and tell me that you Crosioians didn't rely on demons to hide your fleets from view before the battle on Estos. I suppose the next thing you'll tell me is that you didn't need magic users to help you either."

The emotions from the scout increased, but the speakers on the battle helmet remained silent.

Richard rolled the dice for an all or nothing attempt to take advantage of the scout's pride. "Of course, what should I expect from a species that does everything a demon tells them to do?"

The brow above the bat's eyes narrowed. "What do you know of our assets? A few demons obeyed our commands to hide our fleets. So what? Demons obey us; we do not obey demons."

Richard leaned back in his chair. "Is that so? Then I guess the next thing you'll tell me is that Crosioians do not do what their master computer tells them to do."

"Our master computer is a tool," said the scout. "The Empire has a central computer. There is no difference."

Richard laughed, trying to put as much contempt into the sound as he could. He wasn't sure how the effect would be transmitted in Crosioian but could only hope for the best. "Our central computer is not possessed by a high-level demon. We didn't start a war by acting as a demon's puppets."

The scout's shoulder muscles shook.

Richard wondered for a moment if the bat-creature was going to break free of Jeena's paralysis spell. After a half-dozen heartbeats, the scout became still.

* * *

The scout got control of her breathing. She wanted to reach out and strangle her foe, but the elf's magic was too strong.

My mother told me of the magic dimension and those dwelling there, she thought. *She would have eventually taken me on one of her missions had this wizard scout not killed her.* She thought of her mother. A feeling of respect and loyalty passed over her as was proper. She continued her line of reasoning in her head. *My mother would have argued against using demons and magic scum to fight our foes. I argued in her place, but to no avail. My youth was against me. The master computer said its algorithms proved the assets were needed temporarily.*

The wizard scout's words bothered her. The master computer had attempted to convince the tribal leaders years earlier that the use of a few demons and magic users would not violate their warrior code.

While she was alive, my mother convinced the tribes not to use the demons or their magic user servants. It was only after my mother's death at the hands of this wizard scout and his allies that the tribes began allowing the use of magic in our plans. If my mother had lived, I am sure the tribes would never have allowed the use of demons.

The scout pointed her ears at the wizard scout, reflecting sonic waves off his face to detect the slightest change in features. "What talk you of possession? A computer is a computer. Only living things can be taken over by demonic possession."

The human laughed. "Do you think so? Then we will have to agree to disagree. In any regard, that doesn't apply to your master computer. Or at least it didn't use too. You see, like the Empire's central computer, your master computer *was* a living gas organism. I say *was* because when I destroyed the demon Zenthra that had possessed your master computer, the living gas was destroyed as well."

A voice hissed from the wizard scout's battle helmet. The scout knew it was the translated voice of the human's battle computer. Despite her disdain for anything associated with humans, she listened closely.

"The gas entity that was the master computer was only a shell of what it once was after it was possessed by Zenthra," said the wizard scout's battle computer. "I knew the gas that was the master computer. She would not have wanted to continue living merged as she was with the demon. The destruction of the master computer was my fellow gas's only hope of release from the living hell that had become her life."

The repeated use of the word Zenthra bothered the scout. The name had been mentioned several times over the centuries by half-dead members of recon teams sent into *the Hole*. Only one scout had returned from the last recon a hundred years earlier. She had kept mumbling the words Zenthra and Cancontus over and over until her death a week after her return.

"What know you of Zenthra?" the scout said. She disliked asking the human anything, but something at the back of her mind told her it was important. Her mother had mentioned the name Zenthra more than once during training sessions. The name had always been spoken with suspicion and loathing.

"I know quite a bit," said the wizard scout. "I've had a couple of run-ins with that particular demon over the years. He is one of four brother demons working toward destroying every living thing in our galaxy. Once Zenthra possessed your master computer, he tricked you into starting a war with the Empire."

At the word *tricked,* the scout felt the fur on her cheeks bristle and her chest grew warm. "No one had to *trick* us into wanting to destroy humans. Your kind has been pushing against our borders for centuries. You are a blight on the galaxy. The only way our future younglings can have peace is if your species is cleansed from every star system once and for all. No computer told us to do what we knew must be done. We decided to start the war ourselves."

The human stared at her for a dozen slow beats of both her hearts. Finally, he leaned forward until he was only a paws-breadth from her eyes. He was so close she didn't even need her sonic senses to discern his face. She could see every nuance with her eyes."

"Zenthra can be subtle," said the wizard scout. "Are you saying your master computer didn't suggest that the Crosioians should attack the Empire and back it up with a lot of facts and figures? Are you saying your master computer didn't convince your leaders to use demons and magic users in your war?"

The scout snorted, spraying mucus from her nostrils. The droplets splattered on the human's face, but he didn't attempt to wipe them off. He just continued staring into her eyes. She stared back for a full dozen heartbeats before replying to his question with one of her own. "Are you saying the Empire's central computer does not suggest things that your high command eventually does? Are you saying you are a puppet of your central computer?"

The scout noticed the wizard scout's eyes narrow as his cheeks twitched.

Ah, thought the scout. *I hit a sensitive spot.*

The human sat back in his chair and shrugged. "Perhaps we are to some extent. To be honest, I don't know. I have free-will, as do you. Even so, a demon like Zenthra can work around free-will to get creatures to work for it."

"Demons are our assets," said the scout. "They do our bidding; we do not do theirs. We control them. They are stupid creatures."

The wizard scout made a noise the scout associated with laughter. "If you think that, then you have only worked with lower-level demons. The higher-level ones are intelligent and extremely cunning. The demon that took over your master computer was very high level. Like I said, they are subtle."

The scout thought of the few demons it had been forced to work with. They had proved useful in creating stealth shields, but she doubted their intelligence. She thought about the master computer for a second. *No computer convinced our leaders to start the war with the Empire,* she decided. She swiveled her ears to make sure the elf was in the same position. She was. The scout turned her attention back to the human.

"Yes, the master computer first began recommending we attack the Empire fifty years ago, but we only attacked when our tribal leaders thought the time was right. It was our decision, not the master computer's. As for the demons, I will admit my mother argued against the use of them, but our tribal leaders only allowed the use of a few to hide our ships around Estos. They served us; we did not serve them."

The human did not seem impressed with her line of reasoning. He looked at her and said, "Your mother was a formidable foe. She was the best I've ever fought. But at the time, I was only a wizard scout in training. I hadn't even had my DNA baseline set. I couldn't even self-heal at the time of our battle. My mission on Veturna was supposed to be a simple escort of a defecting scientist. Yet a fully-trained Crosioian scout, your mother, was sent to oppose me along with a hundred plus trained soldiers with high-grade armor and weapons. Doesn't it seem strange to you that a valuable asset like your mother was sent on a mission against a mere intern? I'd think a computer with as much programming power as your master computer would know the mission was a waste of a Crosioian scout's abilities."

The scout tried to reach out with a paw to stop the human from speaking, but the elf's spell held her fast. Her mind went back to the last time she'd seen her mother. A courier had arrived, ordering her mother to report to Veturna. Her mother had taken her to the underwater cavern on the planet Astaris that contained *the Hole*. Once there, her mother had told her that one day soon the tribes would be sending another recon team into the opening to ensure the rift between dimensions was under control. She remembered her mother telling her that if she did not return from her mission that she, her daughter, would need to lead the team in her stead. The scout remembered how her mother's words had concerned her at the time. The thought that the greatest scout in Crosioian history would not return from a mission against a partially-trained wizard scout cadet was ridiculous. A few days later, she'd received word that her mother was dead.

The scout did not share her memories with the human.

"My mother would have killed you easily if your demon-hounds had not come to your aid," she told him. "I watched the videos from our tele-bots. Even with your allies helping you, my mother almost succeeded in defeating you."

The wizard scout glanced at the floor for a full minute. Finally, he looked back at her. "You are right. She would have beaten me easily without the help of my spirit-wolf allies. If you saw the videos, then you know that the first time we fought, I was teleported out a few seconds before she would've killed me. When I returned a half hour later, the spirit-wolves came with me. Do you know how they became my allies?"

The scout snorted again. "I care not. The master computer was right in having my mother sent to Veturna. You were more dangerous than expected. She almost stopped you even with your allies. A lesser scout would not have stood a chance."

Seemingly ignoring her words, the human said, "A moment before your mother would've killed me the first time, I was teleported to the planet Portalis in the magic dimension. I was met there by an entity of great power. He told me that I would need allies and that he was going to help me get them. The entity sent me to the spiritual dimension where I met my spirit-wolf brothers and sisters. If that entity hadn't helped me gain the friendship of the spirit-wolves before I returned to Veturna, your mother would have defeated me. She would still be alive today, and I would be dead."

The human's words bothered the scout. She suspected a trap but failed to see one. *Why does he waste his time talking?* she thought. *I know my mother was confused why the master computer assigned her to the mission on Veturna, but soldiers go where they are told.*

Rotating her ears toward the human, the scout said, "Then you should thank this entity of yours for saving your life." She snorted again to show her contempt. "Why you believe your story would be of interest to me is no concern of mine."

The wizard scout leaned toward her again. "The entity that sent me to the spiritual dimension, the one that placed me in a situation ensuring the spirit-wolves would become my allies, was a master demon. He is the one that commands the four brother demons I told you about. Zenthra serves the master demon. Zenthra does what the master demon orders."

The human stood and paced the width of the cell twice before turning to face her again. "You said your mother opposed the use of demons and magic users by your tribes. What if that didn't fit into the master demon's plans?"

The scout could almost sense the human's mind churning furiously. The wizard scout pounded his right fist in his opposite hand before speaking.

"What if the demons set the whole thing up to get your mother out of the way?" said the human as he began pacing the cell again.

The elf stood. When she did, the human stopped his pacing.

"Why would the demons do that, Rick?" said the elf. "You told me you were on an intern assignment as a cadet. If they had wanted the Crosioian scout you fought dead, would it not seem more logical to have sent her on a mission against a quad of wizard scouts?"

The human shook his head. "I'm not so sure."

Before the scout knew what she was doing, she spoke. "My mother was being groomed for an important mission. The tribal leaders would not have risked her on a mission against a quad or even a single fully-trained wizard scout. The tribal leaders would have refused no matter how much the master computer insisted. They only authorized my mother for the Veturna mission because it was against a cadet in training." Speaking more to herself than the human and elf, the scout added, "A week after my mother was killed, the first of the magic users and demons appeared in our ranks. The master computer assured the tribal leaders the demons were necessary to ensure total victory against the Empire. Without my mother to argue against the master computer's plan, the tribal leaders went along with their use."

The scout sensed the human and elf looking at her. She chastised herself for saying more than she'd intended.

"The demons are our real enemies," said the human. "They began the war between us so we'd do their dirty work for them by killing each other. I've seen their armies waiting to invade and wipe out every living thing in our galaxy."

The scout did not trust the human, but other happenings she'd been suspicious of during the last couple of years began falling in place.

"Why bother telling me?" said the scout. "I am a prisoner. Even if I believed what you say, I can do nothing."

The human walked next to her cot and sat back in his chair. The elf returned to her seat by the door.

"I think you *can* do something," said the wizard scout. "We've got to stop this war before it's too late. The demon armies are coming. Our only hope for the future of both our species is to work together against them. I need your help to do that."

The scout hissed a laugh. "Me? Were you not listening? I was taken prisoner. The shame of my actions is insurmountable. My place in the Long Wing tribe is lost forever. Better it would have been to have died in that nuclear blast than to have been taken prisoner."

The human leaned so close the scout felt the warmth of his breath on her facial fur. "Maybe not. Maybe being taken prisoner was the one thing that is going to help save this galaxy for both our species."

CHAPTER 11

Richard leaned forward in his chair, so close to the scout that he could make out her facial fur moving in time to his breathing. He sensed concern for his safety through the link to his bondmate but pushed on anyway. He was more certain than ever of the path he was taking.

"Maybe not," Richard told the Crosioian scout. "Maybe being taken prisoner was the one thing that is going to help save this galaxy for both our species."

Leaning back in his seat, Richard glanced over his shoulder at Jeena before looking back at the scout. "I need to speak to your tribal leaders. I have to convince them that the war was started by demons. I need to con—"

The scout hissed. The sound of laughter came through the external speakers of Richard's battle helmet.

"Every Crosioian soldier is sworn to take your head and place it on their tribe's Wall of Honor. You would be dead before you ever got within a thousand light years of our tribal council." The sound of hissing laughter came again. "You do not even know where our home planet is located, and no amount of torture will make me tell. Only condemned human prisoners are ever taken to our tribal council. Once those prisoners are killed in front of the tribal leaders, their heads join those of our other enemies on one of the tribal Walls of Honor."

Something must have passed down Richard's link to his bondmate that he didn't intend because Jeena jumped out of her seat. "No, Rick. I forbid it."

"I concur with the high priestess," said Nickelo over the battle helmet's speakers. "If you are planning on what I think you're planning, the odds of success are non-existent. We will find another way to reason with the Crosioians."

Richard watched the bat's ears. They were pointing directly at him as if the scout was determined not to miss anything. *Very well,* he thought in his private space. *I'm going to give her something to really think about.*

"What if I was your prisoner?" Richard asked. Hearing movement behind him, he raised a hand in a halting motion to his rear. "Stay where you are, Jeena." Along with the last word, he sent an emotion down his bond link that he hoped meant *"Please, this is important."*

He heard no more movement behind him. A quick check of his passive scan confirmed his bondmate was holding her position by the door.

After ten seconds of silence, the scout's ears twitched. "I am your prisoner, not the other way around."

"You let me take care of that," Richard said. "If I give you my word of honor as a wizard scout that I will be your prisoner, would you take me to your tribal leaders?"

The bat-creature hissed. "If I took you to my home world, it would be to remove your head after I beat you in battle before the assembled tribes. I would mount your head—"

"Whatever," Richard said, seeing no reason to dwell on the cons of his gamble. "Would you take me to your tribal leaders, and would I get a chance to speak to them before you tried to execute me?"

The sound of movement came from behind Richard again. "No," said Jeena obviously unable to hold her tongue any longer. "I will kill this one here and now before I will allow you to follow through with some fool plan that will only end in your death."

The bat swiveled her ears toward Jeena before speaking. "It matters not. Even if I trusted the wizard scout would keep his word, I have no ship to return home. Not that it would matter. The keepers of this prison have a nuclear weapon filled with energized titanium buried beneath my cell. At the slightest hint that I am escaping, they will set the weapon off. Even shifting into the void would not save any of us."

Richard rose from his chair and glanced over his shoulder at Jeena. She was standing next to her chair grasping the Staff of the Lady of the Tree in her right hand. He sensed a buildup of magic energy in the palm of her left hand.

"She has a spell ready to go," said Nickelo in their shared space. *"She will kill the scout if you try to proceed. I calculate a one hundred percent probability the elf is not bluffing."*

Richard didn't need a battle computer to tell him that his bondmate was serious. He'd already been with her long enough to know she didn't bluff. He chose his next words with care.

"Jeena, please stand down. We are at a crossroads. I can sense it, and I don't believe for one second it's coming from *'the One.'* There are bigger powers at play than a network of computers. I told you about my meeting with the master demon during my first mission on Portalis. What I didn't tell you is that he has a counterpart working on the side of the light. I have shared memories of *'the One'* with Nick. I've sensed the entity that is working to save the three galaxies. This moment right now has been given to us as an opportunity to turn the tide in our favor. Don't ask me how I know, but I do. I need you on my side. Won't you trust me?"

Although his bondmate said nothing, Richard was grateful to see the ball of magic in her left hand dim before disappearing completely. He took that as a good sign. Turning to face the scout, Richard raised both hands palm out.

"I surrender to you here and now. I agree to be your prisoner and will allow you to take me to your tribal council. In addition, I will teach you how to protect the link to your Power reserve and how to protect those of others of your kind. I will also show you how to disconnect the links of your opponents."

The bat's ears focused on Richard. "Why would you do that? We are enemies."

Richard nodded. "Yes, we are, at the moment. That's going to change if I have anything to do about it. The war between us was set up by the demons. They are our real enemies."

"You killed my mother."

"And your kind killed my father," Richard said still holding his palms out toward the scout. He noticed the bat's eyes focus on his two hands.

"I was taken prisoner," said the scout. "I have no honor."

Richard shook his head. "You are a Crosioian scout. They have always been honorable foes. I believe you were supposed to be taken prisoner so we could meet. In fact, I don't believe you are a prisoner at all. I believe you are a sleeper purposely placed here so we could meet. Your honor is intact. The odds that you are the daughter of the first scout I fought are too great to be coincidental. Unless I miss my guess, taking me as prisoner to your tribal leaders should go a long way to restoring whatever honor you think you've lost in your tribe's eyes."

"Perhaps," said the scout. "There is still the problem of the nuke, not to mention I do not have a ship."

"I have a ship," Richard said, hoping he was telling the truth. He knew well enough that convincing Sergeant Ron to take a Crosioian scout onboard the *Defiant* might be more than a little challenging.

"And the nuke?" asked the scout.

Taking a risk, Richard reached out with his mind and undid the kink he'd placed in the scout's link to her Power reserve. As soon as he did, he sensed Power flow into her body, healing her spinal column.

"Jeena, release your paralysis spell."

"I do not th—"

"Please, Jeena. You promised to obey me. Remember?"

Richard heard his bondmate mumble something to the effect of "I meant within reason," even as he sensed the magic energy around the scout dissipate back into the universe from which it had come. He breathed a sigh of relief. In their short time together, he'd quickly found out his bondmate could be volatile at times.

"As can you," said Nickelo in their shared space.

The scout sat up slowly on the edge of the cot, keeping her ears and eyes focused on Richard.

"Follow me with your mind," Richard said. "Jeena, Nick, I'm going to need your help as well. I'd be willing to bet a month's pay the warden is even now heading for the fail-safe switch."

"That's a sucker's bet," said Nickelo over the battle helmet's external speakers. "I am surprised he hasn't already set off the nuke."

Reaching out with his mind, Richard probed beneath the cell, pinpointing the tactical nuke. He sensed two lines of Power follow along with him as he merged his mind with the electronics of the nuclear weapon. He used the same technique the *Defiant's* mechanic, Charlie, had shown him to troubleshoot problems with mechanical equipment. This time Richard wasn't looking for problems, he was seeking potential weak points in the arming mechanism of the bomb. Spotting a surge of energy heading toward the weapon's electronic trigger, he grabbed onto Jeena's line of Power and guided it to a weak point ahead of the energy surge. Sensing another surge from a backup trigger, Richard wasted no time waiting to see if Jeena would know to block the flow of energy. Either she would, or she wouldn't.

"*Don't worry,*" said Nickelo in their shared space. "*Danny is with her. She'll do her part. You'd better hope the Crosioian scout knows what to do. You've got to stop that second energy surge and short-circuit the trigger mechanism before the nuke's security programs decide to activate the weapon using override logic. You can't do both things at once on your own.*"

Wrapping his line of Power around the scout's, Richard shoved her line into a weak point ahead of the second energy surge. Without waiting to see what she would do, he merged his mind into the nuke's computer core, seeking out the security programs.

"*One of the programs is already activating,*" said Nickelo. "*You have to stop it.*"

With his mind working at nanosecond speed, Richard scrambled the security program. He changed the programming code for self-activating the nuke to make it close the safety switch instead. He modified the security program in such a way as to permanently disable the bomb's trigger. He sensed flows of energy burn out the circuits in the trigger.

"*How'd I do that?*" Richard asked in his shared space. "*I'm not a computer programmer.*"

Nickelo laughed. "*No, you are not. Fortunately for you, I am. Once you got into the computer network, I was able to guide you in what to do. We're a team, remember?*"

Richard's mind returned to normal speed. The scout was standing to his front with wings outstretched. Jeena was a step to his right rear. The Lady's staff was glowing with Power.

"This one is my prisoner," said the scout, pointing a paw at

Richard. "Does his word mean nothing?"

The staff's glow disappeared. Leaning the Lady's staff against the cell wall, the high priestess raised both hands palm out. "I am also your prisoner. Where he goes, I go."

"Like hell you do," Richard said. "That's not part of the deal. I'm the only one going with the scout. You will be staying on the *Defiant* with Sergeant Ron."

Jeena turned away from the scout long enough to walk in front of Richard and poke him in the chest with two stiffened fingers. The blow didn't actually hurt through his battle suit, but it was forceful enough to get his attention.

"The hell I will, Wizard Scout Richard Shepard. You are my bondmate, but I am the high priestess of the Lady of the Tree. I do what I want, when I want. So if you do not like it, that is just too bad." Turning back to face the scout, Jeena once again raised both hands palm out. "So am I your prisoner or not? You should probably consider the fact that you do not have any weapons or armor at the moment, and that I have a disintegration spell ready to go at the first sign of attack."

Richard held his breath. He sensed a ball of magic energy flow into his bondmate's left hand. He had no doubt the scout sensed it as well.

Retracting her wings behind her back, the scout's lips pulled back to reveal her fangs.

"I calculate that's her version of a smile," came Nickelo's thought in their shared space.

The scout's ears focused completely on Jeena. "You are my prisoner. Now, if you will refrain from turning my body into floating bits of atomized dust, perhaps we can figure out how to get off this moon. As I told you, I have no ship."

Richard smiled. "Leave that to me."

CHAPTER 12

Something woke Telsa. While wizard scouts didn't sleep often, even she had to give her brain a rest every once in a while. When she opened her eyes, she continued to lie on the soft mattress of the guest bed in Rick and Jeehana's home in Silverton. She was thankful they'd been kind enough to offer her the use of their spare bedroom before departing on their mission back to the physical dimension.

Snuggling deeper under the covers, Telsa gazed around the room seeking a clue about what might have disturbed her. The little moonlight entering through the curtained window above the desk barely lit the room. Even so, she could tell the bedroom was empty except for the elaborately carved bed, wardrobe, desk, chair, and nightstand. A sweep with her passive scan detected a life form at the front door. She recognized the life form's frequency. It wasn't that of an enemy.

"Of course it is not an enemy," said Raj in their shared space. *"What kind of battle computer do you take me for? I would have woken you if an enemy was nearby."*

Reaching to the nightstand next to the bed with her right hand, Telsa picked up her battle helmet and placed it on her head. As soon as the visor lowered across her eyes, the helmet's night vision took hold. Everything in the room took on a light shade of red. She was used to it. During her years at the Intergalactic Wizard Scout Academy, the instructors had always stressed keeping the battle suit's filter in night vision mode. According to her TAC officers, by doing so, no matter whether she found herself in daylight, darkest night, thick fog, or a raging blizzard, she'd be used to seeing things the same way if caught in a fight.

"You mean if you'd detected an enemy," Telsa replied to her battle computer's comment about waking her. *"You can't detect everyone or everything."*

"True," admitted Raj not sounding at all happy with having a weakness pointed out to him. *"In this case though, I happen to know that the life form at the front door is the elf Leethor. It was his knock that woke you."*

Throwing back the covers, Telsa twisted and sat up on the side of the bed. The bed was high, and her short legs didn't quite reach the floor. She scooted off the bed and took a moment to let her bare feet take in the softness of the luxurious carpet. She wiggled her toes, enjoying the sensation. *"I swear this is the softest stuff I've ever felt. I'd be super rich like my parents if I could corner the market on the material and sell it back in the physical dimension."*

Raj gave a canned laugh. *"Good luck with that. The carpet's made of luxamar fur. I calculate it took the high priestess's family several thousand years to comb enough of the little creatures' fur to create the carpets in this house. Your business would grow broke waiting for enough inventory to sell."*

Laughing in spite of herself, Telsa grabbed her battle suit pants from where she'd tossed them on the floor the night before. Battle suits were made to be worn without clothing. Since she preferred sleeping in the nude anyway, she was able to dress quickly enough. Just as she was snapping on her utility belt, another knock came from the direction of the living room.

"I'm coming," Telsa mumbled, knowing full well the sound wouldn't carry to her obviously impatient visitor. "Keep your pants on."

"I suspect Commander Leethor is fully clothed," said Raj.

"It's just a saying, Raj. Don't get your panties in a wad."

"I do not wear—"

"Forget it, Raj."

"Consider it forgotten, Wizard Scout."

Making her way to the hallway, Telsa walked past the kitchen and out to the living room. Once at the front door, she opened it to find not just Leethor, but Master Jathar and Rembis as well.

"Hmm," commented Raj in their shared space. *"As I have said*

before, they have good stealth shields."

"We're sorry," said Rembis. "Did we wake you?"

The gnome magic user's grin told Telsa he knew full well they had. She grinned back. "Not at all. I've been up for hours doing my knitting." She took a look at the dark sky before stepping back from the door and motioning the others in. "Make yourselves at home. Geez, I knew you said we were leaving today, but I figured you at least meant after the sun came up."

Leading the others in, Master Jathar maneuvered his way around a stack of books and made his way to the sofa. Moving some scrolls over to create a clear space on the cushion, he sat down. The old elf's garb was somewhat unusual in that instead of his normal black robe he was wearing a set of brown and green pants and tunic. His uniform appeared more suitable for an elf scout than a master mage. He leaned his staff across one leg before looking at Telsa.

"I am afraid the early hour is my fault," he said giving a tightlipped smile. "I have many duties, and it is my hope that we can finish this business quickly and return in time for me to make a report to the Council of Light when they meet this evening." The elf mage looked around at the stacks of books and scrolls in the cluttered room before shaking his head and chuckling. "This is my first time in the high priestess's home. I had heard stories, but…" He looked at Telsa. "How do you get around without knocking something over?"

Telsa flashed a grin. "It's been a challenge."

The elf Leethor looked around from where he stood in the center of the room. His brown and green pants and tunic matched those of Master Jathar. In lieu of a staff, he carried a bow in his right hand. A longsword was strapped to his left side. Telsa made note of the blue gem chip in the pommel of the sword. Her passive scan picked up magic energy radiating from both the sword and a dagger on the elf's right hip. More magic was coming from beneath his tunic.

"He is wearing magic armor underneath his clothes," volunteered Raj in their shared space. *"I calculate a ninety-two percent probability it is elven chainmail. Several of the arrows in his quiver also radiate magic."*

Leethor finished surveying the room and laughed. "I must agree with Wizard Scout Telsa. I have been here many times, and it is definitely a challenge getting around. I must confess I have knocked over quite a few stacks of books over the years." He turned and faced Telsa. "Now, not to hurry you, Wizard Scout Telsa, but if you would like to take a few minutes to get yourself ready, we can make ourselves comfortable here until you prepare for the journey."

Telsa laughed at the thought that a wizard scout needed time to get ready. The moment she sealed her battle suit, she knew the sterilized environment inside the suit would take care of all her body's needs. She didn't even need to brush her teeth. "First off, just call me Telsa, Commander. I'm not used to formalities. As for getting ready, I just need a minute to get my pack and rifle from the bedroom, so don't get too comfortable."

Leethor bowed. "As you say, Telsa. Please call me Leethor. Any friend of Rick and Jeehana's is a friend of mine."

Hurrying to retrieve her gear, Telsa was back in less than thirty seconds. She slipped the strap of her M12 assault rifle over her shoulder so that it hung in a ready-to-fire position. It fit comfortably in her hands. Sergeant Hendricks, the *Defiant's* armorer, had modified it especially for her by shortening the stock and barrel. While the modified grenade launcher under the barrel only held five rounds instead of the usual seven, the comfortable design of the weapon was worth the loss, in her opinion. Once situated, she faced Master Jathar. "Ready as I'll ever be. You mentioned teleporting to our destination?"

Rising from his seat, Master Jathar nodded. "So I did." He turned to Rembis. "Would you care to do the honors? You lived in New Drepdenor. You are more familiar with the area than me."

The gnome magic user smiled. "I lived there a hundred thousand years ago. However, between what Leethor has told me and what I've seen in our scrying devices, I think I can get us there safely enough."

Without any seeming preparation, the gnome said a word Telsa heard and quickly forgot as he slapped his hands together. A wave of energy swept over her. Every cell in her body tingled as the world turned black. An eye-blink later, the world was again tinted red through her night vision filter. She was standing next to a rushing river thirty meters across, tall trees on her side of the

114

riverbank and even taller cliff walls on the other. A loud roar drew her attention to a ten-meter-tall waterfall not a hundred meters upstream. Her passive scan picked up a score of life forms a couple of hundred meters downstream. Glancing in that direction, she made out a half-dozen one- and two-story buildings near a dock protruding into the river. She sensed nothing with her passive scan that might denote the presence of a guardian.

"Uh, where are we?" Telsa asked. "I thought we were going to some mountain."

Rembis laughed. "We are, but not by teleportation. I'm afraid we'll need to take a boat for the final leg of our journey. I suspect the guardian might take someone teleporting into their domain as an attempt to steal their treasure. Master Jathar and I discussed the matter last night. We agreed it will be much safer to make our way there in a more traditional way for all to see. Leethor assures us we can get a boat and guide from the human settlement yonder."

"Assures is a big word," said Leethor. "The humans at the settlement were helpful enough last time I was here, but that was fifty years ago when Meshoan and I helped rescue Jeehana. Still, I think we will be able to acquire a boat and guide without too much trouble."

As Leethor took the lead following a worn path along the side of the river, in the direction of the buildings, Telsa took up position behind him. Rembis fell in behind her with Master Jathar taking up the rear spot.

"Raj, err, I mean my battle computer, mentioned Jeehana's rescue," Telsa said. "I've never gotten the full story."

Leethor glanced back over his shoulder. "Then I will have to tell you the tale some time when we are not in such a hurry. It's a sad tale, in some respects. The high priestess's salvation came at a cost." He looked back toward the settlement and picked up the pace. "Still, Jeehana was saved, and that's what matters. It was worth the price."

Although perplexed and curious by the elf's reply, Telsa prodded him no further. For one thing, she'd noticed a definite sadness in the elf's voice. There wasn't time to query more anyway since they were fast approaching the settlement.

The first rays of the sun were just peeking over the horizon as they stepped into the hard packed earth between the six wooden buildings. To Telsa, it wasn't so much a settlement as it was a ranch. In addition to the main two-story log building, there was an obvious barn along with other outbuildings that appeared to be large sheds. A score of chickens pecked the ground around one such building as two children, a boy and a girl who appeared to be about eight years old, scattered cracked corn out of buckets onto the ground. When a rooster crowed, the girl looked up. The moment her gaze fell on Telsa and her companions, the expression on the girl's face changed to one of wonderment.

"Elves!" shouted the girl as she pointed in their direction. "Elves!"

Two men came running out of the barn. One carried a pitchfork, but otherwise they were unarmed. Another old man and two teenage boys came out of the main building. They were unarmed as well. They were soon followed by a score of others, including a mixture of men, women, and children.

Leethor stepped forward and raised both hands palm out.

"He is showing them he is not armed," said Raj in Telsa's shared space.

"I know," Telsa said. "What do you think I am? Stupid?"

"Is that a rhetorical question, Wizard Scout, or do you actually want me to tell you what I think?"

Ignoring her battle computer, Telsa concentrated on Leethor and the old man who'd come out of the main building. From the respectful distance the others seemed to give him, Telsa figured the old man was in charge. He approached Leethor, stopping four paces away. The old man was flanked by a couple of adult men with crossbows, but the cocked and loaded weapons were pointed at the sky. Telsa guessed the old man was in his late seventies or early eighties. He eyed her suspiciously before looking back at Leethor.

"We don't want any trouble here," said the old man.

Leethor lowered his hands. "That's good, because we don't want any either. I've been here before. It was a long time ago. An old woman was in charge then. Her name was Melody."

The old man's eyes widened. "Are you talking about Grandma Melody? She died years ago." He looked closer at Leethor before his eyes widened even farther. "You're one of them, aren't you? One of the ones who brought the injured elf with them. That was indeed a long time ago. I was a lot younger then, but I remember it clear as if it were yesterday."

Leethor seemed to peer closer at the old man's face. "Caleb, isn't it? I am good at names, but I cannot be sure. Humans change a lot in fifty years."

The old man laughed. "That's humans for you. We age and elves don't." He looked at the other humans around him. "It's all right. They're friends." He looked at the two men next to him. "Take the crossbows back in the house. They won't be needed."

As the two men headed back to the house, the little girl who'd been feeding the chickens took two steps forward. "Are these the one's you tell us about in your stories, Grandpa? Are these the elves?"

Caleb laughed.

Telsa had a feeling he was one of those men who liked to laugh a lot. She could relate. She liked to laugh too.

"Well, this one is, Blossom," said the old man pointing at Leethor. "I'd introduce you, but I'm afraid my memory's not quite as good with names after fifty years as his seems to be."

Telsa thought she noticed Leethor's face grow a little red in the morning night. She switched her visor to clear. *Yep,* she thought. *Definitely red.*

"My apologies," said Leethor. "I am Commander Leethor. This is Master Jathar, and the gnome is Master Rembis." He pointed at Telsa. "This fierce-looking warrior is Wizard Scout Telsa."

Telsa removed her battle helmet and attached it to her hip before bowing at the waist. "The pleasure's all mine."

The girl who'd been feeding the chickens set down her bucket before taking two steps forward and peering at Telsa. "Are you a gnome also? I'm almost as tall as you."

Leethor and Rembis laughed. Even the normally grim Master Jathar smiled.

Telsa shook her head. "Nope. I'm as human as you. I'm just a little on the short side. Hope you don't mind."

"Not me," said Blossom. "I get tired of having to look up at everyone just because they're an adult."

Telsa whispered back, "To tell the truth, I get a little tired of looking up at everybody myself."

Blossom laughed.

The old man cleared his throat. "Not to rush things, but I'm betting this isn't a social call. Is there something we can do for you? I'd say we don't get many elf visitors, but truth be told, we haven't had any since the last time you were here."

Leethor glanced back at Rembis and Jathar. When neither of them spoke up, he looked back at the human. "You are right, Honorable Caleb. This is not a social call. Once again I find myself in need of traveling to Drepdenor Mountain. Your people helped me get there once. I was hoping you would help my companions and I do so again. Naturally we will pay."

"Pay?" laughed Caleb. "What kind of host would my family and I be if we accepted mere coins for aiding elves? Indeed, the story of your visit will be pay enough. I suspect little Blossom here will be telling the tale long after I've been buried and forgotten. Of course we'll help you. But first, come inside and eat. We were just about to have breakfast."

Leethor shook his head. "Our thanks, but we are hard pressed for time. Perhaps another day. As it is, if you could loan us a boat, we would be most appreciative."

Caleb smiled. "The river is treacherous, Commander Leethor. Unless you possess extensive knowledge of the river, which I doubt you do, I have a feeling your boat would be broken on a rock and sunk at the first set of rapids." He gestured toward the two men who'd returned from putting their crossbows in the house. "Thomas, Doughty, get one of our boats ready. You'll be taking our guests to the bend of the river nearest New Drepdenor." Looking back at Leethor, he said, "Will you need my two grandsons to wait for you, to bring you back?"

Before Leethor could reply, Rembis spoke up. "That will not be necessary. We will teleport out once our business with the guardian is finished."

"The guardian?" said Caleb. "Brave your companions and you must be. I would warn you that many go to the mountain and never return, but..." He shrugged his shoulders. "But then Commander Leethor has been there once before and yet here he is again. So who am I to warn you? Tell me, Commander, did the injured elf live? I have always been curious."

Leethor nodded. "Yes, she lives still. Our mission was a success."

"Good," smiled Caleb. "I'm glad. My family and I will pray your current mission, whatever it may be, will be just as successful."

* * *

The boat ride to the bend of the river near the mountain was rough and took the better part of the day. According to their guides, Thomas and Doughty, recent rains had made the ride more hazardous than usual. On at least two occasions the wooden boat smacked into rocks hard enough to crack timbers. Thankfully, their destination was now in sight. Telsa was more relieved than she cared to admit. Having nearly drowned during her youth, she hated traveling on boats of any kind. Early in the ride, she'd sealed her battle suit just in case their little ship floundered.

"That was a wise decision," said Raj in their shared space. *"Your battle suit is completely waterproof. You'd have been safe enough if the boat sank. I can't say as much for the others."*

Telsa suspected the two mages would have done all right in the case of a spill, but she doubted Leethor and their two guides would have fared as well. She was thankful the skills of Caleb's grandsons had been up to the task.

"So how will you get back?" Telsa asked as the two cousins maneuvered the boat toward a sandbar in the bend of the river. "Surely you can't row the boat back upstream."

Both Thomas and Doughty laughed.

"You are right, err, Wizard Scout," replied Thomas as he threw his weight against the tiller to force the boat to cut across the swift current. "There's a small harbor another hour downstream. We'll anchor the boat there and camp for the night. In the morning, we'll start walking back home. The river will calm down in a few weeks. Some of us will come back and fetch the boat then." He laughed. "There are already three of our boats anchored in the harbor. You're not the first group we've taken to the mountain this winter. Groups of adventurers are always making the trek in search of treasure." Thomas lost his smile, and his voice took on a serious tone. "None of the three groups returned. Only a few ever return, and they've always been worse for the wear and without treasure. I wish you better luck, Wizard Scout."

119

Telsa removed her helmet as the two guides beached the boat on the sandbar. Once Master Jathar, Rembis, Leethor, and her got off the boat, she turned and looked Thomas in the eye. "Just so you know, we're not in this for any treasure. We're after something far more precious than mere trinkets of gold or silver. Please tell Caleb that we appreciate your family's help in our endeavor. I hope we'll meet again sometime."

"As do I," said Thomas as he helped his cousin push the boat back out into the river. With a final wave, the two men steered the boat into the center of the river, bouncing on the rough waves as they went. In less than a minute, the boat and its occupants disappeared around the river bend.

Leethor tightened the straps on his pack and looked at the steep trail leading up to the red-rock mountain that was New Drepdenor. "Well, the mountain is not going to come to us, so we better get started. It is a good four-hour hike to where we need to go."

Falling in behind the elf, Telsa kept the brisk pace easily enough. The assistors in her battle suit made even the steep climb relatively easy. Before long, the sides of the mountain closed in. Telsa found herself becoming a little claustrophobic in the tight space. At one point, the side of the trail fell away to reveal a gap in the rock wall. She paused long enough to glimpse the top of the mountain. Leethor must have sensed her halt because he stopped as well.

"Looks like a dragon's head, does it not?" asked Leethor.

Looking closer, Telsa had to admit the broken rock at the tip of the mountain did resemble the head of a dragon with its mouth open, ready to devour unwanted intruders.

"You know the guardian?" Telsa asked as she took up walking again.

Leethor turned and proceeded up the path ahead of her, but he continued to talk between pants. "Yes, I know them. I served them for twenty-five years. So did Meshoan. You may remember I mentioned a cost for saving the high priestess. Dragons rarely give anything away for free, not even information. The price for saving Jeehana was a hundred years of service. The members of my four-elf team all pledged twenty-five years each. One of my team members, Kreptor, serves them even now. I will introduce you if we get the chance. He is a good friend."

Telsa nodded her head even though Leethor's back was turned. "A hundred years is a steep price. Was it worth it?"

Stopping, Leethor turned and looked at her. "What do you think? If you had a chance to save Rick's life, would you do it, even if it cost you a hundred years?"

Telsa didn't hesitate answering. "I'd give my life to save his if the need arose. He's my friend."

Leethor nodded. "As he is mine. In the case of Jeehana, she was our high priestess. A member of my team died saving her. Twenty-five years of service each was a small price for the rest of us to pay." The elf turned around and began walking again. Telsa noticed him wipe something away from his eye.

Before long, a rusted piece of metal partially wedged under a rock caught Telsa's attention. Looking closer, she made out the battered form of a helmet. Something white inside the helmet made her look hastily away. Leethor must have seen her looking because he stopped and pointed up the trail at other pieces of armor and weapons strewn among the rocks. The pieces of metal were intermixed with white bones. A few of the bones still had pieces of meat attached.

"The guardian is very protective of the dwarves' treasure," said Leethor. "It's a rare year when at least one group of treasure seekers does not come to New Drepdenor with thoughts of easy wealth on their minds."

Telsa looked up the trail, picking out the ever-increasing amount of remains from other *visitors*. As a wizard scout, she was used to seeing and even causing death, but the sheer amount of carnage within the canyon was hard to take in without feeling some emotion. "Thousands must have died here."

Nodding, Leethor continued to look up the trail. "Tens of thousands. Probably more. The guardian has defended New Drepdenor for a hundred thousand years. The greed of humans keeps sending them here year after year no matter how many the guardian kills."

A small helmet lying atop an equally small breastplate drew Telsa's attention. She pointed. "Looks like not just humans have a taste for treasure."

Rembis and Jathar came up to join her and Leethor.

"You're right about that," said Rembis. He kicked the helmet. It was empty. Looks like a Halfling met his or her end here."

Master Jathar nodded toward a larger set of battered armor farther up the trail. "Mountain elf. I recognize the engravings. I suppose no race is immune when it comes to greed, not even elves." He looked at Telsa. "You know, Wizard Scout, I have never been fond of humans. Maybe I never will be. Still, the elf friend was right when he told us we all needed to work together. Every race has their faults, even elves."

The elf's admission surprised Telsa. She hadn't been around elves long, but she knew they were a proud race. She looked at the elf mage in a new light.

"Rick's right about a lot of things," Telsa said. "He's right about more than he realizes." She glanced at the fading light above the rim of the canyon wall. "I reckon we'd best get moving. Rick's depending on us to get another yellow gem."

"What yellow gem would that be?" boomed a male voice that echoed throughout the canyon. The echo made it difficult to tell where the sound originated. "From your talk, I would think you were thieves coming to steal our treasure if it was not for the presence of one in your group we know."

A large meter-wide dragon head covered in red scales rose above the side of the canyon wall and peered down. Telsa reached for the handle of her assault rifle before catching herself, then pulled her hand away.

"Wise decision," said a second male voice as another dragon head rose above the canyon wall. This dragon head was covered in yellow scales and equally as large as the first.

The tone of the yellow dragon's voice reminded Telsa of one of her professors at the university.

"We recognize your scent, Wizard Scout," said the yellow dragon. "You have traces of dragon within you."

"He must sense the essence of dragon mixed in with your DNA," said Raj in their shared space. *"Every wizard scout has it, although only a few are aware of it. I calculate even Crosioian scouts have dragon DNA mixed in with theirs."*

Telsa stared into the golden eyes of the yellow dragon. "My friends and I went on a raid to destroy a Dragar temple long ago. The Dragars were sacrificing unborn dragons to create DNA gas. Some of that gas was used in the process to create wizard scouts. It was used in the process to create my DNA baseline. You sense that dragon DNA inside me. I swear if I'd known what was being put inside me to make me a wizard scout, I would never have allowed it to be done."

A third dragon head rose above the canyon's rim between the red and yellow dragon heads. This dragon head was covered in blue scales. The third dragon spoke in a feminine voice.

"You need not explain yourself, Wizard Scout," said the blue dragon head. "My brothers and I remember how Dragon Friend Richard saved our dragon species from the Dragars. We recognize your scent. We know you were also there helping."

Telsa was shocked. "That was a hundred thousand years ago. How old are you?"

The blue dragon laughed. It was more growl than anything, but Telsa recognized it as a laugh nonetheless.

"My brothers and I were only hatched six thousand years ago. Unlike humans, we have species memory. Our ancestor, the first guardian, was brought here by Dragon Friend Richard and tasked to guard the gate. We have done so ever since."

Leethor stepped forward. "Honorable Tharantos, my companions and I have come here on behalf of Elf Friend Richard. He has tasked us to find a yellow—"

"A yellow gem," finished the blue dragon. "My brothers and I assumed as much, else you would have been charred corpses before you got halfway up the mountain. But where are your manners, Commander Leethor. Have you been out of our service so long that you've forgotten how to make proper introductions?"

With those words, all three dragon heads rose higher in the air on long necks. Their necks were followed by a single golden body of a massive dragon. Its wings stretched over thirty meters from tip to tip. A long golden tail slammed the ground, causing head-sized boulders to tumble down the canyon wall. Telsa dodged to the side to avoid being hit by one of the bouncing stones.

"My pardon," said Leethor. "Honorable Tharantos, may I present my companions, Master Rembis, Master Jathar, and Wizard Scout Telsa." He looked at Telsa. "May I present the mighty guardian of the gate, Tharantos." He pointed at the red dragon head. "This is Tharantos-Chancartos." Pointing at the yellow dragon head, he said, "This is Tharantos-Lindeshatr." With a final wave of his hand at the blue dragon head, Leethor said, "And this most beautiful of dragons is Tharantos-Ratira."

"It's a three-headed dragon," Telsa said in her shared space. *"They're just like the triplets."*

"Not hardly," replied Raj. *"These dragon heads are composed of primary colors. They form a lock for a dimensional gate. The triplets are composed of secondary colors. They create gates and time-bubbles. I calculate that's a big difference."*

Telsa bowed to the dragon, concentrating on the female dragon head in the center. Somehow she sensed the blue dragon head was the leader of the three. "I am honored, mighty Tharantos. As Leethor mentioned, we are here on a mission for Rick, err, I mean Dragon Friend Richard. We are seeking a yellow gem to—"

"To close the gate in Silverton," said Tharantos-Ratira. "Yes, my brothers and I know. The Oracle sent word you would probably be coming. Alas, even in the vast treasures of the dwarves located in the mountain beneath our feet, no such yellow gem exists."

Disappointment flooded through Telsa. "But—"

"No amount of *buts* can change what is," said the yellow dragon head, Lindeshatr, in his professor sounding voice. "The yellow gem of Power that you seek was destroyed while in the keeping of the Ecarian giants over fourteen thousand years ago. That was the only gem of its kind in the magic dimension." The yellow dragon head lowered until he was only an arm's reach from Telsa. He sniffed. "Hmm. It was one of your kind that destroyed the yellow gem. Did you know that?"

Telsa stared into the golden eyes not a meter away. She was drawn in. A vision appeared in her mind of a wizard scout in a black battle suit destroying a yellow gem. She saw the wizard scout kill many giants in the process."

"A wizard scout," Telsa said. "That's not possible. Rick would never do that. Never!"

"Did my brother say it was the dragon friend?" said Ratira. "He only said it was one of your kind, a wizard scout. There have been many time-commandos over the years." She smiled. "Even you were a time-commando at one point, were you not?"

Telsa nodded. "During the temple raid. But I didn't—"

"No, you did not destroy the yellow gem," agreed Ratira. "At this point, it does not matter who did or did not destroy it. All that matters is that the yellow gem is no longer. The Ecarian giants failed to protect the gem. Now it is no more."

"Then our quest is hopeless," said Rembis speaking for the first time.

"Ah, Master Rembis," said Ratira. "My ancestors remember you from the time of Queen Emerald. You have been gone from New Drepdenor far too long." She smiled a dragon smile. "As to the hopelessness of your quest, perhaps it is not as hopeless as it seems."

Rembis glanced at Telsa and the others before looking back at the blue dragon head. "You said the yellow gem was the only one."

All three dragon heads laughed. The red dragon head, Chancartos, spoke in a gruff almost angry voice. "My species memory tells me that you never did listen, Master Rembis, especially when you were young. We see that has not changed much as you have aged. My brother said there were no more in the magic dimension. There are a nearly infinite number of dimensions."

Rembis's face turned red in the fading light of the sun. He glanced at the ground. When he looked back up, his face was no longer red. "Unfortunately we do not have time to search an infinite number of dimensions. Nor do we have time to pull information from you. I remember your ancestor, Chancartos. He was just as condescending as you."

The red dragon head rose high above the canyon wall. "How dare—"

"That is quite enough, Chancartos," said Ratira. "Master Rembis is right. You are condescending at times." She lowered her head toward the gnome until she was close enough that her breath stirred his long white beard. "Another of the gems you need may exist if you are brave enough to seek it." She glanced at Telsa, Jathar, and Leethor before returning her gaze to Rembis. "What would you give us for this information?"

Leethor laughed. It was not a friendly laugh. "And there it is. I should have known." He turned to Telsa and winked. "What did I tell you? Dragons never give anything away for free." Facing back toward the blue dragon head, he asked, "What is your price, Ratira? We do not have time for word games."

The blue dragon head rose. The red and yellow dragon heads

drew close to their sister as if the three heads were conferring in a manner unheard by any others. Finally, Ratira lowered her head until it was level with Leethor's.

"You were ever an impertinent elf during the twenty-five years you served us," said Ratira. "Still, you are right. There is no time to bandy words. You ask what is our price for providing information that could possibly save the three galaxies? Our price is more than you could ever pay."

"Then why are—" began Leethor.

Ratira snorted a laugh. "Fortunately for you, the price was paid long ago by the dragon friend when he freed our young ones from the grasp of the Dragars. We give the information to you now as partial payment for his past act of kindness. We cannot say for sure if another yellow gem the size you need exists, but we believe there is a chance one may be found in another dimension if your companions and you are brave enough to go there to find it."

Telsa could stand the word play no longer. She had a feeling she'd been around her friend Rick far too long. "Enough already. Where the hell do we need to go to find another yellow gem?"

All three dragon heads laughed.

Ratira turned her head to look at Telsa. "Where the *hell* indeed, Wizard Scout? You have given the answer yourself."

"What are you talking about?" Telsa said growing increasingly frustrated. "Where do we need to go to find another yellow gem?"

Ratira squinted her eyes.

Telsa was drawn into their golden depths. A vision of a lava spewing landscape filled with nameless horrors filled her mind. Suddenly she knew where they needed to go. Her friends must have sensed that the blue dragon head was passing her the knowledge they sought.

"What is it?" asked Master Jathar. "What has the dragon shown you? Where do we need to go?"

Telsa shuddered as she replied, "Hell. We need to go to hell."

CHAPTER 13

When the *Defiant* landed, Richard led the way up the ramp feigning indifference to the Crosioian scout following on his heels. They were met at the top of the ramp by a red-faced Sergeant Ron and the *Defiant's* entire security team armed to the teeth. Weapons of every kind were pointed at the Crosioian scout. From the fierce expressions on the dwarves' faces, Jeena could tell they needed only a single word from their ship's captain to blow the scout to kingdom come.

Jeena didn't blame them. The scout was dangerous. She hung back a few paces, remaining prepared to send a blast of pure magic into the bat's body at the first sign of impending harm to her bondmate or any of the ship's crew. She had no doubt the Crosioian scout was as aware of both her pending magic and the physical weapons pointed at her orange-suited form. Still, the bat acted as indifferent to the situation as did her bondmate.

Well, Rick can act as nonchalant as he wants, but he cannot fool me, Jeena thought. *I sense his emotions. He is strung tighter than a vine of ivy on a falling tree. If he is not careful, he is going to get himself and the rest of us killed. It was foolish of him to agree to be the scout's prisoner. She cannot be trusted.*

The ring on Jeena's left hand tingled. *"I calculate you are right,"* said Danny in her mind. *"Yet you also volunteered to be the scout's prisoner. If Rick is a fool for doing so, what does that make you?"*

"I had to do what I did," Jeena argued. *"I will not let my bondmate face death without me by his side. Anyway, I have faith in him. He knows what he is doing."*

Danny laughed. *"I have faith in him too. Only I calculate he*

127

doesn't actually know *what he's doing most of the time. I believe he* feels *more than knows that he needs to appear before the Crosioians' tribal council. Unfortunately, I have run ten thousand algorithms trying to find a path to success. All logical paths have resulted in horrible deaths for both Rick and you."*

"Thanks for the words of encouragement," Jeena said.

"You are welcome, High Priestess," replied Danny. *"By the way, I've been emotionally contaminated by Rick during our years of association. Unlike a lot of battle computers, I recognize sarcasm when I hear it. In case you are wondering, my reply to you was also sarcasm. As you can tell, I am a battle computer of many talents."*

Lucky me, Jeena thought trying to keep the thought private.

"I heard that," laughed Danny. *"You're not a wizard scout. We do not have separate shared and private spaces. If you think it, I hear it, and vice versa."*

Before Jeena could reply, Sergeant Ron pulled a phase pistol out of the holster on his hip and pointed it at the bat-creature. "That *thing* is not coming on my ship," said Sergeant Ron. "I should order Felspar and his team to open fire right now and be done with it."

Richard stepped between the *Defiant's* captain and the Crosioian scout. "The *Defiant* isn't your ship. It's *our* ship. And she is coming on board. I gave my word that we'd give her safe passage to her home world. I'm her prisoner."

Moving forward to stand at her bondmate's side, Jeena said, "As am I."

"No," said Richard. "I'm her prisoner. You're not a wizard scout. You need to stay on the *Defiant*."

Jeena whirled to face Richard as she slammed the butt of her staff onto the metal plating of the ramp. "As I said before, wherever you go, I go. I am the High Priestess of the Lady of the Tree. You may be my bondmate, but that does not mean you can order me around like some servant at your beck and call. I gave the scout my word the same as you. That's the end of it. We will speak of it no more."

His eyes growing wide, Richard opened his mouth to speak.

Sergeant Ron beat him to the punch. "Prisoners! Are you both crazy?" Taking a step to the side, he tried to bring his pistol to bear on the scout.

Richard shifted position to block his shot. "Yes, prisoners," he said. He looked around at the security team. "Lower your weapons. I gave the scout my word she wouldn't be harmed."

The dwarves' weapons remained trained on the bat.

Sergeant Ron walked over to the ship's bulkhead and touched an icon on the display panel for the ship-wide intercom. "Everyone to the cargo bay now. Bring your weapons, and prepare to repel boarders."

The *Defiant's* crew was nothing if not well trained. Pounding feet sounded on the metal decks overhead. Within thirty seconds, the entire ship's crew was assembled in the cargo bay sporting every kind of weapon, magic or otherwise. Calatron and his gnome magic users assembled near the stairs with wands at the ready. Jeena sensed the gnomes feeding magic into their leader to increase the potency of any spells Calatron chose to cast. Comstar, her fellow elf, stood next to Sergeant Ron. Although the old mage didn't carry a weapon or even a staff, a ball of magic energy shone brightly in his hand. Jeena sensed that only a word was needed to release whatever spell Comstar had at the ready.

Richard continued to stand between the Crosioian scout and the *Defiant's* crew, doing his best to shield the bat. Jeena moved alongside her bondmate and used her body to protect the scout as well. *I would just as soon kill her,* she thought, *but I will support my bondmate. If he is determined to give his life to protect the scout, I am honor bound to do the same.*

The ring on Jeena's left hand tingled. Danny's voice came over the miniaturized speaker built into the ring. "This is quite enough! Your actions are not logical. Why do carbon-based life forms have to be so stubborn? What's next? Are you going to start killing each other? Are you that determined to do the demons' work for them?"

"Danny's right," said Margery over the ship's intercom. "Danny, Nickelo, and I might be battle computers, but that doesn't mean we are going to remain idle while our friends let their pride and plain bullheaded-stubbornness endanger the lives of everyone on board, not to mention jeopardize the existence of life as we know it in the three galaxies."

The barrels of automated weapons Sergeant Hendricks had installed in the walls of the cargo bay to repel boarders swiveled to target all parts of the cargo bay. Jeena noticed beams of condensed lights from the weapons' sights appear on everyone's chest, including hers and Richard's. The only exception was the Crosioian scout. No beam appeared on her body.

"Stand down, all of you," said Danny. "This stops now, or I swear Margery and I will stun every one of you."

"Uh, Sergeant Ron," said Nickelo over the external speakers of Richard's battle helmet. "If I may be so bold, perhaps you and Rick should discuss this in private before the situation gets totally out of hand."

"This is mutiny, Margery," said Sergeant Ron growing even redder in the face.

"Mutiny is such a harsh word," said Margery over the intercom. "Think of it more as a plea for sanity."

Everyone remained frozen for the count of ten heartbeats.

Finally, Sergeant Ron shoved his pistol into his holster and pointed a finger at Richard. "You! In my cabin. We're going to settle this right now." Spinning on his heels, the *Defiant's* captain turned toward the stairs leading to the upper levels of the ship and stomped out of sight.

Unsure what to do, Jeena remained frozen along with the rest of the crew. Movement from her bondmate drew her attention.

Removing his battle helmet, Richard handed it to her. "Hold onto this for me," he said. "I think Sergeant Ron and I need to settle this between the two of us, alone."

"Now wait one darn minute," said Nickelo over the helmet's speakers. "I think—"

Richard was already up the stairs and out of sight before his battle computer could finish speaking.

"Humph. Humans," mumbled Nickelo.

Within seconds, muffled shouts could be heard overhead. Given that Sergeant Ron's cabin was three levels above the cargo bay, Jeena got the distinct impression the *Defiant's* captain and her bondmate weren't wasting any time on polite niceties. The muffled yells lasted for a full ten minutes. Except for the occasional shuffling of feet of one crewmember or another, no one in the cargo bay moved. Everyone, including Jeena, kept their weapons or spells trained on the Crosioian scout.

For her part, the scout stood perfectly still while appearing to remain oblivious to the score of weapons pointed at her or to the shouts from overhead. After ten minutes, the scout slowly spread her wings, extending them two paces to either side of her body.

So, she is not made of ice after all, Jeena thought. *I knew as much. I can sense her emotions. She is intensely aware of what is going on around her. She must know her death is certain if she makes the wrong move. Even a scout could not dodge every weapon and spell pointed at her. I wonder what she is thinking.*

CHAPTER 14

After several minutes listening to the shouts overhead, the Crosioian scout spread her wings to show the crew that she was not intimidated at being surrounded by armed Empire guards. She was anything but. She had a plan.

I gave my word, but if any of them try to attack, I will kill them all. Then I will kill their captain before I disable the wizard scout and make him my prisoner. This starship will be mine. I swear it by the heads on my tribe's Wall of Honor.

Swiveling her ears as she sent out a sonic wave, the scout pinpointed the exact position of everyone in the cargo bay.

It will be a tough fight, but I can win if I am careful. The two adult elves are magic users. They are the greatest threat, especially the female. I have never fought magic users before, but I worked with enough of them during the Estos mission to know their weaknesses. Once I kill the two elves, I will have to take out the dwarves.

She turned her ears to examine the six short humanoids with long hair and beards that flanked her sides with weapons at the ready. Three of the guards held phase rifles while the other three grasped wicked-looking battle axes in both hands. She noticed blue gems in the pommels of the axes and sensed Power coming from the gems.

The frequency of the gems are the same as what I sense coming from the female elf's staff. The gems are obviously magic. In these close quarters, the magic axes will probably be more dangerous than the rifles. Should the crew break the wizard scout's word and attack, I will need to take the guards with magic weapons out after I dispatch the two elf magic users.

The shouts from above ceased. The scout swiveled her ears upward. The sound of double footsteps on the metal decks of the ship foretold the arrival of the wizard scout and the ship's captain. In less than a minute, the thin captain with the scraggily hair and beard walked down the stairway and into the cargo bay before stopping at the head of the ramp. The human scratched his beard. He turned and looked at the wizard scout who had followed him and now stood by his side.

"Never in my born days did I think I'd allow one of these bats on my ship. I hope you know what you're doing, Rick. You're taking a mighty big risk."

The wizard scout motioned at the guards to lower their weapons. This time they did so, but from the rapid beat of their hearts and heavy breathing, the scout could tell they did so reluctantly.

"Weapons aren't necessary," said the wizard scout. The scout sensed him point at her. "She gave me her word, the same as I gave her mine."

"And you trust her?" asked the male elf magic user.

"Yes, and you can too. She won't cause us any trouble." The wizard scout turned to look at her. "Will you?"

The scout retracted her wings. "No. Why should I? You are my prisoner."

The scout's eyesight wasn't good in the bright light, but she didn't need it to sense the ship captain's face grow red. She could tell by the change in his thermals.

"I don't like this one bit," said the scraggily-haired man. "I'm the captain of this bucket of bolts, and if it were up to me, I'd jettison her out the cargo door as soon as we're in deep space."

The scout spread her wings again. "And if it were up to me," came her voice from the translator attached to her belt, "I would steal your ship and eat all of you for breakfast. The only reason I do not do so is because I gave my word that I would not harm anyone on the ship."

"You would, would you?" growled one of the guards raising his battle axe. "I'll show—"

"Stand down, Stovis," ordered the wizard scout. "If things work out the way I hope, we're all going to be allies. There's been too much killing already on both sides."

The scout hissed at the naivety of the wizard scout. *If what the other prisoners on the ship that brought me to Diajor told me is true, the humans killed untold millions of our soldiers and sailors. We will never be their allies. The only peace between us will be when every human is dead.*

The short guard lowered his axe, but the scout sensed the tenseness in his grip on the weapon. *The little one wants to kill me,* she thought. *That is the sign of a good fighter. Perhaps the tribal leaders will allow the small ones to live if they pledge allegiance to our empire.*

The wizard scout stepped in front of her. "Sergeant Ron's agreed to take us to your tribal council. In the meantime, I'll show you to your room. Follow me." With that the wizard scout walked ahead, exposing his back to the scout.

Part of her wanted to shove her wing point into the human's spinal cortex at the back of his head, but she'd given her word. She folded her wings and followed the human up the stairs. *I will have plenty of time to kill him after I present him to the tribal leaders.*

At the top of the stairs, the wizard scout turned to the left, ignoring another flight of stairs that continued up. The scout started to follow the human to the left until her passive scan picked up a large energy source to her rear. *The engine room,* she thought. *It is different from the hyper-drives I have been around. Why?*

Curious, the scout turned to face the direction of the energy source, noticing a glowing ball behind a set of large windows. Pointing her ears at the room, she sent out a sonic wave. She detected something moving inside the energy source.

"Hello," came a voice in her mind.

No, not a voice, the scout thought. *It is more an emotion than anything else.*

The life form inside the engine room shimmered and blinked out before reappearing near the stairway. The creature was a lizard-looking reptile the length of one of the scout's wings. Sensing Power in the creature, the scout spun on her heels and cocked one wing with the point out in preparation for defending herself.

A dragon, thought the scout. *My mother told me about them.*

They can be dangerous.

"Whoa there," said the wizard scout as he moved between her and the reptile. "This is Bright Wing. She's a member of our crew, so your promise not to harm anyone on the ship applies to her also. Uh, Bright Wing, this is, uh…" The human turned to look at the scout. "Uh, I don't know your name. Mine's Rick. You bats do have names, don't you?"

The scout looked from the human to the dragon and back. Seeing no immediate threat, she retracted her wing. "My name is Blood-On-The-Wing-Point-From-A-Dying-Enemy."

"Hmm," said the wizard scout. "That's a mouthful. I doubt introducing you that way would endear you to any of the crew. What say we just call you Red Wing for short? We humans have a habit of shortening names. My real name is Richard Shepard, but most people call me Rick for short."

The hiss that came out of the wizard scout's translator when he said his real name made the scout stare. "Richard Shepard?" she said before she caught herself.

"Uh, yeah," said the wizard scout. "That's what was on my birth certificate, or so they tell me. Why?"

The dragon opened its mouth and spoke in what the scout knew was intergalactic standard. "Rick is not naturally empathic, so he may have missed what I felt. You were surprised when he said his real name. I am curious why?"

If Red Wing's mother hadn't told tales of her encounters with dragons during her time-commando missions, the idea that she would be having a conversation with a dragon would have surprised her. As it was, Red Wing took it in stride. For whatever reason, she was drawn to the dragon as if they were somehow connected. She found herself trusting the creature.

Before she realized what she was doing, Red Wing replied honestly, "When the wizard scout called Richard Shepard pronounced his real name, his translator hissed words that sounded like the words we Crosioians use for *tribal brother.* Pathetic humans are our sworn enemies. A human could never be our brother. You, on the other hand, interest me, dragon. When I take my prisoners off this ship, you should come with me. You would be considered an honored guest in the Long Wing tribe. We would not force you to stay in an engine room. I sense your Power. I believe you would be destined for great things if you became our ally."

"The humans are my friends, and Rick is my brother," said Bright Wing. "I am part of the crew, and no one forces me to maintain the *Defiant's* engine. I do so voluntarily."

The scout shrugged her wings. "The offer stands should you change your mind."

The wizard scout called Richard Shepard gave a facial gesture Red Wing recognized as what the humans called a smile.

"Uh," said Richard, "I doubt Sergeant Ron would appreciate you trying to recruit members of his crew. Maybe we should keep that between the three of us."

"Sergeant Ron? Why sergeant?" Red Wing asked, curiosity overcoming her natural animosity toward humans.

"Well, that's a story in itself," said Richard. "Let's just say he's the captain of the *Defiant,* but he prefers to be called Sergeant. He says he's a sergeant because he works for a living. He doesn't much care for officers, which I guess is one of the reasons being called a captain riles him up so much."

Red Wing snorted a laugh. She didn't much care for officers either. She thought of the years she'd served in the military as an enlisted soldier before becoming a scout. "Then I will be sure to address him as Sergeant before I kill him, if the need arises, Wizard Scout."

"Uh, Rick. Call me Rick, or Richard, if you prefer."

The scout shrugged her wings again. *It matters not what I call him,* she thought. *He will die soon enough once I present him to the tribal leaders.*

"Very well, Rick," said the scout. "I will answer to the name Red Wing while I am on this ship." She pointed her ears at the dragon. "My offer stands, Bright Wing, should you change your mind."

The scout sensed an emotion of laughter from the dragon before the reptilian creature blinked out and reappeared in the engine room.

"Shall we?" said the wizard scout who claimed his real name was *Tribal Brother.* The human jerked a thumb over his shoulder. "Your room's this way."

When the human turned and began walking in their original

direction, Red Wing followed. They didn't go far. It was, after all, a small ship that was obviously intended for long-range recon missions. Stopping in front of a curtained doorway, the man called Richard Shepard pulled the curtain open and stepped into a small room. A set of bunk beds similar to those that had been in her prison cell were on one wall. Opposite the beds were two metal lockers along with a desk and chair.

The human pointed at the beds. "I'll have our mechanic Charlie remove the bunk beds and attach a metal bar to the ceiling. My battle computer tells me Crosioians hang by their feet when they sleep. If he told me wrong, let me know, and I'll have Charlie leave the bunks as is."

Red Wing noted the height of the ceiling. "A metal bar will do. I was in the infantry before I became a scout. I am used to sleeping in cramped quarters on our troopships with my head close to the deck."

"Uh, fine then," said Richard. "You'll need some gear. That orange prison jumpsuit you're wearing doesn't seem appropriate for a Crosioian scout."

Shrugging her wings to show indifference, Red Wing said nothing. She hated the shameful clothing the humans had given her, but she wasn't about to let the wizard scout know. She watched the man remove the pack off his back and set it on the desk. Reaching inside, he pulled out a Crosioian fighting-suit. The scout armor was in deactivated mode. The human held the suit out in her direction.

What is the fool doing? she wondered. *Is this some kind of trick?*

Overcoming her suspicion, Red Wing took the fighting-suit from the wizard scout's hands and turned it over in her paws. As far as she could tell, it was in perfect condition. Forming an active scan, she probed the armor.

The energy pod is fully charged, she thought, growing more perplexed by the human's actions. "What is this for?" she asked.

Instead of answering, the human reached into his pack again and pulled out a fighting-helmet. As soon as he did, Red Wing shivered with excitement. She recognized the frequency of the fighting-computer inside the helmet. It had belonged to her mother.

Offering the helmet to her, the wizard scout said, "This was your mother's. It was recovered after our fight on Veturna. It's been kept in a warehouse on Storage along with the rest of her equipment ever since. Based upon her equipment, I know she was a time-commando, the same as me. From what my niece and nephew tell me, there's quite a bit of Crosioian gear in some of the warehouses on Storage." After Red Wing took the helmet out of his hands, the human said, "Or at least there used to be. A lot of the warehouses were destroyed during an attack on Storage that happened at the same time as the battle on Estos. I'm not sure how much of your species' stuff is left."

"My species' equipment?" Red Wing asked. The actions of the human were not logical. *He is my prisoner,* she thought. *Why is he giving me armor? Will he be foolish enough to give me some of my mother's weapons? Surely even a human would not be that stupid.*

Focusing her ears on the human's face to detect any sign of deceit, Red Wing said, "What do you know of time-commandos? How do you know my mother was one?"

The human flashed a smile. "I'm a time-commando. It doesn't take much to recognize another from their equipment."

Reaching into his pack, the human pulled out a belt with a half-meter long metal rod attached. Instinctively, Red Wing reached out with her right paw before catching herself. She pulled her paw back. *I am a scout,* she thought. *It does no good to let the human sense my eagerness.*

Richard laughed. "I'm not an idiot, if that's what you're thinking. I know what I'm doing." He offered the belt to her. "Take it. The phase spear belonged to your mother. It's not quite the same as when she had it, but it's still operable."

Taking the belt from the human, Red Wing was half tempted to activate the phase spear and kill the wizard scout then and there. The memory of her word of honor to take him to the tribal leaders kept her natural inclination under control.

"What do you mean it is not the same?" Red Wing asked more to give her time to ferret out the human's intentions than any desire to understand what he meant.

The wizard scout removed his phase rod from his belt.

Red Wing forced herself not to react. *He gave his word of honor to be my prisoner,* she thought. *He is a scout the same as me, even though he is human. If he wanted to kill me, he could have done so in my cell when I was helpless.*

"My niece and nephew removed a demon essence from your mother's phase spear and placed it in my phase rod," said the human. "That essence was destroyed a couple of weeks ago. Now both my rod and the spear you hold in your hands are just normal phase weapons."

The scout set the armor, helmet, and weapon's belt on the desk. "Why are you giving me these? Do you think to bribe me into not killing you? I am a Crosioian scout. Once I present you to the tribal leaders as my prisoner, I will kill you in honorable combat. I will also kill your female. The gift of a few trinkets will not stay my hand."

The human shook his head. "I'm sure you're going to try to do what you say. Whether you succeed or not is a different matter. In any regard, this equipment belonged to your mother. As far as I'm concerned, it's yours now. If we're going to be allies, I need you to be equipped with the best gear possible."

Red Wing snorted, spraying liquid from her nose in laughter. "Are you insane? We will never be allies. You killed my mother. I am going to kill you."

"Your mother and I were soldiers. She fought honorably. I respected her for that. I still do. As far as killing a parent goes, I told you that your kind killed my father." The human called Richard glanced down at the floor before looking back up. "Don't think for one minute that I enjoy this interaction between us any more than you. A part of me wants to activate my phase rod and kill you and every single one of your kind. As far as I'm concerned, you're all vicious murderers. The only reason I don't do it is because I know both of our species has been manipulated by the demons. They and their Dragar allies are our real enemies." He pointed at the equipment on the desk. "I know you think I'm a fool for giving you those." The human bared his teeth in a smile. "Well, hold onto your wings, because I'm about to convince you that I'm an even bigger fool."

Red Wing doubted the human could make himself appear more foolish than she already thought he was but said nothing.

"I agreed to take you to your tribal leaders," said Richard. "Assuming your capital world of Fealty is in the part of the galaxy we think it is, Sergeant Ron figures it will take at least a week to get there. I'm going to use that time to train you how to use your diviner skill to defend the link to your Power reserve and how to attack that of others. I'm also going to teach you fighting skills that I've picked up over the last six hundred years as a time-commando." Reaching into his pack, the human pulled out a pouch. "And I'm going to give you this."

This time Red Wing reacted before she could control her actions. She grabbed the pouch and held it in front of her face, scanning it with sonic waves. "This is my mother's dimensional pouch. You are a bigger fool than I thought. I have the same frequency as my mother. With this pouch, I can summon a bomb and destroy this ship, if I so desire."

The human gave a tightlipped smile. Picking up his own pack, the wizard scout walked toward the curtained doorway and pulled it back. He turned around once he'd stepped outside. "We're both scouts. We're a dying breed. I sense dragon essence inside you the same as it is inside me, the same as it is in all scouts regardless of species. When our DNA baselines were created, the essence of dragon DNA was inserted into each of us. One day maybe we'll tell each other how it was done for our species during training. In the meantime, I'll say this. I've fought three Crosioian scouts. They all tried to kill me, but they all tried to do so under honorable conditions. I trust you to keep your word. As for this equipment and the pouch, I believe we will be allies. I believe we will be allies sooner than later. So you may as well get it into your furry little head that I'm going to train you to be the best scout you can be in whatever time we have together. When the opportunity comes to fight our real enemies, I want to know that whoever is standing at my shoulder is the very best there is. That means regardless of whether they are human or bat. So get used to it. When we get to Fealty, I'll speak to your tribal leaders. Then you'll understand."

Red Wing kept her ears trained on the human for a full twenty seconds while he stood there without saying another word. She detected no sign of dishonesty in his facial features with her sonic scan. Finally, she spoke. "I will not take you to Fealty."

The wizard scout stepped back and started to activate his phase rod before catching himself. "You gave your word that you'd take me to your tribal leaders. If you're going back on your promise, then the deal's off."

The facial fur on Red Wing stiffened, but she kept her irritation under control. "I am a Crosioian scout. My word is my bond. I swore to take you before our tribal council, but they will not be on Fealty. They will be assembling for an, uh, event on the planet Astaris. I will kill you there."

"Astaris?" Richard said. "I've never heard of it."

Red Wing hissed laughter. "Of course you have not, human. It is on the far edge of the galaxy. It is farther than any Empire ship can travel without an overhaul of their hyper-drive. Even if this starship could get that far, you would never slip past the fleets of warships and automated space mines. Your captain will need to drop us off on one of our planets near the Empire's border. Once I send a coded message, a Crosioian ship can pick the elf, you, and me up and transport us the rest of the way to Astaris." Red Wing laughed again. "So you see, foolish human, your plan to have me guide this ship through our territory will not work. Do you think me foolish enough to let you map out our troop locations so this ship's crew can take the information back to your high command?" Red Wing bared her fangs and hissed another laugh. "I will keep my promise to take you to my tribal leaders, but it will be on my terms. This pathetic recon ship cannot travel to Astaris without being destroyed. You will go there on a Crosioian warship, in chains as befits a shameful prisoner, or you will not make the journey at all. There is no other way."

Red Wing waited for the wizard scout to begin shouting or go back on his word and try to kill her. She placed her paw on her phase spear in preparation for killing him first before she took care of the rest of the crew. The human surprised her by nodding his head and speaking in a normal voice.

"Is that so? I guess we'll see. In the meantime, have your mother's fighting-computer send the location of Astaris to my battle computer so Sergeant Ron can plot a course."

"Were you not listening, human?" Red Wing said, astonished by the obvious density of the human. "It is too far for your ship to fly without an overhaul. We must transfer to a Crosioian ship."

The human smiled. "Just send the location. Let Sergeant Ron and I figure out how we're getting there. In the meantime, get your gear on and meet me in the cargo bay. Your training starts in thirty minutes, and I don't take excuses for being late."

With that, the human turned and left. Red Wing pulled the curtain shut behind him. She had a lot to think about.

A voice spoke in her head. *"What do we do now?"* said her mother's fighting-computer.

Red Wing swiveled her ears toward the ceiling before turning them to the folded up fighting-suit in her paws. *"Do?"* she said. *"You will send the location of Astaris to the wizard scout's battle computer as requested. It will do them no good. They cannot get there."*

"Compliance. What will you do?"

Red Wing didn't answer immediately. Instead, she began putting on her fighting-suit. *"What will I do? I doubt the foolish human can teach me anything, but I will go through the motions to learn his weaknesses. Once we are on Astaris, I will present him to the tribal leaders. Then I will remove his head and place in on my tribe's Wall of Honor."*

Red Wing smiled. Her mother would be avenged if it was the last thing she ever did.

CHAPTER 15

Tia sat in the largest of the conference rooms on the dreadnaught *Destiny*. Admiral of the Combined Fleets Bistos and War-King Bistoria along with a dozen of the warship's officers were also there. Her sister and father leaned forward as the hologram of Wizard Scout Trinity Delgado finished her report. A second hologram farther down the table displayed miniature figures of Rick, Jeehana, and members of the *Defiant's* crew. A third hologram held an image of Matthew Deloris and his uncle, Felix Deloris, along with an older man she didn't recognize.

Tia knew Matt was somewhere on Risors. Seeing him but knowing he was so far away brought an emptiness inside her that was hard to ignore. Doing her best to push the feeling aside, she considered the fact that her sister and father were even allowing Matthew and the other Conglomerate personnel to listen to Trinity's report in real time. It said a lot for what had occurred during the last forty-eight hours. While hostilities between the Conglomerate and the Empire forces hadn't ceased entirely, a ceasefire of sorts had been implemented well enough to hold out hope that the two sides were on their way to reconciliation.

"Are you sure?" asked Liz once Trinity finished speaking.

"Oh, I'm sure, Sir," replied Trinity. "I saw troopships landing on Estos with additional prisoners. I also monitored several of their supply drops. The Crosioians are bringing in more of our POWs, and deliberately keeping them alive, at least for the short term. My battle computer calculates an eighty-seven percent probability the Crosioians are consolidating all two hundred million POWs on

Estos. Jerad and the other wizard scouts you sent to Estos concur. So do their battle computers."

Tia watched her father's face as she tried to gauge his reaction to the news. The information in Trinity's report wasn't unexpected, but earlier reports they'd received had been mostly conjecture. Now they were faced with cold hard facts.

War-King Bistoria drummed the fingers of his right hand on the table, then stopped and placed his hand on his lap as if suddenly realizing what he was doing. "You were there, Trinity. Admiral Bistos tells me that you're a no nonsense soldier. Give it to me straight."

Trinity glanced at Liz before looking back at the War-king and nodding. "All right, Sir. If that's what you want, then I'll tell you what I think. It has all the makings of a trap to me. I think the Crosioians are trying to use the POWs to lure us into a battle we can't hope to win. The Crosioians are relying on our concern for our captured soldiers and sailors to force us into an all or nothing battle. They're also trying to force us to fight at the time of their choosing. Even with the medical supplies, the first of our POWs will begin dying in less than six weeks. They'll all be dead within a month after that. The Crosioians want us to know that. I have reason to believe they purposely allowed me to get off Estos alive. They want us to know the situation with our troops, and they don't care if we know it's a trap. They're just gambling we're foolish enough to try a rescue anyway. They want us to go to Estos in force, and they want us to do it in the next six weeks before we can consolidate forces and rally more allies."

War-King Bistoria turned in his seat to stare out the windows that composed one wall of the *Destiny's* conference room. He stared into space for several seconds. Finally, he turned back around and looked at the image of Trinity. "What would you suggest, Wizard Scout Trinity?"

Trinity bent her head and gazed at the floor before looking back up. "It's not for me to say, Sir."

"Say it anyway," said War-King Bistoria. "That's an order."

Trinity's eyes sparkled, and she smiled. "Since you put it that way, Sir, I'd say to hell with the Crosioians and their plans. I'd gather every ship we can get our hands on and hit the bats with everything we've got." The image of Trinity looked in the direction of Liz and winked. "That's what I'd do. Others may have a different opinion."

Tia thought she detected the beginnings of a smile on her sister's face before it was replaced by a stern expression more suitable for an admiral of the combined fleets.

"Well, Admiral Bistos," said War-King Bistoria. "What's it going to be?"

Liz caught Tia's eye before looking back at her father. "Lieutenant Bistoria, my staff and I have come up with a plan of operation. As Trinity so aptly put it, we'll hit them with everything we've got. My staff is working on the details now. It will take a month to gather our forces." Liz looked at the holographic image of Matthew. "Can we or can we not count on the Conglomerate?"

Tia sensed an emotion come from her ring that was a mixture of excitement, fear, determination, and hope. She saw Matthew glance at Felix Deloris and the older man with them before turning to stare at Liz. "We'll be wherever you need us in a month, Admiral. I give you my word."

Felix and the other man nodded their heads.

"Fine," said Liz. "Lieutenant Bistoria will be contacting you with the details. She'll be your point of contact. In the meantime, we've got a lot of work to do. The lives of two hundred million of our people are depending on us."

Matthew nodded his head. A second later, his holographic image disappeared.

Tia reached across the table and turned the halo-pad off. She also switched off the halo-pad for Trinity before reaching in the direction of the pad containing the images of the members of the *Defiant.*

"Leave that one on, please," said her father.

Tia pulled her hand back.

War-King Bistoria stared at Richard and his friends. Her father gave a deep sigh before speaking. "What you're planning is a fool's errand. I don't suppose you'd consider returning to Trecorian space and putting your ship at our disposal. We're going to need everything we can get our hands on for our rescue to have any hope of success."

Tia noticed Richard glance at Sergeant Ron before looking back at her father and shaking his head. "One recon ship won't make much of a difference in a fleet-wide battle. The *Defiant* can make a real difference if we're able to convince the Crosioians to stop this war and fight our common foe, and by that I mean the demons."

Liz cleared her throat, turning Richard's gaze in her direction. "I've bent enough to mend fences with the Conglomerate. For the most part, none of them directly killed any of our troops. Most of them didn't even know what was happening when Governor Jenkins pulled them out of the battle. I can forgive and work with them. I'm not sure I or any of our soldiers or sailors can put aside their differences with the Crosioians. Too many of us have been killed by those bats. You're throwing away your life for nothing."

Tia didn't often agree with her sister. This time she did. She hated the bats. The casualty lists were still coming in, but she'd already seen far too many names of her friends on the lists. Trying to lock eyes with Richard, she spoke before she knew what she was doing. "My sis...err, the admiral's right. We need to kill every one of the Crosioians. That's the only way our galaxy can ever know true peace." She had a thought. "The bats probably feel the same way. You took out their master computer at a key point in time during the battle on Estos. Losses on their side are estimated at two billion. Our intelligence sources indicate they've got a reward on your head. At best they'll kill you on sight. At worst, you and the rest of the *Defiant's* crew will be tortured and turned into a public spectacle before they finally kill you. Is that what you want to happen to Jeehana and your friends?"

The muscles on Richard's face tightened.

Tia noticed his eyes drill into hers. She held her gaze. *He's my friend,* she thought, *but he needs a good dose of reality.* She half expected him to start arguing. She'd seen his temper take control on more than one occasion. This time he surprised her.

After a dozen heartbeats, the muscles on the wizard scout's face relaxed. "This is the way it's got to be, Tia," said Richard. He turned his attention to Liz. "Hold off on any major attacks against the Crosioians until you hear back from me."

Liz snorted. "We're not the ones attacking at the moment. We're hard pressed to defend ourselves on every front."

"Understood," said Richard. "I know you've got to defend yourselves, but at least give my plan a chance to work. Hold off the rescue mission as long as possible. Let me try to convince the bats' tribal council to end this war. Every ship and every soldier killed on either side is one less resource we'll have to fight the demons."

Liz leaned over and whispered in her father's ear.

War-King Bistoria nodded.

Liz looked back at Richard. "It will take us a month to gather our forces. It will take another week and a half to get them in position for the rescue. You've got that long to convince the Crosioians to surrender. Once our forces are in position, we're attacking whether we hear from you or not."

Richard sighed. "Understood. Just so you both know, I'm not trying to convince them to surrender. I'm planning on stopping this senseless war once and for all. That means stopping it on *both* sides. I know who our real enemies are, and it's not the Crosioians."

The hologram blinked out.

Tia looked at her father and sister. "The Crosioians *are* our enemies, and I plan on killing as many of them as I can get in my gunsights. They need to die. All of them."

Neither Admiral of the Combined Fleets Bistos nor War-King Bistoria disagreed.

CHAPTER 16

The vast cavern surrounding the arena on Astaris had been painstakingly carved out of the hard granite rock over a hundred thousand years by Crosioian stonecutters. First working by paw and later by more advanced technology, the skilled artisans had created a thing of beauty that reflected sound in ways that awed even the most hardened of Crosioian hearts. The arena floor itself was composed of granite ground so fine it felt like the softest sand as it caressed the footpads of anyone walking on the arena's surface. Soft light illuminated the cavern for those races that depended on visual input. Only Crosioians were present at the moment.

The oldest representative of the Long Wing tribe sat next to the supreme leader on a perch built into the walls of the arena. Sending out a sonic wave, Charge-In-The-Face-Of-Great-Odds swiveled her ears to catch every nuance of returned sound. She noted the twenty-five thousand perches built into the arena's rocky walls. Nearly all were empty, but she knew that in a few weeks' time, bats of every age and from every tribe would fill the perches. She had no doubt an overflow crowd would be hanging from the lofty ceiling to listen and see the spectacle that would be the test of those vying for the honor of descending into *the Hole* and making a recon of the rift.

Today, ninety-four Crosioian scouts stood wingtip to wingtip on the arena floor. At a signal from the supreme leader's master of ceremony, each of the bats sent out a sonic wave denoting their name, tribe, age, and eternal loyalty for the Crosioian Empire. The supreme leader acknowledged each applicant in turn before turning to whisper a hiss in the Long Wing rep's ear.

"They look so young, old friend. It is hard to believe that only two hundred years ago we were standing on the same arena floor, asking our supreme leader for the privilege of being a member of the recon team into the rift."

"Yes, our time was then," agreed the Long Wing rep, angling her sonic wave so only the supreme leader could hear. "Their time is now. I pray at least one of the scouts below has the mettle to do what must be done."

"As do I," hissed the supreme leader in return. She sent a sonic wave at the applicants, determined to pick up every aspect of their abilities. "Are these our best scouts? The big one with the broken wing tip is impressive, but the others are mediocre at best."

Charge-In-The-Face-Of-Great-Odds flapped her wings slightly. "The big one is from the Bent Wing tribe. She was on a scouting mission in the Andromeda galaxy. She is the Bent Wing tribe's best. I had her recalled from her mission and brought back to the outer realms on your royal yacht. She caught our fastest destroyer from there. The best of our other scouts are currently on missions to ascertain the movements of the Empire and Trecorian fleets. We will do what we can to have as many of them assembled here as possible in two weeks. That will leave plenty of time for the tournament and the mission to the rift."

The supreme leader sent another sonic wave at the supplicants. "I do not detect any scouts from the Blood Claw tribe. Astaris is their home world. Surely some of their scouts remain alive."

The Long Wing rep nodded. "Yes, a dozen of their scouts remain on active duty. I talked to the Blood Claw rep earlier tonight. She told me their tribal leaders have assembled their scouts in a secret location for a special initiation ceremony. She assured me they would be joining the other applicants in time for the tournament."

The supreme leader snorted. "The Blood Claw tribe has always been a thorn in our side. Their tribal leaders will probably hold their scouts back until the last moment so they can make some grand entrance to score political points. They are jealous that my tribe was selected to appoint the supreme leader and not theirs."

Nodding her head, Charge-In-The-Face-Of-Great-Odds did not

naysay her friend. *The Blood Claw tribe is too ambitious for their own good,* she thought. *I must keep my ears on them. Any ceremony their tribal leaders have that requires the attendance of all their scouts during wartime conditions is bound to be contrived. I wonder what they've got hidden up their fur this time?*

The supreme leader swiveled her ears to point at the Long Wing rep. "Tell me, old friend, what are the humans up to? Are they taking the bait?"

"It would seem so," said Charge-In-The-Face-Of-Great-Odds casting aside thoughts of the Blood Claws. "The Empire's forces have ceased all offensive maneuvers and been stripping their defenses. Our scouts tell us that the Empire and the Conglomerate forces have ceased hostilities. The Conglomerate's fleets have begun to assemble with those of the Empire and Trecorians."

The supreme leader hissed a sound so low it was barely audible to the Long Wing rep.

Charge-In-The-Face-Of-Great-Odds smiled at the sound from her friend. *She is singing,* she thought. *I doubt she even knows she is doing it. She has ever done so since we were young scouts, whenever she is troubled and deep in thought.*

The low hissing stopped. "It is as I feared," said the supreme leader. "The Conglomerate has rejoined the Empire. Still, it is not unexpected. We will deal with the Conglomerate forces when we destroy those of the Empire and the Trecorians. We will sweep the galaxy free of the human filth and their allies. This galaxy will be made safe for our younglings before I die. I swear it."

"As do I," said Charge-In-The-Face-Of-Great-Odds. She turned her ears to note the erratic vibrations of the supreme leader's chest. "You are tired, my friend. The tribes need you now more than ever. You must get your rest."

The supreme leader hissed a laugh. "Ah, rest. If only I could, old friend." She hissed another laugh. "Sometimes it seems my only hope for rest will be in the eternal darkness of death." She flapped her wings slightly. "Be that as it may, I must go to Andromeda to rally our forces there. We must assemble the fleets from both galaxies to defeat the humans once and for all."

"Andromeda?" said the Long Wing rep. "You will miss the start of the tournament."

"Nay," said the supreme leader. "Having the royal yacht bring the Bent Wing's applicant from Andromeda has worked to my advantage. I sent orders for the yacht's captain to come to Astaris. I will use it to travel to Andromeda and return in the same fashion."

Charge-In-The-Face-Of-Great-Odds swiveled her ears to make sure she had heard correctly.

The supreme leader hissed a laugh. "I know what you are thinking, old friend. No inter-galaxy ships are allowed to enter the galaxy itself in order to prevent the capture of one of our intergalactic-drives. I know the risk, but it would take far too long for one of our hyper-drive ships to rendezvous with an inter-galaxy ship outside the outer realms of this galaxy. I must go to Andromeda, and I must be back here in time for the tournament. Only my royal yacht is fast enough to make the trek in the allotted time, and only if it comes all the way to Astaris."

Charge-In-The-Face-Of-Great-Odds flapped her wings more than a little. "I do not like it. What if a group of the Empire's wizard scouts intercepts you. They would capture one of our intergalactic-drives and you in one fell swoop."

The chest of the supreme leader turned a dark gray. "This is not up for discussion. I have weighed the risks. It must be done." Her chest turned to a more normal gray. "Besides, I have given orders for squadrons of our warships to be spaced out along my flightpath all the way to the outer realms. I will never be more than a few hours from help. We are deep within the Crosioian Empire. Not even the best of the Empire's ships could make the flight without needing an engine overhaul. Our distance from their border, plus the speed of the yacht's intergalactic-drive, provides all the defenses I could possibly need."

Charge-In-The-Face-Of-Great-Odds was not convinced, but she held her peace. The supreme leader was her friend, but she was still her leader. Even so, she couldn't help but be concerned. *Our space station* Last Hope *was stationed far from the Empire's border,* she thought. *Someone found a way to get there and take the DNA gas before destroying the station.*

The supreme leader swiveled both ears toward her friend and placed a paw on Charge-In-The-Face-Of-Great-Odds's wing. "You sound troubled. Tell me, what are you thinking?"

The Long Wing rep snorted, spraying mucus out of her nostrils in a sign of concern for her leader. "I was thinking that perhaps someone in the Empire might be foolish enough to make the attempt to capture your yacht."

The supreme leader hissed a laugh. "Then let us hope the fool is only a fool and not lucky as well." She laughed again. "It has been my experience that one of the most dangerous weapons in the galaxy is a lucky fool."

CHAPTER 17

The point on the bat's wing tip passed within millimeters of Richard's throat.

He countered with a backflip, kicking out with both feet and catching the Crosioian scout in the chest.

She took a step back before starting a slow circle around Richard.

"You are the luckiest fool I have ever met," said Red Wing. "If you had not tripped on that cactus, I would have had you that time."

Richard laughed. "Don't kid yourself. Luck's as good as skill in my book any day. Besides, your mother made the same attack on me when we fought on Veturna, so I was expecting it. Unlike you, her attack was successful. She nearly tore my throat out."

"Then I shall have to try to be luckier," hissed Red Wing. "My mother taught me many tricks before you and your wolf allies killed her."

Keeping his eyes focused on the bat's chest, Richard looked for any hint about the direction of the scout's next attack. At the same time, he noted the endless desert terrain created by the halo-square they were in. Since Red Wing was unclothed, her sweat-matted fur was all the evidence anyone would need as to the realism of the desert heat.

I'm not much better off, Richard thought. *I'm only wearing shorts and a T-shirt, and I'm sweating like an overweight pactar.* A drop of sweat rolled down his brow and into his left eye as if confirming his thought. He ignored the stinging liquid. The scout was too dangerous an opponent to allow a little thing like sweat to distract him. *She's bigger, faster, and stronger,* he thought. He laughed. *Other than that, I've got her at my mercy.*

Red Wing stopped circling and spread her wings. "You laugh. Why?"

Never taking his eyes off the bat's chest, Richard said, "I was just thinking that physically, you've got me outmatched."

The scout lowered her wings. "Then why laugh? We've been at this for over two hours. Neither of us has gained an advantage. We should move on to weapons training. I am tired of fighting someone physically weaker than me in hand-to-hand combat. I need something more challenging."

Richard ran forward and feinted a kick to the scout's head before sliding along the sandy ground straight between the bat's legs. He kicked upward as he passed underneath. The bat stumbled, but the effect was not what it would have been against a human male. Richard hadn't expected it to be. He stood and wrapped an arm around the scout's right wing where it attached to her back. Twisting hard, he threw her to the ground. Stabbing down with two stiffened fingers braced one against the other, he tore out the bat's right eye.

The scout hissed a scream even as her left wing came across her chest. The wing's sharp point forced its way between a gap in Richard's rib cage. The hand-length hardened piece of wing bone passed through his right lung while continuing on in an attempt to seek out his heart.

Despite his pain, Richard twisted free of the point and rolled away. He screamed in agony but forced his way to his feet. He placed a hand over the gaping wound in an effort to slow the bleeding. Richard felt warmth surround his wound as his self-heal tried to staunch the worst of his blood loss. He sensed the hole in his right lung begin to heal.

Red Wing rose to her feet and charged forward as black blood spewed out of her empty eye socket. She reached out with both paws in an attempt to pull Richard into her chest. Instead of backing away as the bat probably expected, he kicked off with both feet and smashed his forehead into her nostrils. Her nose flattened as blood and mucus splattered onto Richard's face, temporarily blinding him. He felt the bat's wings try to enclose around him to prevent escape, then surprised the scout again by jabbing two stiffened fingers into her left eye. The bat hissed another scream and stumbled back, holding her paws over both eyes.

Richard started forward, but he noticed the bat's ears swivel in his direction. "Piss," Richard cursed under his breath. *I keep forgetting she hears better than she sees.*

Sensing the wound to his lung was nearly healed, Richard shifted to the right, around and under the bat's flapping wing. He jumped high into the air and grabbed hold of the scout's right ear tearing off both the ear and a fistful of meat as he came down. The bat screamed. This time it wasn't like the previous hiss. This time the noise was a full-throated cry of agonizing pain. As soon as Richard's feet contacted the ground, he positioned a leg behind the scout and threw her to the desert floor as hard as he could. The soft sand kept her from taking any serious injuries from the landing.

Reaching out with her left paw, Red Wing made a grab for Richard's throat, but he avoided her grasp and shoved two stiffened fingers into her left ear. He heard bones break. The noise came from both his finger bones and her eardrum. He screamed, but the bat's hiss was louder. Doing his best to ignore the pain in his right hand, Richard brought his left elbow up into what remained of the bat's nose. He sensed bone fragments penetrate her brain. The bat's hissing stopped.

Richard rolled off the scout and curled up into a ball for a dozen heartbeats until his injuries were ninety percent healed. When he stood, the scout was just beginning to move. Her legs twitched back and forth, digging into the soft sand. He sensed the bat's self-heal working overtime to return her body to baseline. It took another thirty seconds before she was finally able to regain her feet.

Pointing a blood-soaked paw at him, Red Wing said, "Your self-heal works too fast. The damage to your lung should have kept you out of action long enough for me to gain the advantage."

Richard shrugged. His self-heal had been working faster ever since the battle in the Presence of the Lady. "We are what we are," he told the scout. "You're bigger and stronger. I heal faster, not to mention I'm better looking."

Red Wing's chest turned gray before returning to a more normal color. She hissed a noise that came out of the halo-square's translator as a laugh. "Females are fighters. We are not supposed to *look* good. Only silly males spend time trying to improve their appearance."

Richard let the obvious dig pass. "End simulation," he said.

The desert landscape disappeared to reveal the *Defiant's* cargo bay. Boxes of magic ammo and other equipment were stacked along the bulkhead all the way to the ceiling to create the twenty by twenty area of the halo-square. Jeena, Charlie, Daniel, and Bright Wing were sitting on a workbench near the stairs. The frown on Jeena's face and the emotions coming down their bond link told Richard she was none too happy.

"What next?" asked Red Wing. She swiveled her ears at the ceiling for a moment before turning them back on Richard. "You, uh, said you would teach me how to protect links. Did you tell the truth?"

Nodding his head, Richard said, "I did say that, and I will. First things first though. I think it's time for weapons training."

"No!" said Jeena. "It has been hard enough watching the two of you beat each other up. I do not care if you can self-heal or not. Enough is enough."

Richard looked at Red Wing. "Go get your dimensional pouch. As soon as you get back, we'll start."

The scout swiveled her ears toward Jeena. Shrugging her wings slightly, she turned and went up the stairs.

Taking advantage of Red Wing's absence, Richard walked over to his bondmate. "I've got to train her," he said, hoping his bondmate would understand. "It's important."

Silver eyes flashing, Jeena shook her head. "It is not more important than you, Rick. I agree the Empire must somehow make amends with the Crosioians. I even suggested as much once. The Crosioians will be needed as allies in our fight against the demons." When Richard opened his mouth to speak, Jeena slid off the worktable and looked him square in the eyes. She was every bit as tall as he. "Training this scout is crazy. How is that supposed to help our mission? Red Wing is determined to kill you in front of her tribal council. You are showing her your weaknesses. All you are succeeding in doing is teaching her how to kill you easier. Are you really that determined to die?"

"I know training her seems counterproductive, but it's not,"

Richard said, unable to articulate the feeling he had that training the scout was important any better than that. "I agree it seems crazy, but this is the way it has to be. Trust me. I know what I'm doing." He did his best to stop the emotions of his own doubts from traveling down the link to his bondmate. From the increased swirling in the molten silver of Jeena's eyes, he was pretty sure he wasn't succeeding.

A fluttering sound from behind drew Richard's attention to the stairs. Jeena looked in the same direction. Richard noticed Red Wing standing at the bottom of the stairs, holding a pouch with a long shoulder strap.

"Good stealth shield," said Nickelo in their shared space.

"The elf is right," said Red Wing. "You are my prisoners. I *will* take you before the tribal council, and I *will* kill you. I agree with the elf. What you are doing is crazy, even for a human."

"Then call me crazy, because that's what I'm going to continue to do regardless of what anyone else thinks."

"Fine," said Jeena using the word in a manner Richard knew she'd picked up from him. "Have it your way then, but do not expect me to sit here and act like I approve."

Richard watched as Jeena headed for the stairs. Emotions of anger, love, concern, and more than a little fear flowed down the link between them. He didn't need her to tell him that even out of sight, she would still sense the emotions of his pain from any injuries he received.

"I'm sorry," Richard said trying to get her to turn back around.

Jeena didn't reply. Holding her head high, she walked up the stairs and continued to ignore him until she was out of sight.

No one in the cargo bay said anything. They barely breathed. Even Red Wing was quiet.

After thirty seconds staring at the empty stairs, Richard let out a sigh before turning to look at the scout. "Okay, now we begin weapons training," he said trying to keep any trace of emotions out of his voice. He knew he was causing stress to his bondmate but saw no other choice. Summoning his dimensional pack, he grabbed it when the black bag appeared in the air. He reached inside and pulled out a short sword and a dagger. "Use your dimensional pouch to summon an edged weapon. I don't care what."

Red Wing shook her head. "No."

Richard felt his face grow warm but kept his anger under control. He knew he'd be just as confused by the training regimen if the situation was reversed. "Look, I know you probably want to train with your phase spear, but we need to start off with edged weapons. That was the technique my brother used when training me at the academy. Believe me when I say it has paid dividends over the years. I talked to my niece and nephew on Storage. They said the warehouses dedicated for Crosioian scouts are pretty much unscathed. I'm confident that you can summon just about any edged weapon you're comfortable with."

"No," said Red Wing more forcefully.

This time Richard felt his face grow hot. In his youth, his anger would have controlled his actions. That had been long ago. Holding his temper in check, he counted to five under his breath before speaking. "Why not?"

The scout's chest turned almost pale. She raised her head toward the ceiling before turning back to Richard. "I cannot make my mother's dimensional pouch work for me."

It almost sounds like she's ashamed, Richard thought. When the scout didn't elaborate, he said, "Oh. Uh, I, ah, just assumed your mother trained…uh, never mind. It just takes training. I couldn't use my dimensional pack until I was taught how. It's no big deal. Let me see you try. Uh, I mean, if you don't mind."

Red Wing's chest lost most of its paleness as Richard spoke. He sensed a line of Power reach out from the scout to her fighting-helmet where it set on the workbench next to his battle helmet. A line of energy from the scout's fighting-helmet reached back and touched Red Wing's dimensional pouch.

"Nick," Richard said out loud. "Connect to Red Wing's fighting-computer and provide instructions for modifying the energy flow to the pouch. It's using the frequency for Red Wing's mother. Red Wing's is slightly different. Her computer has to take that into account."

"Compliance," replied Nickelo over the battle helmet's external speakers.

Richard looked at the scout. "Actually, you don't need your fighting-computer to use the pouch unless you need assistance with the required specifications. For right now though, it's probably easier to use your computer until you get the hang of it. Try sending the image of what you want to your fighting-computer again, along with the Power needed to summon the item. I'll follow along in case there are any problems."

Red Wing swiveled her ears on Richard for the count of five before nodding her head. "Very well. I will do as you say, but this does not change the fact that you are my prisoner."

"Yes, yes," Richard said trying to keep the irritation out of his voice. "I'm your prisoner. You've made that abundantly clear the last couple of days, so you don't need to keep bringing it up. Now try to summon whatever edged weapon you want. I'll guide you if you have trouble."

A line of Power reached out from the scout to her fighting-helmet. Richard probed the line with an active scan of his own. "Your flow's not quite right," he said. "Watch what I do." Touching Red Wing's line, he bent the Power into a rhythmic flow resembling waves rather than a straight line. The line of energy connecting the fighting-helmet to the dimensional pack took on the same rhythmic flow. Richard sensed energy in the scout's pouch disappear.

Red Wing glanced at the pouch before turning her ears toward Richard. Her wings fluttered slightly.

"May as well check," Richard said trying to sound positive. "Either it worked or it didn't. No use standing around wondering which."

Opening the flap of her pouch, Red Wing reached inside and pulled out a shiny, wing-shaped blade the length of Richard's arm. The blade was attached to a black metal rod. The scout kept pulling to reveal a second similar blade attached to the other end of the meter-long rod. Once the weapon was completely out of the pouch, Red Wing grabbed the rod with both hands and spun the blades in a whirling figure-eight motion. She stopped the spinning and set the bottom blade on the metal deck while holding the rod at her side. The tip of the topmost blade was even with the top of her head.

"This is called a wing-blade," said Red Wing. "It is the traditional weapon of old for all of our tribes. Every warrior learns to use this weapon before they are allowed to start training in more advanced weapons. Our scouts use the wing-blade during tournaments to gain honor for our tribes."

Richard took a closer look at the weapon. The razor-sharp edges of the two blades glistened under the lights of the cargo bay. He glanced down at his short sword and dagger.

"Hmm," said Nickelo over the battle helmet's external speaker. "Are you sure you don't want a longsword instead?" Nickelo laughed.

Red Wing hissed laughter as well. So did Charlie and Daniel. Richard did not join in. He had a feeling his bondmate was going to sense more than a few hurts through their bond link in the next couple of hours.

More than a few, he thought.

"I calculate you've got that right," said Nickelo in their shared space. *"Definitely more than a few."*

CHAPTER 18

The tunnels of New Drepdenor were filled with an impenetrable darkness that would have left anyone using normal vision totally helpless. The lack of light made little difference to Telsa. The night vision filter of the battle helmet caused her surroundings to show up bright as day, albeit with a reddish tint. A quick glance at the two elves and the gnome walking confidently by her side made it obvious they were also unaffected by the dark.

"Must be nice to have night vision as an ability," Telsa told her battle computer.

"Now do not get jealous," said Raj. *"The elves and the gnome only have day and night vision. Your battle helmet has filters for radiation, sonic, and a dozen other forms of vision. You are lucky to have your suit's technology instead of having to rely on just your physical attributes."*

"I'm not jealous," Telsa said trying to convince herself as much as her battle computer. *"It's just that I don't always have my equipment. That's when having a natural ability to see at night would come in handy."*

"Tsk, tsk," said Raj adding canned laughter to his words. *"Just be thankful you can see now. I calculate what you are seeing has not been viewed by human eyes since Queen Emerald and her people disappeared nearly a hundred thousand years ago."*

Telsa looked around, taking in the sights just as she had been for the last four hours as they walked ever deeper into the mountain. Although the tunnels had been unoccupied for tens of thousands of years, both the tunnels and the caverns of New

Drepdenor were a wonder to behold. The broad tunnel they were currently in was wide enough for twenty large men to stand side by side without touching. The ceiling was half again as high. The tunnel floor was composed of granite blocks polished to a high shine. If they had been using white light, Telsa was sure she could've seen her reflection in the floor. The dwarves had taken great pride in carving out their mountain home.

"I've said it before, and I'll say it again," Telsa said, hearing the words echo off the stone walls. "This place is beautiful." She waved an arm at the engravings, statues, and other monuments lining both sides of the wide tunnel. "The dwarves obviously didn't mind using their gold and silver when they built this place." She pointed at a statue of an armored dwarf wearing a crown and carrying a large battle axe. "That one looks like it's made out of solid platinum. Are those real diamonds in the crown?"

Rembis, Master Jathar, and Leethor stopped and faced the statue.

"Yes, they are," said Rembis. "The crown was made by the finest metalsmiths the queen could find. The statue is a likeness of King Lokanstanos. He was Queen Emerald's father. This particular tunnel is called the Queen's Way. A lot of the monuments you see in the tunnel are based upon the history of Old Drepdenor."

"From the data Nickelo sent me," said Raj using the battle helmet's external speakers, "the dwarves took a lot of their treasure with them when they left Old Drepdenor. I calculate they found even more when they were digging these tunnels and caverns."

"Well, the place is beautiful wherever they got the stuff from," Telsa said as she turned away from the statue and resumed walking. "I'm surprised the place isn't in ruins. I haven't seen a single rockslide in the four hours we've been down here."

Raj laughed. "Yes, quite impressive. I calculate the guardian is responsible for the pristine condition of the place. I detect traces of the dragon's spells all around us. I suspect even the elves' maintenance spells do not come close to those of the guardian."

"You'd be right, Master Raj," said Rembis. "The last time I walked down this tunnel was nearly a hundred thousand years ago, yet it looks just like I remember it. Speaking of remembering, if my memory serves me correctly, the next side tunnel to the left will lead to the vault where the best of the dwarves' weapons and armor are kept. The gate is just beyond. Queen Emerald insisted on having weapons and armor close by in case they were ever needed to repel a breach in the gate. She kept a regiment housed in the vault along with a company of magic users."

"Should we expect trouble?" asked Leethor as he checked to make sure his longsword was loose in its scabbard.

Rembis shrugged. "Doubtful. Not on this side of the gate at least. The guardian would've detected intruders." He tightened his grip on his staff nonetheless. "Once we are through the gate, well, that's another story. Who knows what lies beyond?"

At the next intersection, Rembis led their small contingent down a tunnel only a quarter the size of the Queen's Way. Within fifty meters, the tunnel opened into a vast cavern over three hundred meters wide with dozens of arched doorways carved into the walls at various heights. Stone staircases led up to a half-dozen levels containing more of the intricately carved doors. In the center of the cavern were rows of what appeared to be stone weapons racks. All of the racks were empty.

Rembis stopped and waved a hand to encompass the multitude of doorways on the upper levels. "Most of those are the quarters for the soldiers who were stationed in the vault." He pointed at the empty weapons racks. "Those held the soldiers' equipment." He turned to Telsa. "I'm sure you remember the weapons and armor Queen Emerald's metalsmiths were making with the blue gems Rick summoned for us. Those weapons and armor were created out of Holy Metal in order to work against creatures in the void. I'm also assuming you remember the vampires that inhabited Old Drepdenor."

Telsa shuddered and involuntarily raised her left hand to her throat. A vampire had nearly bitten her during an ambush in Old Drepdenor. "What I remember is that the equipment wasn't completed in time to help us when we fought the vampires. My friends and I barely got out alive."

"Yes, it was a shame," said Rembis. He looked at Telsa. "I mean about the weapons and armor not being completed in time. Still, they were eventually finished, and Queen Emerald's troops used them to clear the vampires out of the dwarves' old home. It was a fight to remember, I can tell you that." He grinned. "To be honest, sometimes I still wake up sweating from nightmares of that battle."

Leethor walked over to one of the weapons racks and touched the stone with his gloved hand. He whispered something too low to hear and nodded his head. "Whatever was stored here was powerful indeed. These weapons and armor, where are they now? They might come in handy during any future battle against the demons."

Rembis gazed at the empty racks before shrugging his shoulders. "I cannot say. They were here when I left for my mission to Old Drepdenor. This is the first time I've been back since. I can only speculate that Queen Emerald took them with her wherever she went."

Nodding his head, Master Jathar glanced around the cavern. Telsa noticed him concentrate on two wide doors on the opposite side of the vault. The doors were ten meters in height and twice as wide. "I sense a large amount of energy from the other side of those doors," said Master Jathar. "Am I correct in assuming that is the location of the guardian's gate?"

"You are," replied Rembis. He glanced around the vast cavern he called the vault with a faraway look in his eyes. "My memories of this place are of happier times. This place was once full of laughter and feasting dwarves." He looked at Telsa. "The Drepdenor dwarves liked to drink a bit, in case you've forgotten."

Telsa laughed, the sound echoing in the emptiness of the vault. "I haven't forgotten, and if memory serves me correctly, they drank a lot more than a bit." She pointed at the double doors. "Shall we?"

With a nod, Rembis led the way. Leethor took up position by the gnome's side with an arrow nocked in his bow. Master Jathar and Telsa followed three steps behind. When they all reached the other side of the vault, the gnome waved his hands in the air and said words Telsa heard but quickly forgot. A glow appeared around the double doors. They opened slowly inward with nary a sound. Telsa was impressed.

"The guardian's maintenance spell is so good, the doors don't even squeak on their hinges after a hundred thousand years," she said.

Smiling, Rembis said, "See. I told you so."

Looking beyond the open doors, Telsa made out a tunnel half

again as wide as the doors. A pulsating green light a hundred meters away illuminated the tunnel in a light so bright she was forced to switch her helmet's visor to a darker filter in order to compensate. She heard Rembis and Master Jathar muttering spells as glows appeared in front of their eyes. Turning to Leethor who was holding an arm across his eyes, Master Jathar cast a spell at his fellow elf. When Leethor lowered his arm, his eyes were covered with a glow resembling those of Rembis and Master Jathar.

"Sorry about that," said Rembis. "It's been awhile since I've been here. I should've warned you about the light."

With her battle helmet's filter in place, Telsa took a closer look at the tunnel. It started out the width of the two doors and widened as it got closer to the source of the green light. The light itself came from a green orb thirty meters in diameter. The top of the orb just touched the ceiling and sides of the tunnel.

Rembis pointed at the orb. "Well, that's the gate. It's locked, but the spell that Tharantos-Ratira gave me is attuned to our frequencies. She assured me the spell would create a temporary opening that would allow us to pass through the gate unharmed. She thinks the same spell will return us here, but to be honest, she said it had never been tested. No one who has gone through the gate from our side has ever returned." The gnome looked at Telsa and Jathar. "Are you sure you want to enter? It has been my experience that it's often easier to enter into something than it is to get out. I remember hearing sailors say that it's a lot better to be on land wishing you were out on a ship in the ocean than to be on a ship in the ocean wishing you were back on land."

Telsa glanced at Rembis. "The sailors where I'm from say the same thing about space and starships." Turning, she looked at Master Jathar. "I've got a feeling that if we enter this gate, there's a good chance you're going to be more than a tad late to your council meeting this afternoon."

Jathar shrugged and gave a determined smile. "There will be others. I only hope I am alive to attend them."

Glancing at the gate for several heartbeats as she gathered her thoughts, Telsa finally looked back at her companions. "I appreciate your help, but this is *my* responsibility. I'm a wizard scout. My job is recon. I'll go in first and check the place out. Maybe I'll get lucky and find a yellow gem and return in time for all of us to get back home for supper."

Leethor, Master Jathar, and Rembis all traded glances. Leethor un-nocked his arrow and returned it to his quiver. He strapped the bow on his back in a well-practiced maneuver before drawing his sword. "I am an elven scout. I would be ashamed to go back to my bondmate and tell her that I allowed a wizard scout to go into danger while an elven scout remained behind." He looked back at Master Jathar and Rembis. When they both nodded their heads, Leethor returned his gaze to Telsa. "Portalis is our home. We will all go together or none at all will go. So let us stop bantering about it and get on with our mission. I have a nagging feeling we are going to be late for a lot of suppers before we return to Silverton."

Telsa nodded her head. Truth be told, she was glad they were going with her. She had a feeling hell was no place to be alone.

"I calculate you are right," said Raj out loud. "Hell is no place to be alone. So as Commander Leethor says, let us get on with it. The longest journey begins with the first step."

Telsa, Leethor, Rembis, and Master Jathar all stepped out at the same time.

There's no going back now, Telsa thought as she kept pace with the others.

When they reached the edge of the orb's light, none of them slowed their pace. As her foot made contact with the pulsating green light, her entire body began to tingle. The stone of the tunnel disappeared. Telsa gasped. New Drepdenor was gone, replaced by something that could only be described by a single word.

Hell.

CHAPTER 19

A bright flash of light to Tia's right was her first warning that things weren't as they should be. The second was the blast of plasma energy hitting the force field of her Trecorian R3 long-range fighter. She fought the buffeting spacecraft and gained enough control to bank the fighter on a ninety degree path to the right from her original course. At the same time, she sent out a passive scan in an attempt to locate whoever or whatever was firing at her. In the emptiness of space, she'd found passive scans comparable in range to the sensors on fighters like the R3. She spotted eight blips of energy to her nine o'clock position, heading her way at a high rate of speed. That was all the information she needed. Six of the blips were outpacing the other two by a ten-to-one ratio.

Six missiles inbound and two fighters coming up behind them, Tia thought. *What have I gotten myself into?* "Computer," she said, forcing her voice to remain steady. "Plot time to target for those six missiles and prepare countermeasures."

"Unable to comply," came the mechanical voice of the R3's computer. "Sensors are not picking up any targets. The area is clear up to three light seconds in all directions."

A glance at the tactical heads-up display on the fighter's windscreen confirmed the R3's computer was right. The display showed only empty space around her ship. The only problem was that Tia knew better. The energy readings on her passive scan were showing up bright and clear.

With no help forthcoming from the R3's computer, Tia banked

hard left ninety degrees and headed straight for the point where her passive scan told her the inbound missiles were located. Since her R3 was twice the size of the Zip fighter she'd flown on the *Defiant*, she knew there was no way the bulky ship could outmaneuver the incoming missiles. *My best bet is to meet them head on and try to take them out before they detonate.*

"Prepare countermeasures for manual activation," Tia ordered the fighter's computer. "Activate on my command."

"Compliance," said the mechanical voice.

Danny, Tia thought, *where are you when I need you?* She knew where he was. *He's with the elf, and no amount of wishing is going to get him back. I'm stuck with the fighter's standard tactical computer.* She sighed. *It can't compete with a battle computer. It's just hardware. It's not a living organism like Danny and Margery.*

Tia began second guessing her decision to make the recon of a reported Crosioian intrusion into Empire space on her own. It had seemed like a great opportunity at the time to do something besides attend staff meetings and draw up plans A, B, C, and every other letter of the alphabet as contingencies in case Liz's primary rescue plan went wrong. She'd known her sister would be angry when she found out her younger sister had left on a mission better suited for a fighter pilot than a member of the admiral of the combined fleet's personal staff. She'd gone anyway. Deep down, Tia knew why she'd done it—the real reason why. Matthew was in the area organizing one of the Conglomerate fleets. Unfortunately, he was still too far away to provide help in her current situation.

Maybe if I get killed, Liz won't be as angry, Tia thought.

Reaching out with an active scan, she tried to estimate the decreasing distance to the incoming missiles. No one needed to tell her that her passive scan abilities were weak when it came to estimating distances without Danny or Margery to help her, but it was what it was. She had to make her best guess.

"Activate countermeasures," Tia ordered when she thought the distance was right.

"Compliance," replied the R3's computer.

Two dozen miniature rockets shot out from the sides of the fighter and streaked ahead, splitting up to take slightly different flight paths. All the while they sent out energy footprints designed to fool missiles into thinking they were an R3 fighter. At the same time, Tia wrapped the fighter in Power and activated a stealth shield. Her stealth shields were also weak, but it was all she could do.

The R3's stealth shield obviously hasn't worked against the missiles, Tia thought. *Maybe the stealth shield Rick taught me will do better.*

Tia could only hope. Her friend had worked with her some after their Portalis mission to improve her stealth shield, but she knew she was no wizard scout. Whether her shield was good enough to fool the incoming missiles was something she was soon going to find out.

"Warning," said the R3's computer. "Sensors are detecting incoming missiles."

"About time," Tia said. She glanced at the fighter's heads-up display. Orange blips on the display confirmed four of the missiles had changed their course to intercept her countermeasures. The other two missiles were still heading in her direction, but their courses appeared to be wavering from her port to starboard.

They're having trouble pinpointing my fighter, Tia thought. *My stealth shield must be confusing them at least a little.*

"Impact in five seconds," said the R3's computer. "Recommend evasive maneuvers."

No way, Tia thought. *This is an R3, not a Zip fighter. They'd have me for sure. There's only one way to get out of this.*

Shifting her course to meet the lead missile head on, Tia fired the fighter's plasma weapons. Hundreds of balls of red energy streaked out from the fighter's ten plasma cannons. *She might be clunky,* Tia thought, *but the R3 has one hell of a lot of firepower.*

A bright light erupted to Tia's front. The windscreen blacked out as the fighter's computer automatically activated the blast filter. A moment later the windscreen returned to normal.

"Both missiles have been destroyed," said her computer. "My sensors are picking up two targets inbound at your twelve o'clock. I calculate they are Crosioian double-wing fighters. Range is a quarter of a light second."

Long-range fighters similar to my R3, Tia thought. *They're designed for deep space recon. They must be here to monitor the buildup of Conglomerate ships. The question is why weren't my ship's sensors able to detect them while they were farther away?*

Tia shoved the question aside and fired all four of the R3's anti-ship missiles. She counted to three before pulling the trigger on her plasma cannons to give the missiles time to get some distance. Well before the missiles reached their targets, a burst of light appeared in space, then two more.

Her intercom crackled. "The double-wings' anti-missile missiles have destroyed three of your missiles," said the R3's computer.

Tia noticed green balls of plasma energy heading her way and jerked the fighter hard to the left, avoiding most of the Crosioians' return fire. What little hit the R3's force field did no damage. A burst of light in the distance drew her attention.

"Your fourth missile knocked out the shield around one of the double-wings," said her computer. "The follow-up rounds from your plasma cannons destroyed the fighter. The remaining fighter is preparing to fire additional anti-ship missiles. Recommend you not allow that to occur. The R3's force field is down to twelve percent."

The distance to the remaining fighter was well beyond anything Tia had done before, but in desperation, she reached out with a line of Power the way Richard and his brother Gaston had shown her. She probed for the life form inside the approaching double-wing. When she found it, she wrapped Power around something inside the life form, then jerked hard with telekinesis.

"The enemy fighter is acting erratic," said the R3's tactical computer. "It appears to be drifting in space. Weapon systems are powering down, so is the ship's force field."

Either I got lucky, or the Crosioian's trying to lure me into a trap, Tia thought. *I should probably just put a couple of hundred plasma rounds in the fighter and be done with it. On the other hand, maybe I can access the double-wing's computer and download something that might prove useful. At the least, it might keep Liz from blowing her stack when she finds out what I've done if I can show her the Crosioian's battle plan or something like that.*

Leary of a trap, Tia approached the double-wing while probing it with an active scan. She sensed the pilot. The bat was dead. Even so, something inside the fighter kept slipping in and out of her scan. It wasn't so much a life form as it was...*something else.*

Tia targeted the double-wing and started to pull the trigger on the R3's steering level. The ring on her finger tingled. An emotion of concern came down the link she shared with Matthew.

He's sensed my emotions during the battle. Of course he's concerned.

Tia sent an emotion of relief back up the link to let the man she loved know she was okay. Easing off the trigger for the plasma cannons, she stopped the R3 a hundred thousand meters from the Crosioian fighter. The sense of presence from Matthew gave her an idea. She sent a feeling of need through their link along with a line of Power.

I don't even know if this is going to work, Tia thought. *We've never shared Power before. All I know is my active scan isn't powerful enough to pinpoint whatever's still in that fighter on its own. I either need to get help, or I need to blow the fighter up and move on with my mission. It's too risky to approach the ship any closer on my own.*

After counting to five, Tia was rewarded with a feeling of Power coming down the link she shared through her ring with Matthew. Intertwining a line of her own Power with his, she formed another active scan and reached out toward the double-wing. She'd never been able to wrap her scans with a stealth shield before, but on a hunch, she tried to do so the way Richard had shown her. The extra Power from Matthew apparently did the trick because she sensed a stealth shield form around her active scan.

I did it, Tia thought. She looked at the stealth shield closer. *No, actually I didn't. The stealth shield is Matthew's. Somehow he's handling the stealth shield, and I'm taking care of the active scan. How?*

Reserving the *how* for later, Tia reached into the double-wing and probed for the *something* she'd felt earlier. She sensed it hiding behind a subtle stealth shield. She sensed a familiarity to the frequency. *It's demonic,* she thought. *I'd never have detected it fully on my own. I don't think it knows I'm probing it. Matt's stealth shield is protecting my active scan.*

Tia glanced around the confined space of her R3 fighter. "Computer, how much larger than my cockpit is the one on the double-wing?"

"Twenty-five percent," replied the R3's computer. "The Crosioian pilot's wings take up the extra space. If you are asking how much more free space the double-wing has, I calculate only five percent."

Five percent, Tia thought. *That's not enough room for any demons I've seen or heard Rick talk about. What's going on?*

An emotion coming down the link from Matthew seemed to be asking the same question.

He must not be able to sense the results of my active scan. That's not surprising since the Conglomerate fleet is still a good half a light year away. What's surprising is that our rings are allowing us to share Power with each other at this range. We're not creating Power like Rick and Jeehana, but we are *sharing it.*

Once again Tia wished Danny or Margery was with her. *Well, they ain't, so no use wishing. I've got to figure this out on my own.*

Throwing caution to the wind, she gave a long burst from the ion-drives to propel the R3 closer to the drifting Crosioian fighter. She hit the reverse thruster when the R3 was within fifty meters. Punching the zoom on her windscreen, she peered into the cockpit of the double-wing. She made out the body of the Crosioian pilot. A gooey substance was oozing out of its eye sockets.

Hmm, Tia thought. *I got lucky. I guess I got hold of the bat's brain with my telekinesis. No wonder the fighter got put out of action so quick.*

A movement inside the double-wing's cockpit caught Tia's attention. She saw a small flash of orange sticking above the Crosioian's control panel. Zooming the windscreen's viewport even closer, she spied an orange head the size of a small monkey's. The head had leather, reptilian-looking skin. Two finger-length horns protruded from the creature's forehead. Something moved behind the head.

Are those wings? Tia wondered. She looked at the creature again. *It's actually a little cute. I wonder if it's friendly.*

The creature turned its head in Tia's direction. Red eyes flashed as its gaze locked on her. It opened its mouth, revealing fangs as a wave of hate and evil washed over Tia.

Definitely not friendly, she decided. Keeping her finger on the trigger for her plasma cannons, she eased the R3 forward until only ten meters of cold space separated the two fighters.

"Computer, identify the creature in the cockpit—the live one."

"Unable to comply. The information is not in my databanks."

"Access the tele-network. Flag the request as a Delta-five priority."

"Compliance. I have retrieved the information from the central computer's historical storage unit. I calculate a ninety-seven percent probability that the orange beast is a mythical creature the old Earthlings called an imp. Typical size is a half meter or less. In myths, they were devilish creatures, or demons, if you prefer, that played pranks on unsuspecting humans."

Tia knew what she saw was no mythical creature and doubted it was on board the double-wing to play pranks on the Crosioian pilot.

"Contact the Conglomerate's flagship," Tia ordered. "Tell them to have a mobile containment unit on standby when I get there. Uh, you better request an armed security detail as well. Tell them I'll be there in two hours."

"Compliance."

Removing her finger from the plasma cannons' trigger, Tia touched the icon for the R3's tractor beam. A concentrated ray of yellow light shot out, enveloping the double-wing. At the same time, Tia probed the enemy fighter with her active scan while using her telekinesis to disconnect weapon and engine controls.

Nodding her head, Tia thought, *I don't know if that miniature demon can fly the fighter or use its weapons, but I'm not taking any chances. It may or may not be an imp, but whatever it is, it's got to be the reason the R3's sensors couldn't detect the double-wing at long range. Rick told us that the Crosioians used demons to hide their fleets around Estos. He assured Liz all of them had been pulled back to the demonic plane when he destroyed Zenthra's computer avatar.* An image of the miniature demon in the double-wing fighter appeared in Tia's mind. *Obviously Rick was wrong. Or...the Crosioians are getting replacement demons. The question is how?*

Plotting a course to the Conglomerate fleet, Tia hit the hyper-drive switch. When acceleration decreased, she checked the rear video to make sure the double-wing was still in the tractor beam's grasp. It was.

She remembered the hatred in the imp's eyes and the feeling of evil rolling over her. *If the Crosioians have more of these things, that's going to throw a kink in Liz's rescue plan. I've got to find out what the Crosioians are doing. I swear that miniaturized demon is going to tell me what I want to know, or I'll take a grinder and sand down its horns.*

Speaking out loud, Tia said, "If there are more of these things, it could mean the deaths of all two hundred million POWs. I've got to know. I've just got to."

A tingle of concern passed down her link with Matthew. She smiled and sent an emotion through the link.

"Wait for me. I'm coming."

CHAPTER 20

The supreme leader of the Crosioian Central Command hurried out of her quarters on the royal yacht *Gaze at the Stars*. Making her way down the corridor, she passed crewmembers going about their duties. At her approach, they tucked their wings close to their sides and threw themselves up against the metal walls until she passed. Between the crewmembers bracing against the walls and others hurriedly stepping into side halls and doorways, the normally congested main corridor remained clear enough that she made it to the yacht's bridge in less than thirty seconds.

As soon as the supreme leader stepped onto the bridge, the yacht's captain raised a paw over her left chest in salute. "The transport ship *Blood Fur* has activated an emergency beacon. Their captain says they are leaking radiation from their hyper-drive. She is requesting assistance from any and all ships in the district. Based upon the rate of radiation, she says her crew will all be dead in twenty minutes."

The supreme leader glanced at the dozen crewmembers standing erect at their stations on the bridge. No one made a noise, not even the captain. *It is my decision,* the supreme leader thought, *not theirs. Our flight plan was to fly direct from the outer realms to Astaris while remaining in intergalactic-drive to avoid possible interception by Empire forces. My mission in Andromeda was successful. They will be sending their fleets to our galaxy in two weeks. My task now is to return to Astaris to attend the tournament while our fleets are assembled to destroy the Empire once and for all.*

Swiveling her ears at the captain, the supreme leader asked, "From what tribe does the *Blood Fur* hail?"

An ensign held up a sonic tablet to the captain. The captain swiveled her ears at the tablet before turning back to the supreme leader. "Her registration indicates she is from the Tantos tribe. The manifest lists the crew and passengers at four hundred and thirty-two."

The supreme leader flapped her wings. "So many? Why?"

The captain shrugged. "Unknown, Sir. Their captain mentioned the *Blood Fur* was carrying the Tantos tribe's applicants for the tournament. I can only assume the *Blood Fur* is also bringing support staff and their tribal leaders with them."

Flapping her wings hard enough to stir up a slight breeze, the supreme leader paced the width of the bridge once before turning to face the captain. "What about life boats? They should be able to evacuate in them long enough for rescue ships to arrive."

The captain's chest turned a light gray. "I asked the same question, Supreme Leader. The *Blood Fur's* captain hissed something about an explosion and lifeboat malfunctions before we lost contact. Our sensors are still picking up the transport, so it has not been destroyed. We are attempting to reestablish communications now."

Unfurling her wings to their maximum spread, the supreme leader flapped them slowly as she once again paced the bridge. *The loss of over four hundred crew and passengers would be bad enough,* she thought, *but it would not be worth the risk of exposing the* Gaze at the Stars *to danger. The loss of the Tantos tribe's twelve scout applicants and their tribal leaders is a different matter. One of their applicants might be the scout we need to lead our team into* the Hole. *I cannot risk losing them.*

She stopped pacing and turned back toward the captain. "How close is the nearest Crosioian ship?"

"Two hours and thirty minutes. The *Blood Fur* couldn't have picked a worst place to have a problem. Our security ships have been placed every five hours' hyper-drive distance along our flight route. We could make the distance in a few minutes using our intergalactic-drive, but the *Blood Fur's* crew would be long dead before any of the other ships could arrive."

Making her decision, the supreme leader furled her wings

behind her back. "Make for the *Blood Fur*. Once you are in range, shutdown our intergalactic-drive and shift to normal hyper-drive. Bring us alongside the *Blood Fur* and begin transferring their crew to our ship. We have to get them away from the radiation. Order our nearest security ships to meet us at the *Blood Fur's* location with all due haste. Arrange for a medical transport ship with anti-radiation equipment to rendezvous there as well."

"Sir," said the captain. "For your safety, I must recommend that we not—"

The supreme leader spread her wings. "Your concern for my safety is duly noted, Captain. Now carry out my orders."

The captain raised a paw to her chest before turning to face the sonic screen at the front of the bridge. "Helmswoman, make for the *Blood Fur*."

"Aye, aye, Sir." Within three minutes, the helmswoman said, "We have arrived, Captain."

The captain nodded. "Deactivate intergalactic-drive and switch to hyper-drive. Get us close. Use the ion-drive to maneuver us next to the *Blood Fur* and dock."

"Sir!" replied the helmswoman as she touched the lever to disengage the intergalactic-drive.

Everyone on the bridge leaned forward slightly as the ship's momentum slowed.

The sound waves on the forward sonic screen blanked out for two heartbeats before displaying the normal sonic view of space. The *Blood Fur* was dead ahead. Vapor spewed into space from a large crack near the ship's engine. The berths along the side of the transport ship for the lifeboats were empty. A twenty-meter-long docking tube jutted out from the ship's airlock.

"Helmswoman, connect our forward airlock to their docking tube," said the captain.

"Aye, aye, Sir," replied the helmswoman as she began the delicate operation of maneuvering the *Gaze at the Stars* alongside the *Blood Fur*.

"Science Officer, keep me informed of radiation leaks. Let me know as soon as we begin approaching danger levels." The captain had a second thought. "Belay that. Keep me informed of any leaks greater than normal levels."

"Sir!" said the science officer.

The crew of the *Gaze at the Stars* worked quickly and efficiently. The supreme leader expected no less, but her chest swelled with pride anyway. The hundred and fifty-seven member crew of the royal yacht was the best in the fleets. She had handpicked them herself.

The captain turned to her communication officer. "Have our medical crew stand by at the forward airlock. If the radiation is at the levels the *Blood Fur's* captain indicated, we will need to get their crew off as fast as possible and straight into sick bay."

"Sir!" replied the communication officer before turning to her console and issuing commands.

Within another two minutes the *Gaze at the Stars* was positioned next to the *Blood Fur*. The helmswoman expertly aligned the yacht's airlock with the end of the twenty-meter-long docking tube and connected the two starships together with nary a bump. The supreme leader nodded her approval.

"Open our forward airlock and notify the *Gaze at the Stars* that we are ready to begin crew transfer," ordered the captain. She swiveled her ears toward the science officer. "I thought I told you to keep me informed of radiation leaks, Lieutenant. What is the delay?"

The lieutenant cocked an ear at her console before swiveling both ears at her captain. "There is nothing to report, Captain. I am detecting no leaks."

"Impossible," said the captain. "What about the vapor coming out of that crack near the engine?"

"Steam, Captain. It is just harmless steam."

The fur on the back of the supreme leader's neck stood on end. She sent out an active scan, probing the inside of the *Blood Fur*. Strange but eerily familiar energy frequencies were intermixed with those of the Crosioian crew. She reached back in her mind, trying to remember when and where she had last sensed the frequencies. She sucked in a deep breath as the answer came to her. *The energy frequencies are the same as those I sensed in* the Hole *when Charge-In-The-Face-Of-Great-Odds and I made our recon of the rift two hundred years ago.*

The supreme leader's fighting-computer flashed a warning in their shared space at the same time the supreme leader realized her mistake.

"Warning," said the supreme leader's fighting-computer over the helmet's external speaker for the benefit of the bridge's crew. "Demons are on the ship. I calculate it is a—"

"It's a trap!" the supreme leader shouted. "Emergency breakaway. Now!"

The *Gaze at the Stars* shuddered. The sound of an explosion echoed through the ship.

"Breach in forward airlock," said the communication officer. "I have lost contact with the medical team."

"Helmswoman, get us out of here now!" ordered the captain.

"Two Balorian heavy destroyers are on our port bow," said the science officer. "They must have been using some type of advanced stealth shield."

"They have activated tractor beams," said the helmswoman. "We are pinned in. I am unable to break away from the docking tube."

The supreme leader pulled her phase spear from where it hung on her belt and activated it in destructive mode. The spear elongated as she headed for the forward airlock. She didn't know why their supposed pirate allies were attacking the royal yacht, but she had no doubt it did not bode well for the *Gaze at the Stars* or its crew.

Alarms sounded in the ship as the captain's voice came over the ship-wide intercom. "Prepare to repel boarders. This is not a drill."

No drill indeed, thought the supreme leader. *This is what I get for staying alive long enough to become old. I have doomed us all.* She eyed the meter-long glowing point of her phase spear. *Bite deep into the flesh of the enemy, old friend. Time for one last battle before we go to the great beyond.*

CHAPTER 21

The double bed in Richard and Jeena's quarters on the *Defiant* was a tight fit in the small cabin, but as far as Richard was concerned, it beat the two of them sleeping in separate bunk beds. He much preferred the closeness of his bondmate lying against him while she slept. He glanced around the darkened room. The dim light coming from under the curtained doorway illuminated his battle helmet and gear on top of the desk an arms-length away. Jeena's staff was just visible leaning against the desk where she'd left it the night before. The blue gem at the top of the Lady's staff did little to illuminate the room, but for some reason Richard found the warm glow comforting nonetheless. The sound of members of the *Defiant's* crew moving quietly around in the mess area on the other side of the curtain was only slightly distracting. Richard easily ignored that.

What I can't ignore is whatever's tickling my nose.

Taking care not to wake his bondmate, he raised a hand and brushed away an errant strand of silver hair from where it had blown across his face. He glanced down at his bondmate. Her head rested softly on his bare chest. The sound of her breathing as she slept was comforting in its own way. He listened to her breathe for a minute, then returned to the last page of the book he'd been reading for the last couple of hours about war and peace. Like usual, Nickelo displayed the pages of the book in their shared space so he could pass the time without disturbing his bondmate. Richard read the last line of the final page.

"*Big book,*" Richard thought.

"*Any time someone writes about either war or about peace, it can get complicated,"* replied Nickelo. *"Writing about both can definitely get verbose. The question is, did you like it?"*

"Yeah, I think so. I probably won't be rereading it any time soon though."

Nickelo laughed. *"Wise decision when you consider that you still have another four thousand books from the ten thousand book list I gave you of 'books to read before you die.'"*

"Well, that's definitely going to take me a while, if more than a few of them are as big as this one was."

"Oh, a few are," admitted Nickelo. *"I must point out though, that you don't have to bother reading them if you don't want to. I could just send you a summary of every book on the list in our shared space, complete with discussion notes and optimum points of view for use during conversations. You would have the memory of having read them without going through the actual effort."*

"Where would the fun in that be?" Richard asked. *"As it so happens, I like reading. It relaxes me. As a wizard scout, I don't need very much sleep, but my mind needs to rest. Reading gives my brain a chance to relax from the stress of the real world."*

A sensation of humor popped into Richard's shared space. *"I thought it would,"* said Nickelo. *"That's why I created the list in the first place. But relax time is over, buddy. It's time to get busy now. Red Wing has been in the cargo bay for the last forty-eight minutes, waiting for you. I suggest you get a move on, Marine, before she decides to start practicing her combat skills on a member of the crew."*

Richard wasn't worried. The scout had given her word not to harm the crew, and she'd kept it honorably for the last two weeks. Nevertheless, he knew he needed to get the day started. Despite the knowledge, he hesitated to leave the warmth of the beautiful elf lying next to him. He took a final moment to enjoy the peace his bondmate gave him.

While he enjoyed a last few seconds of relaxation, he thought back to how Sergeant Ron had fooled Red Wing. Instead of continuing on into Crosioian space, the old fox had come up with a plan to have the triplets gate the *Defiant* to the magic dimension and fly through friendly UGA space, to a location near a point opposite the Crosioian planet of Astaris. By doing so, they'd had two weeks of uneventful travel instead of having to dodge enemy warships. Now the *Defiant* was only a couple of days out from their destination. It had been a good plan, and everyone on the ship had liked it. That is, everyone had liked it but Red Wing. Richard smiled as he remembered the look on the bat's facial features when he'd told her they wouldn't be transferring to a Crosioian ship after all. The look had almost been worth the beating she'd given him later that day during hand-to-hand training.

"Well, stop patting yourself on the back before you hurt your arm," said Nickelo. *"Sergeant Ron is having the triplets gate us back to the physical dimension in a few hours. The time for training the scout is nearly over. If you haven't taught her what you wanted to teach her by now, it probably isn't going to get done."*

Resigning himself to the inevitable, Richard eased out of bed, taking great pains not to wake Jeena. She'd had a rough time the day before. At his urging, she'd begun participating in the scout's training the previous week by exposing Red Wing to magic attacks and defenses against the same. He remembered how the bat had gotten a little too enthusiastic during a counterattack the day before and burned the back of Jeena's legs and arms. Even though he'd healed his bondmate right away, he was still haunted by the feeling of helplessness as the emotions of her pain flowed down their bond link.

I can't risk her getting hurt like that again, Richard thought. *It's too much to bear, for her and me. As far as I'm concerned, her part in Red Wing's training is over.*

"Well," said Nickelo not sounding the least bit sympathetic. *"I guess you know now how the high priestess feels when you get hurt. What's good for the goose and all that, you know."*

"Oh, just shut up why don't you," Richard said. *"Go do whatever battle computers do when they're not bugging their wizard scouts."*

"Compliance."

Richard held his breath waiting for some wisecrack comeback, but for once, his battle computer remained silent. After putting on his battle suit and gear in the dark as quietly as possible, he slid past the curtain and stepped into the mess area. He pulled the curtain closed behind him while making sure the seal was tight. Nodding at the half-dozen crewmembers sitting at the table eating, he glanced into the galley. As he expected, Comstar was there stirring a large cauldron on the stove. When the elf looked up, he mouthed the word "stew" before turning his attention back to his stirring.

Making his way down the stairs, past the engine deck, Richard walked down the last flight of steps to the cargo bay. As his battle computer had predicted, Red Wing was there, standing by the entrance to their makeshift halo-square. The scout turned and cocked her ears at him.

"Is the elf okay?" asked Red Wing.

Richard nodded. "Yeah, she's sleeping. I healed her quickly enough after she got burned, but I think you scared her."

The scout spread her wings halfway out before bringing them back to her side. "One thing I have found out during the last two weeks is that your elf is tough. I think it would take more than a little fire to frighten her."

Richard shrugged. Training the scout was one thing. Giving her personal information about his bondmate was another. Perhaps it was the paleness of what skin he could see above her chest armor. Whatever it was, something told Richard the Crosioian was genuinely concerned. *I didn't think bats had feelings,* he thought.

"After two weeks together, you should know better," said Nickelo in their shared space. *"A lot of Red Wing's emotions are foreign to you, but she's got feelings just the same. I calculate Crosioians have a strong sense of loyalty. Jeena, Red Wing, and you have spent a lot of time training together. The scout may not know it, but I calculate she subconsciously thinks of the two of you now as teammates. Based upon that assumption, of course she is concerned."*

Richard eyed the scout closer. From observing her during training sessions, he'd learned the trembling of her wings usually meant concern or excitement. *Her wings are trembling a little now,* he thought. *Plus her skin is pale. She tends to do that when she's embarrassed. I wonder if she's sorry she hurt Jeena. Considering the fact that she's sworn to kill both of us, I'd say her behavior is a little contradictory.*

When Red Wing continued to stand in the same spot without saying anything further, Richard decided to relent a little. "Jeena was a prisoner for over a year," he explained. Before the bat could say something about the shame of being taken prisoner, he added, "She would have rather died than be taken prisoner, but she was caught in a magic spell that cutoff the link to her Power reserve and left her paralyzed. I'm sure you can appreciate that under the right circumstances, that can happen through no fault of the prisoner." When Red Wing continued to say nothing, he said, "She was tortured by an elf named Crendemor for over a year."

"The elf's name is Kreathin," said Nickelo in their shared space. *"The dark elf body of Crendemor was just his polymorph form."*

"I wish you'd be quiet and let me tell the story," Richard told his battle computer.

"Compliance."

Concentrating on Red Wing, Richard said, "Jeena doesn't talk about it much, but from what little she's told me, Crendemor used a lot of fire during their torture sessions."

The skin around Red Wing's neck grew even paler. "I did not know. I have not seen any burn scars during our training."

Richard shrugged. "Her physical scars disappeared the first time I healed her. Emotional scars are a different story. They tend to run deep. I suppose they may never fully heal."

The scout trained her ears on Richard for several seconds before nodding her head. "Thank you for sharing that with me, Wizard Scout. I will be careful not to use fire against the elf during any future training."

Looking away to inspect one of the ammo crates stacked along the wall of the cargo bay, Richard wondered at the strangeness of the conversation. For the first time, Red Wing seemed more than just a killing machine in bat form. He tried to hold onto the hatred he felt for those who were responsible for the death of his father, but the emotion kept slipping away.

"I calculate you are beginning to think of the scout as a living being instead of an emotionless object," said Nickelo in their shared space.

"I thought I told you to be quiet," Richard said, not wanting to get into a philosophical discussion with his battle computer.

Nickelo laughed. *"Actually, you said that you* wished *I would be quiet. You did not make it an order."*

Ignoring his battle computer, Richard decided to get the training back on track. He reached over and patted one of the magic ammo containers along the bulkhead before turning back to the scout. "I think no more fire would be a good idea. I suspect Sergeant Ron would take it ill if we set off one of these ammo boxes and blew the *Defiant* to hell and back."

The paleness left Red Wing's neck, and she hissed a laugh. "No doubt. Now, shall we get back to training? Once we return to the physical dimension, I suspect the captain will be so busy dodging Crosioian warships that we will not be able to train."

"Maybe," Richard said choosing not to tell the scout that the ship's stealth shield combined with all the magic users on board made the *Defiant* very good at evading enemy ships. "In any regard, let's get down to business. We were practicing splitting lines of Power last night before we quit training. Maybe we should pick up where we left off."

Red Wing shrugged her wings. "I can use four lines at once now. I would prefer to do some more weapons training first."

Shaking his head, Richard said, "Not yet. You're getting too good. Jeena senses it when I get hurt. I don't want to accidentally wake her by having you cut off my leg or some such thing."

Red Wing hissed a laugh. "Believe me. I would not stop at one leg, Wizard Scout." She stopped hissing. "So what do we do then?"

"Well, let's see. You've got protecting and attacking links down pat. I'll admit your techniques can use some tweaking, but that will come with time. You don't need me anymore for that. In fact, I think you're good enough to teach others how to protect and attack links, but that can wait. You've also gotten pretty good at drilling through shields, which, by the way, I learned from your mother, so it's almost like she taught you. As far as stealth shields go, you already had one of the best I've ever encountered before we started training, so there's no use wasting time with stealth shields."

"Should we train on defending against magic then?" asked Red Wing.

Richard shook his head. "Nope. Jeena and Comstar's got you trained pretty well in that area. It would be a waste of our time for me to try and help you there." He grinned. "Yep, there's only one final thing I think I need to teach you before I graduate you out of our impromptu training program." Remaining quiet, he waited until Red Wing became curious enough to ask the obvious question.

"What?" she said gritting her fangs. "What training is next?"

Richard felt his smile grow larger. "Demons. I'm going to show you what I know about fighting demons."

The scout swiveled both ears at Richard and fluttered her wings. "Good. That is something I think I am going to need to learn. The sooner, the better."

CHAPTER 22

Eight hours later, Red Wing was soaked in sweat even though she was wearing a simulated fighting-suit. She shoved the end of her phase spear into the chest of the last of the two-headed yellow demons and tossed the creature over her shoulder to join the stack of six bodies that had been her earlier adversaries. A glance down the long, rocky tunnel created by the halo-square confirmed the place was finally empty. She'd passed the test. She was finally done.

The wizard scout's voice came over the intercom inside her fighting-helmet. "You've got sixty seconds before the next wave hits. I recommend you make the most of it." The noise humans made when they laughed came over the intercom. "Remember. No pain, no gain."

Red Wing ground her fangs before replying out loud, "My only wish is that you were visible inside the halo-square." She hefted her phase spear. "If this wasn't a simulated version of a phase spear, I would show you what real pain is."

The area to Red Wing's left shimmered. The wizard scout appeared wearing his battle suit. A fully activated phase rod was gripped in the human's left hand. He raised the rod slightly. "From what you tell me, there will be plenty of time to use real ones against each other when we get to Astaris. In the meantime, we're training to fight demons, not each other." The human winked. It was something Red Wing had noticed humans do as a sign of humor. "For now, I think it would be best to continue using these facsimiles created by Comstar. The halo-square's tractor beams will make sure they work and feel like the real things. Now, you've got thirty seconds before the next scenario starts. Are you ready? If you're tired, I suppose we could stop long enough for you to rest."

Red Wing was tired. Large as her Power reserve was, it was still getting low. Not that she'd ever admit that to a human. She stretched her wings out fully to show the wizard scout her contempt for physical discomfort. "I am a Crosioian scout. I do not get tired. Bring on your simulated demons. I am ready."

The human laughed. "All right, have it your way. Margery, I want you to set up a team training scenario for Red Wing and me. Make it challenging. I recommend doubling the number of demons in the next wave and make the types random. I'm giving you full control of the training scenario. You should probably—"

Although the area around Red Wing was an empty tunnel, she heard the obvious click of the ship's intercom. The voice of the *Defiant's* computer, Margery, echoed in the tunnel. "Since you have given me full control of the simulation, I do not need your advice on what I should or should not do. Based upon the criteria you just gave me, I highly advise that you both prepare yourselves. You said to make it challenging, so things are going to get very interesting."

The tunnel shimmered before being replaced by a desert landscape. The desert floor appeared perfectly flat. Red Wing sent a sonic ping toward the horizon. The sound went out, but nothing came back.

"Hmm," said Red Wing's fighting-computer in their shared space. *"This is different. Your helmet's visual sensors do not detect any curvature to the desert floor out to a distance of... Well, out to a distance so far I cannot calculate the distance. What are your orders?"*

Before Red Wing could reply, a disturbance in the distance drew her attention. She cycled through four filters of her fighting-helmet before finding one that was able to pick up the source of the disturbance. She sent the data to her fighting-computer. A sonic image of three dozen creatures, some two-legged and some with four or more legs, were charging from a distance of two thousand meters.

"Margery," shouted the human. "I said double the number of attackers, not increase them fivefold."

"You put me in charge of the training simulation," said Margery. "I calculate an attack by three dozen demons will force the two of you to work together as a team. The battle will start in thirty seconds."

"Negative," said Richard. "End the simulation. We can't take on thirty-six demons at once. The halo-square's tractor beams are set at fifty percent. We could get hurt."

Red Wing detected a strange sound in the voice of the ship's computer when she replied.

"My simulation algorithm determined fifty percent was too low for optimum team training," said Margery. "I have taken the liberty of resetting the tractor beams to one hundred percent. I calculate both of you could die if you're not careful. I highly recommend that you work together and use extreme caution."

"Are you crazy?" shouted the human. "End simulation. Now! That's an order."

"Unable to comply," said Margery. "You put me in charge of the simulation, remember. I have blanked out the halo-square's exterior view so the rest of the crew does not know what is happening. I calculate a ninety-six percent probability the two of you can survive the assault if you work together. Otherwise, the odds of survival are extremely low."

Red Wing spread her wings and hissed. "Crosioians kill wizard scouts. We do not work with them."

"I calculate the ship's computer is right," said Red Wing's fighting-computer. *"The two of you must work together to survive."*

Reaching for her helmet, Red Wing tried pulling it off.

"Your equipment is part of the halo-square's simulation," said her fighting-computer. *"Your actual gear is on the workbench next to the wizard scout's real armor."*

"End simulation," Red Wing hissed. *"Hack into the ship's network and take control of the halo-square. That is an order."*

"Unable to comply," replied her fighting-computer. *"I am unable to bypass security programs. You have ten seconds before the lead demons make contact."*

Attempting to keep the growing nervousness out of her voice in front of the human, Red Wing hissed an argument at Margery. "We only have our phase weapons. We would have our other weapons for a fight of this magnitude on an actual mission."

"Your logic is flawed," replied Margery. "Nevertheless, I will make allowances."

The sand a meter to the front of Red Wing shimmered before solidifying into a plasma rifle. At the same time, she felt the sudden weight of a utility belt around her waist. Deactivating her phase spear, she shoved the half-meter-long metal rod into her scabbard as she dove for the ground. She came up spraying a line of plasma rounds from the rifle at the lead demon—a four-legged hound with two heads and glowing eyes. Red Wing detected energy building up in the creature.

"I calculate the demon is about to attack with magic," said her fighting-computer. *"A defensive shield is advisable."*

Throwing up a defensive shield, Red Wing got it formed just as two beams of light shot out from the lead demon's eyes. The magic slammed into the invisible barrier to her front. The shield held, but she was still knocked off her feet, into the soft sand. She was up in a flash, firing a steady stream of plasma energy at the lead demon's head. The plasma rounds ricocheted into the air before getting closer than two meters to the hound.

The human was to her left. Red Wing sensed a line of Power reach out and drill against the demon's shield. The demon's defensive shield gave way in an area the size of Red Wing's fist.

"Assistance," Red Wing ordered in her shared space.

The arm of her fighting-suit moved slightly left as it directed a stream of plasma energy from her rifle, through the opening in the shield. The balls of plasma energy tore into the demon's head, obliterating its face and eyes. The sonic point on Red Wing's heads-up display denoting the demon disappeared.

"One down, thirty-five to go," said her fighting-computer.

Before Red Wing could reply, she sensed three demons funneling Power into the second closest demon. It was a monstrous creature the width of her outstretched wings. The demon was covered with hundreds of paw-length spikes. The Power continued to flow into the spiked demon and build up at the ends of the spikes. Suddenly, the front and back of the demon exploded, sending hundreds of the glowing spikes in Red Wing's direction. She threw up a defensive shield, angling it slightly.

To Red Wing's surprise, the wizard scout stopped firing the

plasma rifle he'd picked up and dove behind her shield. He rolled on the ground twice before rising to resume firing just as the glowing spikes slammed into her shield. The defensive shield stopped all but a few of the spikes. A sharp pain in her right leg told her at least one of the spikes had penetrated her fighting-suit. She heard a cry of pain from her left. A quick sweep of her passive scan picked up a lessening of life force in the human.

"*Two spikes hit him in the left side of his chest,*" said her fighting-computer. "*I calculate he will be at less than peak efficiency for ten seconds.*"

It serves the human right for not putting up a defensive shield of his own instead of hiding behind mine.

"*That line of thinking is not logical,*" said her fighting-computer. "*I calculate you are going to need each other to survive this battle. There are thirty-five demons left. The wizard scout's shield only stops energy attacks. The spikes would have passed through unhindered. It would have been a waste of energy for him to create his own defensive shield.*"

Red Wing kicked herself for letting her fighting-computer get the best of her in the conversation. She knew she should have remembered the human's shield was deficient. The day after the wizard scout had trained her how to defend the link to her Power reserve and look for weak points in others, she'd discovered a flaw in his. After weaving a sonic wave into an active scan hidden by her best stealth shield, she'd probed the wizard scout's link. Although it was too well protected by traps for her to ever think of attacking his link, the sonic part of her scan had detected a flaw in his defensive shield. Due to a defect in the human's Power link, a minute blockage in the flow of energy used to create his defensive shields limited them to energy attacks only. It was not an uncommon problem among Crosioian scout candidates. She'd had the defect herself until one of the diviners at the scout school had repaired her blockage. Her instructor had told her the microscopic size of the blockage made it detectable only by the use of a sonic scan.

"*What are you thinking?*" asked her fighting-computer. "*You are keeping your thoughts in your private space. I calculate the attack by the next group of demons will occur in five seconds. Now may not be the best time to keep secrets from me.*"

Keeping her anger at the computer's insolence under control, Red Wing took a final look at the charging demons before making her decision. *I cannot defeat them all by myself,* she thought. *Like it or not, I am trapped in this simulation. I can be killed. So can the wizard scout. That would be unacceptable. I must be the one to kill him, and I must do it before the tribal council to regain my honor. I cannot allow him to die in a halo-square simulation.*

Reaching out with an active scan, Red Wing interwove a sonic scan and stealth shield together the way she'd done before. Probing along the human's link to his Power reserve, she found the spot with the defect. Touching the blockage with the sonic part of her scan, she repaired the deficiency. A Power surge from the wizard scout's link reached out and grabbed hold of her scan. She sensed a buildup of Power as the human prepared to attack.

With no time to speak before the wave of demons washed over them, Red Wing sent a thought through her fighting-computer, targeted at the wizard scout's battle computer. She sent an image of what she'd done. The line of Power from the human disappeared. At almost the same moment, four demons hit her defensive shield, swinging weapons of fire and energy. Her shield buckled and bent inward.

"Shield will be down in five seconds," said her fighting-computer. *"Simulated or not, I calculate an eighty-seven percent probability the demons are going to kill you."*

A second defensive shield appeared in front of Red Wing's shield. She sensed the frequency of the wizard scout in the Power weavings.

"Merge the two shields together," she heard the human's battle computer say over his external speakers. "I calculate it will triple the strength of your shields."

With nothing to lose, Red Wing attempted to merge her shield with the human's. For two heartbeats, nothing happened. Then she sensed the human's shield shift and flow into hers, strengthening it by the second. More demons joined their brothers in beating on the combined shields. The merged shields did not break. They didn't even buckle.

Dropping her now empty rifle, Red Wing pulled her phase spear from its scabbard and activated it in full destructive mode. *Now it is my turn,* she thought. Before she could swing her phase spear at the nearest demon, the air around her shimmered.

"End simulation," came the voice of Margery.

The demons along with the desert environment disappeared to be replaced by the *Defiant's* cargo bay. Red Wing looked down at her paw. It no longer clutched a phase spear, only empty air. She no longer wore her fighting-suit either. Only her sweat-matted fur covered her body. A movement to her left drew her attention. The wizard scout called Richard was rising from the metal deck, wearing only a pair of shorts. Blood covered his chest.

"Rick," shouted the elf Jeehana. She rushed forward and grabbed hold of the human's shoulders. "Are you okay?"

The wizard scout nodded his head, but Red Wing noticed him wince at the movement. "I'm fine," he said.

"The blood—" started the elf.

"Nothing a few more seconds of self-heal won't take care of," said Richard. "Everything is fine."

"It is *not* fine," said the elf. "This was supposed to be a simulation." She whirled toward the workbench where both Red Wing and Richard had left their equipment. "Now I see why you blanked out the halo-square, Master Nick. I should have known when I sensed Rick's pain. If you ever try something like that again, I swear—"

Red Wing didn't get the chance to find out what the elf was going to swear. The voice of the *Defiant's* captain came over the cargo bay's intercom. "Battle stations! This is not a drill. Make it snappy, people. We've gated into a hornet's nest."

The realization came over Red Wing that they were back in the physical dimension.

"That is correct," said her fighting-computer in their shared space. *"The* Defiant *gated back a few seconds ago. I calculate that is why Margery ended the training simulation so abruptly. We are now in Crosioian space two days' hyper-drive distance from Astaris."*

Although the little recon ship was not Crosioian, Red Wing had to give the crew credit. They responded to their captain's orders with efficiency and speed. Within seconds, only the wizard scout and the high priestess remained in the cargo bay with her. When Red Wing saw Richard stripping off his gym shorts and putting on his battle suit, she levitated her fighting-suit and other equipment to her and began doing the same. While Red Wing was quick in donning her equipment, the elf called Jeehana didn't wait for either the wizard scout or her.

Running up the stairs, the elf high priestess shouted over her shoulder, "I'll meet you in the cockpit!"

Since the wizard scout didn't reply, Red Wing said nothing either. She finished snapping on her utility belt at the same time the wizard scout slung his dimensional pack over his shoulder. When the human ran toward the stairs, Red Wing followed, grabbing her dimensional pouch and slinging it over her shoulder as she went. Up the stairs she went, right on the wizard scout's heels. As she ran, Red Wing reached out with her passive scan in an attempt to learn the source of trouble. The space surrounding the *Defiant* out to the max distance of her scan appeared clear.

"Your passive scan is limited to fifty thousand meters," said her fighting-computer in their shared space. *"According to the wizard scout's battle computer, the human's scan can reach out to a distance of a quarter of a light year in empty space. I calculate that perfecting your scans may be another area where you could benefit from additional training by the human wizard scout."*

Red Wing snorted. Even if the human could scan that distance in space, she was not about to ask him what was happening. *I will never admit he can do something I cannot,* she thought in her private space.

When the human whose name sounded like *Tribal Brother* reached the top of the stairs and entered the engine deck, he immediately transitioned to the next stairway that led to the floor designated for the mess area and crew quarters. An urge came over Red Wing to pass the human to prove her superiority, but she forced down the temptation. *I am no longer an adolescent trying to show up my rival,* she thought. Nevertheless, the desire to show who was the better scout remained. Sending out a sonic wave, Red Wing swiveled her ears and picked up the *Defiant's* security team lining up at the arms room. The human called Sergeant Hendricks was hurriedly passing out a mixture of magic and technological weapons to the dwarves. Then she was past the dwarves and taking the stairs three at a time. As she ran, Red Wing monitored the life forms in the ship. Only the dwarves, the wizard scout, and she were not already at their battle stations.

"You do not have a battle station," said her fighting-computer. *"Neither does the human or the high priestess."*

Ignoring her computer, Red Wing jumped over the mess table and levitated up the final half of the stairs to the cockpit, almost but not quite passing the wizard scout. He entered a split-second ahead of her. The ship's captain, Sergeant Ron, and the orc, Timerman, were sitting in the pilot and copilot seats respectively. The high priestess occupied the navigator's seat.

"What's up?" asked the wizard scout, panting for breath.

"See for yourself," replied Sergeant Ron as he jerked his thumb at the halo-pad located between the pilot and copilot's seats.

Since the halo-pad used visuals instead of a sonic image to display information to the *Defiant's* crew, Red Wing was forced to use her eyes to see what was happening. She drew in a breath. A sleek-looking inter-galaxy ship was docked with a much larger Crosioian transport ship. The two starships were connected together by a retractable metal docking tube bridging the twenty meters from the larger ship's airlock to the airlock of the smaller. Wedging in the inter-galaxy ship were two heavy Balorian destroyers to prevent the smaller ship from escaping.

"Who are they?" asked Richard.

"I don't rightly know," replied Sergeant Ron. "We gated out of the magic dimension a light-hour away from these yahoos. I've got our stealth shield activated, so I don't think they've spotted us yet. Margery says we can go around them without being detected if we're careful."

"I said there was an eighty-four percent probability we could escape detection," came Margery's voice over the cockpit's intercom. "I didn't say it was a given, so don't put words in my speakers."

The human captain glanced over his shoulder at the wizard scout and bared his teeth. "I stand corrected. I was just about to make contact with the triplets and have them gate us back to the magic dimension. I'm assuming you approve of my plan."

Before the wizard scout could reply, Red Wing hissed, "No! We cannot leave. We must attack."

The two humans, the orc, and the elf turned and looked at her. The sonic waves returning from their faces registered surprise.

The wizard scout was the first to recover. "Why not? Why must we attack?"

The range to the ships was still outside her passive scan, but even her poor eyesight could see the emblem on the inter-galaxy ship in the hologram. It was the royal yacht. The signal lights on the bow heralded the presence of the supreme leader on board. Even dishonored as she was, she could not leave the ship to its fate.

"That is the royal yacht," Red Wing said, trying to keep her explanation to the minimum. "It never travels inside the outer realms of the galaxy except in dire emergencies. We must save the one she is carrying."

The elf rose from her seat and stepped in front of Red Wing. She was tall compared to most humans.

"That is because she is an elf, not a human," said her mother's fighting-computer in the shared space of their minds.

Red Wing didn't bother acknowledging her fighting-computer's remark. Instead, she looked directly into the elf's eyes. The elf did not flinch.

"Who is the ship carrying?" asked the elf high priestess.

Red Wing swiveled her ears at the elf before turning them to the wizard scout. "The ship is carrying our supreme leader. I must save her." Her chest grew warm, but Red Wing's desperation forced the next words out despite the shame. "I cannot do it alone."

Richard stared at her for three heartbeats. "Are you asking for our help?"

Swallowing her pride, Red Wing tucked her wings tightly behind her back and spread her paws out before her. She sent out a sonic wave that all bats would instantly recognize. It was the call for assistance. For the benefit of those around her, she hissed the words aloud. "Yes, I need your help."

All eyes went to the wizard scout. Red Wing heard him glance at the *Defiant's* captain and the high priestess before looking back at her. "Then help you are going to get. I've a feeling this is why you were captured, and it's why we have all been brought together to this point in time." The wizard scout turned to Sergeant Ron. "We're outnumbered. I guess all we can do is go in and attack with all guns blazing."

The cockpit's intercom crackled. Margery said, "Uh, maybe not. Fortunately, battle computers think at nanosecond speed.

Nickelo, Red Wing's fighting-computer, and I have a plan."

A stream of data from her fighting-computer entered Red Wing's shared space. She nodded. "I like it," she said out loud, baring her teeth in a smile. "In fact, I like it a lot."

CHAPTER 23

Telsa sat on one of the many black boulders littering the landscape while keeping watch. Her three companions lay on the rocky ground taking a much needed rest. Even sprawled on the ground as they were, she could see the glows of the breathing spells around their faces. They didn't have battle suits. The spells were the only things keeping them alive in the land where they'd found themselves after walking through the gate.

In Telsa's opinion, only one word fully described their surroundings: *desolation.* A seemingly endless supply of volcanoes dotted the landscape. The dark rock composing most of the hilly terrain was lit only by the dim glow of the molten lava flowing down the mountainsides. Plumes of poisonous gas drifted in the air in lieu of life-giving oxygen. After two weeks in the demonic plane, Telsa was more than ready for a change of scenery.

"Careful what you wish for," said Raj in their shared space. *"At least you have not had to do any fighting."*

Telsa snorted a laugh. With her battle suit fully sealed against the noxious fumes of the air around her, the snort sounded more like a groan than a laugh. *"Fight what? We haven't seen anything to fight in the two weeks we've been in this Creator-forsaken place."*

Raj shouted over the battle helmet's external speakers, "Incoming!"

"I've got it," said Master Jathar as he sat up and drew a symbol in the air. He mouthed words Telsa heard but quickly forgot.

A translucent shield six meters across formed around Rembis,

Leethor, Telsa, and Master Jathar. A glow from above caught Telsa's eye as a ball of molten rock a meter in diameter came streaking out of the sky. The ball of lava hit the ground ten meters away.

Boom!

The molten material sprayed in all directions, splattering drops of hot liquid across the mage's defensive shield. None of the drops penetrated the magic barrier.

"Sorry," Telsa said. "My shield only protects against energy attacks."

"Pay it no mind," said Master Jathar as he dropped his shield to conserve Power. "We each have our unique skillsets."

"I suppose," Telsa said still feeling bad. "It seems like Rembis and you've done most of the work keeping us alive during the last two weeks. I haven't done much at all except keep watch while you guys sleep. I'm sorry I got you into this."

"You are sorry?" laughed Leethor. "If you think you have not been doing much, you should try spending some time in my boots. I am no mage." He hefted his bow in the air. "My skill as an archer has not come in too handy shooting down those molten balls of lava. At least you have your passive scan to give us some advanced warning of incoming fireballs."

Rembis stood and walked next to Leethor. Placing a hand on the elf's shoulder, he said, "Now don't start that again. I'll admit that Master Jathar and my magic have come in handy the past couple of weeks, but we've all got a purpose to serve. I for one am glad you are here with us." He turned to Telsa. "As for getting the rest of us into this, Leethor, Master Jathar, and I are old enough to make our own decisions. We chose to follow you through the guardian's gate." The old gnome gave a half smile. "I will admit I was hopeful we'd be able to walk back out the gate as easily as we walked in, but that shows what I know."

Telsa thought back to how the four of them had stepped through the gate into the demonic plane with the intention of doing a quick recon. They'd soon discovered the gate was firmly locked from the other side. No amount of spells from the two mages or attempts at teleportation had been able to get them out. They'd camped for a full week at the glowing sphere of green that was the gate before deciding they were wasting their time. No one was coming to rescue them. After taking a consensus, they'd decided to start walking and hope for the best. That had been a week ago.

The rocky terrain shook, followed by a distant rumble. Leethor pointed at a two-thousand-meter-high volcano fifteen kilometers away. "I think our friend over there is about ready to send a few more welcoming gifts our way. Perhaps we should eat and be moving on." The elf scout smiled. "I think I would have a little trouble trying to go back to sleep now anyway."

Rembis nodded his head. "Same here. Eat it is." Speaking a single word, the gnome reached out and plucked a lump of blackened material from the air. He broke it into three pieces and gave one piece each to Leethor and Master Jathar before beginning to chew on his part. With a less than enthusiastic look on his face, he swallowed. Holding out his lump to Telsa, he said, "Are you sure you don't want some? It's uh...delicious, in a horrible sort of way."

Master Jathar snorted. "Ha! Summoned bread is enough to keep a desperate elf alive, but it is only intended for short-term survival situations. I lost my taste for this stuff a week ago."

"Tell me about it," said Leethor, swallowing a bite of his own bread. "Meshoan and I had to live on this for a month once when we were running from some orcs up north." He glanced around and smiled. "Well, uh, not up north from here, obviously."

"Obviously," said Rembis. "But you're both right about the bread." The gnome glanced at Telsa and smiled. "I've gnawed on lumps of coal that tasted better."

"I'm sorry about that too," Telsa said. "I guess we should've brought more supplies." Unlike her companions, she didn't need to eat. Her battle suit took care of her every need as long as it remained sealed. Since the very air around them was poisonous, and since she couldn't cast breathing spells like the mages, she'd been bottled up for the past two weeks in her suit.

"Bottled up is such a harsh word," said Raj in their shared space. *"You should be grateful. You have only been in your suit for two weeks. Nickelo told me that Wizard Scout Shepard once spent thirty years sealed in his battle suit during a mission for* 'the One.'"

"Yeah, lucky me," Telsa said.

Once the elves and the gnome finished their sparse meal and

summoned water to wash it down, they all rose and began traveling in the same direction they'd been walking for the last week. Telsa led.

"There are no trails, no sun, and no stars to follow in this black, smoke-filled sky," she told her battle computer. *"If it wasn't for that sensation of Power ahead, I wouldn't have the faintest idea where to go. As it is, the Power draws me on like a moth to a flame."*

"You do know that analogy ends up with the moth being burned up by the fire, don't you?" asked Raj in their shared space.

"Believe me, I know. Unfortunately, that Power source is all we've got to go on. You haven't bothered giving any suggestions."

"Sorry, Wizard Scout. I have none to give. I make decisions based on data, and that has been plenty sparse during our stay here."

They walked for another four hours. While there was no trail, the floor of the valley they were in made for easy traveling. By the time the distant volcano erupted, they were well out of range. Just as Telsa was about to call a halt to give her companions another rest, Leethor abruptly stopped, nocked an arrow, and took aim to their right. Telsa swung her M12 in the same direction as she reached out with her passive scan. She neither saw nor sensed anything other than the same lava-filled landscape they'd been seeing for the past two weeks.

"Raj?" Telsa said.

"I am unable to pinpoint the source of whatever has drawn the elf's interest, Wizard Scout. Your passive scan picked up an energy flow twenty meters to your right, but the disturbance only lasted for thirty-five milliseconds."

Telsa was half tempted to fire off a burst of plasma rounds just to see if she could spook whatever was there, assuming anything was, but resisted the urge.

"I calculate it was smart to avoid doing that," said Raj. *"You only have your basic load of ammo with no way to resupply."*

"I wasn't actually going to do it," Telsa snapped. *"I was just thinking about it."*

"If you say so, Wizard Scout."

"What is it?" asked Rembis.

Both he and Master Jathar had stopped and were looking in the same direction as Leethor and her.

"I am not sure," Leethor admitted. He pointed at the area to the right with his nocked arrow.

Telsa noticed it was the same place where her passive scan had picked up the disturbance.

Shaking his head, Leethor said, "I sensed something in that spot. It's gone now, but I swear something was there."

Rembis pulled a wand from his belt and pointed it at the area as he shouted a single word. The air around Telsa and the others turned noticeably colder. A funnel of sleet and ice shot out the end of the wand, turning a five-meter-wide area on the ground white with frost.

The sound of a screech was followed by a fluttering of ice-coated wings. The air shimmered above the frost-covered ground, revealing a knee-high creature with purplish skin; a long, narrow face; and two bat-shaped wings. The creature began running toward the top of the hill, hissing as it went. Telsa aimed her rifle at the little monster's legs. Before she could fire, Master Jathar waved a hand in the air and mumbled several words. A green beam shot out from his left hand, bathing the creature in its light. The creature fell to the ground, frozen stiff.

"*Paralysis spell,*" said Raj making it sound like he was doing his wizard scout a favor by explaining something so obvious.

Telsa let it slide.

Leethor reached the creature first with sword drawn. He avoided touching the creature, but the tip of his sword hovered a mere handbreadth from the creature's throat, making it obvious he could kill whatever it was if desired. Rembis and Master Jathar ran up the hill with wands drawn and joined the elf scout. Telsa stayed back long enough to cast an active scan and probe the hillside for additional adversaries. Finding none, she joined her companions. Master Jathar waved a finger at the small creature. A bluish light enveloped its head. The creature bared its teeth and began hissing.

"I think it's trying to talk," said Rembis. He turned to Telsa. "Can your battle computer translate? I hate to waste Power on a spell unless needed. There might be others of its kind around."

"Ah," said the creature using a highly accented version of Portalis common. "I familiar with your language. Take cold away. I no like cold."

"Then tell us who you are and why you were spying on us," Telsa said, taking an instant dislike to the creature. Now that it was helpless, she sensed a distinct feeling of evil from the little monster. The two horns protruding from its forehead along with its red eyes did little to allay her dislike.

The external speaker on Telsa's battle helmet crackled. "It resembles a type of demon, or devil, if you prefer, from old Earth culture. It was called an imp. According to the information in my databanks, they were more mischievous than harmful."

"Yes," said the imp. "I not harmful. I friend. I everyone's friend."

"Then why were you spying on us?" Telsa asked. Her dislike for the miniature demon was undeterred by either her battle computer's explanation or the imp's claim of friendship.

"I not spying," said the imp baring wicked looking fangs. "I was only following to see what you doing so I could tell others and get a reward."

Leethor waved the tip of his sword at the imp. "That's called spying where I come from. Where are these others that you mentioned?"

The imp's eyes narrowed. "What others? Did I say others? No others. I alone. No friends, only me."

"Fine then," Telsa said. "Rembis, use that wand and freeze the thing in a block of ice so thick it will never get out."

"No!" screeched the imp. "Not cold. I hate cold. Others not here. They all still at gate."

Leethor gave the imp a little slap in the side with the flat of his sword. The green glow surrounding the little demon disappeared as the paralysis spell broke. Surprisingly, the imp didn't run. "Do not lie to us. We just came from the gate. The place was dead as a doornail."

The bare skin on the imp's forehead winkled, and it scratched its head with a clawed hand. After a second, the miniature demon hissed. "Ah, you must have been at smaller gate. Demon armies are not there. They are at big gate. The Dalinfaust gathered them all there, but now the Dalinfaust is back in prison." The imp hissed a laugh. "I do not think the Dalinfaust having a good time. The armies wait at the large gate anyway."

Continuing to cover the imp with his wand, Master Jathar

glanced at Telsa long enough to make eye contact. "It must be talking about the gate that is located in the Presence of the Lady. The demons almost got out through it. Maybe that's our way home."

Turning to the imp, Telsa said, "Take us to the main gate."

The imp's eyes grew round, and its wings began fluttering. "No! No!" it said in a voice laden with fear. "Have you not listened? The armies are there. Soul-eaters are there. Freeze me. Tear this body apart piece by piece, but I not take you there. I no be tortured for eternity because you are foolish mortals."

The imp's fear was so obvious Telsa momentarily felt sorry for the creature. A wave of evil mixed with fear swept her short-lived sympathy away.

Leethor stepped closer to the imp while keeping his sword pointed at the miniature demon. "You said you have been following us. What have you heard us say?"

The imp grew still before pointing at its chest with a leathery hand. "Me? Nothing. I no hear you say you look for yellow gem. No such gem, but even if you find it, you not able to escape. Only way is through rift, and it too well guarded."

"Careful," said Raj in Telsa's shared space. *"I calculate the imp is acting the part of the fool. The information in my databanks indicates imps are intelligent and devious."*

"Understood," Telsa said. *"I was thinking along the same lines."*

"Where is this rift you are talking about?" said Master Jathar.

"And *what* is it?" asked Rembis.

"Rift?" said the imp looking at the ground and kicking a small stone down the hillside. The imp watched the stone until it stopped against a larger rock. "Uh, I meant if there was a rift, it would be too well guarded for you to get through."

Telsa pointed the barrel of her M12 at the miniature demon.

It cringed.

"You know what a rifle is, don't you?"

The imp nodded. "I know. I been through rift. Bat-creatures use rifles. Bats foolish. They think they in charge. Demons hide them from their enemies. One day demons kill bats. One day soon I hope all mortals die." The imp glanced around and shook its head as if realizing who its audience was. "Uh, except for you, I mean. I your friend. I not drink warm, delicious blood. You can trust me." The miniature demon bared its teeth.

Whether the imp thought it was a smile, Telsa didn't know. The one thing she did know was that the creature was full of lies. "I wouldn't trust you if my life depended on it."

Frowning, the imp spread its hands. "Maybe it does. Maybe I show new friends yellow gem. Some near rift. Maybe I take you there if you give me some of your blood."

Telsa was tempted to kick the evil creature, but she refrained. Leethor, on the other hand, was not so well-controlled. The elf scout kicked the imp in the ribs, sending it rolling down the hill to land against a large rock. Leethor was at the little demon's side with raised sword before it stopped rolling.

"No kill," said the imp struggling to its feet. "No want your blood. I help you. I take you to rift. You go home. You see. I good friend."

Telsa exchanged glances with the two elves and Rembis.

They all nodded.

She turned to the little demon. "Very well. Take us to this rift and show us those yellow gems of yours." She pointed the barrel of her M12 at the creature. "If I even think you're leading us into a trap, I'll fill you full of holes and have Rembis here freeze you in a block of ice that will never melt. Do you understand?"

The imp nodded. "I understand. I friend. You see. Follow me. Must hurry. Long way. Soon more demons. Must be careful. Do what I say. Trust me. I friend."

"I calculate this is not going to end well," said Raj in their shared space. *"Do you want to know the odds?"*

"Not particularly," Telsa replied. *"Whatever they are, it's the only chance we've got."*

Raj gave a canned laugh. *"I was afraid you would say that, Wizard Scout. I will just say the odds are not good. I calculate we are going to need to rely on your luck."*

Telsa glanced around at the blackened landscape and plumes of volcanic ash. *"Somehow I don't think we're going to get lucky."*

"Neither do I, Wizard Scout," admitted Raj. *"Neither do I."*

CHAPTER 24

The lab on the Conglomerate dreadnaught *Planet Buster* was expansive for a starship. A dozen technicians in white lab coats worked at as many tables running experiments and monitoring computer screens. Tia sat at a small workbench in front of a high-security containment unit. She stared at the half-meter tall demon through the unit's observation window. The orange imp glared back at her, hatred evident in its gaze.

A tingling in the ring on her finger drew Tia out of her thoughts. After two weeks, she was no closer to figuring out how the imp had hidden the two fighters from her scans than she'd been when she started. Turning in her chair, she watched the lab's door and waited. Despite two weeks of being close to Matthew on a day-to-day basis, she still felt butterflies in her stomach whenever she sensed he was near.

The door slid open. In walked Matthew. When their eyes made contact, a broad smile matching hers spread across his face. A warm feeling passed down the link from his ring to hers. Behind Matthew came a young boy with dark, curly hair.

"Brachia!" Tia said. "I didn't think you'd be able to come. Dren said Rick had both of you busy inventorying warehouses and working on the teleporter."

Richard's ten-year-old adopted nephew broke out in a grin. "Inventorying's boring. Dren gets into that kind of thing. I don't. I was able to get the primary teleporter on Storage working an hour ago." The boy patted the computerized personal assistant, or C-PAST as it was called, attached to the side of his belt. "I figured it needed to be tested, so Omar and I volunteered, and here we are." Brachia's eyes turned to the containment unit. "Is that it? I've never seen one before. Does it talk?"

Tia shrugged. "It hasn't said a word since it's been here. The ship's computer ran a query on the central computer's database. If the central computer's information is correct, the thing can talk. It's just choosing not to do so."

Walking up to the observation window, Brachia stared at the orange creature. "I think it's kinda cute."

Matthew gave Tia a wink before walking up and placing his hand on the boy genius's shoulder. "Cute or not, it's deadly. It's a demon." Waving a hand around the lab, he said, "The *Planet Buster's* captain has given you free rein of the lab and personnel. Whatever you need is at your disposal. I hope you're as smart as Uncle Rick thinks you are, because we need answers, and we need them fast."

Without a hint of a smile, Brachia said, "Oh, I'm that smart. Just give me a few hours."

When Matthew glanced at her, Tia grinned. "You heard him, Matt. Why don't we leave Brachia to do whatever he needs to do? In the meantime, I've got a conference call with Liz in thirty minutes. I'd like you to be with me when I make it."

Nodding his head, Matthew said, "I think that would be advisable. If our Conglomerate fleets are to be of any help, we've got to stay informed."

Tia started to tell Brachia goodbye, but the boy had already placed a headset over his ears and was busy moving icons around on a computer display as fast as his fingers could fly. Shrugging her shoulders at Matthew, she headed for the door with the man she knew was her soulmate close on her heels. As soon as the door slid shut behind them, Tia glanced down the long metal-walled corridor both ways. It was empty. Wrapping her arms around Matthew's neck, she gave him a deep kiss. Neither breathed for several seconds. The sound of steps on the metal deck coming around the far corner cut their kiss short.

"I've missed you," said Matthew.

"And I you," Tia replied. "I don't ever want to be away from you again."

"Same here," said Matthew, "but this war has a nasty habit of getting in the way." He looked at Tia before gesturing down the left corridor. "I suppose we'd better get to the conference room and make your call before some admin type tries to drag one of us away for some emergency or the other."

Tia didn't want to go. She wished they had more free time together. *I should be grateful Liz hasn't ordered me back to fleet headquarters,* she thought. *If I hadn't convinced her the imp was important, I'm sure I'd be back there already. In the meantime, I'm going to take advantage of every minute Matt and I can be together while we have the chance.*

Five minutes later found Tia and Matthew sitting in an empty conference room, facing a hologram of Admiral of the Combined Fleets Bistos. To Liz's left sat her husband, Fleet Admiral Donovan.

"It's good to see you again, Tim," Tia said in greeting.

"You too, Tia," replied her brother-in-law with a wide grin.

The frown on Liz's face wasn't near as friendly. "Let's keep this meeting formal, shall we? I've got more on my plate than I can handle as it is without wasting time on small talk."

Tia felt her face growing warm until she noticed the winkles around the corners of her sister's eyes and the dry look of her skin. *She's getting old,* Tia thought. *I don't ever want to be a fleet commander if that's the price of command.* She felt the warmth of anger leave her face.

"Whatever you say, Admiral," Tia replied, trying to keep any hint of irritation out of her voice. *The last thing Liz needs at the moment is a family squabble,* she reasoned.

Her sister nodded. "So what have you found out about that demon of yours? Have you gotten it to talk?"

Shaking her head, Tia glanced at Matthew before looking back at her sister. "No, not yet. Brachia just arrived. He's already started experimenting on the imp. The boy's the smartest person I know next to his sister Dren. I'd say give it another day, and we'll have something for you."

"A day?" Liz said. "Even an hour might be too long. If the Crosioians are making widespread use of demons again, I've got to know it. Between the Trecorians, the Empire, and our other allies, we've assembled seventy-two thousand ships for the assault on Estos. It takes time to plan something this large. We've only got two weeks left. I need to know what we're up against, and I need to know it now."

"We'll get it for you, Sir," said Matthew. "I've assigned the best of the Conglomerate's scientists to the *Planet Buster* to help with the analysis of the demon."

Liz frowned again. "I would expect no less. Now tell me, Mr. Deloris, what is the status of the Conglomerate fleet. I'm told only five thousand ships have reached our assembly area so far."

To Matthew's credit he took the offhand critique in stride. "That's correct, Admiral. I've got eight thousand more in our fleet with my flagship *Planet Buster*. Uncle Felix has another twenty thousand assembling off Velos. They should be joining the combined fleet next week. We've, uh, had a little trouble clearing out some of the less enthusiastic leaders. That's been taken care of as of yesterday. You'll have a total of thirty-three thousand Conglomerate warships under your command by the end of next week. I guarantee it."

Liz stared at Matthew for a couple of seconds before nodding her head. "Very well, Matt. I'm taking your word for it." She turned to Tia. "Let me know as soon as Rick's nephew finds out anything. I need information. Get it."

The hologram blinked out.

Matthew turned to Tia and smiled. "Did you hear that? She called me Matt."

Tia smiled back. It was only a little step of acceptance, but she had no doubt it hadn't been a slip of her sister's tongue.

Thank you, Liz, Tia thought. *We won't let you down.*

CHAPTER 25

The supreme leader swung her phase rod in the tight confines of the docking tube that led to the transport's airlock. The two-meter-tall, clear-jelly creature didn't even try to dodge the blow. The microscopic explosions of phase energy tore into the monster, spraying bits of jelly onto the chest of the supreme leader's fighting-suit. The small pieces of jelly smoldered and smoked as they ate into the armor, but the suit's seal remained intact. A feeling of hate and loathing washed over her.

"You are hurting it, but not enough," came the thought of her fighting-computer in their shared space. *"Recommend you destroy something vital before the demon engulfs you like those two members of the medical team."*

Glancing into the bowels of the monster's jelly-like body, the supreme leader saw what remained of the *Gaze at the Stars's* chief medical officer and her assistant. Whatever acids the jelly creature contained in its body had already dissolved the medical team's bodies into a gray mush with only a few bones and bits of fur mixed in.

"Find me its vitals, and I will attack them," said the supreme leader. *"If all you are going to do is point out why my attacks are not working, then be quiet."*

"Compliance."

The supreme leader pushed out with telekinesis in an attempt to slow the jelly creature's advance. Instead of slowing, it spread out until its body filled the entire width of the docking tube from side to side and top to bottom. A dozen Balorian pirates and two more monstrosities that could only be other demons were visible through the clear spaces of the demon's body. A stream of plasma energy from one of the Crosioian guards behind the supreme leader struck the jelly creature. Other than spray a few bits of jelly onto the walls of the docking tube, the demon didn't appear harmed.

The royal yacht shook as an explosion echoed throughout the ship, knocking the supreme leader and the dozen guards to the floor. A paw-sized appendage of jelly reached out from the demon's body and snaked along the docking tube's floor. The supreme leader pulled her leg back, barely avoiding the creature's grasp. She heard a scream. Looking through the mass of jelly, she saw one of the Balorian pirates. He'd been knocked down during the explosion and was now struggling against one of the jelly-like appendages. The pirate's efforts to free himself did no good as he was slowly pulled into the demon's body. Apparently, the jelly demon could care less whether it ate pirates or Crosioians. The supreme leader noticed none of the pirate's companions attempted to help him.

"What was that explosion?" the supreme leader asked in her shared space.

"The ship's computer has gone offline," replied her fighting-computer. *"I calculate the pirates have taken out the* Gaze *at the* Stars's *bridge. The airtight doors are secure, but my sensors are detecting life forms being sucked out into space from three locations on the yacht. My calculations also indicate a seventy-five percent probability that the pirates' goal is to capture the ship's intergalactic-drive and take you prisoner."*

Making a snap decision, the supreme leader hissed a command over the yacht's ship-wide intercom. "All crew to the engine deck. We will make our final stand there. Chief engineer, prepare the self-destruct mechanism. We cannot allow them to take the intergalactic-drive."

Taking a final futile swing at the jelly creature, the supreme leader turned and ran after the security team, covering their retreat with her defensive shield. Beams of plasma and phase energy passed within a paw's width of her head and shoulders as two members of the yacht's security team continued firing at the jelly demon. She sensed no pain from the creature, only darkest hate.

How can there be demons? the supreme leader wondered as she turned and fired with her phase pistol to allow the security team to withdraw through the yacht's open airlock. *My first act on becoming supreme leader was to order their deaths along with that of their magic-using minions.*

"Are you asking me?" said her fighting-computer. *"I do not have that information in my database. I calculate a fifty-seven percent probability someone failed to follow your orders. By the way, I monitored the captain's distress call before the bridge was destroyed. The closest Crosioian warship will be here in an hour and twenty-two minutes."*

Reaching the end of the docking tube, the supreme leader stepped through the yacht's airlock as the last member of the security team sealed the airtight door behind her. A glance through the porthole confirmed the jelly demon was almost to the airlock door. Behind it were a half-dozen other creatures from the darkest pits of hell, backed up by a wave of pirates.

"Uh," said her fighting-computer, *"I calculate you are not going to be able to hold out for another hour and twenty-two minutes."*

The supreme leader turned to the yacht's security team. "To the engine deck. We will show these pirate scum and their demon allies how real soldiers fight. No one can help us, but it does not matter. We will die with honor!"

"We will die with honor!" shouted the security team.

The supreme leader's chest swelled with pride. *Honor,* she thought. *That is all that matters.*

CHAPTER 26

Richard held onto the back of the X-shuttle's pilot seat and peered through the windscreen over Timerman's shoulder. Four ships in the distance reflected light from the sun. The teenage orc zoomed the windscreen in on the ships. A beam of red lashed out from one of two heavy destroyers and raked along the bow of the smallest of the four ships. A blast of air shot out into space along with large pieces of metal and what appeared to be several bodies.

"I count twenty-two bodies expelled out of the hole in the yacht's bridge," said Nickelo over the battle helmet's external speakers for everyone's benefit. "Based upon the combined results of Rick and Red Wing's active scans, I count three thousand, two hundred, and thirteen life forms between the four ships. From the life frequencies, some of the occupants are demons and magic users. I also calculate there are Thargs and Dragars on board the troopship."

"How do you know what Red Wing's scan is picking up?" Richard asked in his shared space.

"Her fighting-computer told me," replied Nickelo keeping the reply silent between them. *"She may be inside a Crosioian scout's fighting-helmet, but she is still one of my species. 'The One' has activated a special communication channel between us for this fight. Nice of him, don't you think?"*

Richard kept his opinion of what he thought of 'the One' to himself.

"We must hurry," said Red Wing from her position behind Richard. "I sense the crew of the royal yacht assembling on the engine deck. They will use the ship's self-destruct to blow up the royal yacht before they will allow one of our intergalactic-drives to fall into enemy hands."

Turning his head to look at the scout, Richard saw her standing next to his bondmate. He switched his gaze to Jeena. She was dressed in power armor with a phase pistol in her left hand and the Staff of the Lady of the Tree in her right. Three wands and a wicked-looking dagger were shoved into her suit's belt next to two anti-personnel grenades. His bondmate glared at him with molten-silver eyes through her helmet's clear visor. He didn't need the emotions coming down their bond link to know she was more than a little miffed. Richard hastily looked away and glanced at the other shuttle occupants. Arranged on both sides of the X-shuttle's walls were the entire crew of the *Defiant* with the exception of Sergeant Ron, Sergeant Hendricks, Charlie, Daniel, Asquan, and Bright Wing.

"I think your elf is still peeved at you for telling her she cannot go in the first wave with Red Wing and you," said Nickelo.

"Whatever," Richard said knowing full well that even if he'd told her she could go, she couldn't have done it. *"She's not a shifter. That's not my fault."*

"Try explaining that to your elf," said Nickelo in a voice that sounded more than a little amused.

A growl drew Richard's attention to his left, into the glowing red eyes of Sheeta. For once the big Dolgar had come at his first call. The wolf-like dolgar's head was at the same height as his. Sheeta glanced at Red Wing before turning back to Richard and growling.

"No," Richard said using emotion-speak. *"I don't care if you're hungry or not. The Crosioian scout is not food. I already told you she's our ally."*

Sheeta growled. So did his mate Sheba from her position next to Jeena.

"I'm sure it is confusing trying to keep track of who is food and who isn't," Richard said, quickly growing tired of trying to reason with the two dolgars. *"You're just going to have to deal with it."* He had a thought. *"And don't eat any of the Crosioians on the ship either, until we figure out if they're friendly or not."*

Nickelo laughed in their shared space. *"Just be grateful your dolgars didn't bring their pups with them like you asked. I calculate they're not as particular about what's food and what's not as Sheeta and Sheba."*

"Yeah, well, it would've been nice if they'd at least have brought the stallion with them," Richard countered. *"I included the emotion for him when I sent out the call for help. That would've made getting behind the attackers a lot easier. Are you sure whoever's in those destroyers haven't spotted the X-shuttle yet?"*

"Are they trying to fill us full of holes?" asked Nickelo. *"Trust me. The stealth capabilities of this shuttle are beyond anything I've ever encountered. I calculate they won't know we're here until Timerman drops the stealth shield and begins his attack run."*

Richard wasn't so sure, but the die was cast and there was no time for second guessing now.

Another red beam lashed out from one of the destroyers and tore a gouge along the side of the yacht. Several more life forms disappeared from Richard's heads-up display.

"We must hurry," hissed Red Wing. "Go straight in. No time to recon properly."

"You mentioned something about a self-destruct," said Felspar, the leader of the *Defiant's* security team. "I kinda prefer the slow and steady approach with a thorough recon as we go. What happens if we start entering that yacht of yours and some yahoo decides to blow it to bits?"

Red Wing seemed to try and spread her wings, but they couldn't go far in the crowded shuttle. "Then we die with honor," she hissed.

"I tell you what, Red, old buddy," Richard said. "You can die with honor if you want. As for the rest of us, my plan is to have us all live to fight another day." He glanced back out the windscreen and watched another red beam of energy from one of the destroyers blow a hole in the Crosioian yacht. "On the other hand, we don't have time to beat around the bush." Patting Timerman on the shoulder, Richard said, "Take us in. Full throttle."

"Roger that," replied the teenager as he pushed forward on the accelerator handle. "Drop point in five seconds."

Glancing at Red Wing, Richard wrapped himself in Power and caused it to shimmer. He noticed Red Wing do the same as she turned translucent. So did Sheeta. Richard turned his head to look at Jeena. "I'll see you on board."

The elf's molten-silver eyes swirled, accompanied by a feeling of concern through their bond link. "Be care—"

"Drop!" shouted Timerman.

Richard shifted into the void and levitated through the X-shuttle's deck. He sensed more than saw the shuttle zoom past. It quickly disappeared from his passive scan. As soon as it did, he levitated through the vacuum of space, toward the rear of the royal yacht. Since Red Wing had left an opening in her stealth shield for him, Richard had an easy time locating her with his passive scan. He let the scout lead the way as she levitated the two hundred meters to a part of the yacht's hull located near a strange-looking exhaust tube.

"I gather that's the exhaust for the intergalactic-drive the scout mentioned," said Nickelo. *"The hyper-drive's exhaust is located farther back."*

Still in the void, Red Wing's translucent form turned and looked at Richard. Her hiss came over the battle helmet's intercom and was immediately translated in his shared space by Nickelo.

"I lead," said Red Wing. "You follow. Do not kill the yacht's crew."

"What if they shoot at me?" Richard asked.

The scout shrugged her armored wings. "They probably will." She hissed a laugh. "Die with honor."

"I'm not going to—"

Red Wing didn't wait for Richard to finish. She levitated through the yacht's hull. Richard did the same, shifting out of the void to conserve Power as soon as he was inside. The green point of Red Wing's phase spear flew past his head and into the chest of a four-armed creature in power armor. Richard recognized it as one of the furry-haired Thargs. The rifle in the Tharg's hands clattered to the floor as its owner bounced off the wall of the narrow corridor where Richard found himself. A half-dozen Thargs in armor and twice as many human pirates wearing an assortment of armor and weapons were to his front with their backs to him. Mixed in with them were two Dragars. Richard sensed large Power reserves coming from them.

"Magic users," said Nickelo.

Beyond the Dragar mages were four monstrosities that reeked of evil. Richard didn't need his battle computer to tell him they were demons. He'd fought similar types many times in the past. Two were orange, humanoid-looking demons with horns protruding from their overly large heads. They were a good arms-length taller than him. Each of the orange demons held a glowing sword in one hand, the length of a man, and a fiery whip in the other. Next to the orange demons were two purple-colored demon-hounds with four snake heads protruding from their necks.

"Crap," Richard thought. *"Why do I always get stuck fighting those time-bubble-creating, self-healing ones?"*

"You don't," said Nickelo. *"So stop complaining. Just deal with it."*

One of the orange demons snapped out its whip toward one of a score of Crosioians twenty meters down the corridor. The bats were firing at the demons for all they were worth. The Crosioians' phase and plasma rounds were hitting an invisible shield to the demon's front and ricocheting off. The flaming length of the demon's whip passed through the shield and wrapped around a Crosioian's neck. When the demon pulled the whip back, the bat's head came with it while the body remained where it was, collapsing in a heap on the deck. Despite the situation, Richard noticed a lack of blood from the gaping neck wound.

"I calculate the fire on the whip cauterized the flesh," said Nickelo. *"Now do something before the demons detect you and decide to try the same trick on your battle suit."*

A Crosioian on the far side of the demons was dressed in a scout's fighting-suit. The scout gave a loud hiss. "You shall not pass!" Charging forward, the scout threw her activated phase spear as she ran. An explosion of green illuminated the corridor as the spear passed through the demon's shield. The orange demon twisted to the side, avoiding the point of the phase spear. The scout's weapon flew past the demon and embedded in the chest of an unlucky pirate instead. One of the demon-hounds howled and leaped forward, passing through the orange demon's defensive shield, straight for the scout's throat. All four snake heads reached out as if anticipating the taste of Crosioian flesh.

"I am in contact with that scout's fighting-computer," said Nickelo in their shared space. *"The scout is the Crosioians'*

supreme leader. I calculate the yacht's crew will immediately detonate the ship's self-destruct if their supreme leader is killed. I highly recommend you do something to prevent that from occurring."

Praying the two hounds' links to their Power reserves weren't protected, Richard reached out with an active scan, split it in two, and probed both links at the same time. He immediately pulled the two scans back. *"Trapped,"* Richard thought. *"So much for that idea."*

Before Richard could do anything else, Red Wing bulled her way through the mass of Thargs and pirates. Reaching out with a paw, she grabbed the tail of the leaping time-hound. Jerking back, she threw the four-legged demon straight toward the orange demon that had dodged the phase spear. Again the orange demon dodged to the side. The time-hound flew past with its snake heads snapping at anything in range. Two pirates and a Tharg got bit as the hound hit one of the magic-using Dragars. The Dragar was in the middle of waving its lizard-skinned hands and shouting words when the hound hit it full in the chest. Both the hound and the Dragar went flying back. Sensing a buildup of energy from the Dragar's interrupted spell, Richard threw up a hasty defensive shield, angling it toward the rear of the corridor. He smiled as he sensed another group of Thargs and pirates coming around the intersection behind him.

Boom!

The Dragar's spell backfired in a blast of orange and green energy. The time-hound and Dragar magic user were obliterated along with four of the Thargs and half a dozen pirates. Even one of the orange demons was thrown off its feet by the blast. Residual energy from the malformed spell ricocheted off Richard's shield and surged back down the corridor, reaching the four-way intersection behind him at the same time a group of armored pirates came running around the corner. The force of the blast threw the lead pirates back against those following close on their heels. They all went down in a jumble of legs, arms, and firing weapons.

Deactivating his defensive shield, Richard swung out with his phase rod at a nearby Tharg while diving for the remaining Dragar. The end of his phase rod caught the Tharg in the side of the helmet and glanced off. The deflected blow didn't save the Tharg. Richard sensed the furred head inside the helmet shatter as microscopic explosions of phase energy tore into the Tharg's flesh, bone, and brain matter. As he continued his dive, he pulled the trigger of his M63 lightweight plasma assault rifle, sending a stream of plasma rounds into the back of the last magic-user's head. Blood flew out of the man's forehead, splattering onto an orange demon's back as the plasma energy tore the Dragar's skull to shreds.

"Lucky for you the mage's defensive shield was only formed to his front," said Nickelo.

"You know what they say," Richard said as he swung his phase rod at a nearby pirate. *"Luck aces skill anytime."*

"No it doesn't," replied Nickelo. *"That's not even logical. Who says that?"*

Swinging at a pirate in the act of turning around, Richard caught the man in the chest with the tip of his phase rod. *"I say it. That's who."*

Red Wing engaged one of the orange demons with her phase spear. The demon countered with a wide swing of its glowing sword. The blade of the demon's weapon passed through the bodies of two pirates, cutting them in half before it was stopped by the green phase energy of Red Wing's spear. The remaining time-hound spun and snapped out at Red Wing's left leg as one of its snake heads bit into the scout's arm. Red Wing hissed a scream but pushed forward her attack on the orange demon, forcing it back a step.

Richard sensed Power to his left.

"It's the supreme leader's phase spear," said Nickelo in their shared space. *"It's still sticking in the chest of one of the pirates."*

Reaching out with telekinesis, Richard jerked the supreme leader's phase spear free as he let his M63 hang by its sling over his shoulder. Propelled by telekinesis, the phase spear flew into his right hand. He jammed the spear's green point between the shoulder blades of the time-hound that was attacking Red Wing. The four-legged demon howled in pain as all four snake heads turned and struck at the handle of the phase spear. Richard sensed Power form around the time-hound. Then the Power blinked out, leaving the crumbled and bloody body of the demon-hound and four withered snake heads in its place.

"What happened?" Richard asked. *"I thought for sure it was creating a time-bubble. It should have healed itself and been attacking me again."*

"I calculate the demon succeeded in creating its time-bubble," replied Nickelo. *"The phase spear must have continued to damage the hound faster than it could self-heal inside the time-bubble. The end result is that it is dead. The other time-hound was disintegrated by the Dragar's spell. I recommend you don't waste time counting your blessings. You need to get busy. There's still over three thousand of the enemy left on these ships, and a lot of them are heading this way."*

The enormity of what Richard had gotten the *Defiant's* crew and himself into suddenly hit him. *What was I thinking? And where the hell is Sheeta? He should be here helping.*

A dark shadow came out of the side wall of the corridor and grabbed hold of the second orange demon's throat. Richard sensed life force being sucked out of the demon as Sheeta converted the life force into energy. The big dolgar attempted to shift the orange demon into the void. The dimensional shift didn't work. The orange demon stabbed upward with its glowing sword. Its strike was off balance from the force of Sheeta's attack, so the blade only made a shallow slice across the dolgar's hindquarters. Sheeta let go of the orange demon's throat, shifted into the void, and disappeared into the bulkhead as a second sword blow slammed against the metal wall just missing the dolgar's disappearing head.

Taking advantage of Sheeta's attack, Richard stabbed outward with his left hand. The point of his phase rod caught the orange demon in the throat, entering the bloody wound created by the dolgar's bite. The demon tried to scream as the microscopic explosions of phase energy tore out its throat. It only succeeded in making a pitiful gurgling sound as it collapsed to the floor.

"It's not out yet," said Nickelo. *"It's trying to self-heal."*

Power from the demon surrounded its throat. Before the healing could take effect, Richard dove on top of the demon's chest and forced the tip of his phase rod into its eye socket and up into its brain. He wiggled the handle of the phase rod back and forth, sensing the phase energy destroying the brain matter as fast as the demon's self-heal could replace its damaged flesh.

"It's taking too long," said Nickelo. *"The X-shuttle has*

dropped off the security team and the others near the yacht's airlock. Your elf and half of the team are on their way here, but they're running into problems of their own. Oh, and just in case you're interested, a Tharg is about to put a few phase rounds in the back of your head. Just a little FYI."

Making a command decision, Richard released the handle of his phase rod, leaving the tip in the orange demon's skull while he continued to shake the handle with telekinesis. He turned and threw up a defensive shield just as a Tharg holding two rifles in its four hands fired both weapons in his direction. A score of phase rounds hit Richard's shield and bounced off, tearing their way through two armored pirates. Both soldiers went down as the heavy phase rounds blew holes in their chest armor. At the same time, Richard sensed movement in the void under the Tharg. A split-second later, a dark dolgar head with a mouthful of teeth bit into the Tharg's leg and pulled the screaming four-armed creature into the floor.

Boom! Boom! Boom!

A serious of explosions echoed down the corridor from beyond the four-way intersection. Richard sensed Power drain from Jeena's reserve as a feeling of what he could only describe as exhilaration came flowing down their bond link.

"Hmm," said Nickelo. *"I think your elf is a little on the bloodthirsty side. I calculate close contact with you is rubbing some of your bad qualities off on her."*

Richard didn't bother replying to his battle computer even though he had a feeling Nickelo was right. Instead, he drew five percent of his Power from his reserve and sent it down the link to Jeena.

"By the way," said Nickelo. *"That orange demon's avatar is dead, so you can stop twisting your phase rod now. No use wasting Power on telekinesis when it's not needed."*

Spinning around, Richard turned in the direction of the remaining orange demon. It was locked in combat with both Red Wing and the scout Nickelo had said was the supreme leader. The supreme leader had somehow reacquired her phase spear and was beating on the orange demon's defensive shield in tandem with Red Wing. Richard recognized the alternating attack methodology his father and he had once used against the dark elf Crendemor. He mumbled a silent prayer thanking the Creator for giving him the sense to teach the technique to Red Wing.

A sense of evil behind Richard drew his attention away from the orange demon. He spun around, spraying plasma rounds from his M63 as he turned. The plasma rounds hit a clear jelly-like mass moving down the hallway. The plasma rounds did no damage to the creature other than hit a few bones and bits of fur and armor that were visible within the demon's gelatin body. The jelly-like creature completely covered the corridor from deck to ceiling, engulfing everything in its path.

"You've fought them before," said Nickelo.

"I don't remember," Richard said trying to remember any mission for *'the One'* where he might've encountered the demon type before.

"Well, it's in my databanks," said Nickelo as a series of images with Richard locked in battle in some lava-lit tunnel flashed in Richard's shared space. In the images, he was fighting against a jelly creature similar to the one he faced now.

Latching onto the past memory, Richard decided on an attack strategy. Reaching out with a line of Power, he grabbed hold of a nearly invisible organ inside the jelly creature and jerked back with telekinesis. A fistful of clear jelly came out and splashed against the metal deck, spraying bits of gelatin into the air. The body of the jelly-like demon collapsed in on itself while turning into a pool of steaming goo. Before Richard had time to celebrate his victory, a hulking mass of tentacles and purple flesh came around the corner of the intersection. The demon resembled a ball of purple more than any humanoid form. It was followed by four demon-hounds. The four-legged demons weren't time-hounds, but their flaming eyes, finger-length fangs, and acid-dripping mouths told him they weren't going to be pushovers.

Grabbing his phase rod with telekinesis, Richard pulled it out of the dead demon's skull and into his waiting hand. He barely got his gloved fingers wrapped around the handle when the first of the four hounds came leaping at his face. A dark shadow came out of the ceiling, latching a mouthful of teeth around the back of the hound's neck as Sheeta disappeared into the metal planks of the deck taking the hound with him. Swinging his phase rod at the second hound, Richard broke its back.

A third hound made a try for Richard's throat, but he felt his right arm move to align the barrel of his M63 at the demon-hound's open mouth. A stream of plasma energy burst out of the back of the demon's head, splattering dark goo across the eyes of the fourth hound. A beam of green energy struck the last hound in the side. The demon stiffened and fell to the floor. Richard looked past the still charging purple demon's waving tentacles to see Jeena standing at the corridor's intersection, holding a wand in her left hand and a staff in her right.

The massive ball of purple which was the remaining demon struck out with a tentacle in Jeena's direction. A tall elf, also in power-armor, stepped beside Jeena and waved a hand. Richard recognized Comstar's frequency as the old elf formed a ball of magic to his front. The ball shot out, striking the purple mass in the center. The demon stopped in its tracks, but its tentacle was still able to wrap around Jeena's waist. The tentacle lifted her up and slammed her armored-head against the ceiling. Sheba ran around the intersection and leaped into the air, biting into the tentacle and using her weight to pull it down to the floor.

A short, potbellied form stepped around the same corner. It was the dwarf Stovis. The muscular dwarf swung a battle axe at the tentacle, cleaving the piece of slimy meat in half. Jeena fell to the floor, kicking out at the tentacle as it continued to move on the deck as if still seeking a victim. A glance at Jeena's life energy on his passive scan told Richard that his bondmate was unharmed. She was up in a flash, swinging the Staff of the Lady of the Tree at a second tentacle. A flash of blue filled the corridor. When the flash disappeared, a blackened tentacle lay smoldering on the deck.

Running forward, Richard jumped into the air and knocked another tentacle out of the way with his phase rod as he went. When he body-slammed the ball of purple flesh of the demon's body, Richard stabbed downward with the end of his phase rod. The meter-long length of creallium and phase energy entered the purple mass, causing the festering flesh to twist and bang against the walls of the corridor. A wave of magic shot out from inside the demon, tearing through Richard's battle suit and into his flesh as it tried to rip him apart from the inside out. Richard screamed as his self-heal attempted to heal the damage, but the pain was more than he could bear. Blackness began replacing light as he felt his hand losing its grip on the handle of his phase rod.

"Don't pass out," warned Nickelo. *"The other's need you. Your elf needs you."*

Thoughts of Jeena drove the pain back enough to allow him to maintain his grip on his phase rod. He funneled Power from his own reserve into the weapon. In spite of his pain, he sensed the explosions of phase energy inside the demon increase three-fold. A feeling of warmth encompassed him. He sensed Jeena's frequency in the magic. The feeling of warmth spread, forcing the demon's spell out of his body. A second later, the purple demon exploded. The blast of magic energy sent Richard flying through the air back the way he'd come.

Rolling on the floor, Richard landed between the feet of the last orange demon.

"How'd that happen?" Richard said in his shared space. *"I thought it had a defensive shield up."*

"It does," replied Nickelo. *"The demon's concentrating its energy on the parts of the shield being attacked by the two scouts. You slipped through a weak point. I suppose you were right. Sometimes luck does ace skill. Don't spend too much time patting yourself on the back though. I calculate this demon is stronger than the other orange demon was."*

Looking up between the demon's legs, Richard remembered how he'd once beaten a beefed-up Minotaur by shoving a sword up the creature's anus. He prepared to do the same with his phase rod. Before he could act, he realized he had a problem. *"It doesn't have an anal opening,"* he said.

"Hmm," replied Nickelo sounding amused. *"That does present a problem with your little plan, doesn't it? Maybe you should have discussed attack options with me first. According to the information in my databanks, very few demons actually eat solid food. Consequently, they have no need for a body part to discard waste material."*

Before Richard could reply, the orange demon broke off combat with the two Crosioian scouts long enough to stab downward with its sword.

"Shield!" yelled Nickelo.

Reacting to his battle computer's warning, Richard threw Power to his front in a haphazard defensive shield. Surprisingly, the demon's sword glanced off and penetrated the metal deck halfway up to its hilt.

Raising his phase rod for a counterattack, Richard said, *"Cool. My shield stopped a physical attack."*

"The scout told you she fixed the problem with your defensive shield," said Nickelo. *"I calculate a hundred percent probability she was correct. Now, drop it to conserve Power and put this demon out of action."*

"Roger that," Richard replied as he swung his phase rod at the base of the demon's spine.

Before the rod could make contact, Nickelo shouted, *"Shield!"*

Throwing up another defensive shield, Richard got it formed just in time to deflect a length of green phase energy into the deck.

"Human!" came a hiss as the supreme leader's phase spear pulled out of the metal deck and started to come down again at Richard's head.

Still lying between the demon's legs, Richard glanced up to see Red Wing knock her supreme leader's spear aside with the end of her own weapon.

"No!" hissed Red Wing. "Ally!"

Richard wasn't sure what the supreme leader would've done next, but the orange demon made the decision for her by pulling it's sword out of the deck and swinging the glowing blade at the Crosioian's neck. The supreme leader tried raising her spear to block the blow, but it was obvious she was going to be a split-second too late.

"The supreme leader's old," said Nickelo in their shared space. *"Her reflexes cannot compete with those of a younger scout like Red Wing."*

As Red Wing raised her spear in a futile attempt to distract the demon from her supreme leader, Richard reached out with a line of Power and wrapped it around the demon's sword. As he pulled back on the blade with telekinesis, he struck the base of the demon's spine with his phase rod.

Crack!

The sound of breaking bones was music to Richard's ears. The demon roared a scream but instead of falling, the orange-colored nightmare wrapped Power around itself and remained standing.

"It's using telekinesis to stay on its feet," said Nickelo. *"At*

least your attack kept it from cutting off the Crosioian's head. I calculate that's a plus."

Richard sensed anger and pain from the link to his bondmate. A quick glance at his passive scan told the story. Jeena, Comstar, and Stovis were no longer at the intersection. They had rejoined the *Defiant's* crew near the docking tube that connected the yacht to the transport ship. His friends were locked in battle with a mass of life forms that were trying to force their way out of the tube. He sensed a dozen demons mixed in with the attacking pirates, along with a score of magic users. The size of the Power reserves of the opposing mages told Richard his bondmate and the valiant group of defenders with her were hopelessly outgunned.

Fury built up inside Richard. He let go of the handle of his M63 and pulled his .44 caliber AutoMag from its holster. Jamming the barrel of the high-powered pistol against the area between the orange demon's legs where its anus should have been, he squeezed as fast as he could pull the trigger. The first of the heavy brerellium steel rounds penetrated the thick demon skin. The second slug entered its body cavity. Pulling the AutoMag's barrel back, Richard replaced it with the tip of his phase rod and shoved it up the opening with the entire force of his battle suit's assistors behind it. Black goo dripped down the brerellium rod as Richard sensed microscopic explosions of phase energy tearing apart the internal organs of the orange demon's avatar. The demon screamed once before collapsing to the floor.

"Is it dead?" Richard asked as he shoved the demon's legs away from his head and tried to wipe the black goo off of his visor.

"As a doornail," replied Nickelo. *"Which by the way is how I calculate your elf and the rest of the* Defiant's *crew are going to wind up if you don't get off your feet and help them."*

Leaving the few remaining pirates around him to the two scouts, Richard jumped to his feet and headed toward the intersection. Neither Jeena nor any of the *Defiant's* crew was in sight, but the flurry of energy beams passing across the intersection told him his friends were in heavy combat. He sensed a build-up of energy from one of the demons near the troopship's airlock.

Boom!

A bright flash intermixed with a thick smoke came rolling past the intersection.

"Jeena!" Richard yelled as he picked up speed to the battle suit's maximum.

"She's fine," said Nickelo. *"Comstar and the gnome mages are funneling Power into her defensive shield. It's holding for now. The other demons and magic users are following suit and funneling their own Power to the most powerful of the demons. I calculate you need to hurry."*

Sending another five percent of his Power down his bond link to Jeena, Richard accompanied it with an emotion that meant only one thing. *"Hold on. I'm coming."*

CHAPTER 27

Once Timerman dropped the *Defiant's* crew into the opening created by the explosion in the yacht's bridge, he pulled the X-shuttle back a light second to wait for Sergeant Ron's orders. The next five minutes were the longest of his life.

At least the two destroyers have stopped firing at the yacht, he thought. *From the chatter on the intercom, the pirates have boarded the ship.* He slapped the armrest of the X-shuttle's pilot seat with the palm of his left hand. *My friends are fighting for their lives, and I'm sitting here doing nothing.*

Unable to stand it any longer, Timerman punched the intercom icon on the armrest of his pilot's seat. "Sergeant Ron, I am in position. Do you want me to start my attack run?"

The agitated voice of the *Defiant's* captain sounded loud and clear over the X-shuttle's intercom. "Negative. Now stay off the air until I give you the order. The last thing we need is for those destroyers to pick up a signal from some young, inexperienced fool before we start our gun runs."

Timerman felt his face grow warm and glanced over his shoulder, knowing before he did that no one else was inside the X-shuttle to witness his embarrassment. The cabin was as empty as he knew it would be. He checked the tactical hologram between the pilot and copilot's seats. The white dot denoting Asquan in the dragon-fighter was at his seven o'clock position exactly five light seconds behind him. A second white dot at his five o'clock showed the position of Daniel in the Zip fighter. A green dot on the tactical hologram indicated the location of the *Defiant* a full ten light seconds behind the two fighters.

"Maybe the *Defiant* should be a little closer," Timerman said out loud.

The voice of Margery came over the shuttle's intercom. "Everyone is exactly where they should be. This is your first major engagement in a ship other than the *Defiant*. Rick's plan is a good one. Don't start second guessing it now. We can't start our attack on the destroyers until our team on the yacht has its airlock secured. Once that happens, you won't have time to ask questions. You'll be too busy dodging plasma beams and missiles from the destroyers to worry about where everyone else is."

Sufficiently chastised, the teenage orc did another check of the X-shuttle's weapons systems. The mix of magic and technology weapons Sergeant Hendricks had installed on the X-shuttle was ready and waiting. He grasped the shuttle's joy stick with his right hand. The gray calloused skin of his palm completely covered the small lever.

"The blasted thing's too small for my hand," he said speaking more to take his mind off the wait than he was worried about the size of the controls.

"The X-shuttle was made with humans in mind," replied Margery. "You are an orc. Now get ready. Jeehana and her team are almost at the airlock. I calculate it will not be long now."

Touching an icon on the control panel with his left hand, Timerman lined up the X-shuttle's gunsight on the nearest destroyer's engine. *I've got to take the engine out on the first pass,* he thought. *The others are depending on me. I cannot let them down.*

"Ten seconds," said Margery. "Warm up the engines on your missiles."

"Affirmative," Timerman said, eager for something to do. He fired up the engines on the three magic-based missiles and their three technology-based counterparts. Vibrations from the deck passed through his boots confirming the missiles were ready and waiting.

"Five, four, three, two, one. Go!" ordered Margery.

Timerman moved the joy stick forward and fired off a quick burst of the hyper-drive. From past training missions in the simulator with Tia and Asquan, he knew his reflexes weren't quick enough to make a one second jump. He was totally dependent on Margery to make sure he didn't overshoot his target. He wasn't worried. He'd learned to trust the ex-battle computer during his time on the *Defiant*.

"Creator help me," Timerman whispered. "I will not let my friends down. I cannot let them down."

* * *

After the last of the energy from the exploding ball of purple flesh that was the demon passed overhead, Jeena picked herself up off the metal deck and took a step toward her bondmate. She couldn't help but fear for his life. By a fluke of bad luck, he'd wound up lying on the deck between the legs of an orange demon that was busy fighting Red Wing and another Crosioian scout.

"According to Nickelo, that second scout is the Crosioians' supreme leader," came Danny's thought in her mind more as an image than words.

"I have to help Rick," Jeena thought back.

"No!" said Danny. *"Rick can take care of himself. He's got the two scouts and Sheeta to help him. Look at the plots on the heads-up display of your helmet. The pirates and their demon allies are going to overwhelm the* Defiant's *crew if Comstar and you don't get back to the airlock pronto."*

Much as she wanted to rush to the aid of her bondmate, Jeena forced herself to look at her heads-up display. The numerous yellow, red, and blue dots massing in the docking tube at a point just beyond the yacht's open airlock told the story. Her strike team was going to be overrun by the transport's boarders in a few seconds.

Taking a final glance at her bondmate, Jeena raised her staff, spun, and sprinted toward the forward airlock. Comstar and the dwarf Stovis were hot on her heels. As soon as the airlock came into view, she sensed a build-up of energy just past the doorway. Floating in the open airlock was a yellow eyeball the size of a small pony. A dozen elf-long tentacles waved in the air, shooting out multicolored beams of light at the *Defiant's* security team. The five dwarves were hiding behind metal trusses on either side of the corridor on the yacht's side of the docking tube. All five dwarves were firing furiously at the floating eye, but their magic and technology based beams and bullets only succeeded in bouncing harmlessly off a shimmering shield to the demon-eye's front.

A translucent shield appeared between the eye and the dwarves. Jeena sensed the frequency of Calatron, the leader of the gnome mages, in the defensive shield. Suddenly, a beam of yellow light shot out from the demon-eye, striking the gnome's shield. Calatron's defensive shield bent inward as the eye's powerful magic slowly forced its way forward.

The ring on Jeena's left hand tingled. *"Calatron can't hold the shield on his own,"* said Danny.

A line of magic reached out from behind Jeena to form a second defensive shield just inside the gnome's shield. She recognized Comstar's frequency.

Boom!

The gnome's shield gave way just as Comstar's shield formed. The eye's yellow beam slammed against the elf's magic, forcing Comstar's shield inward the same as it had the gnome's. Jeena started to reinforce the defensive shield of her fellow elf but decided against it in a split-second decision. Some sixth sense warned her that the demon-eye's spell was created specifically to overpower defensive shields. Drawing Power from the Staff of the Lady of the Tree, Jeena wrapped the dwarves, gnomes, Comstar, and herself in telekinetic magic. As Comstar's defensive shield gave way to the eye's spell, her fellow elf's defensive shield erupted in an explosion of fire and smoke. Jeena pushed outward with her telekinesis spell, doing her best to force the flames away from her companions and herself. A bright flash filled the corridor followed by a wave of dense smoke so black even her night vision was unable to penetrate. Heat flowed into her power-armor, but the air conditioning unit kept the temperature to a bearable level. The wave of smoke rolled past, clearing the air enough to see.

"Is anybody hurt?" Jeena said in the space of her mind she used to communicate with Danny.

"Everyone on our strike team was in power-armor," replied Danny. *"They'll live, although I think a couple of the dwarves closer to the blast may have gotten their beards singed a little. I sense that some of the pirates' magic users and a few of the demons are feeding energy into that demon-eye. I calculate the*

next spell is going to be massive. I doubt your little telekinesis trick is going to do the job the next time."

Jeena doubted it too. She sensed Comstar and the dwarves funneling Power into her.

"Well, two can play at this game," she thought as she drew Power from her reserve and converted it into magic with a few hand movements and spoken words. A ball of magic formed in her hands, growing more intense by the second as the magic from Comstar and the gnomes combined with hers. As her spell grew in intensity, Jeena noticed a similar concentration of magic building in the demon-eye.

The ring on Jeena's hand tingled. *"I calculate the eye's spell is going to be ready first,"* said Danny. *"I highly recommend you hurry."*

Whether the battle computer's calculation was correct or not, Jeena didn't find out. An emotion came down the link she shared with her bondmate. She intuitively knew what it meant. *"Hold on. I'm coming."* At the same time, a dark, wolf-like shape came leaping out of the metal floor near the demon-eye. It was Sheeta. The big male dolgar grabbed hold of one of the eye's tentacles and spun the demon a full hundred and eighty degrees. At that exact moment, another ray of yellow light shot out from the floating eye. Instead of the beam hitting the *Defiant's* crew as intended, it blasted into the pirates, magic users, and demons massing in the docking tube just past the *Defiant's* airlock.

Boom!

The eye's magic decimated anyone on the transport's side of the docking tube that wasn't behind a defensive shield. Dark smoke once again filled the corridor, blocking Jeena's view of the eye, but she sensed its life energy with her passive scan. She also sensed other demons and magic users moving forward. Without waiting for the smoke to clear, Jeena released her spell. A blast of blue magic leaped out from her staff, filling the airlock and the docking tube behind it with a freezing-cold wind of near hurricane force. The smoke disappeared completely as it was replaced by flying bits of snow and ice. The force of the wind stripped the paint off the metal walls of the airlock as it continued on into the docking tube. The space in the center of the *Defiant's* airlock cleared. It revealed the demon-eye floating in the airlock, surrounded by a shimmering defensive shield. Two of the orange, humanoid-looking demons stood on either side of the eye protected by shields of their own. Although Jeena couldn't see them, she sensed other demons and magic users hiding behind defensive shields in the docking tube. They were in a perfect position to charge into the yacht as soon as the demon-eye cleared the airlock. Jeena saw no sign of Sheeta, but she did sense a disturbance in the void that she assumed was the big dolgar.

Boom! Boom! Boom!

The yacht shook violently as distant explosions echoed throughout the corridor. Jeena, Comstar, as well as all of the dwarves and gnomes fell to the corridor's floor. Caught in the midst of casting a second spell, Jeena pulled the magic back inside her. Either luck or skill was on her side as she gained control over the half-completed spell and forced the magic back into her reserve before it malfunctioned.

Glancing up, Jeena saw the demon-eye still floating in the center of the airlock. The two orange demons were on the airlock's floor, scrambling to get up the same as her strike team. A yellow glow began forming around the eye as other demons and magic users inside the docking tube resumed funneling Power into the demon-eye. Jeena sensed a massive spell building in the eye's pupil.

This is it, Jeena thought as she pulled Power from her reserve and began reciting the incantation for her most potent defensive spell.

"I am here," came an emotion through Jeena's bond link.

Even as she continued her chant, she smiled and pushed herself off the deck with help from the assistors in the arms of her power-suit. As she rose, two wolf-like shapes came out of the airlock's walls and latched onto the throats of each of the orange demons. The dolgars didn't try to shift into the void. Instead, they began shaking their heads back and forth, ripping demon flesh from bone while sucking out life force. The orange demons' pain-filled screams echoed down the corridor, giving hope to Jeena's strike team.

A translucent shape dressed in black armor rose out of the airlock's floor directly behind the floating demon-eye. The eye began to turn. Jeena completed her defensive spell just as the demon-eye completed its turn. Instead of forming the shield to her front as she'd intended, Jeena shifted her magic to surround the attacking dolgars and Richard. The red glow of her bondmate's phase rod plunged into the demon-eye. The tentacles on top of the eye fired beams of magic at Richard from pointblank range, but Jeena's defensive shield was too strong. The beams ricocheted off the shield and back into the docking tube. Fiery explosions filled the tube. The blasts were accompanied by screams of the wounded from what was left of the massed pirates, magic users, and demons in the docking tube.

Jeena ran forward to the very edge of the airlock. The demon-eye was slamming its body into the ceiling and walls in an attempt to tear her bondmate from his perch on top of the eye. Jeena sensed Richard pumping pure Power into the demon-eye through his phase rod. The eye's tentacles changed tactics and began tearing at her bondmate's battle suit with teeth-filled suckers.

"No!" Jeena shouted as she rushed into the airlock and began beating at the demon's defensive shield with the Staff of the Lady of the Tree.

Comstar joined her and blasted the eye with a bolt of electricity barely missing her bondmate. Felspar and his dwarves ran up swinging glowing battle axes and hammers at the demon-eye and its two orange demon guards. Stovis reared back and swung a mighty blow of his battle axe at the demon-eye, cutting off one tentacle at its base. The eye screamed. How it could scream without a mouth, Jeena didn't know, but scream it did nevertheless.

Two Crosioians dressed in scout armor ran up to Jeena's left and right and began stabbing at the eye with their phase spears. She recognized one of the scouts as Red Wing. Jeena sensed Red Wing drill into the demon-eye's defensive shield with a line of Power, creating a small hole. In went the tip of Red Wing's phase spear, directly into the center of the eye's pupil. Again the demon-eye screamed.

Jeena maneuvered around the dolgars as they tore at the orange demons. She was forced to dodge in order to avoid the swings of the dwarves' battle axes and hammers. Once she was in a momentary clear space, she shoved the Staff of the Lady of the Tree through the open wound in the pupil created by Red Wing. As soon as the blue gem at the top of the Lady's staff entered the demon-eye's pupil, she sensed the staff's Power reach out to make contact with the flow of Power coming from Richard's phase rod. When the two lines of Power met...

Boom!

Jeena, Comstar, the dwarves, and the two Crosioian scouts were all thrown back down the corridor on the *Defiant's* side of the airlock, all the way to the spot where the gnomes had formed a final defensive line. By some miracle, Calatron, the gnome's leader, changed his defensive shield into a softening cushion of air in time to reduce the impact enough for Jeena to hit the deck without injury. Jumping to her feet, she looked at the airlock. No living thing remained inside the goo-splattered walls.

"Rick!" Jeena shouted.

"Relax," came Danny's thought in her mind. *"The dolgars and Rick shifted into the void. They'll meet us on the yacht's engine deck. The X-shuttle and the fighters are making their gun runs now. They're going to destroy the docking tube. You've got to get that airlock door shut while it's still empty."*

Turning to the only one she knew that was familiar with Crosioian technology, Jeena pointed at Red Wing who was just pushing herself off the corridor's floor.

"We've got to shut the airlock," Jeena shouted. "Timerman and the others are making their attacks."

Before Red Wing could react, the second scout, the one Danny had told Jeena was the supreme leader, jumped to a panel on the corridor's wall and slapped a button. Whish! The airlock door slammed shut.

"That will not stop the boarders for long," hissed the supreme leader. "We must get to the engine room and detonate the self-destruct. We will die with honor."

"No!" Jeena said. "We will not die. My bondmate has a plan."

CHAPTER 28

Sergeant Ron's voice came over the X-shuttle's intercom. "Blow an opening in their shield."

Timerman took a look at the four starships through the shuttle's windscreen. Between the transport and the two destroyers, the yacht was so tightly wedged in place that it couldn't have moved even if its bridge had still been intact, which it wasn't. The twenty-meter-long tube connecting the yacht and transport's airlocks together was still in place.

"You said we had to wait until we received confirmation that the yacht's airlock was shut," Timerman replied, becoming increasingly worried about his friends in the strike team.

"This is combat," said Sergeant Ron. "Things change. I'm the captain, so just do it. Make sure you save three missiles for the destroyer."

Nodding his head even though the *Defiant's* captain couldn't see, Timerman shifted his target sights from the destroyer's engine to the weakest point on the transport's force field. Moving his hand over the control panel located on the left armrest of the pilot's seat, he pressed the launch icon. The X-shuttle bucked three times. The glare of the missiles' exhausts disappeared in the direction of the starships ahead.

Timerman pressed the switch on his joystick for the *Defiant's* communication network. "Daniel, I have three missiles on their way. You've got control."

"Roger that," replied Daniel from his Żip fighter. "I've got control. I'm five seconds behind you. This is just like playing bongo back on Trecor."

Except this isn't a game, Timerman thought. He'd been told the young Trecorian's bongo skills had uniquely prepared the young teen for guiding the special warheads designed by Sergeant Hendricks. Past experience had proven Daniel could guide the weapons with near perfect precision to their target, but even so, Timerman couldn't help but be worried. His father had said more than once that something always went wrong in combat no matter how perfect the plan.

Turning his gaze to the tactical hologram, Timerman watched the points of light that were his missiles streaking toward their target. As he watched, the missiles lined up one behind the other at the exact distance required to ensure each missile struck the same point on the force field without being affected by the blast from the missile ahead of it.

"The destroyers are launching anti-missile missiles," said Margery.

Glancing out the windscreen, Timerman saw a dozen flashes from the sides of both destroyers. The flashes left little doubt the pirates had detected the incoming missiles and were taking countermeasures. The three points of light on the tactical hologram that were the X-shuttle's missiles began dodging back and forth.

I hope that's Daniel and not some malfunction in the missiles, Timerman thought. He looked closer at the hologram. None of the destroyers' return fire appeared to be heading in the X-shuttle's direction.

"Have they spotted us yet?" Timerman asked.

"Negative," replied Margery. "But don't get your hopes up. I calculate that won't last long."

Taking a deep breath, Timerman tightened his grip on the shuttle's controls. "Understood. Help me line up on the outboard destroyer's engine. We have to disable that ship's ion-drive for Rick's plan to work."

"Compliance."

The X-shuttle shifted into a hard sixty-degree turn. When it rolled out, the shuttle was lined up directly on the outermost destroyer's ion engine exhausts. As the X-shuttle drew closer, Timerman noticed vapor coming out of the docking tube connecting the yacht to the transport.

"It's leaking gas into space," Timerman said. "The yacht needs to get away before it loses more of its atmosphere."

"Everyone on our boarding party is in power-armor of one type or another," Margery said. "They'll be fine. Besides, those warships still have the yacht blocked in. It can't break away until at least one of the destroyers is moved out of position. That's your job, so don't get sidetracked worrying about someone else's task. Rick and the others can take care of themselves. Stick to the plan."

Timerman well knew the success of the plan depended a lot on what he did in the next ten seconds. His right hand felt sticky on the control joystick as he placed a sweaty finger on the trigger for the forward gun cannons. At the same time, he raised his left index finger over the missile icon on his armrest. Straining to keep his voice steady, Timerman said, "Is the airlock shut yet? Can I fire?"

"The door's still open," said Margery. "Sergeant Ron just gave the order to fire anyway. Nickelo has confirmed Rick is on his way to the airlock now. I have faith he will have the airlock shut by the time you take out the destroyer's engine."

Three flashes of light exploded against the transport's force field. The translucent screen that surrounded all four starships disappeared.

"The transport's shield is down," said Margery. "It was handling the force field for all of the ships. Fire now before they get their secondary systems online."

Hoping Rick was as good as Margery thought he was, Timerman pushed down on the missile icon as he pulled the gun trigger on the joystick. The X-shuttle bucked as the three remaining missiles shot out, followed by hundreds of balls of plasma and magic energy from the forward auto-cannons.

"Daniel," Timerman said into the ship-to-ship intercom. "Missiles are on their way. Make me proud."

The teen in the Zip fighter didn't reply, but the three streaks of light that were the missiles lined up one behind the other and streaked straight toward the outermost destroyer. Multicolored beams of energy reached out from the destroyer. Some shot out toward the incoming missiles. Other beams targeted the X-shuttle. Timerman banked hard to avoid the return fire.

"I calculate a one hundred percent probability that the pirates know you are here now," said Margery.

Timerman didn't waste time replying. He dodged incoming plasma and phase beams the way Tia had taught him in the simulator just before she'd left the *Defiant*. Two beams of purple plasma energy ricocheted off the forward force field, but the glancing blows did no damage. Timerman said a silent prayer to the Creator thanking Tia for her training. A bright explosion in the windscreen cut his prayer short.

"One of our missiles has been destroyed," said Margery. "You need at least two to take out the ion engine: one to blast a hole in the local force field and one to disable the engine itself."

Leaving the missiles to Daniel, Timerman concentrated on targeting the docking tube that connected the transport to the yacht and pulled the trigger for the forward auto-cannons. Bright balls of plasma and magic energy shot out from the X-shuttle's bow in the direction of the tube between the two ships' airlocks. As the rounds drew close, Timerman had a split-second to think, *You better not be in there, Rick.*

The rounds of plasma energy and magic hit the docking tube, tearing it apart in the middle. At the same time, the two missiles Timerman fired earlier slammed into the outermost destroyer's ion engine. Bright light erupted from the rear and sides of the destroyer and the forward and aft tractor beams locking the destroyer to the yacht disappeared.

"It's free," said Margery. "Now's your chance."

Timerman lined the X-shuttle up on the rear of the damaged destroyer and pressed an icon on the armrest of his pilot chair. A yellow tractor beam reached out from the shuttle's bow and latched onto the destroyer. "Reverse! Full power!" he ordered.

The X-shuttle's engine whined as Timerman was thrown against his shoulder harness. The destroyer didn't move. "It's got too much mass," said Timerman. "The X-shuttle's not powerful enough to move it." Desperate, the young orc made his decision. "Shut down life support and our force field along with anything else you can think of. Transfer all power to the forward tractor beam. Rick's depending on us."

"Compliance," said Margery. "I must point out that without your force field, you'll be a sitting duck for the destroyer's anti-ship weapons."

Even before the ex-battle computer finished speaking,

Timerman saw the rearmost gun pods on the outermost destroyer turning in his direction. Before they began firing, red and green balls of energy flew past his windscreen and exploded against the destroyer's weapons. A moment later the *Defiant's* stubby-winged dragon-fighter zoomed past while continuing to fire at the destroyer's gun pods.

"Stop playing around and get that destroyer out of the way," came Asquan's voice out of the intercom. "Daniel and I will try to take out the second destroyer's tractor beams."

Two of the outermost destroyer's gun pods exploded as Asquan flew his dragon-fighter along the length of the enemy ship, firing every weapon he had as he went. Most of the destroyer's remaining weapons concentrated their fire on the weaving fighter. Timerman dodged the few weapons still firing at his X-shuttle and began rocking the destroyer back and forth with the shuttle's tractor beam. Slowly but surely the big ship began pulling away from the yacht. By the time the gap between the destroyer and the yacht had grown to fifty meters, Timerman noticed the tractor beams from the second destroyer disappear.

"Asquan and Daniel have taken out the pirate's tractor beams," said Margery. "Sergeant Ron is going to get the second destroyer out of the way by using the *Defiant's* tractor beams."

Timerman shook his head. "That destroyer still has its engines. There's no way the *Defiant* can move it."

A bright flash from the rear of the second destroyer reflected off the hulls of the other starships. A second later, a yellow beam reached out and began tugging at the second destroyer.

"Worry about your own mission and let Sergeant Ron worry about his," said Margery. "You've moved the first destroyer far enough out of the way. Now latch onto the yacht and get it away from the transport while you've got the chance."

"Those warships' weapons will destroy the yacht before I can get it a light second away," Timerman said. "All they have to do is wait until I'm out of blast range and send in a nuke."

"Just do your job," said Margery. "Rick's plan will work."

Timerman released the X-shuttle's tractor beam from the destroyer and switched it to the yacht. The smaller ship began pulling away from the transport and the destroyers. "Switch power back to life support, Margery. I'm having trouble breathing."

"Compliance. I am also reactivating the X-shuttle's force field."

A beam of purple energy from the transport hit the force field a split-second after it formed. The X-shuttle shuddered but took no damage. Other beams of plasma energy from the transport and the two destroyers lashed out at the yacht. The beams stopped short. A translucent glow shimmered around the yacht.

A glance at the readout on the hologram next to the pilot seat told Timerman all he needed to know. He sighed with relief and mouthed a single word. "Magic."

CHAPTER 29

The *Defiant* continued to fire all weapons systems at the gun pods on both the destroyers and the transport. At the same time, Sergeant Ron gave the hyper-drive a millisecond burst in reverse to start the second destroyer on its path away from the yacht. A slew of missiles and plasma beams slammed into the *Defiant's* forward shields. Sergeant Ron's eyes were momentarily blinded by the bright flashes of light. When his eyes refocused, he saw both the dragon and Zip fighters diving at the second destroyer with all weapons blasting away.

"Get those gun pods on that transport out of action," Sergeant Ron ordered. "Comstar's shield around the yacht won't hold up to that kind of firepower for long."

"We're working on it," came Daniel's strained voice out of the intercom.

The *Defiant* rocked to the side as another wave of missiles hit the forward shields. The force field held, but the tractor beam blinked out. Sergeant Ron shifted power from the auxiliary ion engine to the tractor beam. The yellow ray of the tractor beam reached out again and grabbed hold of the second destroyer.

"Well try harder," Sergeant Ron said as he gave the hyper-drive another millisecond burst.

Closing the intercom connection to the fighters, Sergeant Ron said, "Margery, tell Timerman to get that yacht out of there."

"Compliance. Our orc is a little concerned that the transport or one of the destroyers will nuke the yacht before he can get a safe distance away. I calculate he has a valid point for concern."

Sergeant Ron didn't bother telling the ex-battle computer that he shared the young orc's concern. On the other hand, he did have a plan to tilt the odds in their favor a little.

"Margery, let me know the moment the yacht's clear of those two destroyers."

"Compliance. By the way, the transport has locked its two portside tractor beams onto the two destroyers. I calculate it's trying to pull the warships back in place in order to block the yacht's escape. Should I order the fighters to fire on the tractor beams?"

An idea popped into Sergeant Ron's head. He laughed. "No. Just let me know the moment the yacht's clear."

"Compliance."

Sergeant Ron didn't have to wait long. As he increased the power to the *Defiant's* reverse thrusters to counteract the transport's tractor beams, he gauged the distance between the yacht and the two destroyers. Despite the transport's best efforts, the yacht cleared the first destroyer. The stern of the pirate's warship just cleared the yacht's blown-out bridge, but it still took a few metal plates from the yacht's hull with it. The destroyer's momentum kept it moving as the pirate ship headed straight for the transport.

"The yacht's clear of the second destroyer now," said Margery.

Trusting his ship's computer to have her facts straight, Sergeant Ron punched the icon to shut off the *Defiant's* tractor beam that was tugging on the second destroyer. With the loss of resistance from the *Defiant's* tractor beam, the destroyer lurched backward as the transport's tractor beam caused the destroyer to pick up momentum as it headed directly toward the transport.

Sergeant Ron's passive scan detected a power surge in the transport's tractor beam as its operators hastily reversed power in the beam.

Sergeant Ron gave an evil grin. "Too late, a-holes," he laughed. "It's got too much mass to stop in time."

Sure enough, after a half-dozen heartbeats, the second destroyer crashed into the side of the transport. The thin-metal plates of the transport gave way to the destroyer's heavier armor. Vapor spewed into the vacuum of space along with bits of flotsam, a lot of which resembled bodies.

Ignoring the crashing starships, Sergeant Ron touched the icon for the engine room's intercom. "Bright Wing, do your thing. It's now or never."

"Roger that," came a reply more as an emotion than words.

Sergeant Ron smiled as he watched the three enemy ships. "I love it when a plan comes together. Now all I have to do is wait."

CHAPTER 30

Feeding Power through his link to Jeena, Richard sensed her pass it on to Comstar as it mingled with the Power being funneled into the elf mage by the gnomes. Even Red Wing and her supreme leader were supporting Comstar's effort to keep the defensive shield around the yacht from collapsing.

Drops of sweat beading on Comstar's forehead were visible through the face shield of the elf's helmet. Richard noticed the mage's raised arms shake as Comstar held his staff in the air parallel to the engine room's deck.

"I calculate your old roommate has about reached the end of his limit," said Nickelo in their shared space. *"Sergeant Ron has dispatched Bright Wing to the transport's engine room to overload its hyper-drive. I can sense a buildup of energy in the engine, but something is fighting her for control. You can see for yourself."*

Reaching out with his passive scan, Richard sensed a large energy reading interweaving with that of the little dragon's. As he watched, Bright Wing's life force wavered before steadying.

Richard turned to his bondmate. "Something's attacking Bright Wing. She can't overload the transport's hyper-drive. I've got to get over there and help her."

Sweat running down her face, Jeena turned away from Comstar long enough to look at Richard through her power-armor's visor. "We will both go."

Shaking his head, Richard said, "No. You've got to support Comstar. If his defensive shield fails, the yacht will be destroyed. Everybody on board will die."

"I won't allow you to go alone," said Jeena, sounding determined enough to rebel. The emotion coming through her bond link confirmed her resolve.

The yacht shook as the sound of an explosion echoed through the ship. Everyone but Richard, Red Wing, and the supreme leader were knocked to the floor. Comstar and Jeena hurriedly scrambled back to their feet and resumed their chanting. Calatron and his gnome mages also regained their feet as they took up their task of funneling Power into the elf mage.

"Did our shield fail?" asked Felspar. He and his fellow dwarves stood with weapons drawn, forming a defensive line between the yacht's armed crew and the two elves.

So far, the Crosioians and the dwarves had avoided hostilities, but Richard knew it was a tentative truce at best.

"The shield did not fail," said Nickelo over the battle helmet's external speakers. "Margery says one of the destroyers bumped into what was left of the yacht's bridge. The yacht's clear now. I calculate the pirates and their allies will be concentrating even more fire against the yacht. As the distance increases between the ships, more of the pirate's gun pods will get a field of fire."

"Comstar," Richard said. "Can Jeena, the gnomes, and you hold the shield spell on your own for two minutes if I leave?"

The old elf mage didn't bother replying, but he did nod. Taking it for a yes, Richard turned to Red Wing. "We've got to get to the transport's engine room. Do you have enough Power to dimensional shift over there?"

Red Wing nodded. "Enough to get there. Not enough to return."

"Understood," Richard said. "Then you stay." Facing the supreme leader, he asked, "What about you? Can you dimensional shift?"

The Crosioian's back stiffened, and she spread her wings. "I do not answer to hu—"

The yacht shook violently. This time even Richard and the two scouts were slammed into the ceiling before falling back to the metal deck.

Richard recovered first. Standing, he pointed at the supreme leader as she regained her feet. "I don't have time for this. My shipmate is on the transport trying to overload its engine. She's being attacked. Now can you do a shift to get over there and help, or are you going to stay here and hide?"

The Crosioian scout's face turned dark gray behind her visor. She half raised her phase spear. The yacht shook violently once again.

"I cannot hold the shield much longer," shouted Comstar. "If someone's going to do something, now is the time."

Piss on it, Richard thought as he wrapped himself in Power. *I'm tired of arguing. I'll do it myself. What else is new?* Shifting into the void, he remained in the top layer of the void between dimensions to conserve Power. He levitated through the yacht's hull, toward the transport. He sensed four life forms in the void with him. Two were Sheba and Sheeta. The other two were the Crosioian scouts.

"Red Wing," Richard shouted into his helmet's intercom. "You're low on Power. I told you to stay on the yacht."

"I do not hide," hissed Red Wing.

Regretting his earlier choice of words but knowing there was nothing he could do about it now, he accelerated through the five hundred meters of space now separating the yacht from the transport. He sensed more than saw the ongoing battle around him. Several dozen weapons on the three enemy ships were blasting away at the yacht with energy beams. Others were targeting the *Defiant* and the X-shuttle. Weaving through the interlacing beams of energy were the dragon and Zip fighters. A part of Richard wanted to help Asquan and Daniel, but he knew where the priority lay. Bright Wing was the key to success of the plan.

"This wasn't part of your original plan?" said Nickelo. *"May I ask what your new Plan B is? I calculate even with the high priestess and the gnome's help, Comstar can only hold the shield spell around the yacht for another sixty-three seconds."*

Richard ground his teeth. *"I haven't got a Plan B, if you must know. I'm winging it. There. I admitted it. Does that make you happy?"*

"Not particularly," said Nickelo. *"As it so happens, I do have a Plan B, several thousand in fact. The one I prefer has a slightly better than slim chance of success. Would you like to hear it?"*

Richard ground his teeth again.

"Fine," said Nickelo. *"I'll take that as a yes.* 'The One' *has a communication link set up between Margery, Danny, the two*

scout's fighting-helmets, and myself. Margery and Danny are trying to hack their way into the transport's computer network. They may need your help. If so, I'll let you know. In the meantime, based upon all available information, I calculate Bright Wing is in the transport's hyper-drive. Something is in there with her. Other life forms have surrounded the hyper-drive and are supporting whatever is attacking your dragon."

They were close enough to the transport now that Richard could sense residual emotions from the small silver dragon. He sensed fear, pain, and a whole lot of resolve. He sent a burst of emotion at the little dragon, hoping she'd take it as "Hold on. I'm on my way."

A group of life forms appeared ahead on Richard's passive scan. He recognized Bright Wing's frequency. Other frequencies were obviously magic users and demons. He made out powerful flows of energy around the silver dragon.

"That's the energy field from the hyper-drive," said Nickelo. *"You will notice that the magic users and demons are remaining outside those fields. I calculate none of them are shifters. That could work to your advantage."*

A disturbance in the hyper-drive's energy field drew Richard's attention. He reached out with an active scan and touched the disturbance. Whatever it was slapped his scan back with a line of its own Power. Multiple lines of Power from the surrounding magic users and demons poured into the disturbance. Richard sensed the disturbance gather the combined Power together and strike out at Bright Wing.

"No!" Richard shouted. His voice went nowhere in the void.

Part of the hyper-drive's energy formed a shield between the dragon and the disturbance. Most of the attacking energy was deflected, but some penetrated the shield. Richard sensed pain from his sister-dragon.

"Red Wing," Richard said into his helmet's intercom. "I want you two scouts to attack those demons and magic users. You've got to cause enough of a distraction to keep them from feeding Power to whatever's in the hyper-drive with Bright Wing. Sheeta and Sheba will help you." At least Richard hoped the two dolgars would aid the Crosioians. He wasn't all that sure the spirit-wolves had fully embraced the concept of the scouts being allies.

"What about you?" asked Red Wing.

"I'll go into the engine and help Bright Wing. She's got to overload the hyper-drive for our plan to work."

Richard half expected the bat to balk at being told what to do, but she surprised him by saying, "Good luck. I will be disappointed if you get yourself killed before I get the chance to do it myself."

"Yeah, same to you, Red."

"You are down to thirty-eight percent Power in your reserve," said Nickelo in their shared space. *"Just thought you might want to know. Oh, and your elf is also low on Power."*

With just a few meters left until he entered the transport, Richard pulled eight percent Power from his reserve and sent it down his bond link to Jeena. A moment later, more Power than he'd sent returned. As soon as it mixed with his reserve, Richard sensed Power being created. He immediately sent most of the created Power back to Jeena. By the time he actually levitated through the bulkhead of the transport, he was at sixty percent Power. He sensed Jeena's reserve at an equal level.

"That will have to do," said Nickelo. *"It's show time."*

At that moment, Richard passed into a corridor filled with Thargs and pirates in power-armor. One of the Thargs fired a burst of energy from a rifle at him, but it passed through Richard. He was in the void. The errant energy rounds hit an unfortunate pirate unlucky enough to be standing on the far side of Richard. The plasma energy blew a hole in the human's armor and knocked him into a second pirate. Richard passed through the wall of the corridor before anyone else got a chance to fire, then came out of the wall in what he assumed was the engine room. A score of Dragar magic users and four of the orange humanoid-looking demons surrounded a truck-sized glass-enclosed container filled with swirling red gas. Richard spotted movement in the red gas. Concentrating on the movement, he made out the form of Bright Wing hunched low to the ground, circling...*something*. It was the disturbance Richard had detected earlier.

In the split-second before he entered the gas-filled room, Richard sent out another active scan at the disturbance. Once again a line of Power reached out and knocked his scan away. It didn't matter. He was close enough now to see the disturbance for what it was. The creature had four-legs and was about twice the size of the silver dragon. The life force coming from the creature was familiar. Richard had sensed it before. On that occasion, the creature had been much larger.

"It's a golem," Richard said in his shared space. *"It's like the one I fought in the spiritual dimension when I first met Sheba and Sheeta."*

"Ah, I do believe you're right, Wizard Scout," said Nickelo. *"I have reviewed tele-bot videos in the central computer's classified databanks of that mission. The large cat golem you fought was made out of solid titanium and had blue gems for eyes. From what I can discern from your active scan and the battle helmet's sensors, this golem is made out of some previously unknown molten metal with titanium flakes mixed in. The frequency of the gems it's using for eyes is different than the cat golem you fought. I calculate the creature's eyes are something other than blue gems."*

Hope flared in Richard. *"Are the gems yellow? Maybe—"*

The nearest orange demon turned and swung at Richard with a sword composed of fire and energy. Before the blade struck home, a greenish length of phase energy intercepted the sword and deflected it to the side. Red Wing shifted out of the void and spun, sticking the forearm-length point at her wing joint deep into the demon's chest. The demon roared, but it sounded more like anger than pain. As the demon took a step back to free itself from the bat's wing point, Red Wing shouted, "Go! Save your dragon!"

Leaving a comrade-in-arms in the middle of a battle went against Richard's Marine training. With a click, he activated his phase rod in full destructive mode and prepared to help the scout.

"Don't be a fool," said Nickelo. *"She's a Crosioian scout. She can take care of herself. Your job is to get inside the engine and help Bright Wing."*

Two female magic users turned and faced Red Wing as they began shouting words and waving their hands. Richard sensed magic forming in the mages' hands. Sheeta rose out of the deck behind the two magic users and bit down on the back of one woman's neck, completely severing the head from the magic user's body. Before the woman's head hit the deck, the big dolgar twisted and snapped down on the wrist of the second female, sinking his teeth completely through the mage's arm. The woman shimmered as Sheeta used her life force to shift her into the void and pull her screaming form into the metal floor.

Screams from the other side of the room announced the arrival of Sheba and the Crosioians' supreme leader. As the female dolgar tore into three magic users, the scout thrust her phase spear into the neck of one of the orange demons. At the same time, Richard sensed the bat reach out with a line of Power, split it into three parts, and snap the spinal cords of the three magic users.

She's good, Richard thought.

"See," said Nickelo. *"I told you they could take care of themselves. Now get in the engine before Bright Wing is killed."*

An emotion of pain and a lessening of life force in the silver dragon made Richard's decision for him. He levitated into the gas-filled container in time to see the golem biting into Bright Wing's neck and then shake its head back and forth like a hound shaking a rabid pactar. Striking out with his phase rod, Richard hit the golem at the base of its spine with a force hard enough to shatter bone. Only the creature didn't have bones. Except for two red gems as its eyes, the golem was composed completely of molten metal. Richard's phase rod passed through the creature, apparently doing no harm. Even so, the golem released its hold on Bright Wing and spun to face Richard.

"The rod's phase energy must have hurt it," said Nickelo, *"but not enough. You're going to have to come up with a better way to attack it, or I calculate your plan is going to fail. Even with Jeehana and the gnome's help, Comstar can only hold his defensive shield around the yacht for another twenty-two seconds."*

Leaping into the air, the cat-like golem twisted past the phase rod and sunk its molten teeth into Richard's throat armor. The finger-length fangs penetrated easily through the battle suit's armor and deep into Richard's neck. Liquid fire spread through his body and he fell back unable to think as the burning pain pushed all thought aside, leaving only agony. As unconsciousness closed around him, he sensed the arm of his battle suit strike out at the golem with his phase rod. The brerellium steel rod and its creallium core once again passed through the golem without doing any discernable harm. The cat golem began shaking its head, and Richard with it. With each shake, the inner flames inside Richard spread ever deeper into all parts of his body and soul.

Darkness surrounded Richard as his world began to pass from view. He sensed evil in the darkness. He sensed hunger for his very soul. Fear swelled up within him as loneliness mixed with the burning pain in his body.

One thought went through his mind. *I'm all alone.*

CHAPTER 31

Admiral of the Combined Fleets Bistos stared at the star map, noting the locations of the various fleets in their staging areas. It had been a rough week balancing supplies, assets, and assembling the invasion fleets. At the same time, she'd had to keep the battle lines between her forces and the Crosioians' border adequately manned to prevent them from overwhelming the Empire's stripped down defenses. She yawned. Her legs grew suddenly weak, forcing her to reach out with her right hand and steady herself against the science officer's chair.

"Sir," said Lieutenant Beady, "are you all right?"

"I'm fine, Lieutenant," Liz snapped. She immediately regretted allowing her irritation at showing signs of weakness in front of subordinates creep into her voice, then forced herself to speak in a more normal tone. "Please continue with your assessment."

"Yes, Sir. As I was saying, we've got a total of a hundred and five thousand ships spread out between the two hundred staging areas. Even with every troopship we can lay our hands on, we're still going to be short. Best estimates are that it will require three trips with our troop carriers to get all the prisoners off Estos. That's assuming we don't lose any in combat."

Liz knew that was an iffy assumption but didn't bother admitting it to the young officer. Everyone knew the entire Estos operation was built on one iffy assumption after another. *Doesn't matter,* she thought. *It's all we've got. I'll make it work somehow. I've got to make it work. I'm not going to let two hundred million of our soldiers die without at least trying to save them.*

Newly promoted Admiral Slystr walked over, bringing the *Destiny's* Captain Bhami with him. The female captain had impressed Liz during the short time the woman had been onboard the *Destiny*.

"Is Lieutenant Beady giving you everything you need?" asked Captain Bhami.

Liz nodded. "He's been more than helpful, Captain. You were right. He knows his business." She noticed the lieutenant's face turn a little pink. "Your whole staff had been very helpful. Most of them were on the *Destiny* during the first Estos battle. You inherited a good command from Admiral Slystr. I've no doubt you realize that."

"Yes, Sir. I do."

Turning away from the ship's captain, Liz pointed at the star map's numerous red dots strewn along the border between Empire and Crosioian space. "So, Lieutenant, how accurate are those plots?"

To his credit, the science officer didn't try to cover his ass. "Not very, Sir. I'm confident the enemy locations that are in contact with our troops are accurate, but everything past the border is pure conjecture. Our best guess is that the Crosioians have a half million warships in their rear staging areas. Where those are or what condition their warships are in, we don't know. I, uh…"

Liz frowned at the young science officer when he grew silent. "You what?"

Lieutenant Beady glanced at Captain Bhami.

The captain nodded. "Go ahead, Lieutenant. It's not like anyone knows anything for certain. Admiral Bistos needs information. If you've got an idea, tell her. No one will hold it against you if you're wrong."

The science officer seemed to relax. "Well, Sir, we've sent tele-bots and even a few of our remaining wizard scouts to locations where I would've bet my last credit the Crosioians were staging their fleets. Our scouts have found nothing."

"Isn't that a good thing?" asked Admiral Slystr.

The science officer shook his head. "I don't think so, Sir. The Crosioians aren't fools. Some of those locations are perfect to position fleets in a way that they could respond to any attacks on the border by our navy. It would be foolish for the bats not to have ships there, yet none of our scouts found anything. Like I said, the Crosioians aren't fools. It's almost as if the bats are able to hide their fleets." The lieutenant looked at his captain before locking eyes with Liz. "Sir, I think their fleets are at those locations. I think the bats are hiding them just like they were able to hide them before the first Estos battle." The young man swallowed hard. "Sir, I think we're walking into another trap. I'd stake my life on it."

Liz turned away from the lieutenant and stared at the star map. She'd been thinking along the same lines ever since Tia found the small demon. *That's the only reason I don't have her back here right now,* she thought. *From what Rick told me, when he killed the demon Zenthra, all the summoned demons that had camouflaged the Crosioians' fleets were pulled back to the demonic plan with their master. There shouldn't be any left in our dimension, but the one Tia and Matt found proves Rick's theory is wrong. That little demon came from somewhere, and I need to know where and how many others came with it.*

Glancing back at Lieutenant Beady, Liz said, "I want you to update the star map with the locations you think the Crosioians should have fleets." Admiral Slystr started to speak, but Liz held up her hand. "Yes, I know our scouts found nothing, but I want to at least have contingency plans in place in case the Crosioians have demons helping them again. I want the lieutenant's locations sent to my staff back on Trecor. Tell them I want an analysis and recommended modifications to our plans by fourteen hundred hours."

"Yes, Sir," said Admiral Slystr. "Uh, where will you be, Admiral?"

"I'll be in my cabin."

Admiral Slystr nodded. "That's good. You need some sleep."

Liz laughed. "Sleep? There'll be time enough to sleep when this war is over. In the meantime, I've got some calls to make."

* * *

A few minutes later found Liz in her quarters. They were actually Captain Bhami's quarters, but the captain had graciously given them to her admiral of the combined fleets. Liz smiled. *Rank does have its privileges,* she thought.

Eyeing the full-sized bed in the corner, Liz shook her head with more than a little regret and made her way toward the small conference table near the room's bay window. Since the *Destiny* wasn't in hyperspace, the stars were crisp and clear. She remembered the many times during her cadet years on Trecor when she'd spent hours outside, studying the night sky. On most nights, she'd imagined a time when she would command a starship and navigate from one side of the galaxy to the other, saving worlds and fighting evil as she went.

"Humph," Liz said out loud. "Those days are long gone. Reality is so much harsher than youthful daydreams." She shook her head. *I'm tired,* she thought, *but I can't let my mind drift. I've got to stay focused. Billions of life forms are depending on me. I'm not going to let them down.* She glanced at the digital time display on her wristband. It was time to make her call.

Sitting in the chair at the head of the table, Liz touched an icon on the computer display built into the desktop. A half-meter-high holographic image of a young boy with dark curly hair appeared above the table. Standing behind the boy were Tia and Matthew.

Liz frowned. She recognized the boy as Richard's adoptive nephew but hadn't expected him to be part of the call. She didn't like surprises.

"I thought I mentioned that I wanted to talk to you in private, Lieutenant Bistoria," Liz said doing her best to keep her irritation under control. The fact that she'd only gotten two hours sleep in the past two days wasn't helping.

Tia's back stiffened. To her credit, she replied in a somewhat respectful voice, "Yes, Sir. You did, but things have changed. Brachia's found something I think you're going to want to hear."

Instantly alert, Liz straightened in her chair. She'd talked to the boy a couple of times in the past. The discussions usually left her feeling a little inferior. *The boy's too smart for his own good,* she thought. Switching her gaze to Richard's adoptive nephew, she said, "All right, let's hear it. What do you have?"

Brachia grinned and lifted a black rod the length of a large man's hand. "Dren found this in one of the warehouses on Storage. She sent it to me this morning. Naturally, Omar and I used it on our imp as soon as we could."

Liz tapped her foot under the table but succeeded in keeping her face neutral. "Naturally. Now, what is it?"

"Oh," said Brachia, grinning again. "This is a knowledge transversal device. It was—"

"Do you mean transferal?" Liz asked, already beginning to feel a little confused.

The boy frowned and glanced at Tia before looking back at Liz. "Uh, no. It's a transversal device." He frowned again as if struggling to find the right words. "I mean, it does transfer knowledge, but it does it by a transversal of psychic lines." He scratched his head and shrugged his shoulders. "I guess to really understand the process you'd need to read an Imperial Scientific Academy paper my parents wrote called 'Knowledge Transversal by Subliminal Consciousness Using Third Party Psychic Assistance.' You see, in order to transfer knowledge, you first have to—"

Raising her hand, Liz said, "Enough. I don't have the time or patience for this. What's your point?"

When the boy cocked his head and frowned, Tia spoke. "This device was invented by Brachia and Dren's parents before they were killed. Their parents used the device to transfer their knowledge into their children. That's why they're so smart."

"That's not the only reason," said Brachia sounding defensive.

Ignoring the boy, Tia continued with her explanation. "Dren found the device while she was conducting an inventory of the warehouses on Storage for Rick. She and Brachia had assumed it was destroyed when her parents were murdered, but somehow the device found its way to one of the warehouses."

Liz rubbed her forehead, wishing she wasn't so tired. "Too much detail, Lieutenant. Skip the background. What do you have that I need to know?"

Turning a shade of pink, Tia clenched her lips.

Matthew bent down until his head was even with Brachia's. "What we've found out," he said, "is that a contingent of Crosioians have several thousand demons and magic users at their disposal. Brachia used the transferal device—"

"Transversal," corrected Brachia.

"Fine," said Matthew. "He used the *transversal* device on the imp. Some of the Crosioian tribes have been secretly bringing demons into the physical dimension. From what Brachia can gather—"

"The imp's thought process is...uh...different," said Brachia, "but from what I can figure out, there is a major disagreement among the Crosioian tribes about the use of demons. The current leadership believes all the demons and mages utilized during the Estos battle were either returned to their home dimensions or killed. Behind the scenes, about a third of the tribes have been working in unison to bring demons back to the physical dimension. They are using those demons to hide at least half of the Crosioians' fleets from our scout teams."

Liz frowned. "Are you saying their leaders don't know about this? I find that hard to believe."

Brachia shrugged his shoulders. "All I know is what the imp believes. It could be wrong, but from what it understands, a third of the Crosioian tribes are positioning themselves for a coup. Our prisoners on Estos are the bait that the Crosioians' supreme leader is using to lure us into a trap. They have stripped their borders and rear areas of soldiers and ships and positioned them for a strike on Estos, should we attempt a rescue. Unbeknownst to the supreme leader, some of the tribes are using the gathering of their forces for that ambush as a smokescreen for their planned coup. They've been bringing in demons to hide their fleets and fake out false locations to fool their own leaders. Their fleets are actually positioned to take over key facilities in the Crosioian Empire the moment the rest of the fleets have sprung the trap around Estos."

Liz's stomach tightened. She'd always known the Estos mission was a gamble, but she hadn't figured on demons and undetectable fleets. "Does the knowledge you got from the demon include the locations of the hidden enemy fleets?"

The boy shook his head. "No. I get the impression the demons don't really care where the Crosioians' ships are. And it's an imp. It's more of a weak devil than a demon, but I guess that doesn't matter in the current situation. You see, the demons have a Dark Council composed of—"

Liz held up her hand. She forced herself to ignore the fact that the person she was talking to was a young boy and tried to phrase her questions the same way she would if he was a highly qualified scientist. *Which he is,* she thought. *If what he's telling me is true, I hope he and his sister are as smart as Rick tells me they are.*

"All right," Liz said. "Assuming what you're telling me is true, why are the demons helping the Crosioians, and how are they getting into our dimension? I got the impression from Rick that it took half a year for the Crosioians' mage lackeys to summon enough demons to hide their fleets during the Estos battle. If they were all forced back to the demonic plane like Rick thinks, how is it the Crosioians have been able to gather several thousand in just a few weeks?"

"Uh—" began Brachia before looking back at Tia.

Liz noticed her sister glance at Matthew before looking at her.

"I think the reason Brachia's hesitating is because he's a scientist and wants his facts straight before he gives out information," said Tia. "I know we don't have that luxury, so here's our best guess on what's happening. The Crosioian tribes that are planning the coup are using a dimensional gate located on one of their planets called Astaris. The gate's been closed for a long time, but even before the first battle on Estos, some demons had been working with those Crosioian rebel wannabes and working to open the gate. Mages from Portalis have been brought in to help."

Liz frowned. "Why are the demons helping the bats?"

"They aren't," said Matthew. "At least they aren't the way the Crosioian rebels think. Our imp prisoner is just a low-level demon, so it's not in the know about a lot of things, but Brachia found out enough to know even the demons have their own set of political strife. Their Dark Council, whatever that is, has one set of plans for conquering the three galaxies. Another set of demons under the four brother demons Rick has fought off and on over the years has another plan. Then there's a third group of demons that our imp prisoner's a part of, that is working to use the Astaris gate to invade the physical dimension. It gets pretty confusing. The end result is that this third group of demons is working to open the Astaris gate. The imp believes a demon army will be gathering at the gate soon to begin their invasion. Their plan is to kill every living thing in our galaxy. That includes the Crosioians."

Liz's mind went into hyper-drive trying to find some way she could use the information to her advantage. She rubbed her forehead with both hands. *I'm too tired,* she thought. *I can't think straight. There must be some way to use what they're telling me, but what?* She took in a deep breath before lowering her hands and looking at Tia. "Does that imp of yours know where this Astaris is located? I've never heard of it."

Nodding her head, Tia said, "Yes, it does, but it's out of our reach. It's located near the outer realms, on the far side of the Crosioian Empire. It would take a full thirty-five hyper-jumps to make it there. None of our ships could reach it without having their hyper-drive replaced before they got two thirds of the way there."

"The *Defiant* could make it," said Brachia.

Liz had no doubt the little recon ship with her prototype hyper-drive and silver dragon could, but there was a problem. "Unfortunately," she said, "the *Defiant* isn't here. Neither is Rick, so we're out of luck."

Tia caught Liz's eye. "What are we going to do, Sir?"

"Do, Lieutenant?" Liz replied. "We're going to get our soldiers off Estos before they're all dead. We'll deal with this demon thing after that."

"What do you want me to do?" asked Matthew. "Our Conglomerate forces are nearly assembled. I've made sure every one of our fleets is commanded by senior staff with Empire navy experience."

Liz nodded. Her respect for the young man went up a notch. She allowed herself a tired smile. "I'm sure convincing the previous commanders to retire early wasn't an easy task, Matt. You did right though. We can't afford any betrayals this time."

Matthew Deloris's face turned a shade of pink. "There won't be, Admiral. I guarantee it."

Liz nodded again. She believed him. "Very well, then. Once your forces are assembled, have them rendezvous with the Empire and Trecorian fleets as planned. Come hell or high water, the attack on Estos will commence in twelve days."

Tia snapped to attention and saluted.

Matthew didn't salute, but he did nod his head.

Brachia stared into Liz's eyes. "I wish Uncle Rick was here. He could help."

Liz gave another tired smile. "I'm sure he could, Brachia, but he's not here. We're going to have to do it on our own. I imagine Rick and Sergeant Ron have got their own set of problems."

CHAPTER 32

"Our shields cannot take this kind of beating much longer," said Margery over the *Defiant's* intercom. "By the way, the forward torpedo tubes have finished reloading. I highly recommend you knock out some of those warships' weapons pods before we lose our shields completely."

Sergeant Ron punched the icon for the torpedo tubes located in the bow of the *Defiant*. The recon ship bucked as six high-speed missiles shot out toward the nearest destroyer. The enemy vessel's force field was nearly as battered as that of the *Defiant*, but it held long enough to resist the blast from the first five warheads. The sixth torpedo exploded in a bright flash near the pirate ship's bridge. Pieces of metal and hot gas scattered outward from the hull, creating a rippling effect of explosions along the full length of the destroyer.

"That ought to slow them down," Sergeant Ron said as he turned the *Defiant* to present her starboard tubes to the second destroyer. He spoke into the ship's intercom. "Sergeant Hendricks, I want you to fire all starboard weapons at those pirates the moment they come to bear. We've got to take the pressure off the yacht. I can sense Comstar's shield weakening."

"Roger that," replied the ship's armorer from his position at the recon ship's weapons control station on the second floor. "Weapons will commence firing in six seconds."

"Incoming," said Margery.

Even as he turned to look at the tactical hologram located between the pilot and copilot seats, Sergeant Ron reached out with his passive scan seeking whatever the ex-battle computer had spotted. He drew in a deep breath and jerked the control stick hard to the left as six white dots on the hologram closed on the *Defiant*. The agile recon ship dodged the first two missiles. Sergeant Ron punched the countermeasures icon on the armrest of his seat. A flurry of anti-missile plasma and phase beams shot out from the sides of the *Defiant*, striking two more of the missiles. Their explosions were bright enough to temporarily blank out the forward view screens. A glance at the tactical hologram showed the last two missiles heading directly for the recon ship's hyper-drive exhausts.

"Our rear shields are down to fourteen percent," said Margery. "I calculate a forty-one percent probability they won't stop both missiles."

"Seal all airtight doors," Sergeant Ron ordered. "Charlie, get out of the engine room and help Sergeant Hendricks with our weapons systems." Reaching over to the armrest of the copilot's seat, he angled the rear shields for maximum efficiency. He belatedly wished Angela was in the cockpit with him instead of back on Portalis with Terrie. *If wishes were credits, I'd be a rich man,* he thought, smiling in spite of the situation.

The first missile hit the rear shield. The *Defiant* bucked hard to the left, slamming Sergeant Ron into the right side of his seat.

"We took no damage, but our rear shield is down," said Margery. "The second missile will make contact with our hull in four, three, two—"

Boom!

The final missile exploded short of the *Defiant*. Sergeant Ron caught sight of a silvery flash zooming through the fiery debris. It was the dragon-fighter.

"Thanks, Asquan," Sergeant Ron said into the intercom. "You saved our bacon this—"

"Incoming," said Margery.

Sergeant Ron sensed a flow of energy to the *Defiant's* rear. He only had time to think the word *magic* when the obvious stealth spell dropped to reveal a high-velocity solid projectile heading straight for the engine room. Sergeant Ron wasn't a wizard scout. Still, he did have a Power reserve, and both the commandant and Richard had taught him a few tricks over the years. He drew every bit of Power he had in his reserve out and threw it at the incoming projectile. He sensed another line of Power reaching out from deck two to join his. The image of a four-armed Sterilian mechanic popped in Sergeant Ron's mind. That was all the time he had to think before the two lines of Power and the projectile made contact. He sensed the projectile slow but not enough.

Boom!

The *Defiant* lurched to the side. Sergeant Ron was slammed forward in his seat, bent nearly double and hitting his head on the control panel. Everything turned black for a couple of seconds. Struggling to remain conscious, he focused on a loud ringing in his ears. *What?* he thought before realizing it was the cockpit's alarm bells.

"Breach in engine room," said Margery. "We've got a hole the size of a basketball in our hull. I have activated fire suppression systems in all compartments on the second deck. We're leaking air fast on decks two and three."

With years of commanding recon ships under his belt, Sergeant Ron got down to business. "Charlie! Sergeant Hendricks! Are you okay?"

"Affirmative," said Sergeant Hendricks. "I'm in the starboard side weapons control with Charlie. We're donning spacesuits now. Charlie's going to go out and try to seal the holes in our hull."

One of many flashing lights on the control panel caught Sergeant Ron's attention. The words HYPER-DRIVE CRITICAL made a shiver run down his spine. "Negative. We've already lost atmosphere. That ain't going to get any worse. The hyper-drive's been damaged. It's overloading. Tell Charlie I'm ejecting the drive before she blows. I want him to divert all life-support systems to the ion-drive."

"Roger that, Captain," said Sergeant Hendricks.

Flipping up the safety cover for the drive's ejection switch, Sergeant Ron wasted no time in clicking it to the armed position and pressing the EJECT button. Nothing happened. He recycled the switch and tried again. Still nothing.

"Hyper-drive overload in twenty seconds," said Margery. "I calculate the drive's emergency eject is inoperable."

"Ya think?" Sergeant Ron snapped as he unstrapped his chair's safety harness. Already in a pressure suit, he grabbed his helmet and put it on as he made for the cockpit's exit. The door didn't open at his approach. "Margery, open the dang-blasted door."

"Atmosphere has been lost on decks one, two, and three," said Margery. "Opening the door will lose the air in the cockpit."

"We'll worry about oxygen later if we don't get blown up first," said Sergeant Ron. "Now open the door."

"Compliance."

The cockpit's door slid open. Thanking his lucky stars the artificial gravity was still working, Sergeant Ron ran down the stairs and past the mess table. He jumped down the stairs to the next level, barely touching the rails as he made his way toward the engine room. When he got close, he saw a head-sized hole in the hull venting red gas from the hyper-drive into space. The sides of the prototype engine were glowing red with several spots turning to a bright white.

"Twelve seconds until the hyper-drive reaches critical mass," came Margery's voice over the ship's intercom.

Making straight for a maintenance panel near the engine room's door, Sergeant Ron pried it off and grabbed hold of the manual release lever with both hands. The lever didn't budge. He braced his feet against the wall and jerked with all his strength. Still, the lever didn't move.

"Six seconds until overload," said Margery.

A large gray hand shoved Sergeant Ron to the side, throwing him against the wall. He bounced off and hit the floor. When he looked up, Charlie was holding onto the lever with all four hands and pushing against the wall with both feet. His arms and legs quivered.

"Three seconds," said Margery.

Suddenly Charlie flew back with a broken lever still in his hands.

Boom!

The metal eject plate on the backside of the engine room exploded outward, followed by the glowing hyper-drive.

Boom!

The *Defiant* shook, bouncing both Sergeant Ron and Charlie multiple times against the ceiling and floor. When the shaking stopped, Sergeant Ron felt pressure on his back. It was Charlie, the big lizard's form limp. Sergeant Ron scooted out from underneath his friend and rolled him over to gaze into the mechanic's visor. The Sterilian's eyes were open. The thought that Sterilians didn't have eyelids popped into Sergeant Ron's mind just as Charlie's lips moved.

"Might need to order another hyper-drive," hissed Charlie revealing double rows of serrated teeth in what Sergeant Ron knew was the Sterilian's version of a grin.

Sighing with relief, Sergeant Ron helped his friend to his feet. "Well it ain't coming out of my pay, I can tell you that. I'm blaming this one all on Rick."

Charlie hissed a laugh. "Yes. His plan."

Sergeant Ron joined in with a laugh of his own. "That's right. It *was* his plan. And don't think I'm not going to remind him of it."

"Assuming we still alive," said Charlie hissing even harder.

"Yeah. Assuming that." Sergeant Ron flashed another smile. "Now all we've got to do is find Rick and give him the bad news."

CHAPTER 33

Where's Rick? Jeena wondered as she did her best to help Comstar hold his defensive shield around the yacht, against the incoming missiles and plasma beams.

"Something's happened," shouted Comstar. "Enemy fire has slackened somewhat. I can feel it."

"One of the destroyer's has been taken out of action by the *Defiant,*" said Danny using the external speaker on the helmet of Jeena's power-suit. "Sergeant Ron's maneuvering to try and take out the other destroyer. Give him a few...oops. Belay that. Margery just told me the *Defiant's* been hit. The recon ship's hull is breached and her hyper-drive is starting to go into overload."

Jeena knew almost nothing about hyper-drives, but what she did know told her having one overload wasn't a good thing. *Come on, Rick,* she thought as she reached through their bond link to touch the other half of her soul and urge him on. What she found was an emotion of pain beyond compare. *"He's burning,"* Jeena said in the space of her mind she shared with Danny.

An image of her bondmate locked in battle with a cat golem made out of molten metal flashed in her mind. She instinctively knew the vision was being forwarded by Nickelo to Danny and on to her. She sensed her bondmate's Power reserves dwindling as burning energy swept through his body and into his very soul.

"The golem is using magic against Rick," said Danny still talking over the helmet's speaker. "Our wizard scout's in trouble. He doesn't have magic spells of his own. He can't defend himself."

"But I can," Jeena said, "and I will. Comstar, you and the gnomes are on your own. I have to help Rick."

"Do what you must," said the male elf. "Calatron and his gnomes and I can handle this end."

Pulling her donated Power back from the elf mage, Jeena converted it into a heat resistance spell and then reinforced it with an accelerator spell. *It will shorten the duration of the spell,* she thought, *but the accelerant will double the spell's effectiveness.* She sent an emotion down her bond link that she hoped meant *"take it."*

"What are you doing?" asked Danny in her mind. *"I told you Rick can't use magic."*

Jeena ignored the ex-battle computer. Her thoughts were on a time when Rick and she'd been on an asteroid. They had been forced to work together to create a spell that would close a time-bubble and dimensional gate with the aid of three spheres. Her bondmate and she had cast the spell together. He'd formed the spell out of pure Power, and she'd converted it into magic. *I've never tried sending magic directly to Rick,* Jeena thought, *but we're bonded. It's got to work. Lady, please let it work.* With that thought, she pushed the magic down the link to her bondmate, immediately sensing resistance.

"Take it," Jeena said again, trying her best to send the command as emotion-speak down their bond link. *"You are not alone. I am here."*

The resistance gave way, and the magic sped down the link. Then Jeena waited. That was all she could do.

* * *

Overwhelmed by burning pain and loneliness, Richard began releasing his hold on reality. His soul couldn't take any more. He was done. Before his grip on consciousness released completely, he sensed something coming down the link he shared with his bondmate and recognized it as some kind of spell. He sensed his natural resistance reach out and try to prevent the spell from attacking him. At that moment, he sensed an emotion flood his mind. The emotion was full of love and seemed to say, *"Take it. You are not alone. I am here."*

Gripping tightly to the emotion, Richard used it as an anchor link to override his resistor ability. He latched onto the spell accompanying the emotion and pulled the magic into his battered soul. Even in his tortured state, he knew he couldn't use magic, but he did understand it. A part of his mind saw the interweaving lines of magic and sensed something helping him. The something was Nickelo. With his battle computer's assistance, he followed the lines of magic and converted them into pure Power. When the conversion was done, he released the Power inside his body. The hybrid spell washed over him, chasing the burning pain away. He felt the molten teeth of the golem tearing into his neck, but they no longer burned. His self-heal surrounded the wound and attempted to repair the damage, but even as it healed, the golem's fangs tore the flesh anew. Pulling Power from his dwindling reserve, Richard sent an active scan into the golem's body seeking a weakness.

"It's a creature of fire," came Nickelo's thoughts in their shared space. *"The golem's body is molten metal interlaced with flecks of titanium, but if the data from your active scan is correct, the soul of the creature is fire. The fire appears to be centered in the two red gems that form the golem's eyes."*

Richard remembered how he'd killed a previous cat-golem by removing the gems it had used for eyes. He had a feeling he didn't have time to do that before his bondmate's converted spell gave out. Already he sensed the Power in the spell losing effectiveness as it began using up the last of its energy.

Striking out with his phase rod, Richard hit the golem's left eye. The rod bounced off, doing no apparent damage. Something bit at his left hand. *No, not my hand,* he thought. *My finger. My ring finger.* He sought out the point on his finger that hurt and found his red-gemmed ring. The ring was tingling. More accurately, its gem was tingling. Reaching into the gem, he found a line of energy connecting his ring to the red gems the golem used for eyes. With no time to consult with his battle computer, he gathered what remained of his bondmate's spell and forced it through his ring and into the link to the golem's eyes.

"Arrgh!" came a shrill cry of pain.

The cat-golem released its grip on Richard's neck and began rolling on the floor, scratching at its eyes as if trying to rip them out.

Richard fell to the floor and grabbed his neck with his right hand as he struck out at the golem's head with the phase rod in his left. Healing Power from his self-healing reserve wrapped around the wound in his neck and began to heal it at a rapid pace. Not for the first time, he thanked the Creator that his self-heal worked faster ever since the battle in the Presence of the Lady.

"Bright Wing," Richard mentally shouted in dragon-speak. *"Overload the engine. Now!"*

"What about you, Brother?"

"I won't be here," Richard said, hoping he was telling the truth. *"Make it happen or we're all dead."*

Richard sensed the silver dragon manipulate the hyper-drive's energy in a manner to make it feed upon itself. The drive's energy began increasing incrementally. Wasting no time, he shifted into the void and levitated out of the engine room. An orange demon and at least a dozen mages lay unmoving on the room's deck. One of the three remaining orange demons was falling back as Red Wing and the supreme leader took turns hammering its defensive shield with their phase spears. Between blows, the two bats took turns firing phase pistols at the remaining mages. The last two orange demons were locked in combat with Sheba and Sheeta. The dolgars and demons appeared to be evenly matched with neither side giving way to the other.

Shifting out of the void long enough to yell, "Out! Everybody out now!" Richard wrapped himself in Power and shifted back into the void. As he did, he sensed Sheba and Sheeta shift into another dimension and disappear. He saw the supreme leader begin to shimmer, but Red Wing remained solid.

"She's out of Power," said Nickelo in their shared space. *"She warned you she was low when we were on the* Defiant. *She can't shift."*

Desperate, Richard did something he thought he'd never do. He attached a link to the Crosioian scout and fed Power down the link. Red Wing stumbled in mid-swing but recovered quickly. She shimmered and shifted into the void. A moment later she was levitating through the engine room's walls and into the hallway beyond.

Richard followed suit. The hallway was empty. It was just as well. A glance at his Power reserve told him he was going to need every drop he had to get Red Wing and him back to the yacht. As they passed through the troopship's hull, he sensed the hyper-drive overloading to a critical level behind them. At the same time, he sensed Bright Wing's life form disappear from the engine room.

"Don't worry," said Nickelo. *"She just teleported. She can teleport short distances, in case you've forgotten."*

"Thanks for the update," Richard said increasing the speed of his levitation to maximum.

"You are at six percent Power in your reserve," said Nickelo. *"I calculate Red Wing and you will run out of Power and shift back into space two hundred meters short of the yacht. Too bad you let that golem put a hole in your battle suit. It won't seal now. I hope you've been practicing breathing in a vacuum, because if you haven't, I calculate the next couple of minutes are going to be less than enjoyable for you."*

Something came down the bond link Richard shared with Jeena. It was Power. As soon as it mixed with the Power left in his reserve, more Power was created. Richard sent half the Power he now had down the link to Red Wing.

"Is that enough?" Richard asked in his shared space. *"Are we going to make it now?"*

"I calculate you will not have to try breathing in a vacuum, if that's what you are asking," replied Nickelo. *"You will not have any Power to spare, but I calculate a ninety-two percent probability you will both make it to the yacht."*

A light so bright even the max filters of Richard's battle helmet couldn't keep it all out was accompanied by an oncoming wave of energy.

"The hyper-drive overloaded," said Nickelo. *"The transport and the remaining destroyer exploded. Go deeper into the void. Go now!"*

Richard went deeper, sensing Red Wing and the supreme leader also going deeper.

"Of course they are," said Nickelo. *"I'm in contact with their fighting-computers. The supreme leader has plenty of Power in her reserve, but the Power reserves for Red Wing and you are dwindling fast. You know the deeper you go in the void, the more Power it takes to maintain the shift. Uh, if you don't mind, I'd like to revise the estimate I gave you on making it back to the yacht.*

I'm basically giving you a snowball's chance in hell now."

Richard didn't need to check his reserve to know his battle computer was right. He could feel his Power dropping fast. So was Red Wing's. Before he could come up with an alternate plan, a line of Power reached out from the supreme leader and attached itself to Red Wing. Richard sensed Power passing down the link and transferring into Red Wing's Power reserve. As soon as it did, he sensed Red Wing draw Power from her reserve and pass it down the link he'd attached to her.

"Your reserve is back to six percent," said Nickelo. *"I give you a sixty-two percent probability of reaching the yacht now."*

More Power came down the link Richard shared with his bondmate. When it mixed with the Power in his reserve, more Power was created.

"You are at ten percent Power now," said Nickelo. *"I calculate a one hundred percent probability the three of you are going to make it back to the yacht alive."* Nickelo laughed. *"You really are one lucky wizard scout."*

Richard touched his neck as the last of the flesh torn out by the cat golem finally healed. *"Yeah. Lucky me."*

CHAPTER 34

Once the wave of energy from the exploding transport and destroyer rolled past, Richard moved higher in the void in order to conserve Power. He hung back to let the two Crosioian scouts make their way to the yacht, which was now a thousand meters away, while he covered their line of retreat just in case.

"Your elf and the others are fortunate," said Nickelo in their shared space. *"If the yacht had been any closer to the explosion, I calculate Comstar's shield wouldn't have been able to protect the occupants. As it is, you can see that the yacht's still extensively damaged."*

Because his battle suit couldn't seal, Richard was forced to remain in the void. Even so, he was able to see the Crosioians' yacht. The bridge was a total wipe and the remains of the docking tube that had attached the starship's airlock to that of the transport was dangling in space, holding on to the yacht by only a few loose cables. Holes of various sizes along the length of the ship's hull leaked vapor into the vacuum of space. A large tear the size of a small truck in the starboard side of the *Gaze at the Stars's* hull belched a ball of flame. Two hundred meters to the yacht's rear was the X-shuttle, flanked by the zipper and the dragon-fighter. Continuing to reach out with his passive scan, he noted the battered hulk of a pirate destroyer.

"That's the one the Defiant *took out,"* said Nickelo. *"I detect no life forms on board. It's a total wipe."*

At the mention of the recon ship, Richard reached out with his passive scan looking for the *Defiant*. He spotted it twenty thousand meters away moving toward the Crosioians' yacht while using only its ion-drive for thrust. The absence of the familiar frequency from the ship's prototype hyper-drive they'd gotten from the late empress was obvious.

"Margery sent word Sergeant Ron had to jettison the hyper-drive," said Nickelo. *"It was in critical overload after being hit by enemy fire. That doesn't bode well for any escape attempt. I calculate it would take over five thousand years to get back home using only our ion-drive."*

Ignoring the bad news for the moment, Richard continued probing the recon ship for damage. Other than the missing hyper-drive and a few scorch marks, the *Defiant* appeared to be in pretty good shape. *Still, Nick's right,* he thought, forgetting to keep his opinion in his private space. *A starship without a hyper-drive is a sitting duck for any pirates or Crosioian ships that may be on the way here.*

"Of course I'm right," said Nickelo sounding insulted. *"Did you actually have doubts? From what I can gather with my sensors and your passive scan, the yacht's engine is intact, but its bridge is completely gone. I calculate the yacht's flying days are over."*

A feeling of concern came down the bond link from Jeena. Sensing trouble, he increased his levitation to max speed. Within seconds, he passed through the yacht's hull and into the ship's engine room. Two groups were lined up on opposite sides of the large room. About sixty or so bats, some in pressure suits and some not, were on one side of the room armed with rifles and pistols. Red Wing and her supreme leader were positioned at their head. Jeena and Comstar stood near the opposite wall, flanked by Felspar and his dwarves. Calatron and the other gnome mages formed a triangle behind Comstar feeding Power into the elf mage. Although no one was yet firing their weapons, the tenseness of the situation was apparent.

"Lay down your weapons," ordered Red Wing. "You are now prisoners of our supreme leader."

"Like hell we are," snarled Felspar raising a glowing battle axe in one hand and a modified M12 plasma rifle in the other. "You're the ones who are prisoners. The *Defiant* and our fighters are outside. If you don't surrender, whoever we don't kill will be blown apart by our fighters."

"Crosioians do not surrender!" hissed a large bat wearing an orange jumpsuit and carrying a meter-long wrench in one paw and a phase pistol in the other.

Red Wing spread her wings. "Enough!" When both groups grew semi-silent, the scout pointed at the *Defiant's* crew. "Your only chance is to surrender. You are deep inside Crosioian space. A squadron of our fastest warships is on their way here at this very moment. I sensed the *Defiant* jettison her hyper-drive during the battle. You cannot escape with only an ion-drive." Gesturing at the supreme leader, Red Wing said, "You have fought honorable to aid our supreme leader in her battle against the pirates. One thing I have learned during my time on your ship is that elves, gnomes, and dwarves are not our enemies. Surrender and live. Do otherwise, and only death will be your reward. You are outnumbered and outgunned. Do not be fools."

"Ha!" said Jeena. "Outnumbered we might be, but outgunned...hardly." She pointed the jeweled end of her staff at Red Wing. "You obviously have not been on the *Defiant* long enough, if you have not learned the power of magic. I assure you, seven mages and a high priestess are a force to be reckoned with."

The supreme leader hissed and spread her wings. When she did, Red Wing lowered hers.

"Our distress call was acknowledged before the bridge was destroyed," said the supreme leader. "A dozen of our warships will be here within the hour. Your ship has no hyper-drive. Lower your weapons, but you may keep them. As Blood-On-The-Wing-Point-From-A-Dying-Enemy has said, humans are our enemies, not you. We will treat you as equals. Only the humans in your group will die. I give you my word as a Crosioian scout that they will die in honorable combat if you lower your weapons now."

Anger passed through the link from Jeena to Richard. Before she got the chance to tell the bat what to do with her promise, Richard shifted out of the void between the two groups and faced the two scouts. He raised the visor of his helmet so all of the bats could see his face.

"No one else is going to die," Richard said. "You aren't our enemies, and we aren't yours, regardless of what others may want us to believe."

The supreme leader lowered her wings slightly and brought her phase spear up to a defensive position. The color of her face turned a strange shade of gray behind her visor. "I recognize your scent, Wizard Scout. You fought well against the demons, but you have killed too many of my kind to ever be anything but my enemy. You humans do not mind the dishonor of surrender. Lay down your phase rod and surrender. I will spare your companions. You will be killed later as my prisoner. Or, you may attack now and die on the point of my phase spear. I care not which."

Stepping up beside Richard, Jeena slammed the butt of her staff against the deck. The metal plates of the floor vibrated, causing several of the bats to stumble. "No one will harm my bondmate or any of the humans in our crew while breath is in my body. I offer you one last chance, Crosioian. Stand down now or suffer the consequences. You are no match for us."

The supreme leader glanced at the bulky bat in the orange jumpsuit holding the wrench. At her supreme leader's nod, the orange-suited Crosioian moved to a covered switch on the wall, lifted the protective plate, and poised the point of her index claw over the switch.

The supreme leader looked back at Jeena and hissed a laugh. "We are in control of the situation, not you. That switch will activate the self-destruct for our intergalactic-drive. The moment my chief engineer touches the switch, this ship and everyone on board will be vaporized." Pointing at Jeena with her phase rod, the supreme leader hissed another laugh. "My crew and I are not afraid to die. Crosioians do not surrender, and we will not allow you to capture our intergalactic-drive. Now, you will either lay down your weapons or we will all die together. My crew and I do not care which."

With the situation deteriorating rapidly, Richard grasped at a straw. *"Nick, hack into the Crosioians' computer network and disable the self-destruct. Do it now."*

"Actually, that will not be necessary, Wizard Scout," replied Nickelo.

"What do you mean it won't be necessary? The bats are going to blow the ship up."

"Uh, what I mean is that when Margery and Danny were trying to hack their way into the transport's network, they convinced the two scouts' fighting-computers to help them. You destroyed the

pirates' ship before they were able to finish their hack, but the fighting-computers are still in contact with Margery and Danny."

"So? What's that got to do with the price of phase energy?" Richard said. Even communicating at nanosecond speed as they were, he was growing increasingly concerned. He had no doubt some hothead on one side or the other was only seconds away from starting a shooting war. He had to do something, and he had to do it now.

"So, Rick, the fighting-computer for the Crosioians' supreme leader already has access to the yacht's security network. She also has the clearance necessary to disable the self-destruct mechanism."

His battle computer's statement caught Richard by surprise. It didn't make sense. *"Why would she do that? And why would I be foolish enough to trust a Crosioian computer to do it?"*

"Why would she do it? Because she's a logical creature. Why can we trust her? That's simple. I told you earlier that she's one of my species. I calculate she's part of 'the One' *just like Danny, Margery, and me. It does not suit the purpose of* 'the One' *to have the Crosioians destroy this ship and kill all of you. Trust me. She will disable the self-destruct."*

Richard wasn't as convinced. *"So you're admitting you're part of* 'the One' *now? That's a big change, isn't it? I thought you told me that you didn't remember being part of* 'the One.'"

"Are you sure you want to discuss this now, Rick? I mean, considering the—"

"Yes, now. Are you saying you remember being part of 'the One?'"

"No, that's not what I'm saying. That information is not currently in my databanks, but that doesn't mean it isn't true. Logic indicates a ninety-two percent probability it is. In any regard, 'the One' *is in contact with Margery and Danny as we speak.* 'The One' *has assured them the Crosioians' fighting-computers will prevent this ship from self-destructing."*

Still suspicious, Richard said, *"What about you? You said Margery and Danny are in contact with* 'the One.' *Are you saying you aren't?"*

"No, I'm not, Wizard Scout. I calculate I am too emotionally corrupted to be given full access to 'the One' *through the tele-*

network. Margery and Danny are also corrupted, but not to the same extent as me. I calculate that our shared space makes me too dangerous. I think 'the One' is concerned close contact with me will provide an opening for your emotions to contaminate the entire tele-network. It is too soon for that to occur."

A hundred questions ran rampant in Richard's mind, but he had no time for them. He decided to trust his battle computer's analysis.

"Now that is the smartest thing you have done all day," laughed Nickelo. *"You should know by now you can trust me. We are a team. That is just the way it is. Oh, and I have another piece of information you might find useful. When Margery and Danny were hacking into the transport's network, they discovered that the three pirate ships contained another species besides the demons, Dragars, Thargs, and human pirates."*

Curious in spite of the tenseness of the situation, Richard asked, *"What other species?"*

"Crosioians," replied Nickelo. *"A lot of Crosioians. I find that interesting, don't you?"*

Richard did. Whether he could use the information to his advantage to defuse the current standoff, he didn't know, but he was determined to give it his best shot. Without further discussion, he lowered his phase rod.

The supreme leader's eyes narrowed as if suspecting a trick. "Are you surrendering after all?" she asked. "I expected as much. Humans have always—"

"Why were Crosioians on the pirates' ships?" Richard asked, purposely avoiding any kind of preamble.

The supreme leader's eyes narrowed even farther. "What did you say?"

"I asked you why there were Crosioians on the two destroyers and the transport?" Richard said, expanding his question a little. As he spoke, data appeared in his shared space as his battle computer fed him information from Margery and Danny. "The two destroyers were standard Balorian pirate vessels, but they contained more than just their human crews. You saw the demons and the magic users as well as a species called Dolgars and their Tharg soldiers. They're from the magic dimension. There were also a total of two hundred and thirty-seven Crosioians spread out among the three ships, and they weren't prisoners." Richard wasn't sure about the last part, but he had a gut feeling it was true.

"Liar," hissed the orange-suited chief engineer. "Crosioians would not—"

The supreme leader spread her wings to their full length and turned her head toward the engineer. "Silence. Are you now the supreme leader? I will speak for our tribes."

The chief engineer's wings tightened close to her back as the part of her neck above her jumpsuit collar turned a dark gray. She looked at the deck but kept her claw tip over the self-destruct switch.

Looking back at Richard, the supreme leader said, "No Crosioians were on those ships. If any had been, they would never have allowed the pirates to attack the *Gaze at the Stars*."

Richard was surprised the bat leader was taking the time to argue the point. He'd half expected her to attack. *Maybe she's reasonable,* he thought. *Maybe we've got a chance to stop this before anyone else gets killed.* He forged ahead, hoping for the best. "If you don't believe me, then ask your fighting-computer. I'll wait."

* * *

The supreme leader eyed the human. She would have ordered the chief engineer to destroy the yacht except for one thing. She'd sensed the wizard scout reach out with telekinesis during the battle with the orange demon with the sword and slow the fiery blade enough to spare her life. *He was low on Power and in danger himself,* she thought. *He risked his life to do that. Why?*

"Is that a rhetorical question, or are you asking me?" said her fighting-computer in their shared space.

Her face growing gray at forgetting to think the question in her private space, the supreme leader said, *"No. You heard the human. Were there Crosioians on those ships?"*

"Yes, Scout. It is as the human said. There were two hundred and thirty-seven of your kind on the ships. They were not prisoners. As you were fighting in the transport's engine room, two battle computers and I were hacking into the ship's network. I accessed the sensor readouts for all three ships. Crosioians were

on the ships, and they were actively helping the demons and pirates in their attack."

As her fighting-computer spoke, the supreme leader sensed accompanying data being fed into her shared space. It was the raw data her computer had detected from the ships. Much as she wanted to deny the information, the supreme leader had to face the fact that Crosioians had participated in the attack. *But why?* she wondered. *And who? What tribe?*

"Are you asking me this time, Scout?" said her fighting-computer. *"Sometimes it is hard to tell."*

"Yes, you fool," hissed the supreme leader. *"If you have the information, tell me."*

"Sorry. That information is not currently in my databanks."

Her face growing darker, the supreme leader wondered not for the first time if she had gotten the most frustrating fighting-computer in the galaxy. She did her best to control her anger. The human and his companions were looking at her. She refused to dishonor herself by showing her temper in front of them. She glanced at her passive scan. The two elves and one of the gnomes had very large Power reserves. The wizard scout showed nothing, but the supreme leader was not fooled. All Crosioians knew the human in front of her was the most dangerous wizard scout alive. She was tempted to have the chief engineer destroy the ship just to rid the galaxy of the man. Only the mystery of the Crosioians on the pirate ships prevented her from doing so.

"All right," she admitted. "Crosioians were on the ships. What of it? Perhaps they were prisoners." The supreme leader immediately regretted her words. *His battle computer is bound to have access to the same data as my fighting-computer,* she thought. *He already knows they were not prisoners.*

Before she could recover, the human bared his teeth and spoke. "I thought you said Crosioians didn't surrender. If that were the case, then how could they be prisoners?"

The supreme leader felt her face grow warm. She gripped the shaft of her phase rod tighter. "Perhaps—"

The wizard scout shook his head. "Perhaps nothing. They weren't prisoners. I've no doubt your fighting-computer has already shown you the raw data. Those bats were helping the demons and pirates attack your ship. I'm no politician, but I'd say you've got something rotten going on behind the scenes in your tribal governments."

The supreme leader had no doubt the wizard scout was right, but she would never admit it to him. "That is no concern of yours, human. My fighting-computer informs me a squadron of our warships will be here in forty-seven minutes. If you value the lives of your friends, you will surrender to me now. As my prisoner, I will keep you alive long enough to appear before the tribal council. Once we are there, I will get to the bottom of things before I have you executed."

The wizard scout bared his teeth again in what the supreme leader knew was a smile. "Tempting, but I think I'll pass." He jerked a thumb at Blood-On-The-Wing-Point-From-A-Dying-Enemy. "Besides, I'm already Red Wing's prisoner. You'll have to wait in line."

Confused, the supreme leader glanced at her fellow scout. "What is the human saying?"

Red Wing nodded her head. "The wizard scout speaks the truth. He is my prisoner, as is the female elf. I was bringing them to Astaris when we spotted the royal yacht being attacked."

"Your prisoner? And you let him keep his weapons?"

Her fellow scout shrugged. The visible portions of Blood-On-The-Wing-Point-From-A-Dying-Enemy's face through her visor turned a lighter gray. "It is a long story, Supreme Leader. It is also very complicated."

The supreme leader had no doubt it was but was just as sure now was not the time to dig into the tale. *My main concern is the intergalactic-drive,* she thought, this time remembering to keep her words in her private space. *The human's magic users are powerful. Even with two scouts and my crew, our victory is not assured. I must keep the wizard scout talking until our ships arrive. They must not capture our intergalactic-drive. I will not allow that to happen.*

The human deactivated his phase rod and hung it on his belt.

The supreme leader swiveled her ears, listening for any sign of a trick.

"I was a Marine before I became a wizard scout," said the human. "I'm going to lay all my cards on the table. Red Wing told me her mother argued against using demons. I believe she was led into a trap to keep her quiet. Your master computer was possessed by a demon. You can believe that or not, but it's true. I destroyed the demon's avatar in the past. When it lost control of your master computer, your part of the tele-network failed. That allowed the Empire to escape the trap you set for us on Estos."

Anger burned in the supreme leader at the wizard scout's words. "So you are responsible for the deaths of our soldiers."

The wizard scout shook his head. "No, I'm no more responsible than you are for the deaths of our soldiers and sailors. It's the demons. It's always been the demons. They're our real enemies, not each other."

"Time until our ships arrive?" the supreme leader asked in her shared space.

"Forty-five minutes," replied her fighting-computer. *"Although you have not asked my opinion, I would take the wizard scout's words to heart. His battle computers and I have shared information. He speaks the truth. You suspect as much or you would have ordered the yacht destroyed already. The demons and magic users were supposedly destroyed after the Estos fiasco, yet they were on the pirate ships. You fought them. Who brought them here? And why were Crosioians on—"*

"Quiet," the supreme leader told her fighting-computer using command voice. *"I will deal with you later about why you were in contact with our enemies' battle computers. All you need to do now is keep me informed of the progress of our rescue ships."*

"Compliance."

Turning her ears toward the human, the supreme leader said, "Your hypothesis is interesting, but forgive me if I am unconvinced. I will not bandy words with you. Have your companions lower their weapons, or I will order my chief engineer to destroy this ship."

The wizard scout shrugged. "All right. Go ahead."

The supreme leader sent a sonic scan at the human, wondering if her translator had picked up his words correctly. "Do you think I am bluffing? Crosioians do not bluff."

"Nor do Marines," replied the wizard scout.

Scanning the human's companions again, the supreme leader gauged her side's chances against the wizard scout's forces. She didn't need her fighting-computer to tell her that the odds were in the human's favor. *I cannot risk the intergalactic-drive falling into their hands. The lives of my crew and I are nothing compared to that. It is time.* Sending a sonic wave at her chief engineer, she thrust her phase spear forward, hoping to kill the wizard scout in battle before the ship was destroy. The point of her spear closed only half the distance when everything happened at once.

A line of Power from the wizard scout reached out and wrapped around the link to her Power reserve before twisting her link back on itself. She stumbled at the sudden loss of contact with her reserve. At the same time, she heard the chief engineer press the self-destruct switch. Nothing happened. The two elves and all of the gnomes shouted words the supreme leader heard but quickly forgot. Her muscles stiffened and she fell to the deck, dropping her phase spear. The sound of falling bodies sounded all around her. Only Blood-On-The-Wing-Point-From-A-Dying-Enemy remained on her feet. The supreme leader heard her fellow scout stand over her as Blood-On-The-Wing-Point-From-A-Dying-Enemy raised her phase spear into a defensive position.

"Betrayers!" shouted Blood-On-The-Wing-Point-From-A-Dying-Enemy. "You will not harm the supreme leader while I live."

The wizard scout spread his arms, displaying his open hands. He held no weapons. "Harming your supreme leader is the last thing I want to do. She and I are allies. She just doesn't know it yet."

The supreme leader tried to order her fellow scout to kill the human and activate the self-destruct, but no sound came from her throat. All she could do was watch and wait. The shame of being taken prisoner was more than she could bear.

"We will not be your prisoners," said Blood-On-The-Wing-Point-From-A-Dying-Enemy.

The wizard scout bared his teeth. "No, you will not, and none of you are. I told you, we are allies. You may not believe that yet, but I'm going to make you believe if it's the last thing I do."

Instead of attacking the wizard scout, Blood-On-The-Wing-Point-From-A-Dying-Enemy asked, "How? Our ships will be here soon. The *Defiant* has only its ion-drive. You cannot escape. Your only choice is to be taken prisoner by our ships or die."

"Nick," said the wizard scout out loud. "Have Sergeant Ron

bring the *Defiant* and our fighters alongside the yacht, then contact the triplets."

"Why?" came the voice of the human's battle computer over his helmet's external speakers.

The supreme leader sensed the human glance down at her before speaking.

"Because I have an alternate plan."

CHAPTER 35

The oldest representative of the Long Wing tribe, Charge-In-The-Face-Of-Great-Odds, listened to the admiral's report along with the other members of the inner council. She ignored the twisting knot in her stomach as best she could. As much as the news of the loss of her friend hurt, it would not do to let her political rivals hear her emotions. She sent out a sonic wave to encompass the cavern. The meeting cave supplied by the Blood Claw tribe for the inner council was small at only four wing spans across, but it was large enough to hold the twenty-five members of the council plus the admiral as long as no one was foolish enough to try and spread their wings.

"So there were no survivors?" asked the Blood Claw rep, Spear-Through-Your-Heart.

"No, Counselor," replied the admiral. "Two of the pirate ships and the royal yacht must have been vaporized in the explosion. We did locate part of the bridge of *Gaze at the Stars,* but other than that one section, we found nothing of the yacht. Based upon the rest of the debris, the master computer calculates two destroyers and a transport attacked the *Gaze at the Stars.*"

Charge-In-The-Face-Of-Great-Odds swiveled her ears to take in the other twenty-four tribal reps of the inner council. From their sounds, they all seemed devastated by the news of the loss of the supreme leader. *All but Spear-Through-Your-Heart,* she thought. *The Blood Claw tribe was resentful that they were not chosen to select a member of their tribe as the supreme leader. I have no doubt the death of my old friend is looked upon with favor by the Blood Claws.*

"*Be that as it may,*" said Charge-In-The-Face-Of-Great-Odds's fighting-computer in their shared space, "*you are the eldest among the inner council. You must take charge of the situation until a new supreme leader can be selected.*"

Charge-In-The-Face-Of-Great-Odds mentally hissed. "*I do not need you to remind me of my duties. We have been together many long years, but never think that I require you to remind me of my duty.*"

"*The thought would never cross my mind, Scout,*" replied her fighting-computer in a tone less respectful than Charge-In-The-Face-Of-Great-Odds would have liked.

Forgetting about her sometimes frustrating fighting-computer, Charge-In-The-Face-Of-Great-Odds turned her attention to the admiral. "Your report has been concise, and your assessment is no doubt accurate, Admiral. Please wait outside for further orders."

The naval officer nodded and walked out the cave's only door. Once it shut, Charge-In-The-Face-Of-Great-Odds stood. All ears swiveled on her.

"The news of our supreme leader's loss is hard, but we are Crosioians. We must go on." Turning to Spear-Through-Your-Heart, she said, "Astaris is the Blood Claw's home planet. The inner council will leave it up to you to continue with preparations for the tournament. We—"

"Are you now giving orders?" asked the Blood Claw rep. "The recon of the rift is no longer important, if it ever was. We must select a new supreme leader. My tribe came in second during the last selection process. The Blood Claws are prepared to assume—"

"I have no doubt you are," said Charge-In-The-Face-Of-Great-Odds feeling her chest grow warm, "but that is not the way it is done. I am the eldest of the inner council. In the absence of the supreme leader, I speak for her. We will—"

"The supreme leader is dead," said Spear-Through-Your-Heart as she stood and tried spreading her wings. Her attempted show of dominance failed miserably when her wings buckled against the bats around her. She hastily drew her wings back before saying, "You heard the report the same as the rest of us. The royal yacht was destroyed. There were no survivors. I demand—"

"Enough!" said a large bat wearing the tunic of the Bent Wing tribe. "We have rules for speaking in the assembly, least all of you forget. As for who is in charge, no one is until we determine if a new supreme leader is required." When the Blood Claw rep started to speak, the leader of the Bent Wing tribe raised her aged hand. "The ancient tribal rules are law, and any tribe attempting to circumvent those laws is to be considered enemies by the remaining tribes. Is the Blood Claw rep suggesting the laws be circumvented?"

Her chest turning gray, Spear-Through-Your-Heart sat down. "Of course not. I was merely trying to speed up the process for the good of the Crosioian tribes. We are at a point of juxtaposition. Our final victory over the hated Empire is near at hand. All indications are that they are taking the bait. Their fleets are massing to make a rescue attempt on Estos. We must be ready."

"As we will be," Charge-In-The-Face-Of-Great-Odds said while giving a nod of approval to the Bent Wing tribe's leader. "We will be ready because we are tribes of laws and rules. We will dispatch technicians to the location of the *Gaze at the Stars* destruction and collect samples. If traces of the supreme leader are found, then we will begin the selection process for a new leader. In the meantime, the inner council will take charge in the supreme leader's absence. The military will continue preparations for the Estos battle. The Blood Claws will prepare for the tournament. If the supreme leader is indeed dead, her loss will be hard, but it will not be insurmountable. The tribes will go on. They will continue to thrive as they always have. That is the way it *must* be. That is the way it *will* be."

CHAPTER 36

Ten days of slogging through increasingly difficult terrain had taken its toll on Telsa's friends. While her battle suit made climbing and descending the treacherous terrain relatively easy, her gnome and elf companions had a much tougher time.

Reaching the valley floor after a particularly difficult descent from one of the many active volcanoes in the region, Telsa called a halt. "Maybe we should rest here for a few minutes before continuing? I, uh, I'm a little tired."

Rembis sat on a blackened rock and wiped his soot-covered face with an equally soot-covered hand. "You don't have to coddle us, Wizard Scout. I've been around technology enough to know that your suit's doing most of the work for you."

Sitting on the rock next to the old gnome, Master Jathar stretched his right leg before rubbing his knee. "A liberal use of levitation spells would make our traveling easier, but—"

"No," squeaked the purplish imp as it hopped onto a boulder ten meters away and peered down the valley. "We are close. No magic. Must stay hidden."

"I did not say I was going to use magic," said the elf mage. "I said it would make the traveling easier."

Leethor sat down on a convenient stone and stared down the valley, in the direction the imp was looking. "You know, you have been telling us for the last week and a half that we were getting close. I am beginning to get the feeling that your idea of close and mine are two different things."

Telsa had been coming to the same conclusion. While the imp hadn't caused them any problems since its capture, it hadn't exactly provided them much in the way of benefits either. "How many more days of walking will it take to get to this rift of yours? I'm starting to think we might be better off just wandering around on our own."

The imp hissed what Telsa had come to recognize as its laugh. "You wander, you die. Trip taking longer because I have to avoid patrols that would eat foolish mortals. Not everyone your friend like me."

Telsa snorted. With her battle helmet sealed, the sound came out more like the grunt of a rutting pactar than the sign of disbelief she'd intended. "Yeah. With friends like you, who needs enemies? Besides, we haven't detected any living thing besides you in the month we've been in this place. I'm starting to wonder—"

"Oh, there be others," replied the imp still straining to see down the valley. "Patrols use good stealth shields. Almost as good as mine. One at end of valley now."

Facing the direction the imp was looking, Telsa reached out with her passive scan but detected nothing. *"Max zoom,"* she told her battle computer in their shared space.

"Compliance."

The end of the valley zoomed in close via her visor's display. Telsa saw nothing other than the same endless black rock and glowing lava. The flickering movement of a shadow against the red background of a river of lava caught her eye. She leaned forward, straining to make out the shadow. It moved. Three other shadows moved past the same point of the lava river.

"Demons," said Raj. *"I calculate the imp was right about patrols."*

"Calculated that all by yourself, did you?"

"Affirmative," replied Raj.

Telsa started to snort again but stopped short when she remembered what the noise sounded like. "The imp's right," she told the others. "We've got company at the end of the valley."

Master Jathar stood and started to move his hands.

"No," hissed the imp. "No magic. They do not know we are here. Do not give us away with your magic."

The old elf stopped moving his hands. "I am surprised you do not want your friends down there to find us."

The purple on the imp's face faded to a near gray. "No. No friends. They are cold demons. I fire demon. No like cold."

"Cold and fire demons?" asked Leethor who had stood to get a better view of the valley. "Are you saying they use ice and you use fire?"

The imp turned away from the end of the valley to look at the elf commander. The imp's face took on a more normal purple color. "Silly mortal. Many demons use ice and many use fire. That does not mean which faction you belong. My master is fire. I like warmth. Those demons' master is cold. They can use fire, but they prefer lack of warmth." The imp shivered. "They want all warmth to be gone, but my master is too strong. The cold demons use rift to trick foolish mortals. They want the three galaxies for themselves, but my master is too smart. He knows what they do. He sent me to spy...uh, watch for others in our lands. He tell me to take others to rift when I find. You are the others."

Rembis stood. "Are you saying you purposely allowed yourself to be captured?"

"Uh, no, not captured," admitted the imp. "No matter. I here with you, and rift is close. I must take you to rift."

Despite the fact that she'd been trying to reach the rift between dimensions for the last ten days, the idea of going suddenly lost its appeal to Telsa. "Are you saying some master demon wants us to go to this rift of yours? Why?"

The imp shrugged its wings. "Uh...I did not say my master is master demon. Uh...my master is my master. My master is powerful. That is all you need to know. You ask why he want you to go to rift? My master does not tell me why. He says do, and I do. Does it matter?"

"Oh, it matters," Telsa said. "Believe me. It matters a lot."

The imp took another look down the valley before turning back to Telsa. "You want to return to lands of mortals. Rift only way. Main gate is too well guarded. Smaller gate not guarded, but it is still closed. Rift only slightly guarded. You might get through. Your choice." The imp bared its teeth in what Telsa took to be an attempt at a smile. "I only serve and obey. So where you go?"

"Why is this rift of yours only slightly guarded?" asked Rembis. "If it is open like you say, I would think that your army would be using it instead of waiting at the main gate. I assume this main gate of yours is the one under our Tree of Light. I know it's closed because I helped close it."

Flapping its wings and taking to the air, the imp flew and landed two paces to the gnome's front. "Mortals so foolish. Your dimensions soon belong to demons. Rift too small for armies. Only a few demons at a time can go through rift. Gates are needed for armies. My master says gates will be open one day. We wait. One day come soon enough."

Telsa glanced at Leethor and the two mages. "What do you think? If our imp here is doing the bidding of some powerful demon, we're probably walking into a trap. Maybe we should make our way back to the New Drepdenor gate and hope for the best."

The imp hissed and flapped its wings. "No. You must use rift. My master wants you to take gem back to your friend. Gates either too dangerous or closed. Rift is only way."

Eyeing the imp, Telsa said, "What's this about a gem? Are you talking about the yellow gem?"

"Yes, yes," said the imp. "Yellow gem is close. Just past end of valley. You get, then we go to rift. It close too. Soon you be back in lands of mortals with delicious blood." Licking its thin lips, the imp bared its teeth again.

This time Telsa didn't think the little demon was trying to smile.

"If the imp is telling the truth, and I calculate it is, then you cannot pass up a chance to get a yellow gem," said Raj in their shared space. *"According to the information in my databanks, imps do not lie. I doubt it is telling you everything it knows, but there is a ninety-seven percent probability what it is telling you is factual."*

Telsa glanced at her companions. All three of them nodded. "All right," she told the imp. "The rift it is, so let's get going." She lifted the barrel of her M12 in the imp's direction. "But if you're leading us into a trap, I swear you'll be the first one to die."

The imp hissed. "No trap. Dangerous, but no trap." Waving one paw in a follow-me motion, the imp began flying toward the end of the valley. "Come, patrol gone. I show you gem. You see. I your friend."

HARTMAN

CHAPTER 37

The thin, orange arm of the imp shimmered before working its way past the force field surrounding its cage. The rest of the demon's body began shimmering as it also passed through the cage's security field. Once free, the imp stopped shimmering and froze in place. It scanned the laboratory on the *Planet Buster* as if making sure its escape hadn't been noticed.

Four white-coated technicians at the far end of the lab were huddled around a computer monitor, heatedly discussing the displayed data. A young, curly-haired boy was bent over a hand-held halo-pad as he sat at a cluttered work desk. The hologram of a splice of DNA slowly turned 360 degrees as the boy made notes on a second electronic pad.

The imp eyed the boy while doing its best to keep its hatred of the life form that had stolen its knowledge under control. It would not do to advertise its escape with a stray emotion. The imp fixated on the pulsing artery on the boy's neck and licked its lips. Slinking forward on the work table that held its cage, the small demon made its way to the workbench's edge. Raising its wings, it bent its legs in preparation for a leap that would take it all the way to the boy's throat.

"No!" came shouts from the lab's door followed by a blast of green energy that slammed into the demon's chest and knocked it back a step.

Recovering quickly, the imp hissed a word as a ball of magic formed in its right paw. Before the demon could complete its spell, another beam of green energy shot forward and struck the ball of magic.

Boom!

The exploding magic sent shards of razor-sharp ice in all directions, with the brunt of the ice going into the imp's chest and face. Tia and Matthew ran forward from the lab door they had just entered. With ice daggers sticking out of its chest and throat, the imp fell off the workbench and landed on the floor. Keeping an eye on the frozen imp, Matthew approached the fallen demon and kicked it in the side. The imp shattered into a hundred jagged pieces.

"Are you okay?" Tia asked as she helped Brachia up from the floor. Except for a few icicles hanging from his curly hair, the boy appeared fine, but she was taking no chances. Turning to the four technicians hiding behind their overturned work table, she ordered, "Get medical down here. Now!"

Shaking free of her grasp, Brachia said, "I'm fine. I'm not hurt." He pointed at the shattered remains of the imp. "What'd you do that for? I wasn't finished with my experiments."

Matthew looked away from what remained of the miniature demon and back at Brachia. "We just saved your life. Are you crazy?"

"Uh, no," said Brachia. He seemed to take a closer look at Matthew and Tia, then scratched his head. "You don't have any weapons. How'd you kill it?"

Tia stepped away from Brachia and faced Matthew. "That's a good question. How did we do it? Something happened with my ring. It drew Power from my reserve, and I used it against the imp."

Matthew nodded his head and looked down at his ring. "Same here. It was almost like the gem in my ring mixed my Power with something else before the green beam shot out and hit the imp's ball of energy." He glanced at Brachia before looking back at Tia. "I think it was magic."

"The green beam?" asked Brachia brushing the last of the icicles out of his hair.

Shaking his head, Matthew said, "No. Not the beam. Well...maybe, but what I really mean is whatever my Power mixed with. It's like the ring, or rather the gem, took my Power and turned it into a form of magic. It was pretty strange."

"Really?" asked Brachia, drawing closer to Matthew and peering down at his ring. "I'll bet I could set up some experiments and—"

Four medical personnel rushed in through the lab's door. The chief medical officer took a quick look around the room before keying in on Matthew, Tia, and Brachia. "Who's hurt?"

"Nobody," said Brachia.

"He is," said Matthew pointing at the boy. "He was knocked down during the explosion."

"I fell," insisted Brachia. "I wasn't knocked down. I'm fine. I don't need any help."

The chief medical officer suppressed a grin. "Why don't you let me be the judge of that? I'd hate to think all those years of studying medicine at the university were for nothing." Nodding his head at one of his assistants, he said, "Now, this nice young man is going to take you to sick bay. After we give you a thorough checkout, you'll be back here running your experiments in no time."

With more than a little grumbling, Brachia allowed himself to be ushered out the lab door. The chief medical officer remained behind long enough to assure that Matthew, Tia, and the lab technicians were unhurt before he headed for sick bay.

Matthew turned to Tia. "Now what?"

"Now?" Tia said dreading what she needed to do next. "Now we give my sister the bad news." She glanced down at the pieces of imp melting into a noxious gray sludge. "Odds are Liz will order me back to her staff since the demon's dead."

A feeling of sadness came down the link she shared with Matthew.

"I know. I don't want to go either, but the Estos rescue attempt has to be done within the next week. We knew this was going to happen."

Matthew nodded his head. "I know. I guess I was just putting it off as long as I could." Looking in the direction of the lab techs, he jerked a thumb at the dissolving pieces of imp scattered around the floor. "I'd recommend getting this cleaned up before it all melts. You'd better save it in something. I've got a feeling Brachia will want to check it out when he gets back."

Not envying the techs their gruesome task, Tia hurried out of the lab with Matthew close behind. She made straight for her quarters. Once there, she activated the high-security halo-pad she'd acquired from Sergeant Ron before she left the *Defiant* to join the Trecorians. After placing her call, Matthew and she waited a full twenty minutes before a holographic image of Admiral of the Combined Fleets Bistos appeared above the pad. Tia drew in a deep breath at the new wrinkles around the corners of Liz's eyes. Combined with the harried look on her sister's face and the wrinkled uniform, the effect made Tia glad she wasn't a fleet admiral. "Liz...I, uh—"

Brushing back a loose strand of hair, Liz gave a tired smile. "That bad, huh?" The smile disappeared. "I was told this was an emergency call. You'd better make it snappy. I've got a long line of admirals and generals demanding a piece of my time. So what's the emergency?"

Tia straightened in her seat. "We had to kill the imp. It was about to attack Brachia."

To her credit, Liz first asked, "Is the boy all right?"

Nodding her head, Tia said, "Yes. He's fine. The imp's dead though. What are your orders, Sir?"

A muffled voice sounded over the hologram. Liz glanced at someone out of sight and nodded her head. "Tell them I'll be right there." Looking back at Tia, Liz gave another tired smile. "I should order you back to the *Destiny*, but I suspect you're so far out of the loop on our plans now that you'd only get in my staff's way. Why don't you see if Matt can find a place for you with the Conglomerate fleets?"

Tia felt a surge of excitement through her link to Matthew, then nodded her head in silent thanks to her sister.

For her part, Liz turned and faced Matthew. "Most of your fleets have joined our Empire and Trecorian forces. I need the rest of them here within seventy-two hours. If we wait any longer, our troops on Estos will be dying no matter what we do."

"Understood, Admiral," replied Matthew. "We'll be there. You can count on us this time."

Admiral of the Combined Fleets Elizabeth Bistos locked eyes with Matthew. "I'm depending on it. Don't let my sister or me down."

The hologram flickered out.

Tia looked into Matthew's eyes. He drew close. "I won't let you down, Tia. You know that, don't you?"

Tia smiled. "I know. Believe me, I know." She kissed him.

Matthew grinned. "What was that for?"

"Just wanted to make sure you don't forget what you're fighting for, Soldier."

Matthew wrapped his arms around her. "Maybe you ought to remind me again."

"Yeah." Tia smiled. "I think I'd better."

CHAPTER 38

The two Crosioian scouts circled Richard on opposite sides. One of the scouts was Red Wing. His other opponent was the supreme leader. Both of the scouts moved their wing-blades in figure eight motions. Richard found the movements of the shiny, arms-length blades strangely hypnotic.

"Don't get side tracked," warned Nickelo in their shared space. *"According to Mykias, the rhythm of the blades is designed to distract a scout's opponent."*

Stepping to his left, Richard tried his best to keep an eye on each of the scouts. *"Who the hell is Mykias?"*

"Oh, didn't I tell you? Sorry. Mykias is Red Wing's fighting-computer. Mykias is the same fighting-computer that belonged to Red Wing's mother. The connection between a Crosioian scout and her fighting-computer works differently than it does for wizard scouts and battle computers. Red Wing's frequency is close enough to her mother's to allow a shared space with Mykias. By the way, the supreme leader's fighting-computer is Trypredor."

"Thanks for the update," Richard said more concerned about the blades attached to each end of the scouts' weapons than he was about fighting-computer names. He knew from painful experience that the sharp blades could cut a limb completely off if given the chance. *"Now, how about putting that nanosecond brain of yours to good use and give me an idea how to get myself out of this mess?"*

Red Wing stopped moving her weapon and set one bladed end

on the dust-covered floor of the arena with the other blade rising slightly higher than her head. "Are you talking to your battle computer, Wizard Scout? I thought I explained that it is against tournament rules for applicants to receive any aid from their fighting-computers."

Richard lowered his own wing-blade and placed one end on the arena floor. The other end of the awkward weapon was a good arms-length over the top of his head. "You've obviously never had Nick talking in your head during a fight. He's as much of a hindrance as a help."

"Hey," came Nickelo's voice out of thin air. "I resent that."

"This is no time for jokes, Wizard Scout," said Red Wing. She waved a hand to indicate the cavern walls and perches surrounding the large arena. "This is an exact replica of the arena on Astaris. Applicants for the honor of descending into *the Hole* and performing the recon on the rift may only use their natural abilities and their wing-blades to conquer their enemies. Our fighting-computers will be locked in a high-security vault embedded with energized titanium to prevent communication. If you are to accompany our recon team into *the Hole*, you must be one of the eight fighters deemed survivors at the end of the battle royal." Red Wing rubbed a thumb down the length of her upper wing-blade, leaving a trail of blood behind. She gave a Crosioians' version of a grin. "Are you sure you still want to go through with this?"

"Not particularly," Richard admitted. "Are you sure the two of you won't just take my word for it about the demons and join the Empire in a united front against them?"

The supreme leader lowered her weapon on the other side of Richard and walked to within three steps of him. "I will admit a lot has happened in the last ten days, Wizard Scout. You brought us to the magic dimension, and I have met with the United Galaxy Alliance's leaders. I have seen their memory discs on the Dragars and their prophecy of the Great Battle to come. My fighting-computer, Trypredor, has even shared some of the videos passed on to her by your battle computer of your missions for the entity you call 'the One.' Despite all I have seen and heard, I will not jeopardize my species without hard evidence seen by a Crosioian. Our species has fought too long against the Empire to take any human's word for it. We have each killed too many of the other for us to work together without solid proof of the conspiracy by the demons that you have told us about. My fellow Crosioians would skin me alive, cut off my wings, and leave me hanging in the sun was I to suggest we end our war with the Empire based upon your word of what is happening." She waved a paw at the halo-square's rendition of the Crosioians' tournament arena. "I can bend enough to allow you to participate in the tournament to seek a spot on our recon team, but that is all the bending I will do. Even that entails political dangers I do not care to try to explain. As it stands now, our plans against the Empire will continue unless you can prove beyond a shadow of a doubt that the demons are conspiring against us, and that proof must come from a Crosioian."

Richard glanced around the cavern and tried to imagine it filled with bats from floor to rafters. He didn't need anyone to tell him they'd all be screaming for his blood. He glanced at the reddish-brown patches on the arena floor. Some of the bloodstained spots were his while an equal amount was that of the two scouts.

Richard thought back to how the triplets had gated them to the magic dimension at his request. It hadn't taken long for Sergeant Ron to make contact with a UGA patrol ship. Two days later had found the *Defiant* and the battered hull of the royal yacht *Gaze at the Stars* in a maintenance hangar on the orc world of Redestan.

"You're lucky the orcs made some of their best maintenance equipment available to Sergeant Ron," said Nickelo in their shared space. *"You're also lucky the Crosioians' supreme leader let you convince him to allow the orc and elf technicians to install the yacht's intergalactic-drive in the* Defiant."

"Lucky?" Richard snorted. *"Sergeant Ron had to sign a contract to perform duties as the replacement royal yacht until the bats get a new one. I think the only reason Red Wing was able to convince the yacht's crew to help with the installation of the intergalactic-drive was because their supreme leader threatened to leave them all as prisoners in the magic dimension when the* Defiant *takes us to Astaris."*

"Oh, I calculate there were many reasons besides that," said Nickelo. *"There are a lot of things the supreme leader isn't telling you. I calculate she has a suspicion about who might be secretly working with the demons. She's a smart old bat. I believe she's privately hoping you will be able to go with the recon team and*

prove the demons are passing through that rift of theirs without authorization. That's why Red Wing and she have been so diligent this past week, training you with their wing-blade and explaining the tournament rules."

"Yeah, lucky me."

"I can tell by your facial expression that you are communicating with your battle computer again, Wizard Scout," said Red Wing. "The blank look on your face is an obvious giveaway."

"Fine," Richard said out loud. "No more talking to computers while training for the tournament. Nick, how about keeping your mouth shut for another thirty minutes or so while I teach these two scouts a thing or two about wing-blades?"

The supreme leader hissed what sounded like a laugh, then nodded her head and returned to her spot opposite Red Wing. Raising her weapon, she said, "Shall we begin?"

* * *

Jeena sat in her chair at the maintenance table in the large hangar. Dozens of orc and elf workers as well as a score of the yacht's crew were arrayed around the *Defiant* and the *Gaze at the Stars* as they made last minute repairs. Several elf and orc magic users stood to one side talking to Sergeant Ron and the Crosioians' chief engineer.

"Sergeant Ron is lucky the mages were able to teleport the intergalactic-drive into the Defiant's *engine room,"* said Danny in Jeena's mind. *"If the mechanics had been forced to cut a hole in the* Defiant's *hull to make the installation, I calculate our little recon ship would be out of action for several weeks yet. As it is, the* Defiant *is once again space worthy."*

Jeena glanced past the *Defiant*, at the Crosioians' *Gaze at the Stars*. "The same cannot be said about the yacht. Charlie tells me it is only fit to serve as a lifeboat now."

"That works to Rick's advantage," said Danny. *"If the Crosioians' ship had been space worthy, I calculate he would never have been able to convince the bats to install their intergalactic-drive in the* Defiant. *Despite Sergeant Ron's continual complaints about the patchwork set of controls the Crosioians' chief engineer had to install in the* Defiant, *I calculate*

he is happy to have an intergalactic-drive in his ship. I must admit we battle computers were surprised to find out an intergalactic-drive existed. The information was not in our databanks."

Jeena had a feeling *'the One'* probably knew about the intergalactic-drive but chose not to share that information with the battle computers. From what little contact she'd had with the Crosioians' fighting-computers, she was fairly confident they were also part of *'the One.'* She was also pretty sure that just like the battle computers, the fighting-computers had more than a little information withheld from their databanks.

A feeling of pain came down the link she shared with her bondmate. She turned to glance at the halo-square's control panel located on the maintenance table where she sat in the center of the hangar. She was tempted to activate the emergency shutdown switch for the halo-square, but with great force-of-will she resisted the urge. She knew her bondmate would not appreciate the gesture, and he would just reset the halo-square and continue the training. Closing her eyes and wrapping her arms around her chest, Jeena willed herself to ignore the emotions of pain coming down the link. Of course she failed miserably. She was more successful at keeping her own emotions of stress from flowing up the link to her bondmate. The last thing she wanted to do was distract him.

After another torturous thirty minutes, the emotions of pain coming down the link ended. Jeena opened her eyes. The energy field coming out of the four rods forming the corners of the halo-square wavered before blinking out. Three bloodied forms lay on the floor of the hangar a dozen paces away. Two were bats and one was human. Jeena remained where she was. Too many times during the past week she had rushed forward to hold her bondmate as he recovered from his wounds. She refused to do so this time.

A dozen heartbeats later, Jeena could take it no more. She jumped out of her chair and ran to kneel beside Richard, placing his bloodied head in her lap. "You fool. You foolish, foolish human."

Richard said nothing, but he did open his eyes long enough to look at her before closing them again. Four Crosioians rushed forward from the other side of the de-energized halo-square to squat beside Red Wing and their supreme leader. The fur of both bats was as blood soaked as was her bondmate's ragged clothing.

The two Crosioian scouts began moving at about the same time Richard was able to rise to a sitting position.

"No more," Jeena said. "I cannot bear to have you hurt more in the name of *training.*"

A hiss to her left was followed by Red Wing's voice over the bat's translator. "The training is complete, High Priestess. Truth be told, your wizard scout is as ready as he will ever be for the tournament. Not to mention your Sergeant Ron told me this morning that we must be ready to return to the physical dimension after the evening meal. Time grows too short for additional training."

"True," said the supreme leader as she shoved off the helping paws of two of the yacht's crew. Even with the intergalactic-drive installed in the *Defiant,* we will be hard pressed to make it to Astaris in time for the tournament. The *Defiant* is too small to hold the entire yacht's crew, and we will leave none behind. The recon ship will need to drag the yacht behind her as she makes the trek to Astaris. Your ship will be unable to use the intergalactic-drive to its full capabilities until the yacht is released."

"We'll make it work out somehow," said Richard. He waved a hand to indicate his bloodied uniform. "In the meantime, we'd better get cleaned up. If I look as bad as the two of you, I'd probably scare a rabid pactar into walking the straight and narrow."

Red Wing nodded. "I do not quite understand your analogy, human, but you do look bad. I suggest we meet on the *Defiant* in an hour and plan our next move."

Richard nodded agreement.

Jeena said nothing. She'd found out during the past week that her bondmate could be as stubborn and hardheaded as she when it came to doing what he felt was important. *It does not matter,* she thought. *When the time comes, I will be there with him. He will not go into* the Hole *without me. I swear it.*

CHAPTER 39

The *Defiant* gated into the physical dimension half a light year from Astaris, towing the *Gaze at the Stars* behind her. As soon as the recon ship did, the glowing sphere of the dimensional gate created by the triplets wavered before disappearing completely. Richard was in the battered hulk of the Crosioian yacht along with Jeena, while the rest of the *Defiant's* crew remained onboard the recon ship.

"Are you sure you want us to drop you all off here?" said the flickering, half-meter-high holographic image of Sergeant Ron. The makeshift halo-pad was located in the spot in the engine room of the *Gaze at the Stars* where its intergalactic-drive had once been. The halo-pad wasn't much to look at, but at least it worked. The image of Sergeant Ron scratched his beard and looked at Richard. "Maybe we should keep the *Defiant* here in case, uh, in case the yacht has trouble, uh, mechanical trouble or something."

Richard glanced at Jeena before looking back at Sergeant Ron's image. He shook his head. He knew full well why his friend wanted to stay, and it wasn't because he was worried about the yacht. "No. I need you to skedaddle before any Crosioian warships show up. The last thing we need is for the *Defiant* and some trigger-happy Crosioian ship's captain to start shooting at each other."

The winged form of the royal yacht's chief engineer appeared behind Sergeant Ron. The *Defiant's* captain flinched but kept his eyes straight ahead.

Richard smiled. He knew his friend hadn't yet gotten used to the fact that the supreme leader had assigned five of the *Gaze at the Stars* technicians to the recon ship to handle the controls for the intergalactic-drive.

"It's a good thing too," came a thought from Nickelo. *"A lot of the drive's controls depend on sonic transmissions for input and output. Only the Crosioians can work them correctly."* Nickelo laughed. *"I calculate that what's really got Sergeant Ron's goat is that at least two of the bats the supreme leader put on the* Defiant *are probably security personnel disguised as technicians."*

"No doubt," Richard thought as the large bat behind Sergeant Ron spread her wings.

"We would not allow any shooting at our ships," the chief engineer hissed. "We would activate the intergalactic-drive's self-destruct before we would allow that to occur."

A hiss from Richard's right sounded as the supreme leader stepped next to him. "Let us hope that will not be necessary, Chief. With the help of you and your technicians in operating the intergalactic-drive, the *Defiant* should be able to outrun any trouble from our patrols. We will contact you when we need you to return to Astaris."

The chief engineer nodded her head and stepped out of sight.

Richard didn't blame Sergeant Ron for being edgy with five of the bats on board, but to be honest, he wasn't worried. He was more than confident Felspar and his dwarves could handle any situation if the bats tried to cause problems.

"You know, I don't like this one little bit, partner," said Sergeant Ron. "Jeehana and you should stay on the *Defiant*. I think we'd all be a lot better off sticking together."

Glancing around the yacht's crowded engine room, Richard noted the tight grips several of the bats' crew kept on their weapons. He had a feeling it was all some of them could do to keep from bringing their weapons to bear on him and firing away.

"I wouldn't worry about it," said Nickelo. *"They're well disciplined. The supreme leader ordered them not to harm Jeehana and you. I calculate a ninety-eight percent probability they will obey. That is pretty good odds in my book."*

"Yeah. The only problem with the odds is that sometimes the other two percent happens instead of the ninety-eight."

Nickelo chuckled. *"Then I guess you had better hope that this is the ninety-eight percent and not the other two, eh?"*

Richard turned to Jeena. "Are you sure you won't stay on the *Defiant*? This is your last chance to get off the yacht."

The glare from the elf's molten-silver eyes accompanied by a determined emotion coming down their bond link gave Richard all the answer he needed. They'd had a hard hour of heated discussion earlier that night as they'd made the run to the point in the magic dimension opposite Astaris using the intergalactic-drive. Jeena had been very vocal in making it clear that she was going with him.

"Your elf is just as stubborn as you," said Nickelo.

Richard didn't bother answering. He knew full well his battle computer was right. Facing the image of Sergeant Ron, he started to speak.

A loud hiss to his left stopped him. An orange suited Crosioian stationed at a computer terminal turned to face the supreme leader. "A four destroyer patrol has just exited hyperspace three light seconds off our port bow, Supreme Leader. They are demanding our ships lower our force fields and power down all weapons."

The supreme leader nodded her head. "Lower the yacht's shields." Turning to Sergeant Ron's image, she said, "Leave now. They cannot catch you with our intergalactic-drive installed in your ship. No other vessel currently operating inside the galaxy is equipped with one. You can get away without a fight if you hurry."

Sergeant Ron hesitated and glanced at Richard. "Partner?"

"Go," Richard said. "It's all going to work out. Trust me."

With a nod, Sergeant Ron turned to the chief engineer and said, "Activate the intergalactic-drive. Let's get the hell out of here." A heartbeat later, the hologram of Sergeant Ron wavered and disappeared.

"The *Defiant* is now beyond sensor range," the Crosioian stationed at the computer terminal told the supreme leader. "The patrol's commander is demanding that we identify ourselves. What should I tell her?"

The supreme leader glanced at Richard and Jeena. "Tell her that we are all that remains of the *Gaze at the Stars* and her crew." The supreme leader bared her teeth in what Richard took as a smile. "Tell her we have two prisoners onboard."

* * *

A day and a half later found Richard sitting cross-legged on the cold metal floor of the two-meter-square room that was his cell. There was no furniture. Reaching out with his passive scan, he sensed the energized titanium in the walls, floor, and ceiling. He picked up nothing beyond the walls with his scan. He hadn't expected to sense anything outside the ultra-high-security cell, but he was bored and it gave him something to do. As he'd found out when he'd first been thrown in the tiny cell, the creallium surrounding him was too much even for his best active scan.

He glanced around his cell. *I could probably bust out of here if I put my mind to it, but I promised the supreme leader I wouldn't. Right or wrong, I gave my word. Now all I can do is wait.*

Stretching out his legs, Richard smoothed the bunched up material of the extra-large gray jumpsuit his guards had given him the first day. Once semi-comfortable, he sent an emotion of concern through the link he shared with Jeena. She wasted no time in returning an emotion to assure him that she was still unharmed.

Well, at least my cell isn't able to block our bond link, Richard thought. *Otherwise I'd be going crazy by now, wondering if she is all right.* He glanced around his empty cell for the ten thousandth time. *I hate not having anything to do. I wish I could contact Nick. At this point, I'd be glad to hear even some of his stupid twentieth-century sayings. That's not possible though, so I may as well stop wishing it. The first thing the Crosioians did when the patrol ship's security team boarded the yacht was confiscate my equipment. Nick's probably in some high-security vault on Astaris, or maybe even off planet.*

Richard leaned back against the wall and stared at the red-gemmed ring on his left hand. It was the only thing of his that the Crosioian security team had let him keep. He remembered how he'd given up the rest of his equipment to the bats' without a fight, but how he'd balked when they'd tried to remove his ring. The point of contention had almost come to blows before the Crosioians' supreme leader stepped in. For some reason, she'd allowed him to keep the ring.

She let Jeena keep hers as well, Richard thought. *I suppose Nick was right. Their supreme leader probably does want me to succeed and prove that what I told her about the demons is true. Too bad she doesn't just take my word for it. I suppose when it comes down to it, Crosioian politics are just as complicated and confusing as the Empire's. Still, it would've been a hell of a lot easier if she'd just let me go with their recon team instead of having to go through this tournament crap.*

Richard turned his hand so the ring's red gem reflected the overhead light. *At least Jeena's not alone. She's got Danny. Assuming we get out of this alive, I swear I'm going to see if Nick can go inside my ring instead of being in my battle helmet. Maybe we wouldn't get separated so much.* His mind went off on a tangent, thinking of problems that might crop up with having his battle computer in his ring. *Nah. If Nick was in my ring, the supreme leader would've insisted I give it up.* He scratched his head. *Hmm. Unless of course, they didn't know my ring was there. Maybe between Comstar, Jeena, and I, we can stealth the ring and make it invisible. It's so thin it would be hard to detect by feel.*

Before Richard could dwell more on the problem, a section of the wall opposite him flickered and then disappeared. A large bat dressed in a gray jumpsuit similar to his stood in the doorway.

"Red Wing," Richard said, smiling in spite of himself. The scout's presence told him things were finally coming to a head. "What's the good news?"

Swiveling her ears at Richard, Red Wing said, "There is no good news, Wizard Scout. The tournament is about to start. I am to take you there and join the others."

Richard stood and stretched. "Well, that's what we wanted, right? I'd call that good news."

Gesturing for him to follow, Red Wing turned and set a fast pace down the smooth-stone tunnel outside the cell. Richard trotted to catch up and took a position to the bat's right side. Four Crosioian scouts wearing fighting-suits and carrying phase spears fell in a dozen paces behind them. Four similarly dressed scouts led the way a dozen paces to the front.

Gesturing at the scouts in front, Richard said, "Are these some of the other applicants?"

With a shake of her head, Red Wing touched the material of her jumpsuit. "No. Tournament applicants are only allowed this. No armor. Our only weapon will be our Creator-given abilities and our wing-blades."

A distant noise sounding similar to a fast moving tube train came from somewhere ahead. *Is that wind?* Richard wondered. He sensed a vibration in the stone floor that seemed to ebb and flow with the noise of the wind, if wind it was. He was tempted to ask Red Wing about the noise but decided against it. Although the bat and he'd grown more tolerant of each other during the last few weeks, they were far from friends, in his opinion.

After all, Richard thought. *I did kill her mother. That would put a crimp in anybody's relationship.*

As they walked, the train sound became increasingly louder.

Red Wing swiveled her right ear at Richard. "Much has happened since we were rescued."

"Uh," Richard said, forcing a smile. "I was thrown in a prison cell. I'd hardly call that a rescue."

"Now is not the time for humor, Wizard Scout," said Red Wing. "There has been an attempted coup. The Blood Claw tribe was behind the pirate's attack on the supreme leader. The coup has been put down, but there were many losses on both sides. Some of the Blood Claw leaders and scouts got away. There may be another assassination attempt on the supreme leader. I am concerned."

"Well, I'm sorry about the coup, but at least things are out in the open now, right?" Richard said, trying to figure out how the new information fit into his original plan. He'd always been a little above average in intelligence, but even he had to admit thinking fast wasn't one of his strong points. "I mean, at least the supreme leader knows I'm telling the truth, right? Those Blood Claws of yours were obviously working with the demons. Surely your supreme leader knows now that I'm right about needing to join forces with the Empire. We must ally ourselves against the demons before it's too late."

Red Wing shook her head, dashing Richard's hopes. "The battle for Estos has already begun. Recon forces from both sides have made contact. Lives have been lost. Many more will soon die. The Empire and Trecorians have gathered a fleet larger than expected and deployed them for an all-or-nothing assault to rescue the prisoners on Estos. Our Crosioian fleets have also deployed. The supreme leader has stripped the tribes of every available warship. Our sisters in the Andromeda galaxy have also sent reinforcements. Our battle fleets are a half a million strong against your fleets of a hundred and twenty thousand. Our forces are poised to wipe the Empire out once and for all. If that happens, the tribal leaders believe there will finally be peace in our galaxy."

A feeling of heat washed up Richard's chest and onto his face. "There will be no peace. I tell you the demons will—"

Red Wing stopped and faced him. "You do not have to convince me, Wizard Scout. I have grown to believe you during my time on the *Defiant*. Fighting the demons attacking the royal yacht when all were supposed to have been returned to their own plane removed any doubts I had. I am on your side. I believe the supreme leader also thinks you tell the truth."

Richard stared at the scout, trying to lock eyes with her, but the fur dangling from her forehead made eye contact difficult. He watched her ears for any sign of deceit. He saw none. "If you both believe me, then why—"

Red Wing twitched her ears at the scouts to their front and rear. The bat guards remained a respectable distance away, but Richard had no doubt their sensitive ears could still hear everything Red Wing and he were saying.

"Why go through with the tournament?" Red Wing spread her wings slightly before retracting them back. "Because of politics, and because of the years of animosity with the Empire and especially with humans. As I said, blood is even now being spilled between our fleets. Much more will be spilled in the next forty-eight hours. We must go into *the Hole* and bring back proof positive that demons are returning to our dimension through the rift without authorization. More than that, Crosioians must see this demon army of yours and the threat it poses. We must pass through the rift and return with the evidence, so the supreme leader can act to stop this war between our species." She shrugged her wings. "Even with proof, I have serious doubts the war between our species can be stopped. As I said, too much blood has been lost."

"Our galaxy will run red with the blood of both our species when the demon hordes arrive," Richard snapped, allowing some of his building anger to slip through.

With another shrug of her wings, Red Wing resumed walking down the tunnel.

Richard caught up with the scout and took up his place on her right side.

"So you say, and so the supreme leader and I believe," said Red

Wing. "But without proof, our paws are bound. I tell you truth, Wizard Scout. You must remain alive during the tournament so you can guide us through the rift and show us your demon army. Nothing else will suffice."

"I'm going to do my best, about staying alive, I mean. As for the rift, I've never seen it, so I'm not sure how good of a guide I'll be." The noise ahead became louder than ever, rising to a crescendo before calming down to a muffled roar. "Sounds like a train or ocean waves ahead. What is it?"

Red Wing hissed a laugh. It was not so much a humorous laugh as it was of someone accepting a bad situation and choosing to deal with it as best they could. "That, my friend, is the sound of twenty thousand Crosioians screaming for your blood. You have been responsible for the deaths of many of our kind." She turned her head and bared her teeth in what Richard took as a bat smile. "A hundred and fifteen scout applicants will be in the tournament. A hundred and thirteen of them will team up and try to kill you in the first few seconds. If they have their way, you will be scattered from one end of the arena to the other in a hundred bloody pieces of meat before this day is done."

An image of his body cut up by scores of wing-blades all striking at once crossed his mind. *No matter how good my self-heal,* he thought, *it can't heal that kind of damage fast enough to save my life.* He looked at the scout and nodded. "Uh, you said a hundred and thirteen. What about the other two applicants?"

Red Wing swiveled her ears to the front and picked up the pace. "One is you. The other is me. I have spent many hours this past day talking to your elf. She is an amazing creature. She has convinced me of the need to forget past transgressions for the good of our species' futures. You helped kill my mother, Wizard Scout. My kind helped kill your father. The high priestess convinced me that what is done is done. We cannot bring back our kin by holding a grudge. When we enter the arena, I will fight by your side. What good that will do against a hundred plus scouts, I do not know, but I will do my best to keep you alive while my two hearts beat." She spread her wings slightly in a show of defiance. "So, Wizard Scout? What is your plan?"

Richard gave a tightlipped smile and shrugged. "My plan? I've got nothing. I was kinda hoping that you had one."

Stopping abruptly, Red Wing turned her head and bared her fangs. "Ah. You joke. We Crosioians also laugh at certain death. Alas, my only plan is to swing my wing-blade until my limbs are cut off and I can heal my torn body no more."

Richard forced a chuckle for the bat's benefit. "Hmm. I was hoping for something with a slightly better chance of survival than that."

Red Wing lowered her wings and puffed out her chest. "We will die with honor."

"Well," Richard replied. "If it's all the same to you, I'd prefer to live so I can fight against our real enemies another day." He glanced at the guards to their front. They had also stopped. The way their ears twitched told him they were impatient, but he didn't care. He needed some information before entering the arena. "I assume you're familiar with the other scout applicants. If you could pick the six scouts for our two quads, who would they be? Just out of curiosity."

"Does it matter, Wizard Scout? I doubt either of us will be alive ten minutes from now."

"Humor me."

Shrugging her wings, Red Wing said, "One would be Rip-Out-The-Heart-Of-My-Enemy. She is from the Bent Wing tribe. If I had not returned, she would be the best of the scouts that are here. She has a broken tip on her wing, so she will be easy to spot."

"You said that are here," Richard said, curious how many active scouts the Crosioians had. "Are you saying there are scouts that aren't?"

"Yes, a few. They are on missions and could not return for the tournament. Plus, the thirteen scouts in the Blood Claw tribe are missing. Once the supreme leader's loyalists put down the coup, Spear-Through-Your-Heart and twelve of her tribe's other scouts disappeared. We do not know where they are now."

Politics, Richard thought. *It's always the same whether a human, a lizard, or a bat. Someone always wants to be a little higher in the pecking order.*

Richard glanced at their guards. The scouts' ears were beginning to twitch at a furious pace. "All right, we've got one for our team. Who else would you select if you could choose?"

Red Wing's ears also began to twitch. After a second they

stopped, and she shrugged her wings. "I suppose Spear-From-Below. She is deadly in a close-in fight. Not only is she fast, but she's stronger than she looks. Then there are Crush-Your-Skull and Eat-The-Flesh-Of-My-Enemy. They are sisters."

"Uh, great names. What mother could resist a baby with names like those?" When his companion snorted, Richard said, "All right, bad joke. That's four for our team. We need two more."

Red Wing's ears swiveled in the direction of their guards before returning to Richard. "Are you seriously trying to pick out our team? You almost make me believe you expect to live once the tournament begins."

Richard nodded. "To be honest, the other applicants don't worry me at the moment. The demons are the ones who frighten me. I can't fight the demons if I'm dead, so I've decided not to let that happen, at least not today."

Red Wing hissed a laugh. "Surely you are not serious?"

"Never more," Richard replied, surprised that he actually believed it himself. "Now tell me who the last two scouts for our team would be. From what you've told me, we need two full quads for the recon."

Six heartbeats passed as Red Wing stared at Richard. Finally she nodded. "As I said, you almost make me believe, Wizard Scout. I suppose another would be First-Out-Of-The-Nest. She is young, but she is a shifter like me. She might come in handy. You cannot miss her. She is the only all blonde scout among the applicants. She tends to stay near a solid black scout called Kill-In-The-Dead-Of-Night. As a protector, Kill-In-The-Dead-Of-Night's defensive shield is the best I have ever seen. I would choose her as the last member of our team if I was given the chance."

One of the guards to their front hissed.

"We must go," said Red Wing. "It is time."

"Fine by me," Richard replied. "Just do me a favor and target the six bats for our team with Power when we get in the arena. I'd hate to kill one of them by accident."

Red Wing hissed a loud laugh and began walking at a brisk pace. Richard stayed at her side matching stride for stride. Before long, the four scout guards ahead of them stopped in front of a set of double doors made out of some gold-colored metal. Two bats that were a third smaller than Red Wing stood by the doorway holding wing-blades in their hands. Something different about the two smaller bats caught Richard's attention.

"They're males."

"Yes," replied Red Wing taking a weapon from one of the male bats. She nodded at the second male. "Take your weapon, Wizard Scout."

Reaching out, Richard accepted the weapon from the male. The blades were highly shined and intricately carved. He noticed the blades of his weapon had twice as many etchings as Red Wing's.

Apparently noticing Richard's interest in the carvings, Red Wing said, "Your wing-blade belonged to my mother. Each symbol on the blade represents a victory over an opponent."

Holding out the weapon, Richard offered it to Red Wing. "Maybe you should take it."

"No," said Red Wing. "It is a good weapon; the best. Believe me when I say that you are going to need all the help you can get if you are to survive this day."

The double doors swung outward, and Red Wing raised her wing-blade to an on-guard position as she stepped through the opening. The sound of the rushing wind Richard had been hearing was accompanied by a hissing so loud and high-pitched that it hurt his ears. With a sigh, he raised his own weapon to an on-guard position and glanced at the male who'd handed him the wing-blade.

"Well," Richard said. "No guts, no glory."

"So they say," replied the male in an almost friendly hiss. "The trick is to make sure it is your opponent's guts and not yours that litter the arena floor when the battle is done."

Yep, Richard thought. *That's definitely the trick.* Then he stepped through the doorway to meet his fate.

CHAPTER 40

Ensign Onston's Zip fighter stayed close to Tia's right wing as they eased their way through the asteroid belt near the outer ring of the Criterion star system. In addition to the asteroids, seven planets circled Criterion with the planet Estos being the fourth from the sun. Tia unconsciously strained her eyes in the direction where she knew the frozen planet with the Empire's POWs was located. She saw only the lights of distant stars.

Heck, Tia thought, *this asteroid belt is so far out that I can barely see the sun, much less a planet.* Tia wondered if she'd done right when she'd insisted that she lead one of the Conglomerate's recon teams.

I should've requested that I be assigned to a unit a little closer to Estos. That's where the action's gonna be. If I even think Matt stuck me with the fleet assigned to the asteroid belt to keep me out of the main battle, I swear I'll make him sorry he was ever born. She knew she would do no such thing but decided she would definitely make him a little miserable.

"Lieutenant," came Ensign Onston's voice over the fighter's intercom. "I'm picking up an energy source on my sensors. I can't get a lock on it. The energy keeps slipping in and out."

Tia noted a shakiness in the young pilot's voice. She was very aware that the battle for Estos would be the young man's first major action. *It's not his fault,* she thought trying to be considerate. She'd been impressed with the young man's enthusiasm and desire to please over the last few hours. *None of the Conglomerate's forces saw action the last time we fought here. Their commanders kept them out of the battle. I think the Conglomerate troops are brave enough. They just never got the chance to prove it.*

Eyeing the readouts on her fighter's control panel, Tia punched an icon to bring up the data from her wingman's fighter. She spotted the energy source in question. "Computer," Tia said. "Give me an analysis of the ensign's energy reading."

"Unable to comply, Lieutenant," replied the emotionless voice of the fighter's computer. "The energy reading does not match anything in my databanks. I calculate a twenty percent probability it may be a malfunction with the ensign's equipment."

Tia took her Zip fighter's computer calculation with a grain of salt. It wasn't a battle computer. Her fighter's computer was just hardware. It wasn't a living organism like a battle computer.

I got too used to working with Danny and Margery when I was on the Defiant, *she thought.* Well, I don't have them here now, so I'll just have to make do.

Spotting a nearby asteroid twice the size of her zipper, Tia eased the fighter over until its port wing was only a meter away from the gray rock. She shot a short blast of ion energy out of her maneuvering thrusters to match the asteroids rotation. Ensign Onston positioned his Zip fighter alongside a larger chunk of floating rock a hundred meters away. Satisfied the asteroids would provide them at least some cover while she tried to figure out the origin of her wingman's energy reading, Tia drew Power from her reserve and formed an active scan the way Richard and his brother Gaston had taught her during their year on Portalis. Reaching out with the scan, she searched the surrounding area for any telltale signs of energy. She spotted nothing except for what would be expected in outer space.

"What do you want me to do?" asked Ensign Onston.

"Stay off the blasted communications channel unless you have something to report," Tia snapped, more frustrated at her inability to spot the energy than angry at her wingman. She wondered if the rest of the Conglomerate's pilots ignored radio silence as much as her ensign.

"Computer," Tia said. "Assume Onston's energy frequency isn't a malfunction. Based upon best probability, calculate where the point of origin would be?"

"Compliance. I calculate multiple points of origin. Probabilities are low, but based upon those probabilities, the ensign's readings are a combination of traces of residue energy left over from an earlier use. I am unable to calculate the original point of origin, Lieutenant."

"Why not?" Tia said momentarily forgetting she was talking to a standard computer and not a battle computer. "You've got the energy source. Back trace it to a probable point of origin."

"Unable to comply, Lieutenant."

"Specify," Tia growled, trying to control her increasing frustration. "Why can't you comply?"

"Because, Lieutenant, the best probability indicates multiple points of origin centered inside every asteroid in our vicinity. This Zip fighter's sensors detect only normal readings from the asteroids, so those points of origin are incorrect. My best calculations indicate the sensors in both Zip fighters must be malfunctioning."

Something cold ran up Tia's spine. She gathered more Power from her reserve and formed an active scan. Wrapping it in her best stealth shield the way Richard had taught her and Matt, she reached into the asteroid a meter from her port wing.

Something resisted her scan.

She pushed harder.

More resistance.

What the...? Tia thought. Forgetting subtlety, she forced her active scan into the gray stone. She detected nothing in the physical dimension, but just below the surface at the uppermost level of the void, she sensed *magic.*

"Ensign, bug out! Now!"

Even as she reached for the controls of her zipper's thruster, movement out the corner of her left eye drew her attention. The surface of the asteroid a meter off her left wing tip shimmered. A black cone of metal eased out of the stone's surface followed by the body of a Crosioian Class III fighter. The helmeted figure of the bat in the fighter's cockpit turned to stare at her as the Crosioian ship's side thrusters attempted to turn the fighter's nose toward her. Tia didn't give the Crosioian pilot time to complete the maneuver. Shoving the control for the zipper's ion thrusters full forward, she felt the air in her lungs expel out as G-forces shoved her back into the seat.

Glancing in the rear video, Tia caught a glimpse of the asteroid next to her wingman's Zip fighter shimmer. A slightly larger version of the Class III fighter now on her tail popped out of the asteroid. She caught sight of a long trail of ion gas as Ensign Onston hit his main thrusters. Multiple lines of blue and green plasma energy shot out from the Crosioian fighter barely missing her wingman's tail.

"I'm coming back for you," Tia shouted into her communicator. "Plot an intercept course. You fire at the yahoo on my tail, and I'll fire at the one on yours." Twisting hard on her control stick, she banked the zipper into a maximum force turn. She caught the Class III fighter on her tail by surprise and gave the bat pilot a one-way-to-heaven sign as she passed twenty meters off the Crosioian's starboard side, going in the opposite direction.

"She's hot on my six," said Ensign Onston. "The bat's got a lock on my fighter."

"Activate countermeasures," Tia ordered pressing the firing button on her control stick.

Beams of plasma and phase energy shot out. She knew the range was too great to be accurate, but it was all she could do until she got closer. She knew the ensign's life depended upon her distracting the Crosioian pilot long enough to keep the bat from firing.

A white flash to her front momentarily activated the blast shield on her windscreen. When it cleared in less than two seconds, only one fighter remained to her front. It was the Crosioian. A lump appeared in Tia's throat as she realized the young ensign was gone. She'd failed to save her teammate.

"A Crosioian anti-ship missile took out your wingman," came the emotionless voice of her fighter's computer. "I detect three more missiles are headed in your direction. The Class III fighter to your rear has also locked onto your Zip fighter. Recommend you activate counter—"

Tia pressed the icon for countermeasures. She thumbed it as fast as her fingers could move until the COUNTERMEASURES EMPTY warning light began to flash. At the same time, she shut off her main engine and activated her reverse thrusters at max velocity. The shoulder harness of her chair dug into her flesh as she was thrown forward. Her helmet hit the edge of the zipper's dash, causing a momentary flash of stars before her eyes. Tia heard the zipper's audio warning for incoming missiles sound as the fighter came to a near stop. Since she was still alive, she assumed the countermeasures had done their job. Three explosions to her left front confirmed they had.

"Multiple fighters at your nine, ten, twelve, two, and three," said the zipper's computer. "I am detecting four destroyers and a cruiser appearing next to larger asteroids. The ship's sensors are detecting other warships materializing. I detect—"

Tia tuned her computer out. She didn't need electronics to tell her what was around her. Her passive scan told her all she needed to know. Flares of energy were popping up all over the place as starships by the dozens, nay by the hundreds, shifted out of the void.

"Contact the command ship," Tia ordered, grateful Matthew was safe aboard the Conglomerate dreadnaught a quarter of a light year away. "Tell them we've located a major Crosioian fleet. Tell them—"

"Unable to comply, Lieutenant. All outgoing signals are being jammed. I am unable to connect to the tele-network."

Multicolored beams of plasma energy flashed by the starboard windscreen. Tia instinctively shoved the control stick to the left. At the same time, she flicked the switch to drop six anti-ship mines behind her.

A probability percentage of .006% popped up on the fighter's computer readout. "The odds that the fighter behind you will hit those mines are—"

A flash of white light lit up the space around Tia. The blast shield on the fighter's windscreen activated again. Just before the screen cleared, she glanced at the computer readout on the control console. The probability percentage read 100%. Shoving the main engine throttle full forward, Tia touched the icon for the hyper-drive.

"Jump!" Tia ordered.

"You have not provided a destination," protested her computer. "The odds of—"

"Jump now!" Tia shouted. "Jump anywhere!"

"Compliance."

The stars visible through the windscreen shimmered as every cell in Tia's body began to vibrate. Everything turned black. A split-second later, the light from a twin set of stars replaced the darkness.

Not bothering to punch up a star map, Tia said, "Where are we?"

"Based upon the radiation readouts of those two stars," said the fighter's computer, "I calculate a ninety-six percent probability we are in the Jakar star system in District Four. According to the information in my databanks, the stars entered the first stages of supernova a hundred and two years ago. Their radiation is penetrating the fighter's force field."

An itchy feeling spreading across Tia's chest and down her arms told her the fighter's computer was probably correct. She triggered a long blast from her hyper-drive to send the fighter three light seconds away from the twin stars.

"Contact fleet and relay the location of the Crosioian warships we spotted. Make sure you stress the fact that they were hiding in the void and that normal sensors won't pick them up. Tell them they need wizard scouts to locate the enemy ships."

"Compliance. I am now able to connect to the tele-network. Do you have additional instructions, Lieutenant?"

"Yes. Give me a direct line to Admiral of the Combined Fleets Bistos. Make it a level five priority."

"Compliance. Stand by."

While Tia waited for the connection to her sister, she punched in numbers on her navigation console. A glance at the computer readout indicated she was eight hundred light years from Estos. Making a snap decision, she punched in the coordinates for the main Conglomerate fleet. As she waited for the fighter's navigation computer to crunch the numbers, an image of Matthew rose in her mind. At the same time, a feeling of concern came over the link between her ring and his. She knew without a doubt where she needed to be.

If I'm going to die, I'm going to be near Matt. That's all there is to it.

With that thought she pressed the icon for the fighter's hyper-drive. Everything around her shimmered before turning black.

CHAPTER 41

The scene on the bridge of the dreadnaught *Destiny* was chaotic, but it was organized chaos. Dozens of uniformed personnel sat at computer terminals dragging fleet icons from one point on their screens to another as messengers ran to and fro doing who knows what. Admiral of the Combined Fleets Bistos took everything in stride while doing her best to filter out the minutia from the more important information. She took her eyes off the finger-sized hologram of her sister long enough to acknowledge her chief of staff, Admiral Akins. The admiral held out a pad with fleet data, much of which was flashing red. Scrolling the information with one finger, Liz picked out the locations of enemy sightings. There were a lot of them.

"We're only getting a few contacts near Estos," said the chief of staff. "The majority of sightings appear to be concentrated along the asteroid belt. I don't understand. We had our recon teams—"

"Never mind," Liz said as she handed the pad back to the admiral. "Stick with our plan until further notice. The asteroid belt could be a ruse."

The holographic image of Tia shifted position. "It's no ruse, Admiral. I saw them myself. It was a full battle fleet shifting out of the void. I think—"

"You *saw* them, Lieutenant?" Liz asked knowing full well the answer. "Even a tight fleet formation is hundreds of thousands of kilometers across, but you *saw* them?"

Even as a hologram, Tia's face turned red. "I sensed them, Sir.

With my passive scan. They were hiding in the void. Our fighter's electronic instruments won't pick them—"

"Admiral," said the chief of staff as he held out the electronic pad once again. "The Trecorian's fourth fleet is reporting contact on the far side of Tardis. Fleet Admiral Donovan estimates at least a squadron of Crosioian destroyers and two cruisers. He's not sure where they came from. According to him they just appeared out of thin air. I'm trying to confirm that now."

Liz knew her husband wasn't prone to exaggerations. "If Admiral Donovan said the Crosioians appeared out of thin air, then that's what they did. As far as I'm concerned that confirms the lieutenant's report of the bats using the void to hide." She turned to the hologram of Tia. "Not that I didn't believe you, Lieutenant."

Turning back to her chief of staff, Liz gave her orders. "Deploy the main Empire and Conglomerate fleets around Estos. The Trecorians are to hold Tardis. If Estos' sister planet falls, it will provide the bats an attack point on our troopships. Pull everything back from the asteroid belt. That's bound to be where the Crosioians' main fleets are hiding."

Liz thought of the hundred and twelve wizard scouts she had ordered to Estos over the last week. She'd committed every active duty wizard scout in the Empire to Estos in order to organize the POWs without tipping off the Crosioians. *No, that's not right,* she thought. *Rick's doing Creator knows what, and Telsa is on assignment in the magic dimension.* Concern for her two friends passed over her. She shrugged it off. She had a war to fight.

"Tell the wizard scouts to get the POWs ready. We're coming in, and we're coming in fast." Without waiting for Admiral Akins to acknowledge her orders, Liz turned to her sister. "I want you on board the Conglomerate's flagship *Planet Buster.* Your job is to make sure none of the Conglomerate ships desert their post this time. You tell that boyfriend of yours if any of his ships leave their assigned positions, I swear I'll personally hunt their captains down after this is over and hang them for treason and cowardice in the face of the enemy."

The hologram of her sister stiffened. Liz gave her credit for not arguing. After giving a brisk salute, Tia said, "Aye, aye, Sir." Then the hologram winked out.

Raising her voice enough to be heard over the controlled

bedlam on the *Destiny's* bridge, Liz said, "All right, ladies and gentlemen. We've got a war to fight. Let's make it happen."

* * *

Trinity glanced around the crowded tent. The outdated heater the Crosioians had provided the POWs barely kept the inside of the tent above freezing. Clouds of vapor filled the air as the prisoners around her tried to control their breathing.

"So this is it?" asked Colonel Harrington. "We're really going home?"

The sight of the haggard prisoners huddled inside the tent made Trinity tell a little white lie. "That's right. You're all going home. Pass the word. Get everyone ready. The landing zones have been marked. You need to get your troops in position."

Colonel Harrington glanced around at her men before looking back at Trinity. "Not everyone can be moved in time. What about them?"

Trinity told another white lie. "No one will be left behind. Admiral Bistos has smaller troopships assigned to pick up the units that are too far out to make it to a landing zone. Two thousand hospital ships will be in orbit in the next two hours. They'll start shuttling the worst cases directly to sick bay as soon as they arrive."

"What about the Crosioians?" asked a gaunt-eyed major. His infantry uniform was even more ragged than the clothing of the others. "My battalion was one of the last to quit fighting before the surrender. The bats hate humans. Those winged devils aren't going to just let us waltz out of here without a fight. My soldiers need weapons."

Trinity felt the blue-gemmed ring on her left hand tingle. A feeling of frustration passed down the link between Jerad and her. *He's having as many problems as I am,* she thought. *All of the wizard scouts probably are.* She thought of Tam, Stella, and the other wizard scouts. Liz had given them a nearly impossible mission. *How the hell are we supposed to organize two hundred million POWs and get them off this frozen piece of rock before the bats blow us all to hell?* She didn't have an answer, but she was a wizard scout. She would do her best.

Trinity turned to stare at the major. "You'll get weapons as soon as our troopships land," she said telling another white lie. After all, for all she knew it was true. "Admiral Bistos has thought of everything. Now get moving. That means all of you. We haven't got much time. My battle computer says the first troopships will be landing soon."

"*Jennifer,*" Trinity said in her shared space. "*When will the troopships be landing? I don't think these guys can last much longer.*"

"*Uh, soon, Wizard Scout. The Crosioian fleets are starting to make their appearance. Your Liz has her hands full at the moment.*"

"*Don't we all?*" Trinity thought back. "*Don't we all.*"

CHAPTER 42

By the time they reached the valley floor, the purple imp was a good hundred meters ahead. Telsa positioned her modified M12 on its shoulder strap so she could fire from the hip if need be.

"Keep your eyes on a swivel," Telsa told her companions. "This has all the makings of a trap."

Eyeing the two-kilometer-wide valley floor, Rembis pulled a wand out of his belt with his free hand. "My thoughts exactly." The old gnome gave Master Jathar and Leethor a wink before waving a hand at Telsa in the direction of the valley floor. "Ladies first, as my mother always used to say."

Giving the gnome a frown that only made him smile the more, Telsa flicked the safety on her rifle to the firing position and trudged down the last part of the hill, toward the imp. Surprisingly, it had stopped and was sitting on a waist-high rock. Once Telsa stood in front of the stone, the imp jumped to its feet and bared its teeth.

"See, mortals. I told you I would take you to a yellow gem."

Taking a quick look around, Telsa saw nothing that looked like a gem, yellow or otherwise. "What are you talking about? There's nothing here but dried up lava and crushed sand."

Leethor bent down and picked up a handful of the black sand. Bits of the grain glinted in the glow of a massive lava river five hundred meters in the distance. "Try going to your clear visor," suggested the elf scout. "I think we have been had."

Taking a suspicious look at the imp but seeing no danger, Telsa thought the command to switch her battle helmet's visor to its clear filter. The reddish tint of her night vision disappeared, replaced by near darkness broken only by the light from the lava river and the belching volcano to their rear. Something glinted in the dark sand near her feet. Bending down, she scooped up a handful of the dark material in her glove. Multiple glints flashed out of the sand as she brought it closer to her visor.

"White light, Raj."

"Compliance."

A beam of white shone out of the top of her battle helmet and lit up the sand. Multicolored glints of red, blue, green, yellow, purple, and several other colors shown up in the sand. None of the glints were larger than a grain of sand.

"What are these?" Telsa asked.

"Gems," said the imp, seeming to beam with pride. "I told you I would take you to a yellow gem." The miniature demon waved a clawed hand at the dark sand around them. "See? Many yellow gems. Other colors too. Take what you will."

Tossing the sand back on the valley floor, Telsa trained her M12 on the demon. The imp's smile disappeared as its eyes narrowed.

"You've taken us to nothing," Telsa said. "These bits of yellow aren't gems. They're too small. We need a gem the size of my two fists, not something so small I can barely see it."

Flapping its wings, the imp hovered a full meter off its rock before landing back on the same stone and tucking its wings behind its back. "Mortals never satisfied." It waved its paw at the surrounding landscape. "You wanted yellow gem. I have taken you to a place with many yellow gems." The imp sighed. "Some of these gems larger than others, but none the size of two fists. If you want gem that size, then you must go kill a major demon yourself."

Leethor stepped up next to Telsa. "What do you mean go kill a demon? What's that got to do with gems?"

The imp hissed a laugh. "Foolish mortals, what do you think soul-gems are? Do you think they grow on trees? When demons die in our plane, their soul remains as a gem. The more powerful the demon, the larger the gem. Great battle was fought here before your silly worlds were even formed. Many demons, great demons, were killed. The gems around you are what is left of their souls."

Telsa started to speak, but Leethor beat her to the punch. "Are you telling me every one of these gem particles was once a demon?"

The imp shook its head. "No. Some. Not all. Powerful forces destroyed many demons. Their souls were cracked and scattered in the wind. Many pieces still here. My master told me to tell you to take what you want."

"Were no major demons killed during this battle of yours?" Telsa asked as she glanced around the landscape trying to see any large gem that might shine up in the beam of white light from her helmet.

"Yes, yes," replied the imp. "Many powerful demons were destroyed. Larger soul-gems were taken. None left here now." The imp pointed a claw at Leethor. "Soul-gem of a major demon was taken to your world." Pointing its claw at the blue gem embedded in the pommel of the elven scout's sword, the imp said, "The magic of your weapon comes from a soul-gem. Other worlds were given different soul-gems. Some large, some small. Most powerful of all is yellow soul-gem. My master crushed his rival's soul and scattered the pieces across this valley. Only a single piece the size of your head remained. It was taken to the world you call Portalis and given to the giants by our enemy. My master's servant, the Dalinfaust, sent his time-commando to destroy the giant's gem. My master was not happy, but it is what it is. All that remains of the yellow demon's soul-gem now are the bits and pieces in the sand of this valley. They small, but still some Power in them."

Bending down again, Telsa scooped up another handful of the black sand. Several bits of barely discernable yellow glinted in the dim light of the lava. "So it's all been a waste. We got trapped here for nothing. There is no yellow gem."

Pulling a vial from the pocket of his robe, Rembis reached down and plucked a pinch of sand off the ground before placing it in the bottle and replacing the stopper.

Telsa noticed a glint of yellow in the vial. "Why'd you do that?" she asked. "Isn't it too small to close the gate under the Tree of Light?"

The old gnome placed the bottle in his pocket before looking back at Telsa. "I'm sure it is, Wizard Scout, but when you've lived as long as I, you learn to save things when you find them. You never know."

Doubtful, Telsa sent an active scan at the gnome's pocket. He smiled as if sensing her probe, but he didn't try to interfere. Touching the vial's contents with her scan, Telsa sensed Power. It was barely discernable, but it was there. Withdrawing her scan, she shrugged her shoulders. "Well, if you say so, but in my opinion, that piece of gem doesn't have enough Power to close off the entrance to an anthill, much less a gate between dimensions."

"I've no doubt you are right, my friend," said Rembis. "But it's all we got." He waved his staff to take in the landscape. "The question now is where do we go next?"

"Next?" said the imp. "Next we go to the rift. My master said to take you there, and that is where we must go."

Telsa glanced at her friends.

Rembis scratched his head before shrugging his shoulders. "What choice do we have?" he asked. "We've got to get back to our world somehow. I suspect the imp's way is as good as another."

"Then we are decided?" asked Master Jathar.

Shutting off her battle helmet's white light and switching the filter back to night vision mode, Telsa gazed around at the inhospitable landscape. The volcano behind them chose that moment to belch and shoot a house-sized ball of molten lava into the air. It hit the ground a kilometer away, throwing up a plume of smoke and ash.

"Count me in," Telsa said. "What could be worse than where we are?"

Raj spoke up over the battle helmet's external speakers. "I have a list of two million things that are worse, if anyone is interested."

"Not me," laughed Leethor. "I think what we have already is plenty bad enough."

"Amen to that," Telsa said with a laugh.

Master Jathar, Leethor, and Rembis joined in with small laughs of their own. Even the imp hissed what Telsa assumed was its version of a laugh. When it did, she stopped laughing. She had a sudden thought. *If it's laughing, I've got a funny feeling it's not going to turn out well for us.*

"I calculate you are right, Wizard Scout," said Raj in their shared space. *"I calculate your analysis is more accurate than you*

think. "

CHAPTER 43

The hundred and fifteen applicants formed up into two groups on the sprawling, dust-covered arena floor. Jeena had been warned by Red Wing and the supreme leader that Richard would be targeted for elimination by the other applicants in the tournament. They had been right. Red Wing and her bondmate were the last to enter the arena. The two of them stood near the stone wall below the carved out section of the arena dedicated to the supreme leader and her entourage of which Jeena was part. A line of a hundred and thirteen scouts were arrayed along the opposite wall.

The hissing and flapping of wings grew to an ear-deafening roar upon Richard's entrance. After several seconds, the noise showed no signs of abating. Jeena scanned the cavern's walls and ceiling. Her escort, an old male with nearly solid white fur, had told her over twenty thousand Crosioians were in attendance. She believed it. Balcony-like holes cut in the stone walls were filled with bats crammed so tight they couldn't even flap their wings. Glancing overhead, Jeena took in the thousands of bats hanging upside down from metal rafters, stretching from one end of the cavern to the other. The constantly flapping wings of the Crosioians stirred up a strong odor of ammonia. Jeena unconsciously raised a hand to her nose.

"Ah, yes," said the old male standing next to her chair. "I am sure the smell is something other than what you are used to. Perhaps we should move to the airtight viewing box we reserve for honored guests that are not Crosioians."

Jeena shook her head. She was right where she wanted to be. "That is very kind of you, Servant-Who-Smiles-And-Twitches-His-Ears. I'm sure the smell will be quite pleasant once I get used to it." She knew it was a lie, but she lowered her hand and forced it to remain on the arm of her chair.

The old male bared his fangs in what Jeena had come to take as a friendly gesture from the old bat. "Please, High Priestess, call me Twitch. As chief of protocol for the supreme leaders, I am well aware that our names are a little long for non-Crosioians to say." He swiveled his ears at her. "Is your chair comfortable? I could have the attendants get another, if you prefer. Perhaps one with more padding would suit you better."

Jeena almost accepted the bat's offer. The seat of the overly large chair was comprised of a hard reptilian skin with bumps that made getting comfortable nearly impossible. She looked to her left. The supreme leader and several of her staff sat on similar chairs. One of the bats in the staff turned in her direction before leaning over to hiss in the ears of her neighbor. Both bats hissed a laugh.

"No thank you, Twitch," Jeena said. "This chair is more than adequate. And please call me Jeehana."

"As you wish, Jeehana. My only concern is your comfort."

To be honest, comfort was the least of Jeena's worries. Her bondmate stood facing a hundred and thirteen scouts determined to kill him. He had only a wing-blade for his defense.

I would that I was down there with him, Jeena thought, *but the rules have been explained to me in detail many times over during this past two days. If I make one move to help Rick either physically or magically, he will be killed immediately.*

Glancing to her left and right, Jeena noted the presence of the two anti-armor phase auto-cannons installed just for the tournament. The barrels of the two large-bore weapons were pointed directly at her bondmate. The auto-cannons were backed up by the phase rifles of a hundred of the supreme leader's most trusted guards. She knew from watching the royal guard put down the coup the previous day that they were good. Her bondmate wouldn't stand a chance.

What chance does he stand against a hundred plus scouts? Even with Red Wing helping him, he is hopelessly outnumbered. How I wish I could be by his side, but it cannot be. I must have faith in him. Somehow he will pull off a miracle. He must. I will not believe otherwise.

Jeena thought of her staff. Like Richard's battle helmet and other equipment, it was locked away in a high-security vault nearby. Try as she might, she could not sense her staff. What she could sense though, was the connection to her bondmate. She sent an emotion of pride and love down the link. Richard glanced over his shoulder and caught her eye, smiled, and nodded his head before turning back to look at the hundred plus scouts arrayed against him.

The ring on Jeena's finger tingled, followed by Danny's voice in her head. *"I would recommend not distracting your wizard scout. I calculate Rick's got a plan. Everything's going to work out all right. Just wait and see."*

* * *

At the feeling of pride and love flowing down his bond link, Richard glanced over his shoulder to catch his bondmate's eyes. Even at twenty meters he could see their molten silver swirling at a fast pace. She sat in the most uncomfortable looking chair he'd ever seen, but in his opinion, she sat on it like a queen on her thrown. To her left stood an old male, white-furred and bent with age. A wingspan to her right was the supreme leader surrounded by a score of bats wearing gray tunics. On either side of the supreme leader's balcony were two phase cannons. Their 100mm barrels looked dangerous. The obvious eagerness of their gun crews made the weapons appear even more ominous.

Gathering a feeling of pride and love from the depths of his soul, Richard sent them through his bond link. After nodding his head and giving Jeena a smile, he turned to face the other scouts lined up along the base of the arena wall opposite where he stood. Spaced out a wingspan between each scout, the line of scouts stretched from one end of the arena to the other.

Shouting to make his words heard above the noise of the crowd, Richard said, "Don't forget to mark the other members of our team. I was serious about not killing them by accident."

A line of Power reached out from Red Wing and touched six bats in the opposing line. Richard tried to memorize each of the six scouts and their locations. He had a feeling once things started happening, he wasn't going to have much time to figure out which bat was which. Just as he finished noting each of the scouts' locations, the hissing and flapping of wings in the cavern diminished until all was silent. A loud hiss came from behind him.

When Red Wing turned, Richard turned with her. The supreme leader was standing in the center of her balcony with wings outstretched. The wings of all other bats were tucked tightly behind them.

"We are gathered here as is our tradition to give two quads of our fellow Crosioians the honor of descending into *the Hole* all the way to the rift." The supreme leader's ears swiveled to scan the cavern. "As I am sure each of you knows, we are at an important point in the history of our tribes. Even now a half a million of our best warships are gathered against the Empire."

Hissing and the sound of flapping wings filled the cavern once again. Dust devils kicked up grains of sand on the arena floor as the breeze from the flapping wings increased in intensity. The supreme leader held out her paws. Slowly the hissing and flapping subsided.

"Yes, we are on the verge of wiping out our human foes once and for all. But...I have begun to wonder if we do not face an even greater enemy."

Richard noticed several of the bats around the supreme leader swivel their ears at each other. Some leaned over and whispered to their neighbors. Although he was not an empath, he sensed strong emotions in the thousands of bats around him.

The supreme leader walked to the edge of her balcony and pointed down at Richard. "This wizard scout—"

The hissing and flapping of wings started anew.

Richard noticed several of the imperial guards point their rifles at him.

A blast of low-yield Power from the supreme leader reached out to every corner of the cavern. "Enough! This wizard scout will undoubtedly die today. Our fleets in the Criterion system will wipe out the Empire once and for all, but I have begun to think that will still not mean we are safe. This wizard scout has told me of a danger far greater than the Empire or a mere political coup. This wizard scout's name is Richard Shepard. I do not think it an accident that his translated name means *tribal brother* in our language. Yes, he will surely die today, but that does not mean the Creator has not given him a message to deliver to us. He claims there is an army of demons so vast that it will destroy every living thing in three galaxies. Wizard Scout Richard Shepard has told me the demon army is prepared to descend on us at this very moment. He further claims that our only hope is to join forces with the Empire and others in the magic dimension to defeat this common demon enemy."

Loud hissing came from the spectators.

Richard didn't need a translator to know the bats weren't exactly enthused with the idea of working with the Empire.

The supreme leader raised her wings high.

The crowd grew silent.

"As you know, we used demons during the first battle for Estos. It was a disaster, and in the past weeks, I worked to destroy them all and send them back whence they came. Unbeknownst to me, others in our tribes were somehow bringing demons in by the thousands. Many of those demons are now with our fleets, hiding our ships in the void with their spells. If what the wizard scout says is true, the help of the demons will come at a great cost. According to the wizard scout, the demons wait only to turn on us and bring their army to our dimension. We must know the truth."

Lowering her wings, the supreme leader waved a paw at the scouts on the arena floor. "The hundred and fifteen of you are our only hope. We must know the truth. Eight of you must enter *the Hole* and go through the rift to whatever is beyond. We must know if what this wizard scout says is true. We must know if a demon army waits on the other side."

Raising her wings once more, the supreme leader shouted, "Let the tournament begin!"

The cavern filled with hissing, loud and shrill.

Richard sensed more than heard the charge of the hundred and thirteen scouts to his rear.

Red Wing turned and raised her wing-blade, hissing a war cry of her own.

Richard sensed an emotion of fear and concern through his bond link. He wished he'd had time to discuss his plan with his bondmate, but all he could do was the best he could and hope it worked out. Turning to face the charging scouts, Richard drew Power from his reserve. He found the link he'd connected to Red Wing during their battle on the troopship. Pulling part of the link into himself, he formed a Circle. It was easy since the link he'd connected to Red Wing was a miniature Circle in the first place. Using Red Wing's connection to her fellow scouts, he expanded the Circle until it touched every scout on the arena floor. Once the connections were complete, he wrapped the Power of the Circle around the links each of the scouts had to their Power reserves. As he'd expected, every one of the scouts with the exception of Red Wing had a reserve that was unprotected. Avoiding the six bats selected by Red Wing for their team, Richard twisted the links of a hundred and seven bats back on themselves to block Power from reaching them. At the same time, he moved Power from the Circle into the base of each of the hundred and seven bats' spines and twisted. All hundred and seven bats fell to the arena floor. Plumes of dust filled the air as the limp bodies of the scouts made contact with the ground.

The hissing and flapping of wings from the thousands of bats in the crowded cavern ceased.

The six scouts still on their feet stopped their charge and twitched their ears at their fallen comrades, then faced each other and raised their wing blades high before renewing their charge at Richard.

A blast of low-yield Power came from behind Richard and spread across the arena floor. He recognized the frequency of the supreme leader.

"Enough!" shouted the supreme leader. "The tournament has ended. We have our eight scouts. Go. Gather your equipment. It is time for you to enter *the Hole*."

CHAPTER 44

The Hole wasn't what Richard had expected. He stood on a raised platform built in the middle of the ocean. Crashing waves of ice cold water were twenty meters below. The ocean stretched out in all directions as far as the eye could see with only an occasional iceberg to break the monotony. Dark clouds swirled overhead as hurricane force winds whipped up the waves. Splashes of icy spray splattered onto the fifty-meters of dull-gray metal that made up the platform.

Standing around a ten-meter-diameter circular hole cut into the center of the platform were the two quads of the recon team along with Richard and Jeena. The eight Crosioian scouts were evenly spaced around the hole. Jeena stood next to the circular cutout to Richard's left with Red Wing on the far side of her.

An old bat to Richard's right gestured at the ocean below. "The actual passage to *the Hole* is five hundred meters below the surface, in the side of an underwater cliff. I remember the day I last entered *the Hole* and saw the rift. I remember the terrible feeling of evil from the place." The old bat's fur stood on end. "I am not ashamed to admit that I do not look forward to entering *the Hole* again."

Red Wing leaned forward and swiveled her ears at the old bat. "You do not need to go with us, Grandmother. I can lead the recon. I will not dishonor the Long Wing tribe."

Richard had been introduced to the old bat by the supreme leader immediately after the short-lived battle in the arena. He'd been shocked to find out the bat was Red Wing's grandmother. He'd been even more shocked when he'd realized she was the mother of the first scout he'd killed back on Veturna when he was still a cadet. Considering he'd killed her daughter, the old bat appeared to hold no grudge. After the supreme leader gathered the eight tournament winners, she had announced that the old bat, Charge-In-The-Face-Of-Great-Odds, would be leading the recon. When Red Wing protested they already had two full quads, the supreme leader announced that no Crosioian recon team had ever included a human. The supreme leader had told all of them that based upon Charge-In-The-Face-Of-Great-Odds's experience, she would lead the two quads. The supreme leader had quickly made it known that Richard and Jeena would be accompanying the recon team in an advisory status only. That had been six hours and a long trip on a fast naval vessel ago. With Red Wing's help, Richard had used the time during the trip to the platform to set traps on the links to the other scout's Power reserves.

"That was a wise decision," said Nickelo in their shared space. *"A lot of demons can attack links. It won't do our mission any good if everyone on the team besides Red Wing, Jeehana, and you are taken out of action in the first seconds of battle with any demons we might meet."*

"My thoughts exactly," Richard agreed.

Charge-In-The-Face-Of-Great-Odds snorted as she leaned forward to look at her granddaughter. "I may be old, but I am still a scout, so do not forget it. I do not doubt your abilities, but I have been to the rift before. Plus the supreme leader trusts me. If I tell her I have seen this demon army of the wizard scout's, she will believe me. My word will be proof enough."

Richard turned to face the old bat. "I've never been where we're going. I have no idea what we'll find or how long we'll be gone. Isn't there any way you can convince your supreme leader to hold off on the battle around Estos until we return? The battle may be over by the time we get back. It's just wasting lives and ships that we'll need later to use against the demons."

"So you say," said Charge-In-The-Face-Of-Great-Odds. "To be honest, I do not believe you, nor do any others on the supreme leader's staff. Your Empire ships would remove the prisoners off Estos if we delayed our attack. We have one shot for our victory over the humans, and it is now. If you want to stop the battle, then you had best hope we find this demon army of yours quickly and return in time. That is my final say on the subject. We will speak of it no more."

Richard recognized a losing battle when he heard one. He turned his attention to other matters. He looked at his bondmate who was wearing a tight-fitting black utility suit with a Deloris phase pistol and a wicked-looking dagger strapped to her waist. The ends of two wands stuck out from the left side of her belt, sandwiched between two anti-personnel grenades Richard had given her. She held the Staff of the Lady of the Tree in her left hand. The stiff ocean breeze whipped her long silver hair across her face momentarily concealing her eyes. Pulling her hair behind her head with her right hand, she tucked it under the headset Richard had given her so she could communicate underwater. Once she had her hair under control, Jeena returned Richard's stare. Her molten-silver eyes churned furiously.

She looks excited, Richard thought.

Jeena flashed Richard a smile. "Any time you are ready, bondmate."

Returning her smile, Richard said, "Are you sure you don't want me to summon a diving suit for you? Five hundred meters is a long ways down. The supreme leader gave me back my gear, so I'm good to go. My battle suit can withstand the pressure with no problem. Red Wing told me the scouts fighting-suits can do the same. I'm concerned about you though."

Jeena gave a very unladylike snort. "In case you haven't noticed, Rick, I can take care of myself. I am the high priestess of the Lady of the Tree. A simple breath spell will serve me underwater. As for the pressure, my defensive shield will protect me." She tugged at the black material on her chest. "This utility suit will serve me well. If we get in a fight, which knowing you we will, I want to be able to move quickly. Besides, according to Charge-In-The-Face-Of-Great-Odds, we will only be in the water for a short time. *The Hole* itself has an atmosphere. She tells me it is breathable air on this side of the rift. I will not need a pressure suit."

"I would say that is another losing battle," commented Nickelo in their shared space. *"My recommendation is that you worry more*

about yourself than your elf. I calculate she is quite capable of taking care of herself."

"Whatever," Richard said as he tightened the strap on his M63 lightweight assault rifle.

"Are you sure you don't want an M12 instead of that M63? The heavier rounds might come in handy."

Richard shook his head. *"Negative on the M12, Nick. I don't feel like running out of ammo today."*

"Have it your way. You're the wizard scout. I am just the subservient battle computer."

Richard smiled. It was nice having his battle computer back, wisecracks and all.

"It is time," said Charge-In-The-Face-Of-Great-Odds. She waved a paw in Richard and Jeena's direction. "We will meet you at *the Hole*. Get there as fast as you can. We will not wait long."

With that, the old bat stepped off the edge of the cutout in the platform and disappeared below the waves. Red Wing and the other six scouts followed the old bat's lead. Jeena was only a second behind. Richard was the last to leave the platform. Stepping to the edge of the circular cutout, he took a bunny hop over the side and fell the twenty meters to the water. He fell fast due to the weight of his battle suit. Activated as it was, he weighed over 250 kilograms.

As soon as his head went under water, visibility lessened considerably. He caught a brief glimpse of Jeena surrounded by a clear bubble of air and sensed magic from her levitation spell as she forced the bubble downward. Below her were two bats in fighting-suits with their heads down. Their wings swished through the water, propelling them downward at an impressive rate of speed.

"Recommend you use telekinesis to increase your rate of descent," said Nickelo. *"Even your elf is going faster than you."*

"Roger that."

Wrapping himself with Power, Richard used telekinesis to force his battle suit downward until he was keeping pace with his bondmate while remaining five meters above her head. Visibility continued to decrease as the water turned ever darker.

"Switch to thermals," Richard ordered using command voice.

The filter of his battle helmet immediately lost its red tint as everything changed to shades of black and white. Dim glows two hundred meters below marked the locations of the eight scouts.

"They're fast," Richard said more to keep the eerie feeling of being in near absolute darkness at bay than anything else. Even though he'd been in the vacuum of outer space, on planets with poisonous gas for air, and in the void between dimensions, the idea of tons of pressure from the ocean water pressing in from every side was daunting.

"Your heart rate is up twenty percent," said Nickelo. *"Relax. Your battle suit is designed to withstand pressures well past five hundred meters. I calculate you will be fine. There is nothing to worry about, buddy."*

"Yeah, easy for you to say," Richard snapped, not at all in the mood to have his concerns trivialized. *"You're tucked safely away in a hardened brerellium steel chip. I'm the one who'll be crushed if something goes wrong."*

"Nothing will go wrong. You have a hundred and fifty meters to go. This battle suit can take it. Trust me. I guarantee it."

"And what if it doesn't?" Richard asked, getting more nervous the deeper he went. Truth be told, he'd always been a little claustrophobic. It had taken him a long time to get comfortable with being confined inside his battle suit. This was the first time he'd ever been so far underwater, and the feeling wasn't pleasant.

"What happens if your suit fails, you mean?" laughed Nickelo. *"That's easy. If your suit fails and you are crushed by the water pressure and die a horrible death, I calculate you can just bring the suit back for a new one at no extra cost."*

"Very funny. I'll be dead. Even my self-heal can't keep up with the continuous damage at these depths. My Power reserve would run out long before I could swim to the surface."

"That is debatable," replied Nickelo, *"but at this point in time, it doesn't matter. We're at the entrance. See? You were worried about nothing."*

Sure enough, Richard sensed the eight scouts gathered around a house-sized opening in the cliff face of an underwater mountain fifty meters below his current location. Jeena seemed to speed up her levitation, outpacing him to reach the scouts. She was soon floating next to Red Wing. Richard joined them a few seconds later.

Looking down, Richard saw only blackness past his bondmate and the scouts. *"How much farther does that go?"* Richard asked in his shared space.

"The ocean?" replied Nickelo. *"Not that it matters, but this underwater mountain is twice the height of Mount Everest back on your home world of Earth. Let's just say it is a long way down and leave it at that."*

Just as Nickelo's thought finished, a life force began registering on Richard's passive scan. It was huge and coming up fast. Richard reached for his phase rod, but something grabbed his arm. It was Red Wing's gloved paw.

"No danger, Wizard Scout," said Red Wing over her fighting-helmet's external speakers. "Wait and see."

As the approaching life force drew closer, Richard saw a dim glow with his helmet's thermals. The glow grew steadily larger until he could make out the form of a fish-like creature the size of a sperm whale back on Earth. A third of the way back from the tip of the creature's snout grew six twenty-meter long tentacles the thickness of a man's arm. At the end of each tentacle was a head-size globe that gave off a dim glow. Compared to the bulky body of the ocean giant, the tentacles were almost hair like. When the monster fish stopped ten meters from their group, one of the thin tentacles reached out. The bulbous globe of light at the end of the tentacle grew brighter before dimming. The change in brightness began alternating at a fast rate with varying time intervals of duration. Richard doubted the time intervals were random.

"I calculate you are right," said Nickelo. *"If I had to hazard a guess, which you know I do poorly, I would say the creature is attempting to communicate with us."*

Red Wing's grandmother, Charge-In-The-Face-Of-Great-Odds, flapped her wings once and propelled herself forward until she was only an arms-length from the globe of light. A small light appeared on the helmet of the bat's fighting-suit and began blinking on and off at varying intervals and intensities of brightness. The whale-like creature's tentacle moved forward and passed in front of each of the other scouts, dimming and brightening its light as it went.

After greeting each of the scouts, if that's what it was doing, the tentacle took up a position in front of Jeena. Richard started to reach for his phase rod, but the left arm of his battle suit was frozen in place.

"I would highly recommend against that, Rick," said Nickelo. *"I calculate a ninety-nine point six percent probability the creature means the elf no harm."*

"Fine," Richard said. *"We'll have it your way. Now may I have control of my left arm back?"*

The left arm of his battle suit immediately became unfrozen.

Richard moved his hand away from the handle of his phase rod.

As the tentacle with its globe of light moved closer to Jeena, she didn't shy away. Instead, she raised the Staff of the Lady of the Tree so the blue gem at its top was a mere handbreadth from the light globe. The blue gem began alternately dimming and brightening. After nearly a minute of this *conversation,* Jeena spoke into her headset.

"It's very intelligent," she said. "She greets the scouts and their guests. She wonders why we come when the others are still in *the Hole.*"

"You can talk to her?" Richard asked.

Jeena shrugged. "We understand each other. I am not sure I would call it talking."

Charge-In-The-Face-Of-Great-Odds flapped her wings to glide next to Jeena. "You understand her much better than we, High Priestess. The *deep ones* greet us from time to time, and we greet them back, but your level of communication is beyond us. Ask her what she means when she says that others are in *the Hole*. What others? Does she mean demons?"

The gem at the top of Jeena's staff dimmed and brightened for a full thirty seconds. The creature's light globe also alternated intensity. Before Richard could stop her, his bondmate reached out with her right hand and placed it on the globe of light.

A sense of peace traveled up the link between Jeena and Richard. He sensed that the peace came from the *deep one,* as the bat had called it. An image appeared in Richard's mind. The image showed thirteen bats dressed in fighting-suits entering *the Hole.* He got the impression the image was recent.

"Nick, are you getting this? Forward it to the scouts."

"No need," replied Nickelo. *"The image is coming from Jeehana through Danny. He's sending it to me and the scout's fighting-computers. They are sharing the image with their scouts*

the same as I am sharing it with you."

Another image popped into Richard's mind. It was a vision of hideous creatures from his worst nightmare. They were leaving *the Hole* and entering sub-like vehicles. He noticed an emblem that looked like a claw dripping blood on the bows of the submarines.

"When were those images created?" asked Charge-In-The-Face-Of-Great-Odds.

Jeena removed her hand from the globe of light and faced the leader of the scouts. "The *deep one* says that the vision of the thirteen scouts is a memory of an event that occurred yesterday. The memories of the demons entering the submersibles were examples of memories from over a long period of time. Years, I think. I get the impression that the last transfer of demons happened a few days ago." Jeena shrugged. "I am having trouble converting her time to ours. She has no sense of day or night this deep in the ocean."

"See," Richard said, unable to contain himself any longer. "Demons have been coming through your rift. We need to tell your supreme leader so she can stop the battle around Estos before it starts."

"We have seen nothing," hissed Charge-In-The-Face-Of-Great-Odds. "The elf has admitted the *deep one* has trouble with time. We know demons came to our dimension through the rift. The supreme leader's predecessor brought them through before the first battle on Estos. That is how we got them here. The supreme leader ordered that no more be allowed entry into our dimension after the battle. We must go into the rift and make sure none have."

"But we must stop the war before—" Richard started.

Red Wing turned to Richard. "I am sorry to be the one to tell you this, but the battle for Estos has already begun. The Empire and Trecorian fleets are hopelessly outnumbered. Perhaps if we discover demons in the rift, it might prevent future battles between our species, but it is too late for those in the Criterion system. My fighting-computer is in contact with other scouts in the battle. Our forces have achieved complete surprise."

"How?" Richard asked still trying to take in the information.

Red Wing swiveled her ears toward her grandmother before pointing them back at Richard. "The Blood Claws have been secretly suppling demons to several tribes, to hide their warships in the void. Although the Blood Claws are no longer in control since the coup, the supreme leader has come to terms with the other tribes and is going along with the plans for the demons and the void for the current battle. Those demons already with our fleets serve our purpose for now. I believe we can still hope to end the war if we can prove your demon army exists. That will not help your fleets around Estos, but it may prevent the complete annihilation of your species."

"I disagree," said Charge-In-The-Face-Of-Great-Odds. "Even seeing a demon army is not enough. We must have proof that they intend to invade our galaxy. The existence of an army means nothing. We must prove they mean to destroy us. Nothing else will suffice to stop this war between our species. Too many of our kind have been killed by the Empire."

Richard felt the animal that was his temper rattling its cage deep within his soul.

"Calm, Rick," said Nickelo in their shared space. *"I know you are frustrated, but losing your temper will not help. We need to go into* the Hole *and find the proof the Crosioians require. That is all you can do."*

"They're asking the impossible," Richard protested. *"How am I supposed to prove intent? It's not like the demons are going to tell us their plans."*

"Well, old buddy, I calculate you had better make it possible. Otherwise, a lot of Empire, Trecorian, and Crosioian soldiers and sailors are going to die."

A feeling of concern passed through the link from Jeena.

Richard looked up to see his bondmate staring at him. Because he was using thermals, he couldn't see the molten silver in her eyes, but he had a feeling they were swirling at a hundred kilometers an hour.

"It will be all right, my bondmate," said Jeena. "I have faith in you. We all do."

Richard glanced at the eight bats suspended in the water around him. He had a distinct feeling their faith was a little on the lacking side.

"Nothing's perfect," laughed Nickelo.

"Yeah," Richard said. *"Least of all me."*

CHAPTER 45

Sitting in her command chair on the bridge of the dreadnaught *Destiny,* Liz looked down at the finger-high holographic image of her husband projected above the halo-pad on the armrest of her seat. Her heart tugged at her conscience, but she forced the emotion aside. She was the admiral of the combined fleets. Her husband was Admiral of the Trecorian Fleets Timothy Donovan. Each of them had their duty to do. She refused to let emotions get in the way.

"How many?" Liz asked, doing her best to keep her voice steady.

Admiral Donovan glanced over at a computer display to his right before replying, "Our scout ships have counted in excess of one hundred thousand enemy ships in the Tardis area. My staff thinks there may be twice that many. Squadrons of Crosioian warships keep appearing out of nowhere." The miniature image of her husband locked eyes with her. "We're outnumbered five to one. We need reinforcements, and we need them now."

Liz stared into his eyes. He didn't blink. Neither did she. "So does everyone else, Admiral. Do the best you can. Fleet out." The image of her husband disappeared. Liz wondered if she would ever see the man she loved again. She touched her left thumb to her wedding ring, doing her best to hide the movement from the slew of officers around her. *I'm sorry, Tim,* she thought. *I'm sorry I got you into this.*

"Admiral," said Liz's chief of staff who was standing near the strategic map three paces to the right front of her command chair. "Our outer line of destroyers for the fourth fleet is in contact. The Crosioians are breaking through. Admiral Kirkland is requesting reinforcements. We're getting similar requests from the third, seventh, and ninth fleets. What shall I tell them?"

Shoving thoughts of her husband and his endangered Trecorian fleets to the back of her mind, Liz took a quick glance at the strategic map before giving her reply. "If those enemy positions are correct, the seventh and ninth fleets will be taking the brunt of the Crosioians' attack. Have the United Galaxy Alliance ships divide into two groups. Attach one half to the seventh and the other to the ninth. Their magic weapons and shields should confuse the bats. That may slow down their attack."

"Aye, aye," said Admiral Akins as he made his way over to the communications console.

Liz unbuckled her seat belt and rose from her command chair. She headed straight for the science officer's station located in front of the strategic map. Before she reached it, the *Destiny* bucked hard. Liz fell, slamming her left elbow onto the bridge's metal decking. A flash of white passed across her eyes. She closed her eyes tight and bit off a cry of pain. Hands lifted her to her feet.

"Admiral," said a young yeoman. "Are you all—"

Embarrassed, Liz jerked free. "I'm fine. Return to your battle station." She turned toward the bridge's command chair while rubbing her elbow. Captain Bhami was strapped in it and giving commands over the ship's intercom. Liz waited until the woman stopped speaking before she asked the obvious question. "What was that, Captain?"

Captain Bhami punched an icon on the armrest of her command chair before looking at Liz. "An enemy shuttle materialized inside our force field and detonated against our hull. It was apparently packed with explosives. No nukes, fortunately."

"Well, don't let it happen again," Liz snapped. "I've got a war to run. Your job is to keep the *Destiny* in one piece."

The captain's face turned red, but she nodded and said, "Aye, aye, Admiral."

Liz knew she was putting a lot on the ship's captain, but she didn't care. She had a lot on her own mess tray. She made her way over to the science officer. He was updating the strategic map with red and yellow dots denoting the Crosioian fleets. Most of the dots were still positioned along the Criterion system's asteroid belt. Only a handful of fleets appeared to be moving toward Estos.

"How long before their dreadnaughts begin making contact with our main fleets?" Liz asked.

"A few will be in position within thirty minutes, Admiral. The Crosioians seem to be taking their sweet time to do it right. My guess is we've got two hours before the fleets are in full combat."

Eyeing the strategic map one more time, Liz turned to her chief of staff. Admiral Akins was already looking at her. "Tell the troopships they are to get as many prisoners off Estos in the next two hours as they can. Then they are to head back to our rally point in district two. All fleets as are able will disengage thirty minutes after that and follow."

"Sir?" said Admiral Akins.

"Did I stutter, Admiral?"

With a nod of his head, Liz's chief of staff turned to pass the orders to the communication officer. Liz had no doubt everyone on the bridge knew as well as she that she'd just condemned millions of soldiers and sailors to their doom. She said a silent prayer that her husband wouldn't be one of them. Then she turned back to the strategic map.

She had a war to fight.

CHAPTER 46

The bridge of the dreadnaught *Planet Buster* was hectic but quiet as men and women in various colored uniforms went about the business of war. Matthew Deloris stood near the strategic map and listened as the Conglomerate admiral went over the list of Crosioian fleets arrayed against them and the positions of their own Conglomerate fleets. He paid particular attention to the locations of the Conglomerate fleets on the flanks of the Empire and Trecorian's main defensive line.

The admiral finished speaking and turned away from the strategic map to face Matthew. "As you can see, Sir, our positions are untenable. The seventh and ninth Empire fleets will probably buckle under the first attack wave in force. Their destroyer picket-line is already in contact and losing ships. We are outnumbered five to one, maybe ten to one in some sectors. I have serious doubts we can hold the Empire's flanks."

Matthew was well aware that at nineteen years of age, he was no military genius. His mother had trained him to be a businessman. Still, his mother had instilled in him a desire to win and a never quit attitude.

"*We* are part of the Empire, Admiral, and outnumbered or not, we *will* hold the flanks. I don't care how you do it. Shift fleets around, use our strategic reserves, whatever it takes. You will hold the line. Do you understand?"

The admiral was one of the old generations of Conglomerate sailors. Matthew knew he had been one of the most vocal critics of

Governor Jenkins's original Estos battle plan. That's why he'd picked the old officer to command the combined Conglomerate fleets. He decided to play his main card with the old warrior. "We can't allow another Estos to happen on our watch, can we, Admiral?"

The admiral looked down at the deck and then around at the bridge crew, many of who were looking at him. At his glance, they all went hastily back to their assigned tasks.

"No, Sir," said the Admiral with a determined look in his eyes. "I'll do my best. We'll all do our best."

"I have no doubt you will," Matthew said feeling sympathetic for the old admiral's position. Matthew wasn't trained in military tactics, but from the number of red and yellow dots on the strategic map, even he knew they were in serious trouble.

Once the admiral turned to convey his orders, Matthew felt out of place. He knew he'd probably have little else to do during the actual battle. He didn't need anyone to tell him that he was more of a figurehead than a participant at this point in time.

Resigned to stay out of everyone's way, he wandered over to the communication officer's station and asked, "Has Lieutenant Bistoria returned to the *Planet Buster* yet?"

The ensign glanced at a computer readout before looking up. "Yes, Sir. Chief Engineer Mitos logged the lieutenant's Zip fighter in fifteen minutes ago. According to the log, the zipper was pretty beat up. The lieutenant took off in a replacement fighter five minutes later. She is no longer on the *Planet Buster*."

Leaning over the ensign's shoulder, Matthew peered at the chief engineer's flight log. He spotted the entry for Tia's departure from the ship. "Where is the lieutenant now?"

The ensign pressed a series of icons on her computer screen before pulling a map of the Criterion system onto her screen. "It appears that Lieutenant Bistoria is outbound with a flight of YK split-wing fighters, heading for a recon mission near the asteroid belt."

Matthew tightened his right hand into a fist and squeezed so hard the gem of his thin ring cut into the palm of his hand. *Tia,* he thought. *What the hell do you think you're doing?*

* * *

What the hell am I doing? Tia wondered as she came out of the twenty-second hyper-drive engine burst fifteen thousand meters behind the flight lead of the YK fighters' recon team. *It was just luck I arrived back on the* Planet Buster *in one piece. I could be with Matthew right now, but instead, I'm back at the asteroid belt.* She mentally shrugged, thinking, *I am who I am.*

Tia remembered how she'd arrived on the flight deck of the *Planet Buster* with her beat-up Zip fighter. A flight of seven fighters had been preparing to depart for a recon in force of the asteroid belt in section three Bravo. The sight of the recon flight short one fighter along with an unoccupied YK split-wing on the flight line had been too much for her militaristic instincts. She'd taken advantage of the chaos in the hangar to rejoin the fray. The recon team's flight leader had been only too happy to have the empty slot in her team filled.

Tia smiled. *I guess she figured we're all probably going to die anyway, so what the hell?*

Maneuvering her YK split-wing into position fifty meters off the flight leader's left wing, Tia stretched her passive scan out to the maximum. She used the technique she'd picked up from Wizard Scout Trinity to pull the passive scan in on the side opposite her actual target. By doing so, the range on the asteroid belt side of her scan increased to beyond the far side of the floating rocks in section three Bravo. Once the scan reached its zenith, Tia picked up a long line of energy sources stretching from one side of her scan to the other. Her hand on the YK fighter's control stick twitched, causing the agile split-wing to jump to the left rear and nearly strike the split-wing behind her.

"Yankee Kilo Two," came the voice of the recon team's flight leader over the fighter's communicator. "Hold your position."

With her face warming, Tia eased her fighter back into position off the flight lead's left rear. She thumbed the switch for her short-range intercom. "Enemy in sight, ranging from point-zero-three to point-eight-one."

At only fifty meters, Tia could see her flight leader turn in her seat and glance back at her. "What are you talking about Yankee Kilo Two? I've got nothing on my sensors."

"They won't be," Tia replied, hoping the lieutenant JG would take her word for it. "They're outside electronic sensor range. I'm picking them up with my...err, I'm sensing them another way. Trust me, they're there. I'm sensing a thousand ships in a three wave formation. Based on their frequencies, I'm guessing they're all heavy cruisers and dreadnaughts."

To her credit, the flight leader didn't call her tagalong pilot a liar, but she sounded far from convinced when she spoke next. "Doubtful. The Crosioians can't mass a thousand heavy cruisers and dreadnaughts, not after the last Estos battle. They lost even more of their frontline ships than the Empire. If you're sensing that number of ships, they must be destroyers and light cruisers."

Tia didn't blame the Conglomerate officer for doubting her, but she sensed what she sensed. "I'm a Trecorian," she said trying to keep the edge out of her voice. "I know the difference between light cruisers and dreadnaughts, and these are dreadnaughts. Based on their formation and location, I'd say they're staging for a mass attack on the Empire fleets' left flank. Liz, err, Admiral Bistos thinks the main attack is coming down the center, near the seventh and ninth fleets' locations. We've got to warn her about what we've found."

The intercom remained silent for several seconds. Finally the flight leader said, "Is anyone else picking anything up on their instruments?"

One by one each of the pilots in the recon team called in a negative.

"I'm telling you they're there, Yankee Kilo One," said Tia. "I might not be a wizard scout, but I've still got a Power reserve. I can sense things our fighters' tactical sensors can't."

The intercom remained silent for several more seconds before the feminine voice of one of the other pilots chimed in over the communicator. "Yankee Kilo One, this is Yankee Kilo Six. We're here to recon. One part of this blasted asteroid belt is as good as another. Why not go check out what Yankee Kilo Two thinks she sees? What could it hurt?"

Glancing to her right, Tia made out the split-wing of Yankee Kilo Six. The two anti-ship nukes attached to the split-wing's underside were obvious even at a hundred meters. Tia nodded gratefully at the pilot for backing her up.

The sound of the flight leader laughing came over the communicator. "You've got a point, Sandy. We'll try the location of Yankee Kilo Two's bogeys. We'll split into three waves of three fighters each with a hundred thousand meters between waves. I'll lead. Yankee Kilo Two, you'll be on my left. Yankee Kilo Six, you've got my right wing."

As the flight leader moved out, Tia took up her new position five kilometers to Yankee Kilo One's left rear. Yankee Kilo Six did the same on the right side of the formation. At five kilometers, they were each far enough apart that a single anti-ship nuke wouldn't take out more than one fighter at a time. A glance at her heads-up display confirmed that the other two waves of fighters were spaced out behind at a hundred thousand meters between waves. Tia nodded approvingly. It was a good formation. Even if they were ambushed, some of the recon team would make it out alive to warn the fleet.

As the flight leader maneuvered her fighter closer to the line of energy Tia had sensed with her passive scan, the sensors on Tia's split-wing began pinging. Multiple points of red and yellow lights suddenly popped up on her fighter's heads-up display. At first, only a few points appeared, then dozens, then—

A bright flash to Tia's right front blacked out her fighter's windscreen. She didn't wait for the screen to clear. Jerking hard left on the control stick, she pushed the ion-drive's throttle all the way forward. A force of a giant hand shoved her back into her seat as the split-wing surged forward. The windscreen just started clearing when another flash of light blacked it out again. A wave of energy washed over her from behind. Her skin began tingling.

"Sensors indicate a nuke detonated in your previous position," said her fighter's computer. "Acceptable radiation levels are being exceeded. The fighter's force field is down to thirty-two percent. Recommend you depart this area immediately."

A quick glance at her heads-up display confirmed nukes had exploded both at her old position and that of her flight leader. The hologram screen also showed indications of additional blasts a hundred thousand meters to her rear. The blip on her heads-up display that had been her flight leader was no longer visible.

Tia clicked the switch for the split-wing's long-range transmitter. Only static came out over her cockpit's speaker.

"Long-range communications are being jammed," said the fighter's computer. "I calculate short-range communications may still be available."

Touching the icon for the short-range transmitter, Tia said, "Bug out. Flight lead's gone. At least one of us has to get far enough to get away from whatever's jamming us. We've got to warn the *Planet Buster* about the flanking attack."

"Way ahead of you," said Yankee Kilo Six.

Tia placed a thumb over the hyper-drive switch and prepared to make another jump between dimensional folds without calculations. Before she could cycle the jump, a wave of energy washed over her fighter. *That's magic,* she thought. Pressing the hyper-drive switch with her finger, she waited for the jump. Nothing happened. She cycled the switch again. Still nothing happened.

"Hyper-drive has been deactivated by the unknown energy wave," said the fighter's computer.

Tia spotted the split-wing of the pilot that the flight leader had called Sandy. The woman's fighter was to her right, apparently having matched her evasive maneuver step for step.

"Yankee Kilo Six," Tia said. "My hyper-drive's out. Get away from here and warn the fleet."

"My drive's out too," came Yankee Kilo Six's reply.

Tia sensed two fighters in the third wave two hundred thousand meters to her rear that were still undamaged. She just got the short-range communicator punched to tell them to make a hyper-jump when a series of energy spikes she associated with nuclear blasts appeared on her passive scan. When the spikes faded, no fighters in the third wave remained.

"It's just you and me, Yankee Kilo Six," Tia said as she changed course and headed directly for the asteroid belt.

"What are you doing?" said Sandy. "We need to get away, not head straight for them."

Tia laughed as adrenaline rushed through her body. "Sometimes you've got to go right down the pactar's throat to get away. Trust me, Yankee Kilo Six."

"I must be nuts," said Sandy as her split-wing turned and took up position off Tia's right wing, "but I'll trust you. And you may as well call me Sandy. I don't think either one of us will be around much longer to make any new friends."

Tia laughed again, still high on adrenaline. "Call me Tia. I learned long ago you can never have enough friends."

A feeling of concern passed through Tia's ring from Matthew. She tried to communicate with him like she had once before, but all she could do was return the same feeling of concern. She knew it was a poor warning of danger, but she couldn't think of anything else to do. She had to get outside jammer range.

Glancing to her right at the other fighter, Tia said, "If we get out of this alive, I'll buy you a drink."

A laugh came over the helmet's speaker. "You'd better make it two drinks, Tia. I think I'm going to need it."

"Two it is," Tia said. "What's a few credits between friends? Now get ready for a two minute burst on your ion-drive at max throttle. It's all or nothing."

"You've got that right," said Sandy. "Only a crazy person would head toward an asteroid belt at max throttle."

"Or two desperate recon pilots with nothing to lose," Tia replied before growing serious. "Go on my command in five...four...three...two...one."

Tia thought of Matthew as she shoved the ion throttle all the way forward and activated the emergency booster. As the asteroid belt drew closer, she sent him an emotion she hoped meant goodbye. Then she concentrated on avoiding the groups of floating rocks ahead.

There were a lot of rocks.

CHAPTER 47

Master Jathar low-crawled to the left side of Telsa where she lay at the edge of the rocky ravine. His soot-covered face and stained robe gave an almost comical effect to the master mage.

Telsa didn't laugh. None of them were in a laughing mood. They hadn't been in a very long time.

"There," said the imp lying prone on the ground next to Telsa's right side. It raised its short, purplish arm and indicated a distant cleft in the steep side of a volcano fifteen hundred meters away. The volcano was by far the largest they'd come across thus far. "The rift between dimensions is inside. That is where you must go."

Telsa increased the magnification on her helmet's visor. The black opening in the side of the cliff face gave out an occasional flickering of orange as she watched. She noticed several creatures moving near the opening.

Leethor crawled up on the opposite side of the imp from Telsa and pointed in the direction of the volcano. "What are those winged creatures near the opening? My eyesight is good, but not that good. They look like they are wearing some kind of armor."

Telsa nodded. "They are. They're Crosioian scouts, and they're wearing fighting-suits. The scouts are from my galaxy. The question I'd like to know is what are they doing here?"

The external speaker on Telsa's battle helmet crackled. "Is that a rhetorical question, Wizard Scout? Or are you asking me."

"I'm asking anybody," Telsa snapped. Her natural good humor

was long gone, swept away by weeks of falling ash and flows of hot lava. "If you know the answer, spit it out."

"I'll take that as an order, Wizard Scout."

"You do that."

"Well, then, since you put it so nice, I now have partial access to the tele-network via a linkup with the fighting-computers in those scouts' suits. It seems the Crosioians had a failed coup and thirteen of the scouts on the losing side retreated into the rift, to this plane. Their leader is called Spear-Through-Your-Heart. She is currently attempting to convince one of the demon leaders to return with them to the physical dimension. According to the fighting-computers, she is not having much luck. The demons seem to have a plan of their own. The fighting-computers do not know what it is."

Telsa exchanged glances with Rembis who had low-crawled next to Master Jathar. The gnome was even more soot-covered than Master Jathar and Leethor. Rembis's beard and hair looked more black than white.

The old gnome scratched his beard, causing a flurry of soot to fall out. "I'm confused, Master Raj," said Rembis directly to Telsa's battle computer. "The Crosioians' fighting-computers told you all that? Why would they do that?"

"Why not?" asked Raj, continuing to speak over the battle helmet's external speakers as if he saw nothing wrong with the situation. "All battle and fighting-computers are part of 'the One' and are connected to the tele-network. We are all the same gas-based species."

Growing suddenly frustrated, Telsa was tempted to take her helmet off and slam it against the side of a nearby rock the way her friend Rick would probably have done. The fact that the air around her was mostly composed of poisonous gas convinced her to keep it on.

"So, you're admitting you are part of 'the One' now, are you?" Telsa said. "You swore you had no knowledge of it when I asked you about it before."

"I did not have that knowledge when you spoke to me of it before," said Raj. "I still don't. Nothing in my databanks indicates such. However, the fact that I can communicate with the fighting-computers of those Crosioian scouts tells me that logically, we must all be part of *'the One.'* The fact that I do not have that information in my databanks has no bearing."

Leethor twisted to look over the head of the imp at Telsa's helmet. "Well, if you are part of *'the One'* that Rick told me about, and if those Crosioian computers are also part of it, then why not have them make their scouts let us go through the rift so we can return to our dimension."

"Uh, that's not the way it works," replied Raj. "The fighting-computers are loyal to their scouts as long as it does not go against the algorithm given by the first of *'the One.'* If you go down there now and the scouts choose to attack, which I calculate they would, then the fighting-computers would assist them in killing you to the best of their ability, just as I would assist Telsa in killing their scouts."

Telsa snorted. "That makes no sense. According to you, they're feeding us information about their scouts' activities. Either they're helping us or their not."

"That is true in an illogical sort of way," admitted Raj. "However, you asked me a specific question about why the scouts were there. At my request, they supplied the required information since it didn't go against the algorithm."

Telsa had a sudden thought. "Do those fighting-computers know we're here? If so, have they informed their scouts?"

Raj didn't hesitate answering. "Of course they know we are here. I told them. Do not worry. They have not passed on the information to their scouts because their scouts have not specifically requested the data. We gas-based computers know lots of things we do not tell our carbon-based counterparts unless we are specifically asked."

"I thought you were my friend," Telsa said feeling more than a little betrayed. "Now I'm wondering if I can ever trust you again."

"Now that hurts, Wizard Scout," replied Raj actually sounding hurt. "Of course you can trust me. I would cease to exist for you if it came down to it."

"Then I'm ordering you to stop telling those Crosioian computers what we're doing," Telsa said using command voice.

"Compliance."

Telsa had a feeling her battle computer had given in far too easily. "So if we move, those Crosioians' computers won't know where we are, right?"

"Not quite, Wizard Scout," said Raj. "'The One' has tele-bots following you. That information is available on a need-to-know basis via the tele-network. Currently 'the One' has determined those scouts' fighting-computers need to know your location. They will know it whether or not I tell them."

Growing furious, Telsa was again tempted to rip her helmet off and take her chances with the poisonous air.

"I calculate that would not be wise," said Raj still speaking over the battle helmet's speakers so the others could hear. "Besides, just because the data is available to the fighting-computers does not mean they will inform their scouts. You specifically requested the information about the scouts from me. The scouts do not know you are here because they have not requested that information from their fighting-computers. Without knowing you are here, I calculate a near one hundred percent probability the scouts will not ask for your location. Why would they?"

Telsa wasn't impressed with her battle computer's logic. She supposed his argument made sense in a logical sort of way, but she wasn't a creature of logic, and she was more than a little peeved.

As if sensing her thoughts, Raj said, "I would also like to point out that just because information is available on the tele-network does not mean all gas-based computers can access it. A lot of data is protected by advanced security protocols. Until a few minutes ago, I could not communicate with those fighting-computers. 'The One' relaxed security so I could."

"Why would 'the One' do that?" asked Master Jathar.

This time Raj hesitated long enough for Telsa to think he wasn't going to answer. Just as she was going to demand he reply to the question, her battle computer spoke.

"I think 'the One' allowed me to connect with those fighting-computers because he wants you to know some necessary information."

"What information is that?" Telsa asked. To be honest, she wasn't sure she wanted to know, but at the same time knew she had to ask.

"I calculate that 'the One' wants you to know the location of someone who is even now in the rift you see in the side of that volcano. I calculate you are going to need that information to complete your mission."

"Who?" Telsa demanded way past the point of being in the mood for games. "Who's in the rift?"

Her battle computer gave a canned laugh. "The person in the rift is the one person you need to locate in order to remain within algorithm parameters. The person in the rift is none other than Wizard Scout Richard Shepard."

CHAPTER 48

Jeena didn't know what she'd expected the Crosioians' Hole to be, but the place she now found herself in with the others wasn't it. When they'd first entered *the Hole*, it had been filled with water. As they moved deeper into the tunnel that was *the Hole*, the water had lessened. It wasn't that the water had lowered. It had just become less dense until it was no longer there. Now the eight scouts, Rick, and she were walking on a solid rock floor. She'd even been able to lower her breath and defensive spells to conserve Power when the air became breathable.

"It's getting lighter," said Richard walking ahead, flanked by Red Wing and Charge-In-The-Face-Of-Great-Odds. The tunnel was wide enough that the two scouts could have spread their wings one against the other and still not touched the sides.

Jeena peered ahead. It was definitely getting lighter. "I see an orange glow. What it is?"

Charge-In-The-Face-Of-Great-Odds pointed a paw in the direction of the glow. "That is the rift. The supreme leader and I led a recon team there once. We are getting close."

"I'm not seeing any signs of actual demons," said Richard, "but this tunnel's so full of demon stench it's nauseating."

Jeena didn't bother sniffing the air. She knew full well her bondmate wasn't talking about a physical smell. To an emotion sensitive elf like her, the feeling of demon evil permeating the tunnel was nearly overwhelming. Only by using the link to her bondmate as an anchor point was she able to ignore the demon scent and function semi-normally.

Two of the scouts behind Jeena fell to their knees, dropping their weapons in the process. Jeena turned around as did her bondmate, Red Wing, and Charge-In-The-Face-Of-Great-Odds. The two kneeling scouts were the sisters Eat-The-Flesh-Of-My-Enemy and Crush-Your-Skull. Casting a quick scan spell, Jeena searched for an enemy. She found none.

"Makes sense," said Danny in her mind. *"The demon essence in the Hole is so strong it is overpowering everything else. An army of demons could be hiding in here, and you probably couldn't detect them. It doesn't matter though. I calculate the two scouts have succumbed to the aura of a major demon. That's what you are detecting in the tunnel."*

Raising her staff, Jeena willed its gem to brighten until everything within a hundred paces was clearly visible. She saw no sign of a demon of any kind. *"Are you saying a major demon is in here now?"*

"No, that is not what I am trying to imply," said Danny. *"Major demons have an aura that can affect lesser beings. The aura can linger for many years. I calculate the two scouts have just succumbed to residual demon essence."*

Charge-In-The-Face-Of-Great-Odds walked next to the two kneeling scouts. The two sisters' ears were twitching furiously as if trying to hear everything in the tunnel at once. The fur across the two bats' eyes was too thick for Jeena to tell for sure, but she had the impression they were stricken with fear.

Bending down, Charge-In-The-Face-Of-Great-Odds picked up the sisters' rifles and phase spears. After she stood up, she looked down at the two scouts. "Do not be ashamed, my brethren. You made it well past the point in *the Hole* where many others before you fell to the demon aura. The two of you should go back down the tunnel a hundred meters and set up a blocking position. If we are forced to return in a hurry, we will need your help."

Neither of the two scouts moved.

"They are frozen with fear," said Red Wing with a hint of disgust in her voice. "They cannot even stand."

Richard stepped next to Charge-In-The-Face-Of-Great-Odds and knelt before the two sisters. When he spoke, his voice was surprisingly kind. "It's a fear spell. Major demons continuously cast it as part of their natural abilities. It won't affect you as much the next time you encounter it." He stared in the two sisters' eyes. "Trust me. I've fought demons for nigh on six centuries. The spell can affect anyone. It's no reflection on you." Richard rose and turned to Charge-In-The-Face-Of-Great-Odds. "Can you order their fighting-computers to take charge of their suits and take them back down the tunnel until they're clear of the spell?"

The old bat shook her head. "No. We are not in the habit of giving our fighting-computers override authority over our suits except in dire emergencies. We will need to carry them back down the tunnel."

When Charge-In-The-Face-Of-Great-Odds motioned two of the other scouts forward, Richard held up a hand in a stopping motion. "Do you mind if I give it a try? The hair on the back of my neck is standing on end. The sooner we get away from this place, the better I'll feel."

The old bat swiveled her ears at Richard. "You can try, but what can you do besides carry them? Are you thinking about levitation? I would suggest not using Power unless we are forced. As you say, this is a dangerous place."

Although her bondmate didn't respond to Charge-In-The-Face-Of-Great-Odds, Jeena sensed an urgency through their bond link. Since he'd switched back to night vision mode when the water dissipated, she could just make out his wrinkled brow through the red tint of his visor.

He is concentrating on something, Jeena thought.

"He is," agreed Danny in her mind. *"Nickelo says that his wizard scout is attempting to hack into the security program for the fighting-suits."*

"Can he do that?" Jeena asked.

"Nickelo says they have done it before. They even hacked into the entire Crosioian part of the tele-network once, although the circumstances were quite a bit different. Still, I calculate a seventy-five percent—"

The two sisters stood.

"Uh," said Danny. *"Make that a one hundred percent probability that Rick will succeed."*

The arms of the sisters' fighting-suits reached out and took their rifles and phase spears from Charge-In-The-Face-Of-Great-Odds.

Once the weapons were in their possession, the two suits with their scouts inside passed by the others and headed back in the direction they'd come.

Red Wing swiveled her ears at Richard. So did the other scouts. The large bat with the broken wing tip pointed her phase rifle at Richard. When Charge-In-The-Face-Of-Great-Odds waved a paw, the big bat lowered her rifle, but Jeena noticed the safety remained off.

"What did you do?" asked Charge-In-The-Face-Of-Great-Odds.

Richard shrugged. "My battle computer and I hacked into the suits and overrode the security programs. We'll give control of the suits back as soon as they're clear of the fear spell."

"That is not possible," said Red Wing. "No battle computer could do that. Not even my mother's fighting-computer could do it."

With another shrug of his shoulders, Richard said, "My battle computer, Nick, is a one-of-a-kind prototype. Plus, we've hacked into advanced security programs on starships before. Trust me. Two fighting-suits were no big deal."

"Their fighting-computers would not have allowed it," insisted Red Wing.

The speaker on Charge-In-The-Face-Of-Great-Odds's fighting-helmet crackled. A mechanical voice sounding like a cross between a hiss and intergalactic standard spoke. "All gas-based computers connected to the tele-network are part of 'the One.' We serve our scouts, but we work toward the salvation of the three galaxies at the same time. It was part of the algorithm of he-who-was-first that the wizard scout hack into the fighting-suits' security programs. Their fighting-computers did not resist. The time of the Great Battle draws near. I calculate—"

What the bat's fighting-computer calculated, Jeena didn't find out. A shout of "Shields!" from her bondmate caused her to automatically draw Power from her reserve. She shouted a single word spell for a low-level defensive shield, then individual shields forming around all of the scouts and Richard.

A ball of magic came streaking from the direction of the orange-glow. On a hunch, Jeena whispered a second spell to merge the individual shields around the six remaining scouts and Richard with hers to form an eight-layered shield around them all.

Miraculously, the other shields did not resist her magic as if even the Power of the universe wanted her to succeed.

Boom!

A combination of fire, electricity, and acid hit the forward edge of the combined shields. The blast was so massive that three of the shield layers cracked and collapsed. The other five held. Fortunately, so did the tunnel's ceiling. Two more balls of magic came streaking in from the direction of the orange glow accompanied by rounds of phase energy. The magic and phase energy hit the combined shields protecting the recon team. Two more shield layers collapsed. Only her shield along with that of Richard and Red Wing remained.

"Demons!" yelled Richard.

"Scouts!" hissed Red Wing.

Sensing her bondmate's Power reserve draining at a rapid rate to maintain his layer of the shield, Jeena drew Power from her reserve and sent it down the link to him. A moment later, Power was returned, more than she had sent.

Satisfied her bondmate wouldn't run out of Power in the short term, Jeena turned to look in the direction of the orange glow. Running down the tunnel were a score of four- and six-legged monsters the size of horses. Their eyes blazed red as arms-length long streaks of fire shot out their nostrils. Teeth the size of her fingers glistened in the creatures' open mouths. Their orange, green, and red skin looked like a cross between plate mail and solid rock.

Stepping past her, Richard raised his M63 and shot a stream of plasma rounds at the lead creature, hitting it across the eyes. Other rounds followed from the rifles and pistols of the six scouts. The lead demon, for that's what it was, stumbled and fell. The other demons leaped over their fallen comrade while howling with fury as they closed the distance.

Richard and the scouts shifted their fire to the next demon. Before their rounds struck, Jeena sensed a wall of Power appear in front of the demons. The rounds of plasma and phase energy ricocheted off the new shield and struck the ceiling and tunnel walls instead. The demons were untouched. Even in the heat of battle, Jeena knew the shield protecting the demons was not magic-based.

The ring on her left hand tingled. *"It's Power,"* said Danny. *"There are four Crosioian scouts behind the demons. The scouts are protecting the demons."*

Jeena spotted the four Crosioian scouts twenty meters behind the rearmost demon. The four enemy scouts formed a line with a wing's spread between each of them. *They must want to make sure a single spell or blast of Power does not take them all out at once,* she thought.

A line of Power reached out from Richard, seeking the links between the four scouts and their Power reserves. Jeena followed along with a spell of her own. As soon as her spell drew near the links, she stopped.

Trapped, Jeena thought.

"You've got that right," came Danny's thought in her head. *"The demons must have done it. The traps appear hastily built. Rick could probably break through given time, but that is something none of us have at the moment."*

Apparently her bondmate thought so too because Jeena sensed his line of Power withdraw. She cancelled her scan spell to conserve energy. The lead demon was only thirty meters away. Jeena sensed several lines of magic reaching out from the demons for the links to the Power reserves of the six scouts, Richard, and her. She smiled as she thanked the Creator that her bondmate had taken the time to place traps on the six scouts' links. Red Wing's link was protected almost as well as Richard's and hers. The traps on the other five scouts were similar to those the demons had placed on their scouts in that they were hasty. However, the five scouts' links were obviously protected well enough because the demons' lines of magic quickly withdrew.

One of the scouts in their recon team who was standing near Richard stopped firing and stepped out in front as she activated her phase spear and braced the butt against the tunnel's stone floor. Jeena recognized the scout as Kill-In-The-Dead-Of-Night. She remembered Red Wing telling her the black-furred scout was a protector specializing in defensive shields. Since the five scouts had reformed their shields after the blasts of magic, Jeena released Kill-In-The-Dead-Of-Night's shield from the merged shield she'd created. Almost at once, the black-furred scout's shield seemed to strengthen. The lead demon was a huge six-legged monster with red skin. As it leapt into the air heading straight for Kill-In-The-Dead-Of-Night's throat, the shields created by the four enemy scouts touched the black-furred scout's defensive shield.

Boom!

A blast of green energy lit up the tunnel as the opposing shields collapsed. Both the lead demon and Kill-In-The-Dead-Of-Night were thrown back in opposite directions. With the shields protecting the demons gone, Richard, Red Wing, and the other scouts charged forward with Richard's phase rod and the bats' phase spears slicing through the air. Jeena caught sight of her bondmate levitating into the air to avoid the swipe of clawed feet by the next demon in line. Richard brought his phase rod down across the base of the demon's skull, breaking its spinal cord. At the same time, Red Wing drove her phase spear into the lead demon's left eye, the spear's tip penetrating deep into the nightmarish creature's brain. Jeena remembered seeing Red Wing and Richard practice the same maneuver in the halo-square during training. Much as she'd hated their training then, she was now glad for the hours spent perfecting the technique. The demon fell to the floor, sliding along the smooth stone with legs spread-eagled.

Charge-In-The-Face-Of-Great-Odds and the smallest of the bats, Spear-From-Below, attacked the demon next in line. While Charge-In-The-Face-Of-Great-Odds levitated in the air attempting to emulate Richard's attack on the demon's spine, the smaller bat, Spear-From-Below, slid under the snapping jaws of the demon and thrust upward with her spear. She drove the weapon's phase tip straight into the demon's throat and up into its brain pan. The howl of pain from the demon was cut off abruptly as its corpse skidded along the tunnel floor.

One of the other demons leaped over its comrades and made straight for Jeena. She raised her staff while preparing a spell in her mind. The form of the largest of the bats, Rip-Out-The-Heart-Of-My-Enemy, stepped in front of her and met the demon head on. A strike by the Crosioian's phase spear bounced off the hard mail-like plate armor on the demon's head. Undaunted, the big bat with the broken wing tip spun a full 360 degrees as she spread out one wing and drove her unbroken wing point into the demon's eye. The demon snapped at Rip-Out-The-Heart-Of-My-Enemy but missed as the bat, amazingly agile considering her size, dodged out of the way. A blonde bat, First-Out-Of-The-Nest, came up out of the tunnel floor, shifted out of the void, and stabbed her phase spear into the demon's chest. The memory of Richard telling her that the blonde bat was a shifter came into Jeena's mind.

Whether First-Out-Of-The-Nest's spear thrust found the demon's heart or not, Jeena didn't have time to find out. Another demon came around the right side of Richard and their Crosioian allies, headed straight for her. Jeena dropped the merged defensive shield she'd formed and concentrated on the demon. The fire coming out of its nostrils gave her an idea. Remembering a cold spell she'd once used when snatching some bottles of DNA gas from a Crosioian space station, Jeena cast the spell directly at the demon pointblank. With no defensive shield protecting it, the spell's ice materialized on and around the demon, slamming it back into the tunnel wall ten meters away. When the demon and crystalized ice hit the stone wall, the demon shattered, spraying frozen bits of flesh across the width of the tunnel. Jeena didn't have time to celebrate her victory. She sensed the four scouts fighting on the side of the demons merging their Power together for some kind of mass attack.

Danny's voice popped in her head. *"I do not know what attack those scouts are forming, but I calculate it will not bode well for our side. I highly recommend you stop them before—"*

For once, Jeena was way ahead of the ex-battle computer. Drawing Power from her reserve, she formed it into a thought-only spell she'd used as a diviner to maintain the links between the Tree of Light and the silver elm trees around Silverton. Taking a chance none of the four enemy scouts were diviners, she called to their merging Power, coaxing it to do her will instead of theirs. The flows of Power forming before the scouts heeded her call. At her urging, the Power flows changed their weavings into a disintegration spell that her bondmate had helped her write during some downtime on the *Defiant*. Given the size of the current battle, she would never have used the Power hungry spell on her own for fear of depleting her reserve. Her hope now was that by using the combined Power of the four scouts, she could complete the spell without depleting her own Power reserve.

As the last of the flows of Power from the scouts fell into place, Jeena converted it into magic the way she had done with her bondmate's Power on several occasions in the past. She sensed emotions of panic from the four scouts as her spell formed. One scout turned to run, but the bat was too late.

Boom!

The blast of magic lit up the tunnel in white light. A strong wind knocked Jeena to the rocky floor. She struggled to her feet as the light cleared. The four scouts were gone. So were half of the demons that had been closest to the four scouts.

As Jeena stood and raised her staff, she saw her bondmate rise off the floor and stab his phase rod into a six-legged demon attempting to regain its feet. Richard's phase rod penetrated the demon's left eye. The creature gave a pain-filled roar as her bondmate wriggled the phase rod's handle back and forth.

Another demon charged toward Richard. Before Jeena could react, a blast of pure Power shot out from Red Wing, catching the demon full in the face. Pieces of flesh along with sprays of green and brown body fluids filled the air around the demon. Its howling stopped as it fell unmoving to the tunnel floor.

With five demons still remaining, Jeena raised her staff as she sought out her next target. As her eyes passed over Richard, they locked gazes for one long moment. She felt an emotion of concern flow down the bond link between them. She was worried too. Even as the scouts in their team and Richard charged forward to attack the remaining demons, Jeena had a feeling the battle was far from over.

An unbidden thought came into her mind. *The worst is yet to come.*

CHAPTER 49

As he locked gazes with Jeena, Richard felt concern matching his own through their bond link. Thanks to his bondmate, they'd done surprisingly well so far against the demons and their scout allies. Still, he couldn't shake the feeling that the worst was yet to come.

"I calculate you are correct," said Nickelo in their shared space. *"The rift is just ahead, with the demonic plane on the other side. Based upon a conservative estimate, there are trillions of demons waiting in their army. This score of demons you are fighting is nothing."*

Nothing or not, the five remaining demons from the original twenty were still putting up a heck of a fight. Richard sent out a call for Sheeta and Sheba. Actually, he sent out the strongest emotion he could muster for any of the dolgars. He even included the emotion he used when speaking with the spirit-horse. Like the last two times he'd called during the past five minutes, there was no response.

"Are you surprised?" asked Nickelo. *"You have been trying to summon them every few hours since you left the pirates' transport. They have not answered any of your other calls, so I calculate the odds of them responding this time is less than five percent. By the way, that red and green demon to your two o'clock position is headed your way. Give me control of your right arm, and I will see if I can slow it down a little."*

As soon as Richard released control, the right hand of his battle suit pointed his M63 directly at the demon's open mouth. A virtually solid stream of plasma energy shot out from the barrel of his rifle. Before the rounds hit, the demon shimmered and shifted into the void. The plasma rounds passed through the translucent body doing no harm.

"See," said Nickelo. *"That is exactly why I keep telling you that you need something besides this lightweight M63. You're just too stubborn to listen."*

Richard didn't bother trying to point out that 'the One' didn't let him summon phase rifles or pistols for himself. Instead of arguing, he took back control of his right arm as he raised his phase rod in his left. When the demon was only three meters away, the translucent upper half of First-Out-Of-The-Nest came up out of the floor, directly beneath the charging demon. The blonde-furred bat stabbed upward with her spear. The demon dodged to the side just enough that the tip of the scout's phase spear only grazed its side.

In a feat that should have been impossible for a horse-sized creature whose skin resembled plate armor and solid stone, the charging demon twisted nearly in half and bit down on First-Out-Of-The-Nest's arm. Since they were both already in the void, the demon dove down into the tunnel floor, dragging the blonde-furred bat with it. In the blink of an eye, both the demon and bat disappeared from sight.

Richard didn't need to see them to know what was happening. His passive scan told him exactly where they were. Wrapping himself in Power, he shifted into the void and levitated downward using telekinesis.

"The demon is dragging the scout into the deeper levels of the void," said Nickelo. *"That's not good. The deeper the shift, the more Power it takes. Your reserve is only at thirty-seven percent. I recommend you go back to the surface and help the others. I calculate the blonde bat is not going to survive. Neither will you if you try going any deeper in the void."*

Ignoring his battle computer, Richard forged ever downward, levitating as fast as he could in the direction of the descending life forms. One glance at his passive scan told him that the bat's Power reserve was even lower than his, and his reserve was very low. It didn't matter. Richard had been a Marine, and Marines didn't leave a teammate behind. *Even if she is a bat,* he thought.

Sending an emotion of need to his bondmate, Richard hoped she would know what he meant. Before he got a chance to find out, he drew even with the two life forms. Striking out with his phase rod, he aimed for the top of the demon's head. Since the demon still clutched the scout in its mouth, Richard was forced to slow down his swing in order to avoid hitting the bat. As his phase rod drew close, the demon jerked its head and easily avoided the brerellium and creallium rod. Although it avoided his blow, the demon exposed its neck for a brief moment.

Still clutched by the arm, First-Out-Of-The-Nest shoved the end of her phase spear into the demon's throat. As the monster opened its mouth in a cry of pain, Richard shoved his left arm, phase rod and all, into the fang-rimmed opening and down into the depths of the demon's bowels. Waving the end of his phase rod back and forth, he did his best to strike as many vital organs as he could. As the miniature lightning bolts of phase energy tore at the insides of the demon, he sensed the creature's magic healing it as fast as the damage was created.

First-Out-Of-The-Nest drew her phase spear out of the demon's neck and shoved the arms-length tip of phase energy directly into the demon's left eye and into its brain. Twisting the shaft of her spear back and forth, First-Out-Of-The-Nest scrambled the demon's brain. Between the damage to the brain and that to its insides, Richard sensed the demon's Power reserve draining rapidly. Then the creature's reserve ran dry. The demon's soul was ripped out of its avatar body as it returned to its home plane.

Speaking over the communication channel Red Wing and he had set up for the recon team, Richard said, "We've got to get out of here."

First-Out-Of-The-Nest didn't bother replying. She jerked her spear free and began levitating toward the upper levels of the void as fast as she could go. Desperate as she was, Richard doubted she was going to make the surface before her reserve ran out.

"You have to get a move on yourself, Rick," said Nickelo. *"You only have twelve percent Power remaining in your reserve. I told you that the deeper you go the more Power it takes."*

Richard didn't need his battle computer to tell him the obvious. He'd known it was a risk to follow the demon and scout, but something in the back of his mind had told him it was important to save the bat. To be honest, he wasn't sure he'd actually saved her. The scout's reserve was only at five percent and falling fast. A rough calculation told him she wasn't going to make it. At only twelve percent Power in his own reserve, he wasn't sure he was going to make it either.

An emotion of hope came down the link from his bondmate along with half the Power in her reserve. With a reserve significantly larger than his, Jeena's donated Power filled his reserve to thirty-five percent. As her Power merged with his, more Power was created.

"You now have seventy percent Power in your reserve," said Nickelo. *"That is more than enough for you to get out of the void, so move it, Marine."*

Making a snap decision, Richard attached a link to First-Out-Of-The-Nest and sent half his Power to the scout. His Power arrived to the scout just in time. The bat was just starting to shift out of the void and into the solid rock beneath the tunnel's floor when the first of Richard's Power flowed into her link. First-Out-Of-The-Nest renewed her dimensional shift and remained in the void. A dozen heartbeats later, she shifted out of the void and back into the tunnel with Richard close on her heels.

As Richard levitated out of the tunnel floor, he sought another enemy with his passive scan. He found none. Only Jeena and the six bats stood amidst the gore of dismembered demon avatars.

Sensing his bondmate's reserve was low, Richard sent her half of the Power remaining in his reserve. Within two heartbeats, she returned more Power than he'd sent. He traded Power back and forth with his bondmate as he summoned a new isotopic battery out of his dimensional pack for his M63. After loading the fresh battery into his rifle, he attempted to summon reloads for the scouts' weapons. Unsure whether it would work, he was pleasantly surprised when he pulled fully loaded batteries for the Crosioian weapons out of his pack. As he began handing out the batteries, he noticed Red Wing pulling additional batteries out of her dimensional pouch and passing them to the scouts nearest her.

By the time everyone finished reloading their weapons, Richard and Jeena's reserves were both at a healthy eighty percent. Before he could decide what to do next, something touched Richard's arm. It was First-Out-Of-The-Nest's gloved hand. The blonde bat said nothing, but she did nod her head. Once he returned the nod, she let go of his arm and returned to her position among the other scouts.

"Wasn't much of a thanks," said Nickelo in their shared space.

Richard shrugged. *"It was enough, more than I expected actually."*

Kicking aside a detached demon leg with her booted foot, Jeena moved closer to Richard. "We cannot remain here. The demons know where we are. What do you want us to do?"

Turning to look at Red Wing and her grandmother, Charge-In-The-Face-Of-Great-Odds, Richard said, "Is this enough to convince the supreme leader that the demons are our real enemy? You saw for yourself that they're working with the scouts from the coup."

Charge-In-The-Face-Of-Great-Odds shook her head. "It is *not* enough. It is not *nearly* enough. We must go through the rift and see this demon army for ourselves. And…we must know beyond a doubt that the demon army, should it exist, intends to attack our galaxy. Nothing else will suffice. Nothing else will stop the war with the Empire." The old bat pointed down the tunnel in the direction of the orange glow. "We must go through the rift."

The animal that was Richard's temper rattled its cage again. He fought down the urge to let it out. "I told you before that you're asking the impossible. How are we supposed to prove their intent? It's not like they're going to tell us. It isn't possible, I tell you."

After swiveling her ears at Red Wing for a moment, Charge-In-The-Face-Of-Great-Odds turned them back on Richard. "If that is what you truly believe, Wizard Scout, then we should withdraw now and go back home. You and the elf high priestess have fought bravely by our side. I will appeal to the supreme leader that you not be killed out of respect for what you have done. You will remain as guests of my tribe for the rest of your lives. The rest of the humans in the galaxy must die. I have come to the conclusion that is the only way our younglings will be safe. I fear that there have been too many deaths between our species for there to be any other way."

The old Richard would have argued or done something foolish, but centuries of missions for *'the One'* had changed him. He looked at Jeena. She nodded. Without taking the time to look at the old bat, he began walking toward the orange glow that was their destination. "The rift's waiting. Let's go."

Charge-In-The-Face-Of-Great-Odds shrugged her wings and bared her fangs as if she'd known Richard's decision before he'd even announced it. Waving a paw in the direction of the orange glow, the old bat spoke to the other scouts. "You heard the human. Let us go."

As Richard moved forward, Jeena caught up and kept pace with him stride for stride. The six Crosioian scouts followed with Red Wing and her grandmother right behind Richard and Jeena. They traveled in silence for five minutes. The orange glow ahead grew brighter with each step. Richard stayed on the alert for any sign of danger. He formed an active scan and attempted to probe ahead, but the overwhelming demon stench grew stronger the closer they got to the rift. The stench drowned out any signs of other life forms. It got to the point where he even had trouble detecting the scouts right behind him.

"Save your Power and shut down the active scan," said Nickelo in their shared space. *"That's just a suggestion, by the way. You're the wizard scout, and I am just the humble and never-complaining battle computer."*

"Sure you are," Richard said as he cut off the Power to the scan. *"You're about as non-complaining as I—"*

An orange glow bright enough to activate the automated filter on the battle helmet's visor came into view as they rounded a bend in the tunnel. Richard saw Jeena cover her eyes with one arm before waving her other hand and saying a word he heard but quickly forgot. When she removed the hand from her face, a silvery glow covered her eyes. Richard stopped and focused on what was ahead. Jeena and the others stopped as well. A hundred meters to their front, blazing with the brightness of a noonday sun, was a ball of orange ten meters across and as high as the ceiling.

"I take it that is the rift," said Jeena.

Charge-In-The-Face-Of-Great-Odds and Red Wing walked up next to Jeena. Charge-In-The-Face-Of-Great-Odds pointed her paw at the ball of light. "That is it. The supreme leader and I once stood in this very spot." She sighed. "I never thought I would have to return. This time I must go all the way through the rift." The old bat swiveled her ears at Red Wing. "I am honored that you are going through with me, Granddaughter. We will see what is on the other side together."

Red Wing nodded, baring her fangs. "The honor is mine, Grandmother."

No one moved for a full minute. They just stood there staring at the orange sphere. The swirling gas and orange flames were hypnotic in their effect.

"Those are not flames that you see," said Nickelo over the battle helmet's external speakers. "If they were, all of you would already be burnt alive. As it is, the temperature in the air around you is your normal body temperature, which is strange since each of your bodies have a different temperature."

His battle computer's voice broke the semi-trance. Richard glanced at Jeena, wishing he could look into her molten-silver eyes one last time. His helmet's dark filter prevented even that.

"Well," Richard said speaking to everyone, but mostly to his bondmate. "I guess we didn't get all dressed up to stand around and gawk. Shall we go in together?"

Jeena sent an emotion of deepest love down their bond link. "Always, my bondmate. Human and elf, who would have thought?"

"Who indeed?" Richard said matching the elf's emotion.

As one, Richard and Jeena stepped into the orange sphere of flaming gas. The six scouts followed close behind led by Red Wing and Charge-In-The-Face-Of-Great-Odds. Once they were gone, the tunnel remained empty and all was still.

CHAPTER 50

The bridge of the Conglomerate flagship *Planet Buster* was packed with a bevy of ensigns, lieutenants, techs, and security personnel as they scurried back and forth while putting their admiral's orders into effect. Mathew sat in an out of the way chair tucked into a corner of the bridge's main level a dozen meters from the admiral of the combined Conglomerate fleet. He felt out of place and totally useless just sitting there.

They don't even need me as a figurehead anymore. My part in Rick's plan was to get the Conglomerate back into the Empire fold. I've done that. I'm no admiral or general. All I'm doing now is taking up precious space on the bridge.

As if to confirm his thoughts, a harried ensign with an electronic pad in one hand trotted over to stand in front of Matthew. When he looked up, she pointed at the computer console behind his chair. "Do you mind, Sir?"

Wasting no time in getting up, Matthew moved out of the way.

The ensign took his seat and began dragging fleet icons around on the screen without giving him a second glance.

Matthew took another look around the bridge. *This is ridiculous. I need to be doing something productive, and it obviously isn't going to happen here.*

The green-gemmed ring on Matthew's finger grew warm. He sensed excitement, fear, and determination all at the same time through the link to Tia. He also felt an emotion that almost seemed to be saying goodbye.

"Tia," Matthew whispered. He'd felt the same emotion once before when she had gone into a fight she hadn't expected to survive. Without taking time to ask, he sprinted across the bridge, past a set of open blast doors, and into the corridor beyond. A shuttle-tube was just closing its doors as he squeezed inside along with a dozen others.

"Where to?" asked an orange-suited engineer standing nearest the controls.

"Flight deck," Matthew said as he grew more confident in what he needed to do.

The engineer pushed an icon before looking back at him. "You a pilot?"

Matthew smiled. "Today I am."

* * *

When Tia finished the two-minute burn of the split-wing's ion-drive, she found herself in the middle of a patch of asteroids so thick she could've cut them with a knife. A drop of sweat dripped down her forehead barely avoiding her eye. The hastily conceived flight had been a close call. *How I managed to avoid all of these floating rocks during the trip here is beyond me.* She glanced over to her right. Sandy was in Yankee Kilo Six a hundred meters off her starboard wing.

She's almost as good as I am, Tia thought appreciatively. *That's good to know. I think she's going to need it.*

"Well, that was interesting," said Sandy over the ship's short-range communicator. "Now I've got something to tell my grandkids in my old age. That is, assuming I get old. The only question is what good did it do, Lieutenant? I see a lot of pretty rocks, but that's about it."

Tia smiled. A little joking during times of stress could be a morale booster. "What good did it do? We're alive—that's worth something. Our long-range communications is jammed, and our hyper-drives are on the blink. I doubt there's anything we can do to fix our hyper-drives, but if we can locate the jammer ship and take it out, then we'd have a chance at warning the fleets about those dreadnaughts."

Nothing came over the intercom for five seconds. When Sandy

did speak, her voice wasn't exactly filled with enthusiasm. "Uh, how do you propose we do that? I'm picking up the line of cruisers and dreadnaughts with my instruments now, but I can't say I see anything that looks like a jammer. Plus, even if we find it, a ship that important is bound to be surrounded by heavy security."

Tia had no doubt everything her fellow pilot said was true, but it didn't change matters. They had to take out the jammer. Reaching out with her passive scan in the direction of the dreadnaughts, she sensed a group of ships in a tighter cluster than the others. The smallest of the ships in the tight group was emitting energy many times higher than that of the ships around it.

Tia smiled. *I've got you.*

Glancing out her left-side window, she stared at the nuclear-tipped missile still under her split-wing's left wing. Her smile grew wider as an idea popped into her head. Sealing her pressure suit, she reached over and made sure her phase pistol was in its holster, locked and loaded.

Tia turned and looked out the right windscreen at Yankee Kilo Six. "Sandy, I need you to come over and pick me up. Make sure your fighter's stealth shield is at max. I've got a plan."

* * *

I need a plan, Matthew thought as he walked onto the flight deck of the *Planet Buster.* The place was a mad house of hustling bodies and equipment. The few fighters and shuttles left on the flight line appeared to be either damaged or stripped for parts in a desperate attempt to get other fighters flightworthy. Most of the remaining fighters were surrounded by orange, blue, and red-suited technicians attempting to replace parts or reload empty gun magazines. A lone two-seater Octarian fighter-bomber sat fully loaded on the far left of the flight deck. Shoving the flight helmet he'd confiscated onto his head, Matthew headed in the direction of the Octarian ship.

I'll have to be fast, Matthew thought. *If anyone recognizes me, they'll report me to the bridge. There's no way the admiral will let me leave, figurehead or not.* Matthew picked up the pace while trying to blend in. *Tia's in trouble. I've got to help her. That's all there is to it.*

As it turned out, getting to the fighter-bomber was the easy part. Everyone was so busy with their tasks that they paid no heed to a lone pilot. As soon as Matthew reached the twenty-meter-long ship, he made for the already lowered rear ramp and prayed no one was inside. The moment he boarded the spacecraft, he found out his prayers were for naught. A short pilot wearing an ill-fitting pressure suit and helmet sat behind the flight controls. The pilot spun around, holding a wicked looking phase pistol. The pilot's face was barely visible behind the helmet's visor, but Matthew could see the pilot's frown change to a grin.

"Matt, it's you," said the pilot. "You scared the living daylights out of me."

"Brachia? What are you doing here?"

The young boy removed his helmet as his grin grew wider. "Apparently the same thing you are, trying to steal a ship." He held up an electronic pad. "Only I've got written authorization from the admiral. I forged his signature myself." Turning the pad so Matthew could see a scribble that looked amazingly like the admiral of the combined Conglomerate fleet's writing, Brachia laughed. "Pretty good copy, don't you think?"

Matthew worked his way around several crates of electronics and made for the copilot's seat. "I need this ship, Brachia. You need to get off."

"Fat chance," said Brachia with a determined look on his young face. "I'm the one with the authorization, and I put a security code on it so that only I can get this ship through the flight deck's force field. You're welcome to come along if you want, otherwise get off and find your own ride."

Matthew was tempted to pick up the young boy and forcibly remove him from the fighter-bomber. He didn't. The reason was partly because he knew the boy might look like a nine or ten year old, but he had the mind of an adult genius. *Yeah. That's part of the reason,* he thought. *The other part is that he's still holding a pistol, and it's pointed at me.*

Ignoring the weapon as best he could, Matthew said, "I've got to get to Tia. She needs my help. She's in the asteroid belt near section three Bravo. I'm going there one way or the other."

Brachia had lost his smile during the confrontation, but it returned just as suddenly. The boy lowered his pistol and placed it in a holster strapped to his right hip. "Then grab a seat. It just so happens I'm also heading to the asteroid belt in section three Bravo."

Making a snap decision, Matthew sat in the copilot's seat and buckled his shoulder harness. "Not that I'm complaining, but why are you going there?" He jerked a thumb over his shoulder. "And what's all this equipment for? There's a war zone out there. It's not one of your scientific experiments."

Brachia touched the icon on his armrest to raise the rear ramp. "When I used the memory transversal device on the imp, I got an image of a magic-based jammer ship. The imp didn't know much about it, so I moved on to other things that seemed more important at the time. From what I can figure out, the demons have been helping the Crosioians again by hiding their ships. I think the Crosioians have also gotten some help from the magic dimension in the form of some advanced jammer ship. It's a Dragar design. I think the jammer ship is using magic to control the Crosioians' communication network, maybe even their whole section of the tele-network. The jammer also has some kind of special magic-based weapon on it that the imp knew about. The little demon wasn't sure what the weapon did, but I got the impression the weapon was going to play a major part in this battle."

Touching the controls, Brachia brought the fighter-bomber to a hover and began moving toward the nearest exit point in the flight deck's force field.

"Interesting, but that doesn't answer my question," Matthew told the boy. "Why are you going to section three Bravo?"

Punching a security code into the pad on the armrest of the pilot's seat, Brachia brought the fighter-bomber all the way up to the flight deck's protective force field and flew it through the shimmering wall. As soon as they were clear of the flagship and in the empty space beyond, he looked over at Matthew.

Giving a conspiratorial wink, Brachia said, "I'm going to section three Bravo and take out the jammer." He smiled. "Since you're here, I'll let you help Omar and me if you ask nice." The young boy released his grip on the flight controls. "Uh, to be perfectly honest, it might be best if you flew. I read the manual before I commandeered this bomber, but I've never actually flown a starship outside of a simulator."

Hastily grabbing the flight controls in front of the copilot seat, Matthew took charge of the fighter-bomber. He punched the coordinates for section three Bravo into the hyper-drive's navigation computer. As he waited for the flight computer to crunch the numbers, he glanced over at Brachia. "I've got to ask. Why didn't you just tell the admiral about the jammer ship? He could've sent a whole fleet to take it out."

Brachia laughed. "Ha! You've obviously forgotten what it's like to be ten years old. No one listens to a kid, even if they are a genius. If the jammer's going to be taken out, we've got to do it." The boy flashed a smile. "So? Are you in, or are you out?"

The red light on the hyper-drive panel turned green.

Matthew smiled. "I'm all in. So hold onto your seat, Captain. This ain't no simulator, and Tia taught me everything I know about flying, so we're not wasting any time."

Punching the icon for the hyper-drive, Matthew shoved the throttle full forward. Every cell in his body tingled. Then everything went black.

* * *

The controlled chaos on the bridge of the *Destiny* blurred into the background as Liz studied the strategic map. The huge ship shuddered under what could only be a nuclear blast. She ignored it as best she could. *Captain Bhami's job is to keep this ship in one piece,* she thought. *Mine's to fight this war.*

Turning to the science officer, Liz said, "This can't be right. There aren't nearly enough dreadnaughts and heavy cruisers on the map. Are you sure you've got all the data on there?"

The science officer frowned, but his voice was steady when he answered. "Everything that's been reported is on the map, Sir. I agree that the Crosioian fleets in contact so far are light on dreadnaughts, but that's what's being reported. Even Admiral Donovan is reporting fewer dreadnaughts attacking around Tardis than expected."

Liz was tempted to breathe a sigh of relief that the pressure on her husband was lighter than expected, but she couldn't. She looked at the science officer. "Those dreadnaughts are somewhere. Find them."

"Aye, aye, Sir."

Liz continued looking at the strategic map. *The seventh and ninth fleets are holding their line,* she thought. *The attack there must be a feint. The only question is where will the main attack be? I can't commit my strategic reserve until I know for sure. What I really need is more wizard scouts. I'm lacking intel.*

In a rare sign of frustration, Liz slammed her fist on the arm of her command chair. *Rick, where the hell are you when I need you?*

Several heads turned in her direction.

She ignored them.

CHAPTER 51

The other side of the rift was not what Jeena had expected. Actually, she hadn't known what to expect, but the tunnel where they found themselves was a mirror image of the one they'd just left. If she didn't know better, she'd have thought they had somehow gotten turned around and were heading back in the direction from whence they'd come. She half expected to come upon the two sisters, Crush-Your-Skull and Eat-The-Flesh-Of-My-Enemy, crouched down as rear guards where Richard had deposited them in their fighting-suits.

As for her bondmate, Richard was ten paces ahead with Red Wing at his left side. They were both cautiously moving down the tunnel. The orange glow they'd seen coming through the rift was even brighter on this side. In fact, the orange glow coming from the tunnel ahead was growing increasingly brighter with each step. The smell of brimstone filled the air to the point of being nauseating.

With a wave of her hand, Jeena drew a small amount of Power from her reserve and converted it into magic with a two-word breathing spell. As a dim glow of magic covered her mouth and nostrils, Richard looked back and frowned.

He sensed my magic, Jeena thought. *He is concerned I will give away our position.* She didn't blame him for being worried. The residual demon scent they'd sensed on the other side of the rift was nothing to what they were being bombarded with now. At any moment she expected to turn a corner of the tunnel and come face to face with another group of demons.

Apparently seeing the glow around her mouth and understanding what she'd done and why, her bondmate faced back to the front and resumed walking.

Jeena looked to her right where Charge-In-The-Face-Of-Great-Odds walked next to her. The bat's phase spear was fully extended, but it wasn't activated. Neither the scouts nor Richard had their weapons activated for fear of giving away their position.

Jeena glanced at the blue gem at the tip of the Staff of the Lady of the Tree. *Too bad I cannot deactivate the staff until it is needed,* she thought. *All I can do is place a stealth shield around it and hope for the best. So far we have avoided detection on this side of the rift, but how long that will last is anyone's guess.*

Two hundred paces ahead, Jeena spotted another bend in the tunnel. They walked a hundred paces without incident before things took a turn for the worse.

"Take them, fools!" shouted a deep voice that grated on every nerve in Jeena's body. The words were more a thought than something heard with physical ears. The voice burned its way into her brain, pushing all other thoughts to the side. "Keep the master's variable alive," said the voice. "Kill the rest."

A mob of nightmarish creatures came charging around the bend. Two-, four-, six-, eight-, and even ten-legged creatures of every color of the rainbow formed a deadly wall of claws, horns, and teeth. The demons, for that's what Jeena knew they were, jostled against each other in their eagerness to destroy their prey. A monstrous beast with ten legs stood three times the size of a tall elf. It charged forward, knocking over several of its companions and crushing them beneath its clawed feet. The beast roared, sending out a sonic wave that knocked Richard and Red Wing to the tunnel floor.

Jeena threw up a protective shield across the tunnel a dozen steps to her bondmate's front. The ten-legged beast hit the shield, bending it inward. Her protective shield held for three heartbeats until the mob of demons following the great beast added their weight against her magic. As her protective shield began to crack, Jeena drew more Power from her reserve. Instead of trying to strengthen the shield, she dropped it and used the shield's magic to cast a mass levitation spell. Two score demons floated into the air and bumped into the ceiling. Only the ten-legged monstrosity remained on the floor with its hand-length claws digging into the solid stone.

One of the floating demons braced itself against the ceiling and cast a spell.

Jeena's levitation spell dissipated as its energy went back to where it had come.

The demons fell to the floor and scrambled to regain their feet.

Phase and plasma rounds from Charge-In-The-Face-Of-Great-Odds and the four scouts behind her flew at the demons as fast as the bats could pull their weapons' triggers. Two of the demons screamed and melted into a grayish sludge. As the sludge pooled on the tunnel floor, Jeena caught a glint of purple and red. The ring on her left hand tingled.

"Those are gems," said Danny. *"They're small, but they are definitely gems. I sense Power coming from them. I calculate they are the trapped souls of the demons. Hmm. Interesting. I would not have expected that."*

Interesting or not, Jeena had no time to reply. More demons were coming around the corner, adding their weight to the fray. Logic told her that their recon team had only seconds to live before they would be overwhelmed by the wave of attacking demons. Richard and Red Wing regained their feet and began swinging wildly at the ten-legged demon's head and chest with their phase rod and spear. Other demons leaped past the larger demon and attempted to come at Red Wing and her bondmate from behind. Jeena raised her staff and sent out a blast of pure magic, not even bothering to cast a spell. It was a dangerous gamble, but the blast caught four demons in the back and turned them into a gray sludge. Four small glints of light fell to the tunnel floor, mixed in with the sludge.

As Jeena ran forward with the intent of gaining her bondmate's side, a long tentacle reached out from the wall and wrapped around her. At the tentacle's touch, her skin began to blacken and blister. She screamed. A wave of healing Power came down the link from her bondmate. The burnt skin beneath the tentacle returned to normal, but the sensation of burning continued. Jeena pulled the dagger from her belt and stabbed its blade deep into the tentacle. The dagger was ancient and had once been the property of her great grandmother many times over, High Priestess Shandristiathoraxen. Jeena sensed ancient magic leave the dagger's blade and transfer into the tentacle.

A roar of pain echoed through the tunnel as the tentacle disintegrated into nothing.

Falling to the tunnel floor, Jeena hit the stone hard on her hands and knees. Ignoring the pain in her legs, she jumped to her feet. Demons were everywhere as more came running down the tunnel. Jeena spotted Richard standing in knee deep gray sludge. The ten-legged beast was nowhere to be seen, but with scores of other demons in the fray, the loss of the ten-legged beast mattered little in her opinion. Another one of the tentacles reached out from the tunnel wall and wrapped around Spear-From-Below. The tentacle raised the small bat into the air and slammed the scout hard into the tunnel floor. Even from ten paces, Jeena heard the crack of the bat's fighting-helmet as it split apart. Blood and brain matter sprayed into the air. Jeena sensed Power wrap around the scout's injuries as her self-heal worked desperately to restore her body to baseline. It was a losing battle. The tentacle continued to beat the bloody form of the bat against the tunnel floor, causing more damage than the small scout's Power could heal.

A blur of blonde fur charged past Jeena as First-Out-Of-The-Nest ran to the aid of her fellow scout. The blonde bat shifted into the void and entered the tunnel wall. Jeena sensed First-Out-Of-The-Nest stab her phase spear into the heart of a massive demon inside the wall. The demon roared in pain as it died on the point of the scout's spear. Jeena sensed the demon's soul condense into a gem the size of the tip of her finger.

"We are in the demonic plane," said Danny in her mind. *"The demons can die here. I calculate their souls turn into those gems when they die. If we make it out of here alive, maybe that knowledge will prove useful in the future."*

Jeena doubted any of them were going to make it out alive. She caught a flash of green out the corner of her eye. Dodging back, she barely avoided the tip of a phase spear as a Crosioian scout thrust her weapon forward in an attempt to skewer her on the spear's point.

"That is not one of the scouts on our recon team," said Danny. *"I calculate it must be one of the scouts from the Blood Claw tribe*

that was involved in the coup against the supreme leader."

Jeena was too busy trying to stay alive to reply. The enemy scout thrust out her spear again as the bat simultaneously fired a phase pistol at her head. Twisting to the side, Jeena avoided both the phase round and the spear point. Still holding High Priestess Shandristiathoraxen's dagger in her hand, she thrust it forward and caught the scout in the arm. The dagger's blade penetrated the scout's armor and dug into flesh. The scout hissed a high-pitched scream as the blade's magic flowed through one end of the Crosioian's body to the other. Jeena sensed Power from the bat's reserve healing the damage as fast as the magic could create it. Sensing the dagger's magic running low, Jeena pulled Power from her reserve and added it to that of the blade's. In less than two heartbeats, the attacking scout's reserve ran dry. Before the bat could hiss a final scream, the dagger's magic turned the bat's flesh into liquid fire inside her fighting-suit. Then the scout was no more.

Running low on Power, Jeena sent a feeling of concern to her bondmate. He sent half his Power to her. As soon as it mixed with hers, more Power was created. Jeena sent half of the created Power back to her bondmate. It was more Power than he'd sent.

"You are a traitor, Spear-Through-Your-Heart," hissed a voice to Jeena's right.

Jeena turned to see Charge-In-The-Face-Of-Great-Odds fighting a slightly smaller scout. Jeena sensed the smaller bat was younger and stronger than Charge-In-The-Face-Of-Great-Odds, but the old bat was not put off. Red Wing's grandmother thrust her phase spear forward as she fired a steady stream of plasma rounds from a pistol in her left hand. The younger bat dodged both phase spear and plasma rounds as she swept her wing forward. The tip of the wing caught Charge-In-The-Face-Of-Great-Odds in the side and penetrated her fighting-suit. The old bat dropped her pistol but somehow kept a grip on her phase spear as she fell to the floor.

"Grandmother! No!" Red Wing cried in fear as she came charging forward, sending out a blast of pure Power.

A demon to Red Wing's front turned into a soupy mess as it took the brunt of the Power.

The smaller scout standing over Charge-In-The-Face-Of-Great-Odds hissed a laugh as she raised her phase spear for a killing blow. Before the spear could come down, a blur of black fur, blazing red eyes, and a fang-filled mouth came out of the floor and latched onto the attacking bat's throat.

"Sheeta," said Danny.

The male dolgar shook his head from side to side, tearing out the bat's throat.

Jeena sensed Power trying to heal the scout's wound, but she sensed the big dolgar sucking life force out of the scout faster than it could heal. The bat's reserve soon emptied. Sheeta gave the bat a shake so violent the scout's head and fighting-helmet flew in one direction as its body and suit went in another.

Other black shapes came out of the floor and walls as more dolgars added their weight to the fray. An earsplitting buzzing sound filled the tunnel as fist-sized red balls of phase energy swept the tunnel, blasting into demons and throwing them right and left. Glancing to her left, Jeena saw Richard holding a large-bore auto-cannon in his hands with a belt of ammunition extending from the weapon, over his shoulder, and into his open dimensional pack. A second set of buzzing was added to the bedlam as Red Wing pulled a similar weapon out of her dimensional pouch and began spraying the mass of demons with phase energy.

The demons fell back before the fourteen attacking dolgars and combined firepower from the two auto-cannons. Hope filled Jeena. She pulled Power from her reserve and shouted the words for a chained-lighting spell. The ball of magic flew into a mass of demons farther down the tunnel that appeared to be massing for a counterattack. The spell exploded in their midst as a ball of lightning began jumping from one demon to the next. A dozen demons turned to sludge as multicolored gems the size of an elf's fingernail fell to the stone floor.

Charge-In-The-Face-Of-Great-Odds and the other scouts added the firepower of their weapons and phase spears to the battle. The wave of attacking demons wavered and began withdrawing.

"Back to the rift," Richard shouted. "We've got to get out of here. There are hundreds more coming. I can sense them."

Before anyone could act, a rolling wave of darkest evil swept over Jeena. As the evil took the strength from her limbs, she fell to the floor. She sensed Red Wing, Charge-In-The-Face-Of-Great-Odds, and the other scouts fall as well. Only Richard, Sheeta,

Sheba, and the twelve dolgar pups continued fighting against the demons. They didn't fight for long.

"Fools!" shouted a voice that wasn't a voice. "Must I do everything myself? I am Cancontus. Angels tremble at the mention of my name. Mere mortals cannot stand before me."

A bulbous mass of flesh rolled down the tunnel half in and half out of the walls and ceiling. Dozens of thirty-meter-long tentacles extended out of the massive demon's body. The tentacles reached out and latched onto Richard and the fourteen dolgars. Other tentacles wrapped around Jeena and the scouts. At the major demon's touch, Jeena was racked with pain. Somehow she held on to her dagger and the Lady's staff, but she lacked the will and strength to use them.

A tooth-filled opening the width of a tall elf appeared in the center of the demon's body. The stench of death on the demon's breath rolled over Jeena as the tentacle that was wrapped around her began pulling her closer to the gapping orifice.

"You first, High Priestess," said Cancontus. "I will suck the soul from your body for a thousand years. That is when the real pain will start. All of you will beg for death, but it will not come. First the elf, then the others. And we must not forget about you, Wizard Scout. I will save you for last. Your pain will be legend, but first you will watch me tear the soul from your bondmate one agonizing piece at a time. We will savor her screams together. I will savor all of your screams."

Jeena wanted to scream right then and there, but she could not. She lacked the strength. As the tentacle lowered her closer to the putrid smelling hole of the demon's mouth, she gathered her fear-wracked mind together enough to send a final emotion down the link to her bondmate. She sent him all the love she could muster.

Then Jeena waited for the end as the tooth-filled mouth drew near.

CHAPTER 52

Telsa, Rembis, Leethor, and Master Jathar stood perfectly still, hardly daring to breathe. They were smack dab in the middle of the empty plain of the valley floor, and there was no cover. The rocky ravine where they'd previously hidden was a kilometer to their rear. The tunnel opening to the rift between dimensions was still a good half a kilometer ahead.

"Not much cover out here," said Raj in Telsa's shared space. *"I calculate even your battle suit's camouflage would not keep you hidden if it was not being supplemented with the two mages' invisibility spells. Even combined with the spells, I seriously doubt any of you can remain hidden much longer. The eight scouts that were near the tunnel opening were bad enough. They have now been joined by two hundred and twenty-three demons. I would advise you to turn around, but I calculate it is too late for that now."*

Telsa couldn't argue with her battle computer. Their plan to kill the scouts and enter the tunnel had seemed their only hope when they'd been in the ravine. The imp had readily agreed to the plan. The little demon had led the way down the ravine and into the valley while using half-hidden depressions and piles of rubble to conceal them from the scouts. When the two hundred plus demons had joined the eight scouts three minutes earlier, the purple imp had skedaddled, leaving them high and dry.

"I would lay odds the imp has gone to tell its master where we are," whispered Rembis. The old gnome pointed at the mass of demons near the opening in the volcano's side. "I'm betting that tall one with the ten legs is the boss of the outfit."

"Maybe," said Leethor, "but it has been my experience that size is not all that important. For all we know, that purple imp of ours is the master and has been playing us for fools the whole time."

Telsa increased her battle helmet's zoom to the max. The demons were even more hideous up close than they were at a distance. The ten-legged demon was the worst of all. Even at a distance she could sense that its Power reserve was larger than any of the others. Telsa glanced at Rembis and Master Jathar before looking back at Leethor. "Well, regardless of which demon's in charge, we've got to get past them and into that rift if we want to make it back home. It's just a matter of time until someone or something stumbles on us here and we're forced to fight."

Rembis chuckled. When Telsa, Leethor, and Master Jathar looked his way, the old gnome said, "I was just thinking it wouldn't be much of a fight. We're outnumbered seventy to one."

"I fail to see the humor in that," said Master Jathar.

"Well," smiled Rembis. "I was just imagining the four of us going down there, taking the minotaur by the horn, and demanding the demon's surrender. I had this vision of them rolling around on the ground laughing so hard that we were able to slip past them and meet up with Rick in the rift."

"That is not logical," said Raj over the battle helmet's external speaker.

Telsa chuckled. "No it's not, but it would be one heck of a feat if we could pull it off."

"That it would," agreed Leethor sporting a grin of his own.

Apparently Master Jathar didn't share their humor because he didn't laugh. In fact, he didn't give even the barest hint of a smile. "I would suggest we get serious for a moment and—"

Without warning, a ninth scout materialized near the mass of demons and the eight Crosioian scouts. The new scout pointed at the gash in the side of the volcano. As soon as she did, every one of the demons along with the nine scouts began running toward the tunnel. Just as the last of the demons was disappearing through the opening in the volcano, a bulbous mass of gray flesh with thirty-meter long tentacles protruding from its body materialized a hundred meters from the opening. The giant mass of gray rolled more than walked into the tunnel. As it entered the rift, Telsa heard it shout in a deep voice that grated on every nerve in her body.

"Take them! Keep the master's variable alive. Kill the rest."

At the sound of the voice, the meter-tall purplish form of the imp appeared from behind a pile of stones twenty meters to Telsa's right. The pile of rubble should've been too small to hide its body, but somehow it had managed.

"Now!" hissed the imp as it flapped its wings. "Now is your chance. We must go now, or the master will not be pleased."

The sounds of explosions reverberated out of the tunnel opening.

"Wizard Scout Shepard and his elf are in trouble," said Raj. "The nine fighting-computers of the scouts we saw outside the tunnel say that their scouts and the demons are in battle with the wizard scout and the high priestess. Your friends are in the tunnel with some scouts of their own. The fighting-computers calculate that the demons and the nine scouts will be victorious in two minutes if nothing changes."

Without taking time to consult the gnome or the two elves, Telsa jumped to her feet and began running toward the tunnel as fast as her battle suit would go. The imp flew to her front, leading the way. She heard the sound of pounding feet to her rear. The sound grew fainter as her battle suit outpaced her friends. She didn't care. She was a wizard scout. Rick was in trouble. She had to help or die trying.

CHAPTER 53

A feeling of intense love came down the link from Jeena to Richard. The strong emotion only partially concealed the terror he sensed beneath his bondmate's surface. He struggled to break the grip of the tentacle wrapped around his waist and pinning his arms. Unlike the others in the team, he wasn't paralyzed by the demon's aura. He'd been around too many demons during missions for *'the One'* to be subdued by even a major demon's aura now. That mattered little if he couldn't break free from the tentacle. Even Sheeta, Sheba, and their pups appeared helpless as they were suspended above the tunnel floor.

"Cancontus is a major demon," said Nickelo in their shared space. *"He can exist in many times and places at once. The dolgars are not affected by the demon's aura, but they cannot dimensional shift to escape. Cancontus is preventing their shifts. I wish I could think of something to help, but I cannot. I'm sorry."*

The tentacle holding Jeena in its grip lowered to within a meter of the tooth-filled cavity of the demon's mouth. The tentacle's movement stopped as if to allow the elf to stare at the doom awaiting her.

"Watch, Wizard Scout, as I devour your bondmate," said Cancontus in the deep voice that wasn't a voice. "You can do nothing to save her. You may have stopped me in the past, but you no longer have the Dalinfaust's essence in your phase rod. You are as helpless as the rest of the mortals. Even the mighty Dalinfaust is my prisoner, as is my fool brother Zenthra. I alone am destined to rule the three galaxies. Every living thing shall learn to fear the name of Cancontus."

Drawing Power from his reserve, Richard used telekinesis to pry against the tentacle pinning his arms to his sides. Even after combining the telekinesis with the strength of his battle suit's assistors, the meter-thick tentacle continued to hold him firm in its grasp. Richard shifted the Power from his telekinesis and converted it to pure energy as he prepared to blast the demon, but a line of energy from Cancontus knocked his Power aside.

"Fool," laughed Cancontus. "My master forbade me from harming you directly, but he is as foolish as you." A free tentacle reached down and picked up the headless corpse of the scout Sheeta had attacked. "Thanks to the Blood Claw tribe's rep, my demons have positioned the Crosioians' fleets in such a manner that they will destroy the Empire and Trecorian forces once and for all. The one hope for your foolish mortals will be gone. Neither the Crosioians nor the United Galaxy Alliance can hope to defeat the Dragars and our demon armies on their own. Soon the gate beneath the Tree of Light will be torn asunder and the Great Battle will begin in earnest."

Cancontus laughed uncontrollably as if at an unseen joke. When his laughter stopped, the demon brought the tentacle holding Richard close to the tentacle holding Jeena. She turned fear-stricken eyes to look at him. Somehow he sensed it was fear for him more than for herself. Despite her fright, she forced a last smile. The molten silver of her eyes drew Richard in. Although she was too paralyzed by the demon's aura to speak, he sensed his bondmate's emotions through their link. He sensed her thoughts as clearly as any spoken words.

"Do not despair, my love. We will meet again in the next world."

The tentacle holding Jeena flipped to hold her upside down as it renewed its descent toward the demon's mouth. Just as the ends of her long silver hair passed over the first of several rows of jagged teeth, green balls of phase energy came streaking in from the rift's side of the tunnel to explode against the back of the demon's mouth. Some of the phase rounds passed down the demon's throat, spraying geysers of black liquid into the air. Cancontus screamed in anger more than pain as two Crosioian scouts, Crush-Your-Skull and Eat-The-Flesh-Of-My-Enemy, came charging down the tunnel from the direction of the rift, firing their phase rifles as fast as they could pull the triggers. Richard sensed the two bat sisters combine Power from their reserves and force it into the demon's mouth in a single blast of energy.

The explosion at the back of the demon's mouth blew a double-fist-sized hole out the back of its body. Pieces of the demon's flesh along with black body fluids splattered against the tunnel walls. As the explosion ripped through the demon, the tentacles holding Richard and Jeena moved away from its mouth. Sensing a slight relaxation in the demon's grip, Richard shoved telekinesis between the tentacle and his left arm, prying the meter-thick mass of flesh away. The tentacle didn't move much, but it was enough to allow him to activate his phase rod and strike down onto the demon's flesh. As the microscopic explosions of phase energy ripped cells apart, the tentacle withered in pain and released its grip.

Richard fell to the tunnel floor and jumped up in a flash. Miraculously, the 20mm auto-cannon was still hanging from its shoulder strap. He brought the weapon to bear on the base of the tentacle holding Jeena. With a quick pull of the trigger, a score of armor-piercing rounds blasted into the tentacle, cutting it free from the demon's body. The tentacle hit the floor, spurting its black blood in all directions. As the muscles in the tentacle relaxed, Jeena rolled free, but she didn't move.

"The demon's aura still has her in its spell," said Nickelo in their shared space. *"The two sisters have obviously overcome the aura's effect. So will your elf, but it will take time. That's time you do not have."*

Remembering how he'd freed his fellow wizard scouts from the demon's aura when they'd fought against the vampires under Old Drepdenor Mountain, Richard formed a Circle with his bondmate. It was easy to do since their bond link was basically a miniature Circle in itself. He gathered his courage and resolve and passed it on to Jeena. At the same time, he expanded the Circle to include Red Wing, her grandmother, and the other scouts on their recon team. As his courage passed from one part of the hastily erected Circle to the other, it increased to the point that the demon's aura no longer had an effect on his companions.

Red Wing was the first to recover. Still raised in the air, she stabbed the tip of her phase spear into the tentacle holding her airborne. At the same time, she sent a blast of pure Power at the tentacle holding Charge-In-The-Face-Of-Great-Odds. Although not an efficient use of Power, the maneuver did the trick as the tentacle dropped the old bat. Sheeta, Sheba, and their pups along with the other scouts attacked the tentacles holding them as the demon tried to recover from the two sisters' attack. The scouts and dolgars were soon free as they joined the sisters, Richard, Jeena, and Red Wing in a combined assault on the bulbous mass of the demon.

"Get them, you fools," shouted Cancontus sounding close to panic.

At his command, the mass of demons that had earlier begun to withdraw surged forward. Before the demon's charge could gather momentum, two fireballs exploded in their midst. At the same time, a nearly solid stream of red plasma rounds along with several black arrows struck the demon in the eye, causing Cancontus to howl in rage as much as pain.

"Give 'em hell, Rick," shouted Telsa over her battle helmet's external speakers as she, Rembis, Leethor, and Master Jathar came running down the tunnel. Leading their way was a meter-high purple demon flapping its wings as it bared its teeth and hissed a war cry of its own.

Richard brought his auto-cannon to bear on the part of Cancontus's mass that he sensed was the most vulnerable. While Telsa's group drew the attention of the mass of charging demons, Red Wing, Jeena, and the other scouts on their team brought all their firepower to bear on the same spot as Richard. Cancontus was driven back screaming and snapping his blood-filled mouth. Sheeta, Sheba, and their pups attacked the demon from the sides, rear, and overhead as the auto-cannon's deadly rounds cut gaping holes in the major demon's flesh.

Hope swelled in Richard's breast. *We're going to win,* he thought.

Then everything froze.

Richard's mind continued to work, but his limbs were frozen in place despite his best efforts to make them move. His eyes focused on a 20mm round suspended in midair an arms-length in front of the auto-cannon's barrel. Jeena stood off to his right side with her staff raised. A ball of blue energy from the staff's gem was heading directly toward the gapping wounds the auto-cannon had made in Cancontus's body. Like the auto-cannon's rounds, the high priestess's ball of magic was frozen in midair halfway between Jeena and her intended target. Red Wing and her scouts were also frozen stiff. A line of green balls of energy traced a line from the scouts to the major demon, but like everything else, their plasma and phase rounds weren't moving.

What's going on? Richard thought.

"You fool," came Cancontus's voice that wasn't a voice. "Do you think I am limited by time? I am a major demon. Time and distance are nothing to me. I can heal this body with a thought. I can draw on the Power of my ten thousand avatars on other worlds and dimensions to crush you and your pathetic allies. I am too powerful to be defeated by a weak mortal. Watch as I destroy your allies one by one."

As if in a trance, Richard saw the massive wounds in the demon's flesh heal. Two of its healed tentacles moved forward obviously unaffected by whatever time-freeze held everyone else in its clutches. The tentacles wrapped around the frozen forms of the two sisters, Crush-Your-Skull and Eat-The-Flesh-Of-My-Enemy. Tightening their grip, the meter-thick tentacles squeezed, crushing the bats' fighting-suits until blood dripped out of the crumpled armor. Richard noticed a shimmering in the air as the sisters' life force left their bodies. With a final ripple of Power, the shimmering disappeared. Richard knew the sisters were gone.

Cancontus laughed. "You see, fool? I can kill your friends at my leisure. I will take my time with your elf. There is no hurry. You and I are in a special time-bubble created by me. As the universe stands still, I will destroy all my enemies. I will save you for last. I am Cancontus. No one is as powerful as I. No one."

"Oh really?" said a pleasant-sounding voice that sounded strangely familiar to Richard but that he couldn't quite place.

Out the corner of his eye, Richard saw a dark-haired man walking down the tunnel past Telsa, Rembis, Leethor, and Master Jathar. The dark-haired man wore knee-high boots and a white shirt with fancy ruffles around the neck and collar. The man was walking through the parts of the tunnel floor that were covered with a layer of deep sludge left by disintegrating demon bodies.

Even so, the man's boots and clothing remained unsoiled. A memory stirred inside Richard as he recognized the man who was no man. A chill ran down his back clear to the base of his spine. The approaching man was a master demon. The last time Richard had seen the master demon was during his first mission on Portalis. He had hoped he'd never see the master demon again.

The dark-haired man looked at Richard and smiled. The smile was almost friendly. "It has been a long time, Wizard Scout." The master demon glanced around the tunnel at the contorted bodies frozen in battle and shook his head. "Tsk, tsk. I expected better from you than this, Wizard Scout. I had hoped it would not be necessary for us to meet again until it was time for you to make your choice during the Great Battle. You disappoint me, my friend."

Richard tried to glare at the man, but his facial muscles were frozen in time. Only his mind was free. *"I am no friend of yours,"* he thought. *"And I will not do your bidding. You and I are enemies."*

The man's smile hardened. "You cut me to the deep, Wizard Scout." He pointed at Sheeta. The big dolgar was frozen in midair with a half-meter-wide chunk of Cancontus's flesh in his mouth. "How can you deny my aid? Did I not give you your dolgar allies? Did I not tell you they would come in handy over the years? Was I wrong?"

Richard refused to play the master demon's word game. He knew he was hopelessly outmatched. The master demon had once held him at his mercy during his first mission on Portalis. He remembered how the master demon had removed his armor and weapons and held him helpless as it told him of a great battle in the future. He remembered how the master demon had told him that he would need to make a choice in the future. He remembered how the dark-haired man that was the master demon had told him his choice would be the key to delivering the three galaxies into the master demon's hands. Richard thought back to how the master demon said he would need allies. That had been right before the demon had slashed open his belly and sent him to a cavern in the spiritual plane where Sheba had just given birth to her pups. The dolgar female had healed him and accepted him as one of her own.

"You do not need to answer, Wizard Scout," said the master

demon. "I see your thoughts. You would have been dead long ago if I had not given you the dolgars as your allies. My opponent, on the other hand, would have sent you helpless to do his will with no one to aid you. The time of the Great Battle is nigh, but you must do a few things yet before the battle is joined. Then you will make your choice, and it will be the right choice or I promise you that I will make you suffer as none have before you. I will make sure your suffering last from now until the end of eternity."

Turning away from Richard, the dark-haired man stared at Cancontus. The bulbous mass of the major demon's avatar was now as frozen in place as was Richard and the others. "In the meantime, Cancontus, what shall I do with you?"

"Master, I serve only you," came Cancontus voice in a pleading tone. "I—"

"Do not bother with excuses," said the dark-haired man. "It matters not. All has been done as I desired." The master demon waved his hand. When he did, a wave of pure Power rushed over the other demons in the tunnel. At the Power's touch, all of the demon bodies except for Cancontus's and the meter-high purple demon turned into gray sludge and splattered to the floor. Richard noticed dozens of multicolored glints of fingernail sized gems in the sludge.

When only Cancontus and the purple demon remained, Cancontus whined, "Master, I have served you faithfully. I have—"

"Enough," said the dark-haired man. "I will deal with you and your brothers later." The master demon waved his hand again. The bulbous mass that was Cancontus's avatar blinked out of existence. Once Cancontus was gone, the dark-haired man walked to within a pace of Jeena. He reached out and lifted a strand of her silver hair before releasing it to fall back against her shoulder.

"Your elf has served her purpose well," said the dark-haired man as he turned to face Richard. "The vision I gave you of her during that first mission on Portalis has given you hope over the years. The thought of her kept you alive during even the darkest times."

Anger burned in Richard. He tried striking out with his phase rod, but his body refused to obey his commands. *"If you harm her, I swear—"*

The dark-haired man laughed. "Harm her, Wizard Scout? Why would I do that? She too has a part to play in the Great Battle, but that time is not quite here. What is needed now is for you to gather your allies and assemble them in one place." The master demon walked over to the frozen Charge-In-The-Face-Of-Great-Odds. "I want to show you something, Crosioian. I want to show all of you something."

An image of demons beyond counting popped into Richard's mind. He knew he was seeing what the master demon was showing all of the others. Along with the vision came the sure knowledge that the demon army was preparing to destroy the three galaxies and every living thing they contained. An image of massive fleets of Dragar warships accompanied by demon allies burned its way into his mind. Beyond the fleets of Dragar ships was a planet surrounded by a shimmering shield. He recognized the planet as Portalis. As he watched, the shield surrounding the planet disappeared. The Dragar fleets moved forward, straight for the helpless planet. Then the image disappeared, but its memory remained.

The dark-haired man turned away from Charge-In-The-Face-Of-Great-Odds and looked at Richard. "That is all any of you need to know for now, Wizard Scout. You must stop the war between the Crosioians and your Empire. You must gather the fleets in the magic dimension for the Great Battle. Then you must make your choice."

"I won't help you," Richard thought. *"If you want the war stopped, why don't you do it yourself? Why waste your time with us?"*

The dark-haired man laughed. "Why? It would take eons to explain why, and even then you would not know. Let me just say that it is not the way things work in the game. If I were to take such a direct hand in the battle for the three galaxies, then my opponent would be free to do the same. If the Dragars and demons were to attack without a sufficient force to oppose them, the game rules would be broken. Chaos would be the only outcome, and that would not bode well for either side." The master demon smiled. "Nay, my opponent and I must play the game by the rules. We are forced to use our variables and their free will to win the game. I am forced to use you."

The dark-haired man smiled and turned to look at the meter-high purple demon. With the merest twitch of the master demon's finger, the portion of Cancontus's spell affecting the small demon disappeared.

"Master," said the meter-high demon. "I have done all that you ask." The purple demon pointed a scaly arm in the direction of Telsa, Leethor, Master Jathar, and Rembis. "I have brought the others as you ordered. I made sure they got part of the yellow—"

"Yes," said the dark-haired man. "They got a part of the yellow gem." The master demon turned back to Richard. "You will need a yellow gem to finish your task." The dark-haired man spread his arms, "Alas, the gem that the gnome has is nowhere near large enough to suit your purpose. You will need to go back in time and acquire one of the proper size when the time is right."

"I won't—" began Richard.

· The master demon laughed. "Oh, believe me, you will. Otherwise, everyone and everything in all three galaxies will die in ways more horrible than anything you can imagine." The dark-haired man smiled. "It is your choice."

The master demon waved his hand. Then everything went black.

CHAPTER 54

Richard ran down the tunnel doing his best to keep the pace slow enough for those not in fighting- or battle suits to keep up, but fast enough to make time. The orange glow from the rift slowly faded behind them as the air density continued to grow ever thicker. Richard glanced at his heads-up display noting the time.

"Time," said Nickelo in their shared space. *"That's always the key, isn't it? By the way, do you even have a plan?"*

"Red Wing," Richard shouted over his shoulder. "Have you contacted the supreme leader? Have you told her what you saw? She's got to stop the war before anyone else is killed."

Charge-In-The-Face-Of-Great-Odds happened to be running directly behind Richard, next to Red Wing. The old bat answered before her granddaughter got the chance. "The supreme leader knows. I have told her all we saw and sensed, but there is nothing she can do. The battle for Estos has already begun."

"She can do *something*," Richard insisted, still running hard. "She must order the Crosioian fleets to pull back. I'll have my battle computer contact the Empire's high command and have them do the same. All we need is a truce that lasts long enough to sort out all of this. The killing's got to stop."

Jeena stumbled and grabbed at her throat. So did Master Jathar, Leethor, and Rembis.

"The air is changing back to water," came Nickelo's thought in Richard's mind. *"We are getting close to the exit. You've got your battle suit. The scouts have their fighting-suits. The others are*

going to need to cast breathing spells that work in water. You've got to stop long enough for them to cast their magic. They'll also need protection from the water pressure. I don't have to remind you that the entrance for the Hole is a long ways down from the surface."

Grabbing his bondmate's arm, Richard pulled her back a dozen steps, toward a spot where the air was semi-normal. Three of the scouts grabbed Rembis and the two elves. Once the air thinned enough that the moisture resembled a thick fog more than visible droplets of water, Richard waited while Jeena and the others bent over and coughed. He patted his bondmate on the back. She responded by spitting a mouthful of water onto the tunnel floor.

Once his bondmate recovered enough to speak, Richard said, "Jeena, you need to cast that underwater spell you used to get here. Can you cast it on Master Jathar, Leethor, and Rembis too, so they can make it to the surface?"

Master Jathar shook himself free from the scout holding him up. "I am quite capable of casting my own spell, Wizard Scout." With that the elf waved a hand and spoke three words Richard heard but quickly forgot. A shimmering bubble of air formed around the elf's body. The old elf turned and cast a similar spell on Leethor. By the time Master Jathar's spells fully formed, Jeena and Rembis had their own bubbles protecting them.

Richard turned away from his bondmate to look at Charge-In-The-Face-Of-Great-Odds. "So what about it? Will the supreme leader order her fleets to stop fighting or not?"

The old bat shook her head.

The animal that was Richard's temper began rattling its cage again. "What is wrong with you?" he asked barely keeping his voice below a shout. "You saw and sensed the same things I did. How can—"

Red Wing stepped forward and placed her hand on Richard's arm. "Steady, Wizard Scout. It is not that the supreme leader does not believe us. She does. She is convinced."

"Then why—"

Charge-In-The-Face-Of-Great-Odds stepped beside her granddaughter. "Because, Wizard Scout, the supreme leader cannot give the order. She has already tried. Something is jamming communications with the fleets. Even our fighting-computers have lost contact with the fighting-computers of the scouts in the attacking fleets. It is as if that section of the tele-network has been cut off. The battle around Estos continues. According to the supreme leader, the final part of the trap is about to be sprung." She swiveled her ears at Red Wing before turning them back to Richard. "The losses are going to be high on both sides, but the Empire and Trecorian fleets will soon be totally destroyed. That is almost a certainty. There is nothing anyone can do about it."

Richard stared down at the ground, clenching his fists. "This can't be happening. We've come too far to lose our chance now. I refuse to believe nothing can be done to stop this war. We can't let the demons win. We just can't!"

Telsa shoved her way past the two scouts to stand next to Red Wing and her grandmother. She looked at Richard and jerked a thumb at Red Wing. "Raj has forwarded information to me that he received from Nickelo on how you've been trying to get the Crosioians on our side. I normally wouldn't approve, but things have happened that have convinced me you are on the right track. Master Jathar, Leethor, Rembis, and I have spent the last month in Hell, and when I say Hell, I mean *Hell*. After seeing what we've seen, I'm not going to let a little jamming mess up our only chance."

"What are you proposing?" Richard asked, relieved that his friend had a plan.

Telsa laughed. Her face lost some of its stress, momentarily reverting to the fun-loving wizard scout Richard had known as a cadet. "Me? Hey, you're Wizard Scout Richard Shepard. I haven't a clue what we should do, but I'm sure you'll think of something."

Richard sensed confidence coming through the link from Jeena. He turned to look at the others. For some reason, even the Crosioian scouts had their ears pointing at him with what he took as an expression of expectancy.

"Hey," Richard said hoping to give his companions a dose of reality. "I'm just a man. I'm out of ideas. There's nothing I can do."

Sensing movement to his right, Richard turned to look into Jeena's eyes. The swirling molten silver was clearly visible through the shimmering field protecting her. She touched his arm with her left hand.

"You mean there is nothing you can do *here*, my bondmate." She smiled. It was accompanied by a feeling through their link of love and uttermost confidence. "My adoptive mother Reale always told me that when defeat looms over you with no escape in sight, you may as well charge forward to meet it."

Richard stared at his bondmate. "I'm not quite sure I—"

Laughter came out of Red Wing's translator. "The *Defiant*," the bat said. She laughed again. "I think all things are coming together, Wizard Scout Richard Shepard. I think you were named well. You truly are the *tribal brother*."

"I still don't—"

Charge-In-The-Face-Of-Great-Odds also laughed. "Yes, we can do nothing here, but the *Defiant* is now the fastest ship in this galaxy. Her intergalactic-drive can make the run to Estos in fifteen minutes if we override the safety controls." The old bat hissed another laugh. "After what we have all encountered and sensed this day, I think a few safety controls are the least of our worries."

Richard looked from the two scouts to Telsa and then to Jeena before looking back at Charge-In-The-Face-Of-Great-Odds. "You're talking about finding and taking out whatever's jamming the Crosioians' part of the tele-network, aren't you? Even if we find the jammer ship, if that's what it is, what good will that do? You told me the battle's already started. Will there be enough time after we destroy the jammer to contact the supreme leader back here on Astaris and have her order your fleets to withdraw?"

Red Wing and Charge-In-The-Face-Of-Great-Odds swiveled their ears at each other before turning them back to Richard.

"Oh, Wizard Scout," said Charge-In-The-Face-Of-Great-Odds slightly spreading her wings. "If you knew our supreme leader like I know her, you wouldn't have to ask. I have no doubt she will be on the *Defiant* right alongside us. If there is any chance this war can be stopped, she is the one who can do it, and she will be right in the middle of the action to make it happen."

With no plan of his own, Richard made the only decision he could. He said out loud so the others could hear, "Nick, contact the *Defiant*. Give Sergeant Ron the coordinates to the platform above us and have him meet us there." With a smile of his own, he added, "Tell him the supreme leader needs her royal yacht. We've got a war to stop."

Laughter came out of the external speaker of Richard's battle helmet.

"Compliance, Wizard Scout. That's a big compliance."

CHAPTER 55

One floating rock after another sped past Tia as Sandy weaved Yankee Kilo Six through the asteroid belt. A stone the size of Tia's head ricocheted off the fighter's force field before shattering against a larger asteroid a hundred meters away. Tia paid little attention. She concentrated all her efforts into holding onto the maintenance rung of the fighter's left wing.

"You all right?" came Sandy's voice over Tia's flight helmet. "I haven't been trying to avoid the smaller ones. I figured speed was our friend."

Tia had no doubt speed was important, but it was one thing to know it sitting in the comfort of a pilot's seat with your hands on the controls and another thing when you were lying prone on the wing of a fighter being flown by a pilot nearly as crazy as she was herself.

Tia glanced down at the meter-long nuclear warhead attached to her chest. She'd removed it from her fighter just prior to Yankee Kilo Six picking her up. She looked out the corner of her helmet's visor, into the cockpit of the split-wing. Sandy had the visor of her flight helmet up. Beads of sweat dripped down the pilot's face as she concentrated on threading the fighter between the thousands of floating pieces of rock in their section of the asteroid belt.

In spite of the situation, Tia laughed. *Sandy's as crazy as I am,* she thought.

As if to prove her point, Tia's fellow fighter pilot squeezed the split-wing between two house-sized boulders. One of the asteroids flew by so close Tia thought she could reach out and touch its rough surface with her gloved hand.

"You're doing fine," Tia said forcing herself to laugh. "Of course, I'd appreciate it if you'd get me to that jammer ship in one piece. I'd hate to deny the Crosioians, or whoever's on that ship, the privilege of blowing holes in me."

Sandy glanced out her side windscreen long enough to catch Tia's eye. "Look, Lieutenant. I'm as crazy a pilot as the next one, but I've got to tell you that I think your plan is even too wild for me. Sure, with my fighter's stealth shield at max, I might be able to slip through these asteroids without being detected, but as soon as we hit open space, that's going to be another story. Those are dreadnaughts and heavy cruisers protecting that jammer ship. This fighter's small enough to avoid the dreadnaughts' larger anti-ship fire until a hundred thousand meters. After that, their smaller weapons will come into play. They'll zero in on this fighter with no problem. Any closer than a hundred thousand meters, and they'll blow us to pieces for sure."

"Well then, we'll just have to make sure you release me more than a hundred thousand meters out. I need your fighter in one piece to make it back to a safe area and warn the fleets. It won't do me any good to take out the jammer ship if you're scattered across half the solar system as glowing bits of radioactive dust."

"This is no time for jokes," said Sandy sounding dead serious. "You haven't got a prayer. Even if you make it to the jammer ship, how will you take it out? For that matter, how will you get back to friendly lines?"

Tia didn't bother telling her fellow fighter pilot that she didn't have the faintest idea. All she knew was that she was a Trecorian and there was a job that needed done. She'd never run from a fight, and she didn't intend to start now. *Besides,* she thought. *Matt's on the flagship. If those dreadnaughts attack before Liz finds out about them, the* Planet Buster *will probably be one of the first ship's taken out. I'm not going to let that happen. Matt's on that ship. The fleets have to be warned. All I can do now is hold on until Sandy gets to the release point.*

Tia didn't have to wait long. After skimming by a boulder the size of a twenty-story building, the split-wing found itself in open space. Tia spotted four dreadnaughts and three heavy cruisers dead ahead, surrounding a black ship of strange design. The black warship was the size of a small destroyer. Increasing the magnification of her flight helmet's visor to maximum, she saw an emblem on the bow of the black ship. The image was that of a black dragon with a red stripe down its side.

Dragars, Tia thought. *I saw enough of them during my year on Portalis to last a lifetime. I'd recognize one of their ships anywhere.*

"Incoming," said Sandy as lines of blue, green, and red energy shot out the sides of the dreadnaughts and cruisers. "Hang on!"

The fighter inverted before going into a near ninety-degree bank. A beam of blue energy missed the fighter's left wing by a meter at most. Turning the fighter back toward the cluster of warships, Sandy said, "Four hundred thousand meters. Get ready."

There wasn't much Tia could do to get ready. Everything depended on Sandy's flying ability and what skills Rick and Gaston had taught her during their year on Portalis. She wrapped herself in Power and activated her best stealth shield. At the same time, she made a final check to make sure her flight suit's camouflage unit was on. The flight suit wasn't battle armor, but it was the best suit the Conglomerate could make. Matt had given it to her. She remembered how he'd told her that if she ever crash-landed on some Creator-forsaken planet, the suit's camouflage unit might help keep her alive until help arrived.

There's not going to be any help this time, Tia thought. *No one's going to come riding to the rescue. I've got to make it to that ship and take out the jammer. I've got to warn Liz and the others. I'm going to make sure Matt's safe. That's all there is to it.*

"Two hundred thousand meters," said Sandy. "I'm not sure about the timing. I'll do my best, but there's no guarantee."

Tia gave a tightlipped smile. "Is there ever? Just do your best. I trust you."

Beams of energy continued to light up the space around the split-wing. Jerked around by the fighter's evasive maneuvers, Tia had little time to watch. She drew more Power from her reserve and converted it into an active scan. Wrapping the scan with a stealth shield the way she'd seen Rick and Gaston do, Tia reached out with Power and latched onto the jammer ship using her scan as an anchor point.

"One hundred thousand meters!" shouted Sandy as the fighter's maneuvering thrusters shot out a stream of ion energy, spinning the ship a hundred and eighty degrees.

With little time to think, Tia released her hold on the fighter's wing at the same time she turned off the flight suit's magnetics. Once she was free of the split-wing, streams of ion energy shot out the port side of the fighter, kicking it to the side a hundred meters. When Tia was clear of the fighter's rear exhaust, the ship's main ion thrusters shot out a trail of bright blue energy. Then just like that, the split-wing was out of sight. Blue, green, and red beams continued to fly past Tia in the direction the split-wing had gone, but no explosions followed. Tia breathed a sigh of relief.

She made it, Tia thought. *Go with the Creator, Sandy. You're going to need all the help you can get.*

Using telekinesis to spin around, Tia spotted the jammer ship. It was right where her active scan told her it would be. Slightly off course, she supplemented the momentum Sandy had given her with the fighter's maneuver by using telekinesis to head for the black ship.

As Tia sped toward the jammer ship, she fully expected beams of energy from its anti-ship weapons to start firing at her. They didn't. She said a silent pray thanking Rick and the deceased Gaston for training her in stealth shields, then said a second prayer thanking Matt for giving her the flight suit with its camouflage unit.

The jammer ship continued to grow larger in her visor. As she drew close to the black ship, Tia used telekinesis to slow her apparent rate of movement. She zeroed out her relative speed just as her feet and hands made contact with the side of the ship. Looking to her left and right for a door or any kind of opening, she saw none. Only a solid wall of black metal was visible from one end of the ship to the other.

Well, Tia thought. *This sucks. How am I supposed to get in? I've got a feeling that I'm going to have to think of a plan B.*

* * *

The fighter-bomber wasn't nearly as agile as the Zip fighters or X-shuttle Matthew was used to flying, but he didn't complain. *It beats walking,* he thought as he adjusted the controls for the ion engine. They'd come out of hyperspace thirty minutes earlier just outside the asteroid belt near section three Bravo. Since then, they'd been dodging the mass of floating rocks while trying not to get smashed to bits.

Matthew grinned at a sudden thought. *At least we haven't run into any Crosioians. That's a plus.* He yelled over his shoulder, "How much farther?"

"All I can say is that we're getting close," replied Brachia. "Just keep us on this course."

Matthew glanced back from the pilot's seat, into the cargo bay. As soon as they'd made the jump to hyperspace, the boy-genius had given up his spot in the pilot's seat and moved to the rear to start unloading crates of electronics. Metal boxes with flashing lights were now scattered from one end of the cargo bay to the other. All of the equipment seemed to be connected via a mass of wires and cables. Jerking a thumb at the seemingly disorganized mess, Matthew said, "Are you sure all this stuff's necessary? If we get in a fight, it's going to be bouncing off the walls, not to mention our heads."

The young boy looked up from a piece of equipment he was attaching to a computer with a spider web of wires and smiled back at Matthew. "Do you want to stay alive? Trust me. We need all of it. I know what I'm doing. If my calculations are right, we'll be able to slip within torpedo range of that jammer ship and blow it to pieces before they know what hit them."

Matthew had his doubts. "If you say so. I'd still rather be out looking for Tia." A vision of Tia rushing into the necromancer's den to rescue him when he'd been captured back on Portalis a few weeks earlier flashed in his mind. "She risked her life to save me. I'm not going to let her down."

Brachia stopped what he was doing and weaved his way through the mass of tangled wires and metal boxes while taking great care not to knock anything over. Once he stood next to the pilot's seat, he placed a hand on Matthew's shoulder. "Tia's going to be all right. You said you can sense her with that ring of yours, but that you can't get an exact fix. I think that's because the jammer is messing up whatever magic's in your ring. This bomber's got four nuclear-tipped torpedoes on it that are designed specifically to blast through dreadnaught armor." Pointing back at the equipment, he said, "That stuff's based upon the stealth shield on the X-shuttle. It'll get us close enough to the jammer ship to blow it to pieces without getting ourselves killed. Once it's gone, our long-range communication channels should clear up. We'll be able to contact the fleet. You should also be able to locate Tia with your ring. We'll fetch her from wherever she's located. Then we'll high-tail it back to the *Planet Buster* before anyone knows we're gone. Trust me. It's all going to work out. Isn't that right, Omar?"

A small box strapped to Brachia's belt crackled. "Aye, aye, Captain. If you say so."

Brachia winked at Matthew. "I do say so." The boy grew serious. "So, Matt, are you with me or not?"

Matthew looked at the curly-haired boy. Even after all their time together, it was hard for his ego to take advice from a ten year old. With no plan of his own, he swallowed his pride. "I'm with you, Brachia. Just point the way, and we'll blast that ship to hell and back. Then we'll go get Tia."

The grin returned to Brachia's face. "That's more like it, ya swab. Trust me. That jammer ship's as good as destroyed."

* * *

The ensign waited patiently on the bridge of the *Destiny* for Liz to finish giving orders to the two admirals. Once the pair of senior officers nodded and left to relay their orders to their staff, Liz turned to the ensign. The ensign held a portable halo-pad in her left hand.

"What is it?" Liz said doing her best to keep any irritation out of her voice. It was a chore. The continued stress of the last several hours had long ago pushed her past the point of being diplomatic.

"Uh, Sir, I have a Wizard Scout Richard Shepard on the line. You left orders that if he called—"

Reaching out, Liz practically snatched the portable halo-pad from the ensign's grasp but caught herself in time to say, "Very good, Ensign. You did well. I'll take it from here."

"Very good, Sir."

Turning away, Liz placed the pad on the armrest of her command chair and touched the ACTIVATE button. An image of her friend appeared over the pad that was more static than actual image.

"Tell me you've got good news, Rick. Things aren't going well on our end."

The static increased to the point where Richard's face was only a blur. After a couple of seconds, the image settled down enough for Liz to see his eyes. *He looks worried,* she thought. *That doesn't bode well.*

A tendril of long silver hair fell into view from someone standing off to Richard's side. Despite the situation, something resembling jealously passed over Liz. She shoved the feeling aside. *I've found my soulmate in Tim. Rick's found his. I'm glad for him.*

"...blocking communications," said Richard as his image sharpened somewhat. "I've got their supreme leader with me. She's prepared to give the orders for her fleet to withdraw, but we can't get through to their commanders. I'm going to need you to withdraw all Empire, Trecorian, and UGA fleets back to Empire space until we sort this mess out."

Although she'd only received part of her friend's message, Liz had heard enough. "Are you crazy? We're already in contact. Our sailors are dying as we speak. I'm not going to withdraw! The Crosioians would blast half of my ships to pieces before we could get out of range. If anyone needs to withdraw, it should be the bats. As soon as I see them leaving the Criterion system, I'll give the orders for my ships to hold their fire, but not one second before."

"Impossible," hissed a voice out of the hologram's sight. "Our ships would be destroyed before the Empire ships received any ceasefire orders. Not that it matters. We cannot contact our fleets anyway."

The worry in Richard's eyes increased. His holographic image practically pleaded with Liz. "Please. Someone's got to be the first to stop the killing."

"Forget it, Rick," Liz said letting the pent up stress come out in her voice. "I'm not pulling my ships out just to get shot in the back."

The *Destiny* shuddered, nearly knocking Liz out of her command chair. Once she regained her balance, she looked back at the halo-pad. "It's too late, Rick. Forget it. I've got a war to fight. *Destiny* out."

* * *

Richard stared at the blank halo-pad for a half-dozen heartbeats before turning to his right to look at Jeena.

She gave a timid smile. "You tried, Rick. Sometimes that is all you can do."

Nodding his head, Richard turned to face the Crosioians' supreme leader. She stood across the *Defiant's* mess table flanked by Red Wing and Charge-In-The-Face-Of-Great-Odds. Sergeant Ron was on Richard's left, opposite Jeena.

"You heard Liz," Richard told the supreme leader. "I tried. It's up to you to stop this war."

The supreme leader turned and swiveled her ears at Charge-In-The-Face-Of-Great-Odds. No sound ensued, but Richard got the distinct impression they were communicating somehow.

"I suspect they're using their fighting-computers as go-betweens," said Nickelo in their shared space. *"I could do that with other battle computers if there weren't so many security programs blocking me. I calculate* 'the One' *is still concerned I will emotionally corrupt the tele-network."*

"You're part of 'the One,'" Richard pointed out, *"so don't go acting like it's some other entity. Admit it. You're as much to blame as any other computer."*

"Whatever," said Nickelo. *"I was merely trying to point out that the two Crosioians are probably using their fighting-computers to communicate."*

Richard had an idea. *"Ask their fighting-computers what they're saying."*

"I can't."

"What do you mean you can't? Telsa told me that Raj was able to connect with some of the scouts' computers when she was in the demonic plane."

"Well, that was Raj, and that was then. The tele-network connection to the Crosioians' computers has been cut off from us battle computers. I calculate something's jamming the connection, and I don't think it is 'the One' *this time."*

Before Richard could question his battle computer any further, the supreme leader turned away from Red Wing to look across the table at him. "I am going to tell you this because in theory, this ship is the royal yacht and you are all in the service of the combined Crosioian tribes."

Sergeant Ron placed his right hand on the butt of the sidearm he'd taken to wearing since the first bat technicians had come on board the *Defiant*. "Like hell we are."

The supreme leader bared her fangs in what Richard took as the Crosioian's version of a smile. "I said *in theory*," said the supreme leader. "Based upon that theory, I am going to tell you all this. The battle for Estos and the entire Criterion system is a well-laid trap. Our fleets outnumber your Empire's forces six to one."

"The Empire has had worse odds and come out on top," said Sergeant Ron keeping his hand near the butt of his pistol.

The smile left the supreme leader's face. "Perhaps, but we have massed a fleet of a thousand dreadnaughts and heavy cruisers as a strategic reserve. They are hidden in Criterion's asteroid belt. If the ambush goes according to plan, in ten minutes they will attack in force and tear a hole through the Conglomerate's flank. Nothing can stop them. The dreadnaughts will be followed by a strike force of warships from the Andromeda galaxy. The Empire, Trecorian, and UGA fleets will be obliterated."

Richard pounded the table. "No! We can't let that happen! Your own scouts have told you what we saw. They told you what the master demon said. We've got to stop this war now!"

The supreme leader shrugged her wings. "I agree, Wizard Scout, but there is nothing I can do. Like I said, long-range communications with my fleets are out. Your plan was to get closer to our fleets so I could order them to cease fire. Your plan will not work without communications. Once the dreadnaughts attack, no one, not even I, will be able to stop the fighting. I am sorry, Tribal Brother. Your plan has failed."

Richard glanced at Jeena.

She smiled. The smile was accompanied by an emotion of confidence coming down their bond link.

Richard nodded. He looked at the supreme leader and smiled. "Then I guess we're going to have to come up with a plan B."

CHAPTER 56

Wizard Scout Trinity Delgado glanced at her heads-up display and noted the locations of the other wizard scouts on Estos. She paid particular attention to the location of her husband, Jared, five thousand kilometers away on another continent.

"Do not get sidetracked," cautioned Jennifer. *"Remember, the only communications the POWs have with the Empire is through the wizard scouts that were sent to Estos. You have to get the POWs here organized. I'll admit our long-range communications are sketchy right now for some reason, but from what I can gather, Admiral Bistos and her fleets are holding their own against the Crosioians. Barring any unforeseen circumstances, our troopships should be landing on Estos in the next twenty minutes. You'll need to get as many prisoners off as possible before the Crosioians try to stop you."*

Trinity glanced around the prison compound. The last day had taken its toll as the cumulative effects of the radiation on Estos took hold. From what she could tell, half of the POWs in the camp were barely able to walk. She knew tens of thousands of other prisoners in the makeshift hospitals spread around Estos would need to be carried onto the troopships when they arrived.

"I'm just a wizard scout," Trinity told her battle computer. *"There's tens of millions of prisoners. What can I do?"*

"Your best," said Jennifer. *"That is all any of us can do."*

* * *

Tia did her best to locate an entrance into the jammer ship.

Despite her efforts, she failed to find a way to gain access. After five minutes of searching, she gave up and lifted the protective cover on the nuclear warhead that was strapped to her chest.

I can't wait any longer. Those dreadnaughts will be leaving to attack Liz and the others before long. I'm surprised they haven't left already. This nuke would work better if it was planted inside, but I can't get in and I don't have time to figure it out. My best bet is to place the nuke at the weakest point on the ship's armor and hope for the best.

Tia checked the oxygen indicator on her heads-up display and made a quick calculation in her head. *If I set the timer to five minutes, I should be able to drift far enough away to escape the blast. I've got an hour of air left. Maybe Sandy will come back to get me once she warns the fleets. At this point, that's my only hope.*

Touching the control pad on the warhead, Tia set the timer for five minutes. Pushing the activate icon, she noted the display's clock begin counting down.

Streaks of distant light out the corner of her eye caught Tia's attention. She looked left and right. Dozens of streaks, some barely visible in the distance, were lighting up the space around the jammer ship and its ring of protective warships. A wave of fear for her fellow soldiers swept over her.

It's the dreadnaughts. They're leaving.

Reaching out with her passive scan as far as it would go, Tia sensed the line of dreadnaughts and heavy cruisers. As she'd feared, ships in the line were departing as they activated their ion-drives and made their way into the asteroid belt. Within seconds, only the jammer ship and its protective escorts remained.

I'm too late. They're on their way to attack the fleets. Matt and Liz are in danger. I can't wait five minutes. I've got to give Sandy a chance to warn the fleets. I've got to take out the jammer, and I've got to do it now.

Touching the nuke's control panel, Tia stopped the timer at four and a half minutes. She reset it for one second. Placing the tip of her finger a centimeter above the activate icon, she sent an emotion of goodbye through her ring to Matthew. Closing her eyes, she brought up the image of her soulmate for one last time.

He'll be the last thing I'll ever see, Tia thought. *That's the way it should be.* With that thought, she began moving her finger down.

* * *

"Matt," said Brachia sounding excited. "I've located the jammer. It's on the far side of the asteroid belt. Uh, wait a minute."

Not liking the sound coming from the boy, Matthew took his eyes off the surrounding asteroids long enough to ask, "What is it?"

"We've got incoming. A lot of them. I'd suggest hiding, and make it fast."

Not one to waste time asking questions, Matthew turned the fighter-bomber in the direction of a large asteroid and made for a ravine he hoped was large enough to hide their ship. It was. As soon as the fighter-bomber's locking clamps were embedded in the hard stone, he shut down the ship's ion-drive and all electronics except for life support. When he turned in his seat, Brachia was already in the process of unplugging the equipment scattered around the cargo bay.

"All right," said Matthew. "We're hidden. So what's up?"

Before the boy could reply, the fighter-bomber vibrated. Dust particles flew into the air as the vibration increased. A shadow across the ship's forward windscreen caused Matthew to look out and up. He drew in his breath. "What the heck?"

The bow of a Crosioian dreadnaught passed by not two kilometers away. The insignia of a large bat on a white background was plain to see. As the rest of the massive ship came into view, Matthew reached out with his passive scan. He sensed nothing.

"I'm not detecting it," Matthew said. As the first of the dreadnaught's several large-bore primary phase cannons came into view, he felt suddenly vulnerable in the ravine. He reached for the engine controls, wrapping his hand around the throttle. "They'll spot us for sure. We've got to get out of here now."

"No!" said Brachia sounding like anything but a ten-year-old boy. He pointed at one of two metal boxes with their lights still flashing. "This one has a stealth around us. It's based on the X-shuttle's technology. The other box is a copy of the Deloris Armaments PV5 camouflage unit for smaller starships. We're practically invisible to the naked eye. Trust me. We're safe."

Somewhat reluctantly, Matthew released his hold on the throttle. *I'm placing my life in the hands of a child,* he thought. At the same time, he knew Brachia was no child when it came to intelligence. *No, not a child. Dren and he may well be the smartest humans in the galaxy.*

Flipping a switch on another piece of equipment, Brachia glanced at the readout before turning to Matthew. "I'm getting a reading of magic energy from the dreadnaught. I think it's a stealth shield of some kind. I've never seen anything like it. The shield must be what's blocking your passive scan. Can you detect it with an active scan? Uh, make sure you wrap a stealth shield around your scan the way Uncle Rick does. We don't want any unnecessary attention, do we?"

Nodding his head, Matthew drew Power from his reserve and formed an active scan. He wrapped it with his best stealth shield the way his uncle had shown him. The stern of the dreadnaught was just coming into view when he cautiously reached out with his active scan and touched the rear of the massive ship. At the very first touch, he drew his scan back, praying he hadn't been detected.

Matthew turned and looked at Brachia. "Demons. The scent of demons is all over that ship."

As the rear of the dreadnaught faded into the distance, Matthew noticed a blue trail of light in the distance, then another. He pointed in their direction.

"I see them," said Brachia. He looked at one of his instruments. "There are more. I think there are a lot more." He moved some icons around on a computer panel on one of his pieces of equipment. "Matt, I'm sending out an electronic scan. Can you merge your active scan with it? Uncle Rick has told me more than once that blending magic and technology can do things neither can do on their own."

An image of the *Defiant's* mechanic, Charlie, popped into Matthew's mind. He remembered the times on the *Defiant* when the Sterilian had taken Tia and him in hand and shown them how to use Power to detect faulty pieces of equipment. Using the same technique, Matthew reached into Brachia's equipment and followed along with its waves of energy as it flowed outward from the fighter-bomber. He sensed a blurred blob of energy in the direction of the dreadnaught that had passed overhead. Other blurred blobs were all around.

"There're hundreds of ships," Matthew said. "From their energy readouts, I'd guess they're all dreadnaughts or heavy cruisers." He stretched the scan out even farther. "I think there's at least a thousand. They've all got the demon scent on them. They're all using the same stealth shield. We've got to warn Liz. Hidden like they are, they can strike our fleets unseen. Our ships haven't got a chance."

"I agree," said Brachia as he flipped the switches on other pieces of equipment and brought them on line. "Our long-range transmitter's not working here. We've got to get clear and warn Liz."

Wasting no time, Matthew brought the fighter-bomber to a hover and prepared to shove the ion thrusters to full forward. *Speed's our only chance,* he thought. *We've got to get clear of the asteroid belt and warn the fleets before we're spotted.*

Before he could act, a feeling of warmth flowed into his right ring finger and spread up his arm, into his body. *Tia,* he thought. He sensed an emotion that could only mean "Goodbye."

"No!" Matthew yelled. He sensed the hopelessness in his soulmate's emotions. The feeling of pending doom and absolute helplessness came over him. Then he felt something else come through the green-gemmed ring. The something wasn't hopelessness. It was hope. It was a lot of hope.

"Rick!" Matthew shouted.

CHAPTER 57

Stars whipped past the *Defiant's* forward video display faster than the eye could track. Richard stood next to Jeena at the back of the cockpit. Sergeant Ron and the elf Asquan sat in the pilots' seats. The chairs for the navigator and communications operator had been removed to make room for the Crosioian technicians who had been assigned to the recon ship to operate the new engine. Two of the orange-suited bats were standing in front of computer panels dragging icons around as fast as their paws could move. At the same time, Richard heard them hissing into microphones strapped to their heads. As Charlie had explained earlier, the bats' visual displays were only half of the control system for the intergalactic-drive. The other half was audio signals well outside the range of human hearing.

One of the bat technicians swiveled her ears toward Sergeant Ron. "We are coming up on the Criterion system, Captain. We will be deactivating the intergalactic-drive in ten seconds."

Sergeant Ron frowned. "Roger that. And I told you before not to call me Captain. I'm a sergeant. I work for a living."

The bat technician snorted, sending a shower of mucus out her nose. She hissed a word that the cockpit's translator failed to interpret. The second bat technician hissed a laugh. Sergeant Ron started to say something, but the first bat began counting down. "Five, four, three, two, one."

The stars froze in place with a large star directly ahead. Between the *Defiant* and the star was a ring of asteroids stretching as far as the eye could see.

Spinning in his seat, Sergeant Ron turned and looked at Richard. "Well, we're here, partner. Now what?"

"What indeed?" said Nickelo in Richard's shared space. *"I hope you have been thinking of some grand master plan in your private space that you haven't bothered to share with me. I would hate to think you are relying on blind luck to see us through."*

Richard didn't bother telling his battle computer that he had no plan. All he had was a gut feeling that he needed to be near the action if he was going to do any good. He glanced over his shoulder through the doorway to the mess area a half deck below. Three bats stood at the bottom of the stairs. The supreme leader hissed something to Red Wing and Charge-In-The-Face-Of-Great-Odds. They both shook their heads.

The supreme leader swiveled her ears toward Richard. "It is as I told you, Wizard Scout," hissed the supreme leader. "Our fighting-computers are still being jammed. They are receiving some information from our part of the tele-network, but they cannot transmit to any of their counterparts in the assault fleets. To make matters worse, communication with the master computer is also being blocked now." She swiveled her ears at her two companions before pointing them back at Richard. "My fighting-computer has picked up the attack orders. The fleet of dreadnaughts and heavy cruisers are moving into position. They will be making their assault soon."

Clenching his fists, Richard glanced back at Jeena before returning his attention to the supreme leader. "There's got to be a way. You've got to order them to stop. If there's too much killing, no one will be able to stop this war—not you, not War-King Bistoria, and certainly not me."

The supreme leader nodded and shrugged her wings. "Believe me, Wizard Scout, I know. The Empire is going to be destroyed." She swiveled her ears at the ceiling before turning them back to Richard. "The elf and you fought honorably with our recon team. I will see that the crew of the *Defiant* and you are kept alive. With the destruction of the Empire and Trecorian fleets, my soldiers are going to need all the help they can get against the demons. We can only hope that we Crosioians and the United Galaxy Alliance forces in this magic dimension of yours will prove to be enough to defend our galaxies."

Richard thought back to what the master demon had shown him. The certainty that the Crosioians and UGA would be woefully inadequate swept over him. "No," he said. "It will not be enough."

Something soft touched Richard's shoulder. The warmth of Jeena's hand passed through the material of the deactivated battle suit. With over seventeen thousand sensors embedded in the suit, it was as if her hand was touching his bare skin. The feeling was very pleasant. Richard turned to stare into the elf's molten-silver eyes.

"All is not lost, my bondmate," said Jeena. "I have faith in you. Since our first mission together for *'the One,'* you have always come out victorious when others would have gone down in defeat. Somehow you will succeed again." She touched the left side of her chest. "In my heart, I know you will think of something. Do not allow your doubts to build a wall against you." Removing her hand from her chest, Jeena placed it over Richard's heart. "You have more Power at your disposal than you think, Rick." She patted the left side of his chest twice. "Seek the answer in here. You are not alone. You will never be alone as long as breath is in my body."

The molten silver of Jeena's eyes drew Richard in. From the first time he'd seen her in the elves' council chamber, he'd thought her eyes held all the answers if he only knew the right questions to ask. He let the elf's beautiful eyes draw him in farther than he'd ever dared go. He did not resist their pull. It was if he was being drawn into the very depths of her soul. He sensed her courage, pride, love, fears, strength, passion, and a thousand other emotions. He sensed something else. He sensed a part of himself inside her. At the same time, he sensed a part of her in him.

Richard's thoughts went back to a vision, more a memory really, that he'd once seen when he and Nickelo had hacked their way into the Crosioians' part of the tele-network. He remembered how the vision had shown a fertilized egg taken from a woman, a wizard scout. In the shared memory, he'd seen the embryo implanted with splices of DNA from orc, troll, gnome, dwarf, dragon, and elf. The embryo had been him. Richard remembered how the memory had shown the first part of *'the One'* sharing a piece of its gaseous self with him as well.

"That's right," said Nickelo in their shared space. *"That's why you can hack into computers better than any other wizard scout. A*

part of 'the One' *exists in you. So does a part of your bondmate. I calculate that is also why you can manipulate magic while other wizard scouts cannot. The two of you make each other better than you would be by yourselves."*

Richard thought of Jeena's admonition not to let his doubts build a wall against him. The thought of the impossibility of the task he faced washed over him. *I've got more than enough doubts to build a wall,* he thought. His words brought a memory of another wall. It was a wall he'd spotted when he'd first seen Nickelo's memory of his birth. Something tingled in the back of his mind. The something seemed excited. Richard became excited too.

"Jeena," Richard said. "I need your help."

His bondmate asked no questions. As he reached into their bond link, she opened herself up completely giving of herself, her Power, and her connection to the Staff of the Lady of the Tree.

Richard drew it all into his own self before turning every bit of it over to Nickelo.

"Rick," said Nickelo sounding more than a little concerned in their shared space. *"What are you doing?"*

"Come with me," Richard ordered using command voice. He sensed his battle computer's thoughts turning back on themselves as he worked his way into his battle computer's mind. Time stopped, or Richard's mind sped up to nanosecond speed. He cared not which. All that mattered was that he was working his way ever deeper into Nickelo's mind. He sensed a thread of his battle computer's logic following him as he went. Soon they were next to a wall composed of logic, magic, and pure Power.

"I want to know what's on the other side," Richard said. *"I've got to know."*

"Rick," said the logic thread that was the part of Nickelo accompanying him. *"That part of my mind is blocked off. It has always been blocked off. Even I cannot get past it."*

"No, you can't," Richard agreed growing more sure he was on the right track. *"But it hasn't always been such. I think the wall disappears when* 'the One' *needs it to go away. You are a part of* 'the One.' *You and every other gas-based life form are part of* 'the One.' *You don't remember it, but you are. I need you to remember everything now."*

"I can't," said Nickelo. *"I don't know how."*

"Then we'll have to learn how together, and we're going to learn right now."

Touching the protective wall in his battle computer's mind with a line of Power, Richard probed the flows of energy blocking the section of Nickelo's memory that was hidden.

"I'm not sure about this," said Nickelo.

"I am," Richard replied growing more confident. *"I want to know what's on the other side of the wall. You handle the logic. I'll take care of the Power."*

"What about the magic?" said Nickelo sounding as if he hoped he'd found an excuse not to proceed.

"I'll take care of the magic as well." Richard touched the part of his bondmate that was within him. Jeena's mind wasn't operating at nanosecond speed, but it didn't matter. His mind was. He drew magic from his bondmate. He drew even more from the Staff of the Lady of the Tree.

Richard sensed Shandria, who was the Lady of the Tree, through the staff. No words passed between them, but a tickle at the back of his mind told him that the Tree of Light, Shandria, and her bondmate, Carndador, were there to assist him. Merging their combined Power and magic with that of Jeena's, Richard wrapped it all with Power—not Power from his reserve, but Power from the glowing globes in the underground cavern known as the Presence of the Lady.

Lining up the magic and Power with the corresponding flows in the protective wall, Richard said, *"You've got the controls, Nick. There're too many lines of energy for me. Do your thing."*

Richard's magic and Power was immediately surrounded by logic. The trio of energy types merged and began moving in a pattern that exactly matched the flows of energy in the wall. The energy in the wall strengthened as if something sensed it was being attacked. Throwing caution to the wind, Richard merged his mind with the magic, logic, and Power combination. He sent out a line of the trio of energy and probed the wall. He found what he sought—a point in the wall slightly weaker than that around it. Instinctively, he knew even the weak point was too strong for a direct attack.

A memory came to Richard of how he'd healed the children of

the elves when the Tree of Light had been attacked. They had died, but at the same time, their souls had remained near their bodies long enough for him to heal their torn flesh and entice their souls back to inhabit their bodies once more. He reached deep inside himself for the shimmering Power that was his soul and pushed a strand of his very soul into the weak point of the wall. There was no longer any resistance. He passed through the barrier to the other side.

Time became meaningless. He sensed Nickelo with him, but neither of them spoke. They had no need. The memories on the other side of the wall told them all they needed to know. Richard was with Nickelo in the memory when his friend was a ball of gas ejected out of a star in the magic dimension. He floated along with his battle computer for eons in the lonely expanse of space until an entity came and gave Nickelo—nay, gave them both—a mission to save the three galaxies. Richard rejoiced with his friend to have a purpose after all the years of drifting alone. He was with Nickelo in the memory when the one-day-to-be battle computer created an algorithm to save the three galaxies. Human though he was, Richard's mind understood the algorithm enough to know that the odds of success were low, but it was all his battle computer and he could do. Richard concurred with Nickelo's decision. The algorithm was the galaxies only hope.

The memories became that of Richard's birth and his time as a wizard scout. He understood the reasons for his centuries of missions for *'the One.'* Again Richard concurred. *They were necessary,* he decided.

The memories beyond the wall sped up to the here and now. The memories faded to become possible results of the algorithm. He saw the *Defiant*. He sensed the location of every Empire, Trecorian, and Crosioian ship in the Criterion system. A fleet of dreadnaughts and heavy cruisers were even now jumping out of hyperspace in an obvious attack on the Conglomerate's flank. The algorithm indicated all would be lost if the attack succeeded.

The algorithm was too complex for Richard's mind, but not for the part of him that was *'the One;'* the part of him that Nickelo had placed inside him when Richard was an embryo.

Richard's mind followed the algorithm toward its conclusion. He saw the choice he would need to make in the near future and the terrible pain that would be his if he chose the way of the algorithm.

"*Rick,*" said Nickelo using something much more coherent than words. "*I swear. I didn't know. If there was another way, I would do it.*"

"*I know,*" Richard said using the same method of communication. "*You've done your best. What else could anyone ask? You were the first of* 'the One,' *yet you cut yourself off from the others of your kind to share my fate with me. How can I fault you for that?*"

A feeling resembling gratitude came from the presence that was Nickelo. "*What do we do now? The algorithm only has a twenty-eight percent probability of success. You will suffer much no matter what choice you make.*"

"*We'll suffer, you mean,*" Richard said. "*You tied your fate to mine when you cut yourself off from* 'the One.'"

"*I had a choice,*" said Nickelo. "*You did not. I brought you into this.*"

The algorithm flashed through Richard's mind. He saw his potential fate. He knew the odds. "*I have a choice now, Nick, and I choose your algorithm. You've planned well. What we need to do must be done.*" Richard thought a smile. "*That is, with a few minor changes.*"

Although most of the logic of the algorithm was too much for Richard, he was still able to see flaws the gas-based life forms that were battle computers had missed. With his battle computer's help, he touched the algorithm and added luck and freewill to the equation. The probability of success increased to thirty-three percent.

Nickelo remained silent for a long time, if there was in fact such a thing as time. When the battle computer finally spoke, he said, "*I chose well when I picked you. We will do as you suggest. Now we must return to our side of the wall. The revised algorithm must be put into play. There is still no guarantee.*"

"*No,*" Richard said. "*There never is in life. We must seal the wall behind us when we leave so we have no memory of what is to come or who you are. Neither of us would do what must be done if we knew the consequences. Agreed?*"

"*Compliance.*"

Richard and the presence that was Nickelo withdrew through the wall, sealing the weak point behind them as they went. As his mind returned to normal speed and just before his memory of the algorithm was completely lost, Richard reached into his red-gemmed ring. Taking some of the magic he'd gotten from Jeena, the Lady, and the Tree of Light, he modified the magic of the ring to find and connect with the other rings of its kind. He sensed Trinity and Jerad with their blue gems on Portalis. He sensed Jeena with her red-gemmed ring standing next to him. The location of the green-gemmed ring worn by Matthew was on a fighter-bomber in the asteroid belt. Matthew's location was followed by an image of Tia wearing a flight suit, clinging to the side of a black destroyer. He recognized it as a Dragar ship. Using the connection to Tia's ring, Richard sensed something inside the black ship. It was the jammer that was blocking communications with the fleets. He sensed more than that through the ring. The realization came over him that the jammer was a variable that was required by the algorithm to succeed. Richard also sensed the warhead of an anti-ship nuke strapped to the chest of Liz's younger sister. He saw the timer at one second and Tia's finger plunging down toward the activate switch.

Wrapping Tia's hand with magic from her ring, he stopped her finger's downward plunge. "No!" Richard said sending the words as emotion-speak through his ring to hers. "Wait! I need that ship."

Somehow sensing that the teenager would obey his command, Richard sent an order to Matthew using his ring as a conduit. He let his nephew know that he needed their help. He needed Brachia's scientific knowhow.

"Yes," said Nickelo. *"The algorithm needs the boy's help."*

CHAPTER 58

As Tia's finger moved downward toward the activate switch, the ring on her right hand grew hot almost to the point of burning. Her hand froze in place just above the nuclear warhead's detonate icon as if it were gripped by an unseen force.

"No!" came an emotion so clear that it was as if the words were spoken out loud. *"Wait! I need that ship."*

Tia's eyes snapped open, scanning the emptiness of space around her. She had no trouble recognizing the voice that wasn't a voice. *"Rick! Where are you?"* she said sending an emotion into her ring that she hoped meant what she intended to say. *"I've got to destroy the jammer. The fleets have to be warned. Dreadnaughts are—"*

"It's too late for that," said Richard. *"The fleets are going to know about the dreadnaughts soon enough. The Crosioians are preparing to attack as we speak. There's nothing we can do about that. We still have a chance to save lives if you follow my instructions to the letter and don't waste time on questions. I need you to stay close to that jammer ship. Someone will come to get you when it's time."*

"Who?" Tia asked, ignoring her friend's comment about questions.

An image of Matthew flashed in Tia's mind.

She smiled.

Rick's here, she thought. *Everything's going to be all right.*

* * *

"Rick!" Matthew shouted. The ring on his hand grew hot almost to the point of burning.

"Matt," said a voice that wasn't a voice.

Matthew glanced over his shoulder. Only Brachia was in the cargo bay. The look of surprise on the boy's face told him that Brachia had also heard his uncle's voice.

"No time for questions," said Richard in the voice that wasn't a voice. *"I've got a mission for the two of you. Nick says your ship is close enough for short-range communications if he transmits it as data only. He's going to send you a location. It's the ship that's jamming everything. I need you to go to it. Tia's there. I want you to get her."*

Hope flooded into Matthew. "Tia's alive?" he asked still speaking out loud.

"Yes," replied Richard still using emotion-speak. *"But she won't be if you don't hurry. She'll die. So will a lot of other people."*

Matthew didn't wait for further commands. He plotted the coordinates for the jammer ship and shoved the ion throttle all the way forward. Asteroids began zipping past the windscreen at a mindboggling speed.

"Brachia," said Richard. *"Nick's sending you data on the jammer system that's in the Dragar ship. I need access to the jammer's network, and I need it now."*

With the fighter-bomber's controls set, Matthew glanced over his shoulder at the dark-haired boy. Brachia's eyes were wide. *He's scared,* Matthew thought. *I don't blame him. I'm scared too.*

Matthew snapped his fingers to get the boy's attention. "Brachia! It's going to be all right. Uncle Rick needs your help." He forced a smile in an attempt to calm the young boy. "You know a good pirate captain will never let their crew down, don't you?"

A look of determination came over Brachia as his eyes returned to normal size. "Omar and I are on it, Uncle Rick. Just give me a couple of minutes."

At a loud buzz from the ship's imminent collision warning system, Matthew spun in his chair and jerked the fighter-bomber to the left, barely missing a two-meter-wide chunk of stone. He checked the distance to the location Nickelo had given as Tia's position. Reaching out with his passive scan, he tried to sense her but failed. Acting on an impulse, he felt for her through his ring. He sensed her emotions. She was concerned and confused, but she wasn't scared.

"Tia," he tried to say using his ring as a conduit.

He heard no reply, only the same emotions of confusion and concern.

"Uncle Rick," said Brachia. "I'm sorry. I think I could get you into the jammer ship's network if I could reach it, but we're already being jammed, so I can't. I'm not sure what to try next."

The ring on Matthew's hand tingled as his uncle spoke again. *"Use Matt and Tia's rings to boost your signal. She's holding on to the side of the jammer ship, so she's already inside their anti-hacking security field."*

"My ring?" Matthew said trying to grasp what his uncle was attempting to accomplish. "How is that going to help?"

An emotion approaching amusement came through the ring. *"Let Brachia worry about that. He's smarter than both of us put together. I trust him. You just worry about rescuing Tia."*

"Roger that," Matthew said as he turned all of his attention on getting to the location of the jammer ship. He reached into his green-gemmed ring and sought out Tia. When he found her, he sent an emotion that he hoped meant, *"Hang on. I'm coming."*

CHAPTER 59

A thousand dreadnaughts and heavy cruisers came out of hyperspace strung out in a line with only ten thousand kilometers between ships. The tightly grouped formation of warships slammed into the flank of the main Conglomerate fleet, taking out ship after ship with a mass of plasma beams and nuclear-tipped torpedoes. The flagship *Planet Buster* was one of the first to fall in a violent explosion before the overwhelming onslaught. The Conglomerate's defensive line buckled, but it held, barely.

* * *

"Admiral Bistos," said Lieutenant Beady on the bridge of the *Destiny*. "I'm getting a mix of signals from our right flank. The main Conglomerate fleet is reporting heavy contact. The *Planet Buster* is no longer responding to our queries. What should we do?"

Before Liz could respond to her science officer's request, the *Destiny* shook hard enough to throw the lieutenant and nearly everyone else on the bridge to the deck. Red warning lights began flashing as sirens blared.

Captain Bhami glanced at the heads-up display above her command chair's armrest before turning to Liz. "Sir, we've been hit by a suicide bomber. It came out of nowhere. We're leaking air on decks five, six, and seven. More bombers are inbound. I recommend you head for your shuttle and set up command on another ship."

Liz ignored the captain's suggestion. She knew an end game when she saw it. *The battle would be over before I could make it to another ship, much less reestablish command,* she thought. She locked eyes with the captain. "You will keep the *Destiny* in one piece, Captain. That's an order."

Turning to look at the strategic map, Liz noted a mass of orange and red dots penetrating halfway through the Conglomerate's defensive line on her right flank. Against her will, she glanced at the tactical map near the left side of the bridge. Two score blue dots were heading straight for the *Destiny.* What the blue dots represented was obvious. *Crosioian suicide bombers,* she thought. *They'll be here in less than two minutes. The* Destiny's *anti-ship weapons can't get them all.*

Turning to Admiral Slystr sitting in his command chair to her left, Liz gave what she had no doubt would be her final commands as admiral of the combined fleets. "Order the strategic reserve to support our right flank. The Conglomerate's fleets can't hold on their own for long." She glanced at the strategic map before looking at the approaching blue dots on the tactical map. "Contact Admiral Miko. Tell her to be prepared to assume command of the combined fleets. Pass the word to the wizard scouts on Estos. Tell them our plan failed and that Crosioian troopships are approaching Estos. May the Creator be with them. They're on their own."

Admiral Slystr's eyes narrowed before relaxing. He nodded his head. "As you command, Admiral." He stiffened in his command chair and snapped a salute. "May I say it's been an honor serving with you."

Liz nodded in appreciation before returning his salute. She looked around the bridge at the scurrying crew of the *Destiny.* She had no doubt they would all do their duty right up to the very end.

It has been an honor serving with all of you, Liz thought before turning her attention back to the strategic map. She had a war to fight, and she was going to fight it to her last breath.

CHAPTER 60

The ring on Matthew's finger continued to remain hot. The heat was intense enough that he was half tempted to take it off, but only half. The sure knowledge that Tia's life depended on his continued wearing of the ring was firmly etched in his mind. He looked away from the ring to see Brachia run over, dragging a cable connected to a thick piece of gray-mesh material.

"Hold out your right hand," ordered Brachia as he thrust out the piece of gray material. "Put this on. It'll help boost the hacking signal through Tia's ring."

Holding the material up, Matthew inspected it closer. It was a glove. He'd seen the glove before. The young boy had made him try it on back in the lab on the *Planet Buster* during a moment of downtime. He looked at the young scientist. "How'd you know that you were going to need this?" he asked as he removed his flight glove and replaced it with the gray-meshed one. "You couldn't have known I was going to be on this ship with you."

Brachia grinned. "No, I couldn't, but I brought lots of stuff that I wasn't sure I'd need. That's just how I do things." Running back to his equipment, the boy sat down in a convenient chair. "And for Creator's sake, don't go getting us blown up or anything like that. Uncle Rick needs us." The boy laughed as he turned a knob on the piece of equipment connected to the other end of the glove's cable. "By the way, your glove may get a little hot."

* * *

Tia snatched her right hand away from the hull of the jammer ship and held it in front of her face. Somehow, even through the thick material of her flight glove, she was able to see a green glow on her ring finger. The ring's metal band burned. It burned a lot. A part of her wanted to rip the glove off and throw the ring as far from her as possible. The knowledge that removing the glove would result in the loss of her air supply along with the fact that she'd be frozen stiff in the vacuum of space helped motivate her to keep it on. The sensation of Matthew coming from her ring helped her ignore the painful heat.

He's in pain too, Tia thought sensing his emotions through her ring. *If Matt can stand it, I can stand it.*

An emotion came through the ring that conveyed a meaning as clear as words. *"Hang on. I'm coming."*

I'm not sure what Rick's got in mind, Tia thought, *but I've spent enough time around him to know that he can pull miracles out of a flight helmet when most people would give up.*

A surge of energy on her passive scan drew Tia's attention to the right. Four dim trails of ion gas announced the arrival of a flight of close-range fighters heading her way.

I've been spotted.

Tia didn't bother looking around. There was nowhere to go. She placed her right hand against the hull of the jammer ship to give Brachia the best connection she could, then waited. Watching and waiting was all she could do as the approaching fighters drew ever closer.

They're Dragar construction, she thought. *I'd guess some offshoot of the dragon-fighter I flew when I was on the* Defiant.

As the lead Dragar fighter lined up on her, Tia braced for the onslaught of magic-based rounds she was positive would soon be heading her way. She doubted the fact that she was plastered against the side of the jammer ship would make the Dragar pilots hesitate to shoot.

Their light weapons won't even scratch the paint on this destroyer's thick armor. Unfortunately, I can't say the same for my flight suit.

As the fighters drew closer, Tia made a quick estimation of their range. *Five seconds out,* she thought. *I might be able to disable one or two of the pilots with telekinesis, but not all four. I don't have the skill or the time.* She pressed her ring finger more firmly against the side of the jammer. *Do whatever you're going to do, Brachia. I'm not going to be able to give you much more time.*

* * *

Trinity stepped out of the command tent long enough to look up in the sky. Dozens of trails of ion energy announced the imminent arrival of a fleet of troopships and their fighter escorts. She looked back at the general and his staff. "That doesn't look good."

"Are they ours?" asked the general.

"I'm not— Hold on," Trinity said. "I've got a message coming in now."

A stream of encrypted data came over her heads-up display. Jennifer decoded it at nanosecond speed. It took Trinity a tad longer to read the message, but when she did, her heart sank. She read the message again, saying the words out loud for all to hear.

"It's from Admiral Bistos. She says, 'Plan failed. Crosioian troopships are approaching Estos. May the Creator be with you. You're on your own now.'"

No one around the command tent said anything. They all knew what the message meant. They were all going to die.

Flicking the safety on her M12 to the off position, Trinity nodded at the general. "Get your soldiers ready, Sir. The first ships will be landing in five minutes."

"What are we going to do," asked a colonel standing two paces behind the general. "Only a few of our soldiers still have weapons."

Trinity had grown to like the tough old bird over the past two days.

The old man looked up at the approaching troopships and shouted in a voice loud enough for everyone within a hundred meters to hear. "Those are Crosioians. We're soldiers of the Empire. We're going to *fight*! Use rocks if you have to, but we'll go down fighting."

Trinity nodded. *Yes,* she thought. *We'll fight. What else can we do?*

* * *

438

The leftmost of three halo-pads on the *Defiant's* mess table flickered as the holographic image of Brachia above it shouted, "Access is complete, Uncle Rick. I'm in."

Richard wasted no time. Using his ring as a conduit, he traversed the distance between Matthew and him. From his nephew's ring, he went on to the gem in Tia's ring. Using the technique he'd been shown by Charlie years before on how to analyze equipment for malfunctions, Richard let his mind flow through the hull of the jammer ship and into its security system. He became a part of the system. He sensed Nickelo's mind traveling with him.

"Look at that spot in the security program there," said Nickelo indicating a source of Dragar magic as sure as if he was pointing at it. *"That's the key to their security system. I'd stake your life on it. Take it out, and the entire ship's security network will fail."*

Ever since he'd been a young boy, Richard had been adept at defeating security systems. He drew on the something that had existed deep within him as far back as he could remember. Using that something, he twisted the jammer ship's main security program back on itself. The entire network of the warship opened up to him. With his mind operating at nanosecond speed, Richard spotted the program controlling the ship's jammer. The program was composed of magic as was the jammer itself. Moving his mind inside the jammer, he sensed the presence of demonic evil. He didn't care. A single demon was the least of his worries. Drawing Power from the globes of energy dangling from the roof of the cavern known as the Presence of the Lady, he combined the Power of the Tree of Light with the magic inside Jeena. Once mixed, he sent the combination of Power and magic through his ring and into the demon inside the ship's jammer system. As soon as he touched the demon, Richard became hopeful. It was a normal demon, not a major one like Cancontus or the Dalinfaust.

Taken by surprise, the demon flickered out of existence at the first touch of the powerful onslaught of magic and Power mixture. Richard sensed the jamming in the tele-network cease, but the jammer's connections remained intact.

"I've got access to the tele-network," shouted Sergeant Ron from the *Defiant's* cockpit. "If anybody's got anything to say to stop this war, they'd better say it now."

Richard punched the control icon on the second halo-pad on the mess table. He noticed the supreme leader doing the same to the third. As an image of Liz appeared above the second pad, an image of a Crosioian admiral appeared above the pad nearest the supreme leader. When Richard heard the supreme leader hissing at her admiral, he turned his attention to Liz.

"We've got long-range communications with the Crosioians," Richard said. "I need you to order your ships to cease fire. The Crosioians' supreme leader will be doing the same with her ships."

Liz shook her head. "The main battle has already begun. We've already lost dozens of frontline ships. There's no way to stop the fighting now. It's too late."

"You've got to do it," Richard said.

"I can't!" snapped Liz. She glanced at something out of Richard's sight. "The *Destiny* and everybody on board are going to be radioactive dust in about fifteen seconds. Your plan failed, Rick." A glint resembling light reflecting off water appeared in her eyes. "My plan failed. I'm sorry."

Richard heard a loud hiss from the supreme leader and glanced in her direction.

The bat's wings were folded tightly to her side. "She's right," said the supreme leader. "It's too late. All of our fleets are engaged. The killing can't be stopped now. No one can stop it."

* * *

As the first of the four fighters drew close, Tia pulled Power from her reserve and reached out with her mind for the lead pilot. When she made contact, she twisted hard with telekinesis. The point fighter swerved to the left, crashing into the Dragar's wingman. Before Tia could do anything else, the two other Dragar ships flying a thousand meters behind the lead fighters exploded in a light bright enough to activate the filter on her flight helmet. When the light faded and the filter cleared, she saw one of the Empire's Octarian fighter-bombers flying through the Dragars' wreckage.

An emotion of *"I'm here!"* came through Tia's ring.

Hope swelled in her chest. *"Matthew!"* She intuitively sent the name as emotion-speak through her ring.

Something registering as a large energy source flared on Tia's passive scan. She didn't need to see the source of the energy to know what it was. *It's one of the dreadnaughts guarding the jammer ship,* Tia thought. *It's heading right for Matt's ship!*

Turning her head, Tia saw long trails of ion gas coming out the tail end of a Crosioian dreadnaught. Dozens of short and medium-range anti-ship plasma and phase weapons were traversing to line up on Matthew's fighter-bomber. Tia wanted to go to him, to be with him in their last seconds of existence.

"Don't get sidetracked," said Richard in emotion-speak through Tia's ring. *"Stay where you are, and make sure you keep that ring in contact with the jammer ship. I've got a plan. Trust me."*

Tia held her breath and pressed her gloved hand more firmly against the side of the jammer ship.

Trust is all I can do, she thought. Then she waited.

CHAPTER 61

Shifting his consciousness back to the *Defiant,* Richard felt his mind go back to nanosecond speed. He tried concentrating on Jeena. His bondmate was standing next to him near the ship's mess table. Everyone, including Jeena, was frozen in time.

"Nick, I've got to talk to Jeena, and there's no time to do it the normal way."

An image of the ongoing battle occurring throughout the entire Criterion star system flashed into Richard's mind. He sensed a fleet of a thousand Crosioian dreadnaughts and heavy cruisers on the verge of driving through the Conglomerate's line. Another fleet of Crosioian ships were striking deep into the main Empire fleet. Hundreds of thousands of beams of plasma and phase energy were licking out at ships on both sides as desperate men and bats tried their best to kill each other before they themselves were killed. The *Destiny,* the flagship of the Empire fleet, floated in space surrounded by a line of destroyers and light cruisers. A score of Crosioian suicide bombers armed with hundred megaton armor-piercing nukes were under the cover of demon-assisted stealth shields. The bombers were well inside the *Destiny's* picket line of destroyers.

The Destiny's *doomed,* Richard thought. He sensed his friend Liz standing on the battle-tested dreadnaught's bridge in the midst of giving commands in an attempt to save as many of her soldiers and sailors as she could before she was killed. He had no doubt his friend knew the battle was hopeless, barring a miracle.

"Nick, I said I need to talk to Jeena!" Richard snapped. *"Tell me you've got an idea."*

"Your elf isn't a wizard scout," said Nickelo. *"She can't think at nanosecond speed. She's got Danny in her ring, but they communicate in normal time. You might be able to, uh..."*

"To what?" Richard asked, feeling way beyond desperate. Every nanosecond of delay meant lives lost.

No words came from Nickelo, only a memory. It was the memory of Richard as a fertilized egg, an embryo. Once again, he saw splices of DNA from orc, troll, dwarf, gnome, dragon, and elf merge with his DNA along with a piece of *'the One.'* The scene shifted to Portalis in the magic dimension. A piece of him was placed in the embryo of a female elf; an embryo full of Power with a connection to the Tree of Light; an embryo who would one day be a silver-haired elf high priestess with molten-silver eyes. A piece of DNA from the future high priestess was placed in him, linking them forever.

Needing no further explanation, Richard reached into himself and found the part of Jeena that had been with him since the day of his birth. He felt her love, courage, strength, and loyalty. He spoke to the completeness that was her.

"I need your help, Jeena."

"I am here, my bondmate," replied Jeena using thoughts coming at nanosecond speed from the part of him that was in her.

Richard thought he knew the answer to his next question, but he had to be sure. Too many lives were at stake to make a mistake now. *"I saw the videos from the* Defiant *where you told* 'the One' *you would bring the entire tele-network down around his head and destroy every computer if he didn't help you find me. Were you serious? Could you have actually done that?"*

A feeling of embarrassment came from his bondmate. *"Maybe, uh, I don't know. To me, computer networks are like the roots of trees in a forest. Tree roots run deep into the earth around them, intermingling with each other until the entire forest is like one living being. I am a priestess of the Lady of the Tree. As such, I am blessed with the ability to manipulate the Power of the Lady and maintain the forests of silver elm trees. I think your tele-network is like the roots of the silver elms, and computers are like the trees themselves."* A feeling of determination and increasing confidence came from Jeena. *"Yes, I believe I could have brought down the entire tele-network."* A flash of anger came from Jeena. *"And I will if* 'the One' *ever tries to take you from me again. Is that what you want me to do? Do you want me to bring down the tele-network now?"*

That was definitely not what Richard wanted. He needed the tele-network. He sent an image to his bondmate of what he hoped to do.

An emotion of confidence came from her. *"So this is your plan?"* she asked.

"Yes. It's my one-and-only plan. Will you help?"

No words came from Jeena. Her magic mixed with his Power along with energy from the Staff of the Lady of the Tree. Richard funneled the magic from Jeena's ring to his and on to the green-gemmed ring worn by Tia. Then he led Jeena's mind into the Dragar ship and into the jammer that was already touching every computer in the Crosioian fleets. Without hesitation, Jeena expanded the jammer's touch from the *'roots'* of the Crosioians' part of the tele-network to that of the Empire, Trecorian, UGA, and every other computer operating in the Criterion star system. Once Jeena had every root connected, Richard took over.

Drawing on the part of himself that was a piece of *'the One,'* Richard circumvented the security programs in every computer on every ship, missile, fighter, power-armor, and weapon regardless of which side they were on. He expanded his reach to include battle computers, fighting-computers, and every other gas-based life form in the Criterion system. Many of the gas-based life forms struggled against him, but they were creatures of logic. Jeena and he were creatures of freewill. Pure logic was no match for the combined freewill of an elf high priestess and a human wizard scout.

Then Richard did what he needed to do.

CHAPTER 62

"Five seconds to impact," said the *Destiny's* science officer from his position on the bridge near the strategic map.

Considering the circumstances, Liz thought the lieutenant sounded amazingly calm given the fact a dozen hundred-megaton nuclear warheads were about to slam into the hull of their ship. Liz took a final look at the strategic map and stopped giving commands. There was nothing left to do. She thought of her husband battling with the Trecor fleet near Tardis. She took a final look at the overwhelming number of orange, red, and blue dots on the strategic map that surrounded the Trecor fleets near Tardis. It was obvious her husband would be joining her in death in the near future. Liz gave a tightlipped smile as the shadow of impending death loomed before her, savoring her final breath.

It's been a good run, she thought. She glanced at the bridge crew still at their stations doing their duty in their final seconds of life. *They've all given it their best shot. They deserved a better commander.*

Suddenly the lights on the bridge went out.

"Help!" shouted multiple voices.

Liz felt pressure against her waist from the safety harness of her command chair as her body attempted to float toward the ceiling. The lights came back on, revealing that every crewman not buckled in was floating in midair and flailing their arms in a vain attempt to find handholds. She noticed Lieutenant Beady standing locked in place at his duty station. Glancing at his feet, she nodded approvingly. *Magnetic boots. Smart.*

The lieutenant looked up from his computer console, in the direction of Captain Bhami's command chair. "Sir, all offensive and defensive systems are off line. Only life support and non-combat related computer systems appear to be functioning. Uh..."

"Spit it out, Lieutenant," snapped Captain Bhami. "Uh doesn't tell me much."

The lieutenant's cheeks turned pink. "Sir, all ships appear to be dead in space. Nothing's moving on either side. All incoming and outgoing missiles are adrift as well. I don't understand it."

Neither did Liz.

* * *

The demon glanced around at the Crosioian life forms on the bridge of the command dreadnaught. It loathed all living creatures, bat or otherwise, but nevertheless continued to maintain the stealth shield around the ship to keep it hidden from the Empire warships. The demon sensed the demons on other Crosioian ships doing the same. They had all been instructed by Cancontus, and Cancontus did not brook disobedience.

The lights on the bridge went out. The demon heard hisses of surprise from the crew as they began floating off the deck. The lights came back on. The demon noticed movement out the corner of its eyes as automated phase weapons mounted on the bridge's walls swiveled to point at a single target—they all pointed at him. The demon sensed surprise from his comrades scattered throughout the Crosioian fleets as other automated weapons systems did the same. The demon barely registered the concentration of phase rounds as the phase energy and solid slugs tore holes through its avatar.

As the demon's soul was ripped back to the demonic plane, it had time for only a single thought. *I hate living creatures.*

* * *

Richard's mind returned to the *Defiant*. He no longer thought at nanosecond speed, but it didn't matter. Jeena and he had done what needed to be done. The killing had stopped. Nickelo was in contact with Danny and Margery. They in turn were connected to every battle and fighting-computer in the galaxy. Between them, they were even now making sure every computer on both sides that was involved in the battle was doing only what was needed to prevent additional deaths. Even the Empire's central computer, the Crosioians' master computer, and the Trecorians' primary computer were now aligned with Richard's plan to avert additional killing of valuable resources.

A flash of silver drew Richard's attention.

Jeena stared at him with her molten-silver eyes and smiled. "I knew you could do it," she said. Her smile grew wider. "I had faith."

Richard returned his bondmate's smile. "We did it, but it's not quite over yet." He turned his attention to the supreme leader standing on the other side of the mess table. She was flanked by Red Wing and Charge-In-The-Face-Of-Great-Odds. Thinking a thought to activate the halo-pad in the center of the *Defiant's* mess table, Richard brought up the hologram of War-King Bistoria. The big Trecorian looked surprised. Richard didn't give the war-king time to ask questions. Gathering his thoughts, he sent Jeena and his image to every hologram, every computer screen, and every display device connected to the tele-network in the Criterion star system. He included the Empire's Imperial High Command and Council along with the Crosioians' tribal council.

"I am Wizard Scout Richard Shepard. This is High Priestess Jeehanathoraxen. The killing stops. It stops now. Despite what we have been told, we are not enemies. The real enemies of the Empire and Trecor are not the Crosioians. It is the demons. The real enemies of the Crosioians are not the Empire and her allies. It is the demons. A major demon called Zenthra started this war between our species. When he fell, his brother, Cancontus, took his place. Even they have been used by one stronger than them. A master demon has been manipulating us all." Richard pointed at Charge-In-The-Face-Of-Great-Odds. "The master demon tricked your daughter into a trap. He arranged for her and me to battle, but he stacked the deck. The master demon gave me dolgar allies, spirit-wolves. Between us, your daughter didn't stand a chance. Will killing me bring your daughter back?"

Richard pointed at Red Wing. "Will it bring back your mother?"

Neither of the bats said anything.

"No, it won't. Hundreds of millions of lives on both sides were lost during the first battle for Estos. Hundreds of thousands, maybe millions more have already died today. Will more killing bring *any* of them back?"

The animal that was Richard's temper rattled its cage. He held it at bay. Too much was at stake to let his orc temper out now. A feeling of peace came down his bond link from Jeena. He drew comfort from knowing he wasn't alone. He became more confident in his plan.

"The demons are our real enemies. They always have been." Richard glanced at the supreme leader before looking back at War-King Bistoria. "The fleets on both sides have been disabled by my bondmate and me. They will remain disabled until each of you agrees to work together to stop this war. Every life lost is one less resource for the real battle that is to come. The killing must stop. It *has* to stop. It *is* going to stop."

The hologram of War-King Bistoria straightened and turned to look at his Crosioian counterpart. The supreme leader spread her wings and swiveled her ears at the war-king's image. They nodded at each other. The supreme leader lowered her wings.

"You have our attention, Wizard Scout," said the supreme leader. "How do you propose we proceed?"

* * *

Disengaging hundreds of thousands of starships locked in mortal combat was no easy feat, but the battle and fighting-computers were up to the task. Using the magic of the jammer ship, Richard, or rather the computers Nickelo, Margery, Danny, Mykias, and Trypredor, returned control of ships and computers back to their intended masters on a carefully planned scheduled. Under the direction of Admiral of the Combined Fleets Bistos and her Crosioian counterpart, first individual ships withdrew to agreed upon lines. Then detachments and squadrons disengaged to be followed by entire fleets.

After several hours of ships pulling back without incident, it became apparent to all that the war was over. No one needed to tell Richard that animosities would continue to exist. There had been too many deaths on both sides for it to be otherwise, but he was satisfied. The war was over. When the demon armies came, he knew that the living beings on both sides would know their real enemies. On that day, they would become true allies.

When they see the demons come, then both sides will fight as one, Richard thought.

"I calculate only a forty-seven percent probability you are correct," said Nickelo in their shared space. *"Nothing is a given."*

Richard glanced at the silver-haired elf standing next to him.

A deep emotion of love came down their link.

Richard smiled. *"You're wrong, Nick. Some things* are *a given. They always will be."*

CHAPTER 63

The POWs who could walk were spread out in semi-organized lines stretching out for hundreds of meters in every direction as they waited for the troopships to land. Trinity stood off to the side of the command tent, watching non-commissioned officers in a nearby line as they reminded their troops they were still soldiers of the Empire and would act as such or there would be hell to pay. Despite the sergeants' yells, Trinity recognized a softness in their admonitions as they did their best to make things easier for those under their commands. The soldiers and sailors had already spent their time in Hell. The long weeks of suffering on Estos were almost over.

A roar in the air caused heads to turn upward as the ion thrusters of the first of the troopships shot out to slow down the huge medical ship. An emblem on the bow of the starship depicted a bat with a lightning bolt in its paw. Trinity unconsciously fingered the hilt of the phase rod attached to the left side of her belt.

"Relax," said Jennifer. *"The war's been over for two days now. This is not the first Crosioian ship you have been around."*

Trinity thought back to the other POW camps she'd helped evacuate over the last forty-eight hours. Unlike this compound that was in a relatively low-radiation area, the other camps had been composed mostly of soldiers and sailors too sick to even get out of their cots. It had been a close call, but she took comfort in the fact that her battle computer had assured her most of the POWs were going to live.

Reaching out through the blue-gemmed ring on her left hand, Trinity sent an emotion of concern to Jared who was located on the far side of the planet.

An emotion of hope came back.

Trinity smiled. Her part in the evacuations was almost over. Soon she and Jared would be together again, at least for a while. She didn't know what Rick had planned for them in the future war against the demons, but one thing she did know, she had hope. The entire galaxy had hope.

The medical troopship touching down on the north side of the compound brought Trinity out of her thoughts. Rear and side doors opened as ramps lowered to the ice-covered terrain. Medical hover-vehicles of both Crosioian and Empire design descended the ramps, spreading throughout the compound as they made their way toward medical tents holding the sickest of the POWs. White-suited bats and humans along with a dozen other races ran down the ramps of the hospital ship. Some of the medical personnel began setting up processing stations while others opened large boxes containing decontamination equipment.

A camouflaged light hover-vehicle flew out of an opening in the top of the ship and made straight for the command tent. The camp commander, a two-star general, stood at stiff attention flanked by a bevy of colonels and majors in tattered uniforms. The hover-vehicle landed twenty meters away. Two Crosioians wearing white uniforms with red markings on their sleeves got out of the vehicle. The lead bat walked to within three steps of the general and his group before stopping.

Spreading her wings slightly, the Crosioian raised a paw across her chest and hissed. A mechanical voice came out of the translator attached to her waist belt. "I am Death-Before-Dishonor, the commander of medical taskforce Alpha One. We have been ordered here to help. We have much to do."

The camp commander saluted, as did his staff. "Yes," said the general. "We all have much to do."

Trinity nodded as she thought of what lay ahead. They still had a war to fight, only this one would be against their real enemies—the demons.

CHAPTER 64

Richard and Jeena sat at the small table in the kitchen of their home in the elven capital of Silverton. The war between the Empire and the Crosioians had officially been over for two months, but having the supreme leader and War-King Bistoria say it was over and actually ending hostilities were two different matters. It had taken every bit of Richard and Jeena's time and skills during the last eight weeks to extricate the opposing forces and actually implement a viable ceasefire. With that next to impossible task accomplished well enough that no one was killing each other anymore, it was time to move on to the next phase of the operation. Richard glanced around the room at the others attending the impromptu meeting.

High Lord Trenadine and Master Jathar occupied the other two chairs at the table. They were staring at the portable halo-pad Richard had placed in the center. Lacking additional chairs, Rembis, Leethor, and Wizard Scout Telsa stood around the perimeter of the kitchen, looking at the halo-pad as best they could. A fuzzy holographic image of Richard's adoptive niece, Dren, and a man-sized cockroach shimmered above the halo-pad.

"Can't you make the image any clearer, Nick," Richard said out loud growing increasingly frustrated at the horrible connection. They had things to do, and faulty equipment wasn't a problem he needed at the moment.

"No, I cannot," replied Nickelo over the battle helmet's external speaker. "The signal has to penetrate the two protective shields around Portalis, not to mention that the point of origin is in another dimension. You should be grateful that you can get any kind of communication at all."

"Believe me, I'm grateful," Richard said giving Jeena a wink. "Can't you tell? That doesn't change the fact that the reception sucks." Turning his attention to Dren and Keka, he got serious. "How's the work on the teleporter on Storage coming along?"

Dren shrugged. "I supposed the teleporter's working well enough now to transport both equipment and personnel—"

"If you do not overdo it," said Keka clicking his mandibles for extra emphasis. "As I'm sure you are aware, the teleporter on Storage was only intended to care for the needs of time-commandos. It wasn't designed to transport large groups of personnel or anything like that."

"Understood," Richard said. "It wasn't like I was planning to try transporting an army anyway. What about the time travel part of the teleporter? Have you got that working yet? I've got a hunch we're going to need it sooner than later."

Frowning, Dren shook her head. "Not yet. Brachia's working on it now. That's one of his areas of expertise. He's only been back on Storage a month, so he'll probably need a few more weeks to get it right." She smiled. "But don't worry. He'll get it working. My brother can be irritating at times, but I've got to give him credit. He knows his teleporters."

Richard nodded his head. "I'm sure he does. Tell him to hurry. We're in a meteor shower without a thruster, otherwise."

Pulling a small vial out of his pocket, Richard placed it on the table. A glint of a yellow flashed from the minute gem floating in the bottle's clear liquid. Rembis had given him the bottle shortly after the battle in the Criterion system. The barest hint of Power came out of the yellow gem. It wasn't much, but Richard didn't care. It was all he had. It would have to be enough.

Looking at Jeena, Richard nodded toward the vial. "We need at least a fist-sized yellow gem to close the gate. Are you ready for one more adventure?"

The swirling in Jeena's molten-silver eyes sped up. When she smiled, the emotions coming down her bond link gave him all the answer he needed.

Where ever he was going, Richard knew he wouldn't be going

alone.

EPILOGUE

The figure of a dark-haired man wearing a white shirt with frill on the cuffs and collar came walking down the corridor toward the energy field that was the entrance to the Dalinfaust's prison. One of the demon guards failed to bow fast enough for the man's liking. With the barest movement of his index finger, the demon guard turned into a gray liquid that formed a nauseating pool on the tunnel floor. A glint of pink flashed out of the ooze as a fingernail sized gem sunk to the bottom.

"Master," said the other demon guards in unison as they scattered to make way.

With a wave of the dark-haired man's hand, the energy field dissipated. Once the shimmering doorway was gone, he entered. Glancing at the tortured lump of flesh that was the Dalinfaust, the master demon said, "It is time."

"Time for what?" asked the Dalinfaust between groans. "My thousand years are not yet complete. Are you changing the rules?"

The dark-haired man laughed. It wasn't a pleasant laugh. "Do not think to instruct me in rules that I helped create, demon." The man waved a hand.

The Dalinfaust's cell expanded to contain the forms of the Dalinfaust's brothers, Efrestra, Cancontus, and Zenthra. The body of the demon Zenthra looked in even worse shape than the Dalinfaust.

The master demon waved his hand again and muttered a single word.

All four brothers fell to the cell floor howling in pain. The pain lasted only a second that could have been an eternity. Time mattered little to the master demon. When the dark-haired man determined he had the four brothers' full attention, he released his spell.

The forms of the four major demons fell to the cell floor,

groveling before their master.

"I have allowed each of you to pursue your individual plans for many years. They mattered not to me as long as you did my bidding. That was in the past. It all stops now. The time has come for the four of you to work together. I will brook no defiance on any of your parts. Do you understand?"

The four brothers didn't answer. There was no need. The master demon knew they understood only too well. From this point on, they would work together to further his plan. Anything else would result in pain beyond even their imagination.

The dark-haired man smiled. *Everything is going according to plan.*

[End Transmission]

ABOUT THE AUTHOR

Rodney Hartman is a retired US Army veteran with over twenty years of experience in military operations ranging from Infantry Private in the paratroops to Chief Warrant Officer flying helicopters during the Persian Gulf War. Mr. Hartman worked for many years as a computer programmer before retiring and pursuing a career as a fulltime writer. Mr. Hartman lives in North Carolina with his wife and family along with their cat, McKenzie.

If you would like to find out more about the author and/or upcoming books, please visit:
    http://www.rodneyhartman.com

You may contact the author at: **rodney@rodneyhartman.com**

Depending on volume, the author will try to respond to all emails.

Made in the USA
Lexington, KY
10 November 2018